blue
rider
press

Saratoga Payback

Also by Stephen Dobyns

Saratoga Payback

A CHARLIE BRADSHAW MYSTERY

Stephen Dobyns

BLUE RIDER PRESS ▪ NEW YORK

blue
rider
press

An imprint of Penguin Random House LLC
375 Hudson Street
New York, New York 10014

Library of Congress Cataloging-in-Publication Data

Names: Dobyns, Stephen, 1941– author.
Title: Saratoga payback / Stephen Dobyns.
Description: New York : Blue Rider Press, [2017] | Series: A Charlie Bradshaw mystery
Identifiers: LCCN 2016041987 (print) | LCCN 2016051670 (ebook) | ISBN 9780399576577
(hardcover) | ISBN 9780399576584 (epub)
Subjects: LCSH: Bradshaw, Charlie (Fictitious character)—Fiction. | Private investigators—New York
(State)—Saratoga—Fiction. | Murder—Investigation—Fiction. | BISAC: FICTION / Mystery & Detective /
General. | FICTION / Mystery & Detective / Traditional British. | GSAFD: Mystery fiction.
Classification: LCC PS3554.O2 S267 2017 (print) | LCC PS3554.O2 (ebook) | DDC 813/.54—dc23
LC record available at https://lccn.loc.gov/2016041987
p.   cm.

Printed in the United States of America
1   3   5   7   9   10   8   6   4   2

Book design by Gretchen Achilles

For my daughter, Clio Bize Dobyns,
who knows Saratoga

Saratoga
Payback

One

Mickey Martin had what an acquaintance called "urinous" breath: a potent alkaloid whiff mixed with the aroma of rotting meat, which caused those whom he had snared in conversation to stumble back in search of relief. He had a square head, a fringe of short graying hair and wore a pair of thick horn-rimmed glasses, which magnified his eyes, giving him an owl-like expression more suggestive of cunning than wisdom. Apart from his small insurance and realty business, he specialized in gossip, slander and scandal, as well as back biting and stabbing. It was assumed to be a mix of these traits that led him into terminal difficulties, because at an hour or so past midnight during an October cold snap, someone had slashed his throat on a quiet street in Saratoga Springs, leaving his body sprawled on the sidewalk. Then, before disappearing, the killer had reached into Mickey Martin's mouth and sliced out his tongue. Mickey's urinous breath would trouble no one any longer.

It was Charlie Bradshaw's misfortune to discover the body. He had gone to sleep at eleven thirty, nodding off over a book about Sacco and Vanzetti; then, at three thirty, he woke with a start to realize he hadn't taken out the garbage. The truck rumbled past between seven and seven thirty every Tuesday morning, and more than once Charlie had been forced to run down the street in his pajamas and slippers, holding out a black bag of trash like a belated Christmas gift toward the truck's green and rusted maw. Usually, when the driver saw Charlie, he would accelerate and his reflected grin in the side mirror would diminish to a gray speck as the truck proceeded down the block.

So at three thirty-five, Charlie unpeeled himself from his cocoon of blankets—being careful not to wake Janey—put on his robe and slippers and headed downstairs. The two trash cans were at the rear of the driveway, filled with the accumulated detritus of husband, wife and teenage daughter. Then there were two recycling bins. On this night, however, the bins never reached the street, because as Charlie dragged out the trash cans he caught sight of Mickey Martin lying at the juncture of the sidewalk and the concrete path leading to the front steps, though he didn't at first realize it was Mickey. The only streetlight was half a block away, which made the figure more resemble an oversized parcel than a corpse, but Charlie had spent enough time investigating the darker side of human behavior to guess the nature of this particular parcel.

Leaving the trash cans, Charlie made his way across the grass while holding his robe closed at the neck as protection against the chill. A dark stain made an irregular circle on the concrete and half surrounded the dead man's head like a shadowy halo. Mickey wore a long, dark overcoat, dark pants and small dark Italian shoes with tassels, for he had been vain about his feet. Charlie pondered them briefly and sucked his teeth. Then he walked back to the house to turn on the porch light.

When he returned a moment later, the dark stain had taken on a red shimmer and he saw that the man's glasses were lying in the grass. Bending over with his hands on his knees, he identified the corpse as Mickey Martin. The slash across his neck was like a lipsticked, toothless smile. He didn't notice Mickey's tongue was gone—that discovery would come later. Mickey's eyes were open and he wore a dreamy, somewhat confused expression.

Charlie straightened up and massaged the back of his neck. The neighboring houses were dark and he heard no sound beyond the distant yowl of a cat. For a moment he wondered if it would be possible to drag Mickey out to the curb or even a few houses down the street to be left on someone else's front walk. It was not a thought he entertained for long. The spilled blood on Janey's sidewalk marked Mickey Martin as Charlie's very own dead man. But as someone who'd disliked Mickey and who had been the victim of his slander, Charlie felt no great grief for his passing; rather, he believed, as would others, that the course of Mickey's life had made early and violent death close to inevitable. Still, it was murder, and no matter how much Mickey might have deserved his fate, such conduct couldn't be permitted in the Republican community of Saratoga Springs. The trouble for Charlie was that Mickey had apparently been on his way to see him. Although Charlie hadn't laid eyes on Mickey for at least six months, he could foresee a range of personal disruption, the least of which being that he'd get no more sleep that night. Along with turning on the porch light, Charlie had grabbed his cell phone from the hall table. Once more sucking his teeth, he punched in 9-1-1.

Victor Plotz also woke up shortly after at three a.m., opening his eyes with a start. But it wasn't because of garbage. Years bef~ in what he thought of as another life, he had been the super ~

East Side tenement in New York and garbage had occupied a large portion of his time, lugging out thirty cans of it once a week, then lugging them back and cleaning up the messes left from the passive-aggressive and overpaid hulks who worked on the garbage truck—spilled plastic bottles, splops of unrecognizable food and containers redolent of sour milk. Victor had had enough of garbage. It was for him a religious conviction. And a benefit of living with the Queen of Softness, his long-term fiancée, was that he could leave the garbage to her or to one of the men or women employed at the lunch counter—"Family Eats Can't Be Beat"—attached to her house. Vacuuming, washing clothes, refreshing the cat box, Victor would do it all. But not garbage. And, thanks to his New York tenement, he had finished life's requisite burden of manhandling garbage cans at a relatively young age.

No, what woke Victor was a guilty conscience, a phenomenon experienced so rarely that he had lain awake for a minute wondering what the problem was. Beside him on the king-sized water bed, the Queen of Softness made soft purrs and grunts. The room was dark except for a mural of Elvis on black velvet on the opposite wall, which soaked up the glow from the bathroom night-light, giving the late singer's open mouth and ruby-red tongue a ghostly iridescence.

Then Victor remembered why he felt guilty. It was Dave Parlucci, who had accosted him earlier in the evening at the Parting Glass as Victor had been chatting up a waitress, Paula Something, trying to catch a glimpse between the open top buttons of her man's white shirt, down, down to the pink wonder of cleavage dividing her humongous breasts. Circus high divers, Victor felt sure, had leapt into smaller spaces.

Parlucci had slapped him on the back. "Hey, Vic, don't you rub noses with Charlie Bradshaw, you know, the busted gumshoe, or whatever he calls himself?"

The interruption was annoying on so many levels that Victor hardly knew where to begin, except that Charlie was his best friend. "Hunh," he said as he searched his mental repertoire of derision for a suitable response. Parlucci bounced on the balls of his feet in front of him, a red-haired young man with close-set eyes wearing a Harley motorcycle jacket. Lobster eyes, thought Victor. Parlucci was a day bartender someplace and at night he worked as a bouncer at a kids' bar, the Tin and Lint, where he was known for tricking out Skidmore cuties with promises of grass.

"I was out at his place on the lake," continued Parlucci, "and some colored family was living there. Bradshaw don't have any colored blood, does he?"

Here were more verbal provocations to deal with. In the meantime, Victor was aware of Paula Something drifting away and taking her humongous breasts with her. Soon somebody less deserving would be chatting her up.

"He's renting the place," said Victor. "The guy's a doctor."

"Jeez, who'd go to a colored doctor? How'd you like him to shove his fingers up your ass?"

"If you don't get lost, I'll spit in your drink," said Victor as politely as possible. The doctor was in fact Victor's own doctor and he had recently warned Victor that losing his temper was bad for his blood pressure and might lead to a paralyzing stroke.

"Touchy, touchy," said Parlucci.

Verbal insult wouldn't rid him of Parlucci, while the bloody alternatives could land him in jail for what he called "the duration"—Victor admitted to being on the cusp of seventy. So he struggled to content himself with the compromised path. "What's on your mind?"

"I'm looking for Bradshaw. I already said."

"Why are you looking for him?"

Parlucci was drinking a green concoction with a maraschino cherry. Ducking two fingers in his glass, he drew out the cherry by its stem. A lime-green sludge clung to his fingernails. "Have I ever shown you how I can tie the stem of one of these suckers in a knot just with my tongue?" He stuck out his tongue, the same green color as his drink, though a shade lighter.

Victor repeated his question and Parlucci tossed the cherry in his mouth. "Maybe it's none of your business. I mean, I got business with Bradshaw, not with you."

Victor turned back to his Guinness. "Then forget it."

"Hey, don't be so sensitive. I owe him a hundred bucks going back a few months. I hit a lucky horse at the simulcasts this afternoon and thought I'd pay what I owe him. It's easier than avoiding him all the time."

Victor didn't necessarily believe Parlucci, but he wanted to end the conversation without further delay. "Why'd he lend you the money?"

"Come on, Vic, I needed a coupla tires for my truck."

Although an irritant, Parlucci seemed harmless. Let Charlie deal with it. "He's married now and living with his wife in town. Over on the west side." He gave Parlucci the address. As he did so, Victor swore he'd have to remember to tell Charlie about it. In fact, he knew he should have asked Charlie *before* he gave Parlucci the address. Still, Parlucci could have just used the phone book, except, as Victor then realized, the phone was in Janey's name.

"Did he ever get his detective license back?" asked Parlucci.

Charlie had lost his license, or so the district attorney had claimed, for constantly sticking his nose into police business.

"No, he's retired."

"He's doing nothing?"

"He's thinking of opening a bar." This possibility had just occurred to Victor. Charlie himself had never spoke of such a thing.

"That's what I'd like—free drinks and waitresses scared of losing their jobs. You pinch 'em and they can't complain."

After Parlucci left, Victor turned his attention to luring Paula Something back into his immediate environment. She had breasts the size of a pair of Maltese pups and Victor imagined throwing himself into their pink gully and wiggling his feet in the air—a fantasy that sped the blood through his geriatric veins. Soon he forgot all about Parlucci; that is, till three o'clock that morning when he woke from a sound sleep to realize he had forgotten to call Charlie.

Also at three a.m., a dark blue Ford F-350 pulling a horse trailer drew to a stop on a dirt road ten miles east of Saratoga. The truck's lights had been off as it moved slowly forward, its path lit only by the half-moon and a flashlight that the man riding shotgun flicked on and off to make sure they weren't heading for a ditch. Anyway, the driver knew where he was. For the past week, he'd been taking practice drives.

"That's it—five-point-eight miles," said the driver.

"Make sure the door light's off," said a man riding on the bench seat in back.

The driver made an exasperated noise. "I already told you. It's out." He opened the door. Although no light came on, a ringing sound chimed through the night.

The man riding shotgun cursed. "For shit's sake, take out the key."

The driver removed the key and the ringing stopped. The three men sat quietly, listening. The only sound was a distant roar of a tractor-trailer downshifting as the driver descended toward the Hudson River on Route 23.

"Remember," said the man in back, "one bark and they're on their way. They won't bark again."

"What if they're bitches?" said the driver.

"They're not."

"What if one of them's gay?"

The man in back had a harsh smoker's laugh. "You dumb shit, whoever heard of a faggot Rottweiler?"

"Let's get moving," said the third man.

Once out on the road, the third man went to the rear of the trailer, removed a backpack, a few burlap bags and another bag in which a creature was squirming and whining. The man slapped the bag. "Shut up." The whining stopped. He tossed a couple of burlap bags to the driver. "Wrap these around your arm just in case."

"Aw, fuck. What about the bitch?"

"Like you said, one of them might be gay."

The driver fixed the bags around his arm, securing them with string. The other man did the same. The one who'd ridden on the bench seat was on his knees by an eight-foot fence, pulling squares of sod away from the soil. Then he began shoveling. "Don't forget the electric fence."

"Yeah, well, don't you forget to cut it," said the driver.

"Just give me the sign when you're coming back. We'll only have a couple of minutes after I cut it." In another moment, he'd finished digging, having made enough room for the men to crawl under.

"Can't you dig a little more?" asked the driver.

The man put the shovel back in the truck. "Suck in your gut and don't drink so much beer."

"You ready, Hank?" said the driver.

"I'm just listening to you jaw."

"Then let's do it." The driver and Hank got down on their bellies and began to crawl. It had rained in the afternoon and the ground was wet. "Aw, fuck," said the driver. When Hank began to crawl under the fence, the creature in the bag started whining again. Hank slapped it so it yelped.

"Not so hard," said the third man.

"You a dog lover? Just make sure you're here when we get back."

By the time the two men had crawled under the electric fence and stood up, they were only dim shadows to the man by the truck. He wanted to give them more advice, tell them to walk carefully and not talk, but the occasion for that was past. In the right-hand slash pocket of his jacket, he felt a small pistol and closed his fingers around it. The pistol didn't make him less nervous, but it changed the nature of his nervousness. Instead of worrying about getting shot, he worried about shooting someone else. Well, they'd deserve it, coming to mess with them at three thirty in the morning. They'd get a bullet in the gut and it'd be their own fault.

The two men inside the fence set off across the field at a slow lope, slightly crouched to keep closer to the ground. They'd spent half an hour studying the field in daylight and knew the relative position of the dozen trees and a few bushes. It was just over half a mile to the barn—"a straight shot," the other man had told them. They stayed quiet as they waited for the Rottweiler's single bark. The driver wanted to ask whether both dogs would bark once or if just one would bark for the two of them, but he knew Hank disliked him and he didn't want to do anything else to make Hank think he was a dope. Guys like Hank annoyed him, guys secure in their toughness who talked down to everyone else. What he wanted was to smack

Hank in the head with a brick, but if he messed up, Hank would follow him to the ends of the earth. He'd heard about stuff Hank had
done, both in prison and out. If he smacked Hank with a brick, he
had to make sure he wouldn't get back on his feet.

Hank stayed ahead, gripping the bag with the bitch. He used to
run some years after he first got out of prison and the jog through the
field brought it back. He tried to recall the name of the woman he'd
lived with in those days—Carol or Karen. Anyway, they'd had a fight
after she'd shrunk three of his best shirts in the wash. In fact, she was
lucky he hadn't slapped her instead of making her pay for the shirts,
but the upshot was she had moved out and he'd stopped running.

Hank heard the driver clomping behind him like a fuckin' Clydes-
dale. Ahead, he could see the barn, a dark shadow against the hori-
zon. The split-level ranch was about fifty yards beyond. God knew
where the Rottweilers were. Just lurking. With any luck the dogs
wouldn't hear them till they got close.

As it turned out, they heard the bark when they were twenty
yards from the barn: one deep bark and then silence. It had come
from up ahead, but who knew how the dogs were trained. Maybe
they were circling behind them even now. The driver felt his knees
getting watery. He was sorry he hadn't brought a gun no matter
what he'd been told, but he had a hunting knife under his coat. No
way was he going to let a dog drag him down.

Hank untied the top of the bag but held it shut with his hand. An
outside light by the house cast a faint glow. The security light above
the barn door would go on when they got closer. Hank made his way
toward the side of the barn, meaning to approach the door at the last
minute.

"Fuck, there they are!" said the driver.

"Shut up," said Hank. He'd seen them to his left—two big dogs running across the grass about ten feet from each other. They didn't even growl; they just ran. The driver ducked behind Hank, who was holding up the bag and turning it over. Then the bitch tumbled out, a mutt combination of beagle, collie and maybe ten other breeds. Hank gave it a kick to get it moving. The bitch yelped, took one look at the Rottweilers and raced off across the field. The Rottweilers slowed as if uncertain. Then one of the dogs turned after the bitch and disappeared.

"Jesus," said the driver, "it's all about pussy."

"Watch out," said Hank. Maybe the second dog was a faggot after all, or maybe he was some kind of celibate Rottweiler, because he didn't swerve from his path. Hank raised his left arm wrapped in the burlap bags, but when the dog hit, he was knocked back against the wall of the barn. He started to fall, dragged down by the dog's jaws. His pistol, however, was already in his right hand and he smashed the butt against the dog's head. But even after being knocked unconscious, the dog kept hanging on and the driver had to pry apart the dog's jaw to free Hank's arm.

"That's one mean dog. They don't get dogs like that from the puppy store."

"Shut up," hissed Hank. "If anyone comes out of that house, he'll get shot."

The security light came on when Hank reached the front of the barn, illuminating the driveway and yard between the barn and house. He slid open the door, then made his way to the third stall on his right. There was a clumping and snort or two from the stalls as the horses registered the intrusion. Hank removed a halter, strap and mask from his backpack as the driver opened the door to the stall. The horse stood back against the wall, pawing at the hay on the floor—a tall, black stallion with a white diamond shape on his forehead and three white stockings. The driver took out a small light, focusing it on the horse, as Hank attached the mask and bridle. Then he hooked on the strap. "Let's go. And look out for the dog."

The horse noisily clomped across the floor as Hank gripped the strap, holding it near the horse's jaw so he wouldn't rear up. Once outside, Hank pulled the horse away from the security light. There was a light on in the house that hadn't been there before. Hank broke into a run across the dark field, pulling the horse. He heard the driver bumbling along behind him. From the distance came the sound of barking—the Rottweiler getting acquainted with the bitch. When they were halfway across the field, Hank pulled his phone from his coat pocket. "We're almost there. Start cutting."

The third man had cut the chain-link fence and was just cutting the electric wire when Hank and the driver arrived with the horse. They pulled apart the sides of the fence so the horse could get through. The third man kept saying, "Hurry, hurry," as if he had forgotten every other word he'd ever learned.

The ramp was down on the trailer. Hank led the stallion inside and attached it to three swivel tie-rings that folded flat against the padded walls. Then he shoved the ramp back in place and locked the doors. When he got to the truck, it had begun to move.

"Not so fast, not so fast," said the man in back.

The driver hardly slowed, but it was enough to let Hank inside. The door slammed shut. All he wanted was to get away. Until the horse was delivered, he wouldn't get a fucking cent.

"I said not so fast. You want to hurt the horse?"

"Okay, okay," said the driver without slowing down. The dirt road was a dark blur against the darker blur of night.

Hank stared across the field to the house and barn. "There's more lights on."

"For shit's sake," said the man in back.

The truck surged forward. The road was bumpy, but it turned left onto a paved road after a quarter of a mile.

"I see headlights," said Hank. "There's one vehicle, no two, coming down the driveway."

"Jesus," said the man in back. "Hit the lights. No more fuckin' dawdling!"

Two

Charlie still wore his slippers, though over the past few hours, pebbles and leaf-bits had collected between his toes and under his instep. He leaned with his back against a tree. A maple, he thought, and most of its leaves had fallen. In fact, over the weekend, he had raked them. He wore a down jacket over his pajama top, but the wind blew through his pajama pants as if he were naked. At the moment, however, the cold was not among his complaints. Instead, he was thinking with some surprise that it was *his* maple. The tree belonged to him. Even when he modified this thought to say that actually it was Janey's tree, he would again emend it to say, no, it was also his. Without any deferential emphasis, Janey had said when they married that what was hers was his. It had been a casual remark meant to make him feel comfortable, to stop him worrying about breaking a dish or sitting down too heavily on a fragile chair left to her by a favorite aunt. Charlie had now lived in the house for two years—he still thought of it as Janey's house—and before that there'd been two years of commuting from his house on the lake.

But at last it had begun to sink in—it was his tree, his fragile chair, his house: a narrow, three-story Victorian a mile west of downtown. Even though he'd never had trouble thinking that his small house on the lake also belonged to Janey, the reverse had been hard to grasp. Now it clicked: *his* tree and, in consequence, his grass under his slippers and his pebbles and leaf-bits irritating his instep. With Charlie's first marriage, which had ended some twenty years before he had known of Janey's existence and when he'd still been a sergeant in the Saratoga police department, his wife had never made any secret about claiming most of the objects in their house. They belonged to Marge, and when they divorced she took them and took the house as well. She would grow angry if Charlie sat in her Kennedy rocker, used her good china, accidentally stole her pillow at night or didn't wipe his feet before walking on her grandmother's Turkey carpet. It was her property, her stuff, and she had a drawer full of guarantees, titles, certificates and testimonials to prove it.

Janey had none of that and in consequence—it was Charlie's tree, Charlie's grass. Just her three daughters weren't his, although Emma, the youngest and the only one still at home, could be Charlie's as much as he wished in terms of sharing responsibility, escorting her to movies and helping her study for her SAT exams. Never having had children of his own, Charlie found it odd but pleasurable.

What caused Charlie's gush of possession and ownership at five o'clock on an October morning was the finger hoisted five inches from his face, not pointed at him but upward, as if its owner wasn't just inflicting his own condemnation, but the Almighty's. The finger belonged to Lieutenant Frank Hutchins—Hutch to his friends, a select group from which Charlie was excluded. Near them, four sheriff's department crime scene investigators were examining the sidewalk and grass lit by high-power lights and marked off by yellow tape with black lettering telling the general populace they must not cross. Mickey Martin's body had been removed and most of the twenty or so bystanders had gone home. The two patrolmen assigned to keep back the remainder were nodding off on their feet. The tape cut across Charlie's sidewalk, which would force Janey and Emma to use the back door when they left the house later in the morning. This, too, contributed to Charlie's growing sense of indignation, although, in his own time as a policeman, he had spread yellow tape far and wide.

Charlie's feelings about the upraised finger, which had led him to think, My tree, my grass, now led him to the further thought that Hutch and his cronies were tramping on Charlie's grass and making free with his property in the same way that Mickey Martin had made free with his property by getting his throat cut on the front walk. This in turn led to the third stage of Charlie's proprietary thinking: He had had about enough.

Pushing himself away from the tree, Charlie said, "Take your damn finger out of my face."

Now it was Hutchins's turn to be surprised. "Watch it, Bradshaw." He was tall and lean with a hawk-like aspect that was for him a major source of pride. His dark hair was cut in a Harvard Clip, just long enough to be brushed to one side. Charlie knew this because he'd heard men joking about it in the Y locker room.

"Why? Are you going to take away my license?" And so Charlie arrived at the fourth and last of his liberating realizations: The police chief, Ron Novak, with the help of the district attorney, had already taken away his private investigator's license, along with his permit to carry a gun. Consequently, Charlie no longer had to worry about losing them. His license was gone, meaning he was now a plain citizen. He had rights.

"Also," said Charlie, "if you don't have any more questions, I'm going back inside. I'm cold and I have to pee. I've already told you twenty times that I don't know what Mickey Martin was doing on my sidewalk."

But this was what Hutch had trouble believing: that Mickey could have been coming to Charlie's house without Charlie knowing what he wanted. Charlie *must* have known and, accordingly, more pressure must be exerted. In addition, the lieutenant made no secret of the fact that he considered Charlie a liar, as if Hutch had long since bought Mickey's obnoxious fabrications concerning Charlie's general sleaziness.

Charlie understood that another obstacle was their age difference—Hutch was thirty years younger. The Vietnam War had ended while Hutch was still watching *Captain Kangaroo*. And there was the chafe and grind of different life experience. Hutch had spent a dozen years in the FBI before arriving in Saratoga. As he probably told himself ten times a day, he was a professional. What Hutch didn't know about fingerprints would fit into a thimble. He was computer savvy and used words like "network," "interface" and "microprocess" as verbs, as well as having absorbed such military and cop jargon as "pacify" and "terminate," "perps" and "grabs." In the police department that Charlie had left years before, no one called anyone a perp. In Hutch's eyes, Charlie was a cop hobbyist, an amateur. These were opinions shared by Chief Novak, even though Charlie had at times embarrassed them by solving cases they had been unable to solve. So, after Charlie had overreached himself one time too many by actions that Novak found inappropriate to cop hobbyists, Charlie had lost his license and his right to carry a gun, an old .38 that had mostly stayed in his office safe. When Charlie first heard a Saratoga patrolman refer to his Glock, he had thought it was a musical instrument, perhaps derived from "glockenspiel," and so the sentence "I popped 'im twice with my Glock" had had a certain musical charm.

Hutch raised the offending finger a little higher. "Look, Bradshaw, we can either talk here or I can take you downtown."

"There's nothing I can tell you that I haven't told you twenty times."

"Perhaps I'd like to hear it again."

"No," said Charlie. "I have a lawyer and I know my lawyer would like me to go inside. He would tell me I should pee. I'm sixty-seven; I have an elderly bladder."

Hutch seemed ill at ease at the mention of a bodily function, as if he himself never had to pee, as if he had patrolmen to do it for him. "You know what would happen if the DA found out that you were working as a private investigator without a license?"

For Charlie this was a version of the threat he had heard for over twenty years. "You mean he'd cancel my trip to Disneyland?"

Hutchins blinked several times, but before he could answer, Charlie turned and walked to the house: his house, sort of. Through the glass of the front door, he saw Janey sipping a cup of coffee and looking worried. Charlie half expected the lieutenant to call him back with a further threat, but no threat came. He passed through his front door, shutting it and locking it behind him, and then he gave Janey a hug.

But at six thirty, when Charlie had already been back in bed with his eyes shut for thirty minutes, sleep seemed as far away as it had been when talking to Hutch. Why had Mickey Martin come to see him? What had he wanted? Why had he been killed and who had killed him? Turning over on his back, Charlie stared at the ceiling now smudged with the gray blur of dawn. His questions made him again realize that he'd be unable to discover the answers on his own. He couldn't nose around and gather information about an ongoing police investigation. He would have to read about it, like everyone else, in *The Saratogian*, a mediocre source of information even in the best of times. This galled him. His right to act on his curiosity had been restricted. But surely, he told himself, the police will find the murderer even before I wake up, or at latest by the end of the day. That's just simple statistics. And so Charlie turned over for the thirtieth time and stuck his head under his pillow.

But each time he felt poised on the cusp of sleep, another question popped into his head. When had he last seen Mickey Martin? Had it been on the street or in the YMCA? Had it been at a restaurant? Then he remembered. He and Janey had been having dinner at Lillian's on Broadway. It had been in the spring, late March or early April, a rainy weeknight with the restaurant nearly empty. Mickey had been having dinner with a young woman across the room and was berating her for having done something stupid to a car, like driving without releasing the hand brake. Then, as his voice got louder, he had begun to berate her for having no fucking taste in clothes, for dressing, as Mickey had said, like a nun. The woman had short black hair and was in her late twenties, probably fifteen years younger than Mickey. She wore a gray silk blouse that Charlie thought looked very pretty on her, and a black skirt with vertical gray lines. These he had assumed were the offending articles of clothing.

"Do you think they're married?" Janey had asked.

Charlie didn't think so. He'd never heard of Mickey being married and it seemed unlikely that any woman would have him, though, as he had learned long ago, a person's faults had little connection with his or her sexual success.

"And that fuckin' rabbit-fur jacket," Mickey had continued. "It leaves a trail of fur wherever you go. It's got bald spots. How could you be so dumb to buy a fur coat from a jerk on the street?"

Waiters glanced grimly at one another; customers hurried to finish their food.

"Make him stop, Charlie," Janey had said.

"I can't just go up and—"

"If you don't, I will."

So Charlie had crossed the room to Mickey's table, feeling foolish.

Mickey caught sight of him. "Hey, Charlie, what're you doing in a dump like this? Everything's overcooked." Then he nodded toward his companion. "Though I bet Lizzie'd eat anything stuck in front of her."

Charlie had known Mickey for six years, but he knew few details about his life. When he had arrived in Saratoga no one was sure where he'd come from; one man said he'd heard Mickey had been in prison, another said he had originally come from Cleveland. Charlie hadn't cared one way or the other until he had found himself caught up in Mickey's general slander.

Standing at Mickey's table, Charlie tried to force his face into a genial but modest expression. "You're making too much noise, Mickey. Tone it down, okay?" Even from five feet away, Charlie had caught a whiff of his urinous breath. Perhaps that was why Mickey had never married. It made Charlie a little sorry for him.

"Fuck that business, Charlie," said Mickey loudly. "I got as much right to talk as anybody."

The young woman stared down at her plate, on which was an uneaten T-bone. She looked miserable.

"Of course you've a right to talk," said Charlie. "You just don't need to bother everybody else."

Mickey looked angrily around the room. "Just show me one person who doesn't like it."

"Come on, Mickey, let's just go," said the woman.

Belatedly, Charlie saw that Mickey was drinking a double whiskey, with an empty whiskey glass to one side of it. Taking his time, he sat down at Mickey's table and began fishing through his pockets for his cell phone. Though he'd carried a cell phone for a few years, he still hadn't gotten used to it, so when it rang he was never sure which pocket it was in. Finding it, Charlie set the phone before him on the white tablecloth.

"You driving, Mickey?"

Mickey had looked at the phone, but didn't speak.

"You ever have a DUI? They make you go to a bunch of AA meetings now. If you're good, you get your license back after a year. In the meantime, you'd have to ride a bike or ask friends to give you a lift. I'd keep it down, Mickey. You never know who might make a call. There must be a lot of people here fed up with your noise." Charlie had counted to five, retrieved his phone and got to his feet. "See you around."

But that hadn't been quite true. Mickey and the woman soon left and Charlie had never seen him again. Alive, that is. He'd heard, however, that Mickey's real estate and insurance office wasn't doing well and some people wondered where his money came from. That was a problem with a small town, especially out of tourist season. Nosiness. The scrutinizing conversations that helped pass winter evenings in a local bar—so-and-so's divorce or a kid arrested for smoking grass or an inheritance from Uncle Cedric—had occasionally focused on Mickey. Where did his money come from? It made Charlie wonder, in a casual way, if Mickey had really been in prison. It hadn't been a big question, not big enough to do anything about it, but now Mickey had been murdered on Charlie's front walk and idle speculations were no longer idle.

———

Charlie had been asleep for half an hour when, at eight fifteen, there was a crash at the bedroom door and his friend Victor Plotz stumbled into the room, having jumped to avoid the cat, Twinkle, that had scuttled between his feet just past the upstairs landing. These days Victor sometimes carried a cane as a concession to his sore knees, so when Charlie woke, the first thing he saw was Victor leaping toward the bed with the cane upraised.

"What's up?" he asked. After all, he'd known Victor a long time and it wouldn't have occurred to him that he was under attack, though he was glad Janey had already left for work at the hospital.

Stumbling forward, Victor half turned and sat down heavily on the bed, sat down in fact on Charlie's feet. Charlie pulled them out from beneath his friend. "I said, what are you doing?"

Victor wiped his brow. "You know it's against the law to let cats run between people's legs. The FBI could easily confiscate your cat."

"Then they'll have to deal with Emma. It's her cat." Charlie didn't feel like swapping jokes so early in the morning. His eyes felt stuck together.

Victor took several deep breaths. During his middle and late middle age, his hair had resembled a gray dandelion clock, but as he'd moved toward seventy, the clock had grown somewhat patchy. Accordingly, Victor now shaved his head, which made his baldness appear his own choice rather than nature's. In addition, he had joined a concept gym called Nietzsche's and wore a white sweatshirt with a drawing of the philosopher over the motto "What does not kill me makes me stronger." Bulked up and bald, he no longer looked like a senior citizen but a lifer in Attica with a lot of time in the weight room. Even his round plum of a nose looked different; it looked like a weapon.

"So what's with the yellow cop tape? You kill somebody or was it Dave Parlucci?"

"What's Parlucci have to do with it?" Charlie swung his feet to the floor and felt for his slippers. Unless he could grab a nap in the afternoon, he knew he'd get no more sleep that day.

"He's why I'm here. I did a bad thing just because I was trying to glom a girl's tits."

"What sort of bad thing?" Charlie'd had experience with Victor's bad things. The two men sat side by side—Charlie in his pajamas and Victor in his Nietzsche sweatshirt.

"I saw Parlucci in the Parting Glass. He wanted to know where you lived and thought you were still out at the lake. I wasn't going to tell him. I mean, I'd have asked you first. But he said you'd lent him a hundred bucks and he wanted to pay it back."

"You kidding? I'd never lend him money. He'd drink it or put it up his nose."

"He said he'd needed to buy tires for his truck and you helped him out." Victor's voice began to contain elements of complaint.

"I don't believe he has a truck. Last time I saw him he was on foot. Anyway, I've never lent him a cent."

"So I did a bad thing. I'm just saying I did it and I'm sorry."

"I wonder why Parlucci wanted to know where I lived."

"Beats me. So was he killed out on your sidewalk or not?"

"No, it was Mickey Martin."

"Old Piss-breath? You kidding?"

Charlie grimaced. "You're the one who kids; I'm the one who endures."

"Hey, don't get trendy on me, who killed him?"

"I've no idea."

"Are you up to your old tricks? You know what the DA said about playing detective."

"Really, I don't know anything about it. I was taking out the trash around three thirty and there was Mickey with his throat cut on my sidewalk."

"You tell the cops you were taking out the trash at three thirty in the morning?"

"Of course I did."

"And did they roll their eyes? Why were you taking out the trash at three thirty?"

So Charlie told him, describing each minute, beginning with waking abruptly at three thirty, as he remembered his need to take out the trash, to the arrival of the police and his realization that the two maples between the sidewalk and the street belonged to him and Janey together.

By this time Victor had moved to a rocking chair across the room. "That's great, Charlie. Your very own maples. Have you given them names? I've always thought Melvin was a good name for a maple, Melvin and Marcus, the Maple boys. So what was Mickey doing here?"

"I don't know, but the police will find out. There'll be no lack of suspects."

Victor wasn't convinced. "That might be the problem, sorting through the people with a grudge against him. You're not planning to 'poke around,' as you call it?"

Charlie gave a slight laugh. "I'm a different person these days." He wondered if Victor believed him. Actually, he wondered if he believed himself. Victor was staring at Charlie as if he had said the earth was flat.

"And you're not curious?"

"Not really, no. I'll wait to read about it in the paper."

"He must have wanted to talk to you about something and, considering the time he was showing up, it must have been important."

"Maybe."

"He probably wanted your help."

"That's possible."

"And you've no curiosity."

"Only mildly."

"Have you upped your dosage of antidepressants?"

Charlie got up and put on his robe. "I'm not taking antidepressants."

"Then maybe you should, though they can play hell with your sex life. So Mickey can get killed on your sidewalk while engaged in a post-midnight mission and you've got no desire to find out why? You'll just wait for *The Saratogian* to enlighten you with its limpid prose?"

"That's about it."

"Jesus, you're full of shit. What are you, a eunuch?"

"Victor, I'm out of that world. I'm just a regular citizen."

"What about Parlucci?"

"What about him? He knows where I live, thanks to you. If he wants to contact me, he's free to do it."

Victor looked at his friend with disappointment. "Maybe he never meant to contact you. Have you thought of that? Maybe he was finding out where you lived for Mickey. I've seen those two together more than once. Parlucci did some work for Mickey now and then, fixing up houses that Mickey was trying to sell. I bet that's how it happened. Mickey wanted to talk to you and he asked Parlucci to find out where you lived."

"Victor, slow down. Can't you see? I don't care. It's up to Hutchins to figure it out. Not me. Let's go downstairs and get some coffee. You want eggs?"

"I'm not supposed to eat eggs. Just coffee's fine. You know, this isn't like you."

Charlie led the way to the kitchen, which got the morning sun through a pair of large windows, each with a shelf for flowerpots containing red bougainvillea. Straggly and with few blossoms, they reached up over the curtain rod and then dangled down so the sun shone through their leaves. Janey had made a pot of coffee before she left and Charlie poured a cup for Victor.

"Did you see much of Mickey?" asked Charlie.

"Socially? I avoided him like genital warts. He told people I was sponging off Rosemary, pawning her trinkets to buy scratch tickets. Not only does the lady get my Social Security check, but she's also taken charge of my so-called nest egg. The fact is, the Queen of Softness puts me on an allowance and if it weren't for one or two hidden, but trifling, checking accounts, I'd hardly have a dime. But sponging? Far from it. I'd see Mickey in the Parting Glass or around town, but he could take a simple hello and twist it into the claim that you were part of the bunch that bumped off Abe Lincoln."

Charlie laughed. They were sitting at a yellow Formica table. Victor tore open two small bags of sweetener and poured them into his cup. "He used to say I was a blackmailer," said Charlie. "He said that's what I did as a PI, that I scraped together bits of embarrassing information that people paid me not to reveal. Then a year ago I heard he'd told people I was in trouble for improper conduct with my stepdaughters, though he never said what it was. He'd just let the statement hang and let people guess what they wanted. I had a conversation with him."

"What did you say?"

"Well, I was cross."

"I can imagine. What did you say?"

"I promised to have his knees broken."

Victor whistled. "Impressive. Would you have done it?"

"No, no, of course not. At least I don't think so. I just felt I needed to talk to him in language he'd understand. In any case, he stopped spreading that particular story."

"So the cops might put you on their list of suspects?"

"Maybe, but why kill him on my own front walk?"

"To make it seem someone else had killed him. It'd be the perfect place."

Charlie poured Victor another cup of coffee and then filled his own cup as well. "Actually, I never thought Mickey's slander had much point behind it. He slandered the way other guys talk about baseball."

Victor wasn't so sure. "Nah, it was mean. He was a bully and he wrecked some lives. And I guess he did some of the blackmail he accused you of. I'm not a fan of murder, but I'm glad I won't be seeing him anymore."

"You really think it was Parlucci who told Mickey where I live?"

"Stands to reason, doesn't it? They were cut from the same mold."

"I've always found stuff that 'stands to reason' can lead to a lot of unnecessary trouble." Charlie got to his feet. He'd remembered several blueberry muffins were in the bread box. "Would you like a muffin?"

"Jesus, Charlie, I can't eat that stuff anymore. Besides my knees, the doctor says I'm nearly cheek to jowl with diabetes."

"No ice cream?" Charlie couldn't imagine Victor without ice cream.

"I've been eating this stuff that's got no sugar and no fat."

Charlie was skeptical. "How does it taste?"

"Like medicine, but really good medicine. The doctor keeps telling me I got to eat more fodder."

"You mean fiber?"

"That's it. Beans and grains. But it fucks with my pipes. Last week it jammed me up for three days. When I finally made it to the crapper, I dropped a turd the size of a nuclear submarine. I felt I should've snapped a photo, but I flushed it nonetheless. Then there was strange stirring in the water and a rat poked up its paw waving a white flag of surrender."

Three

The horse's head lay on the black leather seat of a BMW 760 with its neck propped up on the armrest. Blood had run into the sedan's controller, and had then pooled and dried in the two burnished metal cup holders. The horse's head was also black with a black mane so, in a perverse way, it seemed meant to match the car's interior. The cut was ragged and Charlie guessed it had been done with a chain saw. He placed the photograph back on the desk and picked up another.

This head had been set inside a child's crib, though no child was in evidence. A dark stain of blood had spread across the blankets with Disney images of Pooh Bear, Piglet and Eeyore. The horse's head was chestnut with a white splash on its brow and a dark mane. Its muzzle was squashed against the bars at the top of the crib, while the severed neck was pressed up against the bars at the bottom, fitting the crib as neatly as a foot in a sneaker.

"Was a child in the crib when they stuck the head in there?" asked Charlie.

Sitting across the desk from Charlie, Fletcher Campbell leaned forward to look at the photograph. "Fortunately not. They were visiting friends in Cold Harbor and the maid had the night off."

The third picture showed a horse's head wedged on the top of a flagpole in front of a large stone house with a green mansard roof. The pole stood in a grassy area surrounded by a circular drive. The head was tilted to the left and blood had run down the pole. Charlie guessed the pole was about twenty feet tall—a gray horse's head facing away from the house like a macabre weather vane, facing, presumably, anyone driving up the driveway.

Charlie put the picture back on the desk. "How'd they get it up there?"

"The cops weren't sure. A crane would have attracted too much attention. Maybe a ladder and a couple of strong men."

"They certainly have a flair for the dramatic. This is pure *Godfather* stuff."

"They're crazy people, that's all. Crazy sadists."

"Maybe." Charlie pushed his chair back from the desk. "But the more dramatic the pictures, the faster owners like you will pay up."

"So you'll help me?"

"I already told you, I'm not a private investigator anymore."

"And I told you, Charlie, I don't want anything investigated. I just want to pay them and get my horse back. Even if he never races again, Bengal Lancer is worth over a million in stud fees. All I ask is for you to deliver the money."

"What makes you think they won't keep the hundred thousand and then either kill or sell the horse?"

"Because no one would pay if horses hadn't been delivered. These scumbags are businessmen. They may kidnap horses but otherwise

they're on the up-and-up. The guys who owned these horses"—
Campbell gestured to the photographs—"they all went to the cops
and this was the result. Hey, I know them. They told me what
happened. I just didn't think it would happen to me. I mean, I had
big dogs."

Charlie had been acquainted with Campbell for about ten years:
a Long Island contractor who had retired young to buy a horse
farm near Saratoga and raise and train thoroughbreds. Although
mildly friendly, they had never been friends. After all, they moved
in different circles. Charlie drove a Golf, now five years old. Campbell drove a Mercedes SUV, the G550 model with over 400 horse-
power. Charlie had barely one house and Campbell had three or four.
And it went like that: cashmere versus cotton, vintage wine versus
Budweiser.

But Charlie felt little envy. So much money would make him anxious, and in his present financial decline he'd never be in a situation
where somebody might threaten to decapitate his prize stallion. The
only animals he had to watch out for were his stepdaughter's cat,
which had nearly crippled Victor, and her Chihuahua puppy, Bruiser.

Campbell was in his late fifties with a white moustache, a shock
of white hair and one of those healthy tans unaffected by the passage
of time, as golden in January as in July. Buttoned over his substantial
stomach was a blue-and-green vest, with the double-black lines of the
Campbell tartan. Campbell wasn't so much fat as thick, having a fire
hydrant shape. Charlie had first met him at the Saratoga YMCA
before Campbell had quit to join an expensive health club. He played
racquetball, lifted weights, swam and seemed one of those men
who excelled at all sports despite his size. Given half a chance, he'd
launch into vivid descriptions of playing football at Yale back in the

seventies. As for Charlie, swimming was his single athletic activity, unless one included worrying and trying to stay out of trouble.

Then, about eight years earlier, Campbell had hired Charlie to discover the identity of an employee who was stealing equipment from one of his barns. Charlie had come to the farm as an apparent stable hand and a day later he found the culprit—a fellow who had been paroled the previous year from the Adirondack medium-security correctional facility in Essex County. He'd been working as a part-time groom for several months and had a drug habit. A sheriff's department investigator made the arrest and the groom was sent back to prison as a parole violator. Charlie couldn't remember his name.

But now it was Thursday morning, and the previous evening Campbell had called Charlie, asking him to drop by "about a money issue." Then it turned out the money in question was, as Campbell had added, "a delivery issue." Campbell reached into his drawer and put a checkbook on top of the photographs. "All you do is deliver the cash. A guy like you in his sixties—no offense, Charlie—they're not going to worry about you jumping them. A grand for an hour's work, who's it going to hurt?"

Charlie glanced at the checkbook, a piece of soft green leather with the initials F.C. embossed in gold. His retirement consisted of Social Security, a small pension from his twenty years as a cop, the rent from his cottage at the lake and a handful of CDs—"chump change," Victor called it. He thought of the various uses to which he could put a thousand dollars, the bills he could pay.

"The horse is insured?"

"Are you saying I should let them lop off its head and settle for the insurance money?" Campbell had raised his voice, and this was another characteristic that Charlie remembered. Campbell was always ready to get angry.

"Not at all, I was just curious." Charlie turned his gaze away from the checkbook to look back at Campbell. "How many owners d'you think have been paid off?"

"It's hard to tell, since they don't talk about it. Maybe half a dozen, maybe more."

"Were all the victims in New York?"

"Those guys are New Yorkers." Campbell gestured again to the photographs. "The others I don't know."

"And how did these people contact you?"

"They sent the pictures as an attachment from some cyber café."

Charlie wasn't sure what was meant by "cyber café," but he didn't ask. He felt increasingly left behind by the technological revolution, if that's what it was called. Every time he used e-mail, he felt like Columbus crossing the Atlantic.

"What kind of security did you have?"

"Electric and chain-link fences, security lights and two big Rottweilers too horny to do their job." Campbell explained how the horse-nappers had brought along a bitch in heat. "Now I'm putting in more electronic stuff and a full-time watchman."

As Campbell described what happened, Charlie realized the theft had occurred right around the time he found the body on his sidewalk. "By the way, did you know Mickey Martin?" It seemed only the coincidence of time that led him to ask the question.

Campbell pushed a box of cigars across his desk, offering one to Charlie, who refused, and then took one for himself. "Not really. I ran into him now and then, that's all. I hear he got his throat cut in front of your house."

"That's right." Charlie was surprised that Campbell hadn't mentioned this bit of knowledge earlier, but perhaps Mickey's death hadn't struck him as significant.

"Was he coming to see you?"

"I think so, but I don't know why."

"He had a big mouth. I don't suppose he'll be missed."

"Did you have trouble with him?"

Campbell snipped off the end of his cigar with a small knife. "Very little. A few years ago he was saying some stuff about me and I had a chat with him. Or some of my guys did. How'd he know where you live? You're not even in the phone book except for that crummy office of yours."

Charlie wondered about the stories Mickey had spread about Campbell and how Campbell had made him stop—more muscle than verbal, he guessed. "I'm pretty sure a man named Dave Parlucci told him."

"Never heard of him."

"He works at some local bars, either as a bartender or bouncer."

"Hanging out in bars isn't one of my bad habits." Campbell drew a kitchen match from a small brass box on his desk. "So what about Bengal Lancer, will you take care of the money for me?"

"When does it have to be delivered?"

"They wouldn't say. Sometime in the next few days."

Charlie wished he were someplace else, maybe in town at a movie or getting one of those latte things at the Common Ground, someplace without excessive temptations. Though he understood the job wouldn't interfere with his role as a defrocked PI, it still might lead to trouble. On the other hand, there was the checkbook right in front of him. And perhaps an element of defiance affected his decision. He disliked Chief Novak telling him to keep his nose clean. He disliked the very banality of the expression. "Okay, I'll do it." But he didn't feel good about it.

For years Eddie Gillespie had seen himself as a young swinger about town, a man who activated palpitations in the hearts of the sexy and susceptible. But the birth of his first grandchild when Eddie was only forty-two had put a dent in his image. As Eddie had begun fast out of the chute, so had his son, born out of wedlock when Eddie was barely twenty. Accordingly, Eddie's pride in the apple of his eye had turned a trifle sour, as his son became a father while still in community college. At this rate, Eddie thought, by the time he got to Charlie's age he'd be a great-grandfather a few times over.

In addition was the problem of Eddie's hair, which had once been his Saratoga Springs trademark as much as the Empire State Building and Eiffel Tower were illustrative of their respective cities. Eddie hadn't simply had hair; he'd had a glossy pompadour of black locks rising above his scalp like Godzilla over Manhattan. But that, figuratively speaking, was yesterday. Now Eddie had to borrow, and each day he was obliged to borrow a little more, with the result that the hair on the sides and back of his head, if left to its own devices, would dangle past his neck, while the top of his head would shine like a fortune-teller's crystal ball. But with the application of sufficient gel and hair grease, Eddie could cover his Sahara of scalp and shape his last locks into designs reminiscent of the glories of the past, as long as the wind wasn't blowing or you didn't get too close. The resulting coiffure had the texture of an overcooked meringue and was hard enough to knock down doors, if such had been Eddie's pleasure.

Third was the problem of Eddie's paunch. Where had it come

from? One morning when he was forty, Eddie had awoken from rest-less sleep and unsettled dreams to find it perched, or at least attached, to his waist, like a gigantic succubus, though the term Eddie had used was "wart." It wasn't his; he was certain of this. He must have stumbled through a time warp and caught a bad case of someone else's karma. In the months to come, he'd learned that exercise and diet did nothing to shrink it. Regrettably, it had become as much a part of him as a child born late in life, and Eddie even began to refer to it in the third person—"me and my pot," "me and my paunch," and also "my paunch would like another piece of chocolate cake." But Eddie didn't like it; he didn't like any of it.

These changes had led Eddie to rethink his life's direction, or lack of it, and his plans for the future and still-to-be-realized nest egg: his retirement in a Tampa condo. Nowadays he drove a truck for the city, plowing and hauling snow and salt in the winter, transporting gravel and sand during the rest of the year. For this activity he thought himself lucky, except for his hair loss, grandchild and paunch. Nowadays he discussed health benefits as he had once dis-cussed fast women; he talked about his retirement package in the same hushed tones with which he had once discussed his genital package. No longer did Eddie yearn to carry a pistol and follow Char-lie down dark alleys and into dangerous situations. Danger had lost its allure. In fact, he wasn't even supposed to *see* Charlie, according to his wife, while Victor Plotz was off-limits completely. If the powers in city maintenance knew that Eddie was consorting with known low-lifes, his retirement package would become as fragile as a debutante's orchid. As for his genital package, it now formed part of his wife's material goods as much as her vacuum cleaner, plasma TV and Honda Civic. Eddie felt lucky just to use it to take a piss, and even that, these days, was problematic, as middle age began to close the tap on his once powerful flow, leading to occasions of urinary trifurcation as one stream hit the wall, one the bathroom rug and the third dribbled down his pants.

But dissing Charlie and Victor was going too far. Despite Eddie's limitations, he was still loyal, or loyalish, though he now mostly saw his old friends late at night in out-of-the-way bars while wearing a large hat to obscure the ruined glory of his former hair. Still, he saw them less often and always with an eye on the door, as if his wife with a SWAT team drawn from her church's ladies auxiliary might burst into the room waving Bibles.

Even today, as Eddie made his way to Charlie's office on Phila Street while on his lunch break, he worried about being spotted. It wasn't that he worried about his wife, who was presumably painting, decorating and extending a variety of fingernails at Gail's Nails in Ballston Spa, but she had spies, a circle of friends whose only wish was to catch Eddie violating what his wife called the "marital contract": a document only a trifle smaller than the *Oxford English Dictionary*.

The day itself was overcast and cold, with the wind energetically sending the last leaves skittering along the street. Days like these led Eddie to fantasize about his future Tampa condo, which in turn intensified his wish to do nothing to rile up the powers in city maintenance. His lunch hour was his lunch hour only within narrow parameters and conditions, and Charlie lay outside them.

Charlie, of course, no longer had any need for an office and Eddie knew that he only hung on to it for sentimental reasons. Charlie would read, entertain friends and play solitaire. Very rarely someone would appear looking for a private detective and Charlie would have to say he was retired. Sometimes he would give out PI-like advice—lawyers to call and options available—but he didn't charge for it. Janey had never asked why he kept the office. It was enough that he thought he needed it.

The office was on the second floor of a brick building, above a used bookstore, and the stairs and hall Charlie swept himself as a goodwill gesture to his landlord, who wanted to raise his rent. On the opaque glass occupying the upper half of his door, Charlie's stepdaughter had stenciled in black paint: "Charles F. Bradshaw—Consultant."

Inside was a small anteroom with two straight chairs and a brown couch with springs so collapsed that it was scarcely an improvement over sitting on the floor. On a table were ancient issues of *National Geographic*. A second door with a pane of opaque glass on which was written the word "Private" led to the office itself. The door was open and Eddie passed through it.

The room was austere, not to say shabby: a threadbare brown carpet, two gray metal file cabinets, a small safe, a cot where Charlie sometimes took naps, two wooden chairs for visitors, a bookcase, an oak desk, a squeaky office chair and Charlie himself, who at the moment was in his shirtsleeves eating a tuna salad sandwich. Behind him on the wall was a framed photograph of Jesse James, looking like a red-tailed hawk on the prowl for baby rabbits. Many years before, Charlie had thought it necessary to have such a photograph; now he wondered why he kept it.

"You busy?" asked Eddie, pausing by the door.

Charlie held up his sandwich. "You like tuna salad? I got another if you want it."

"The wife doesn't like me to eat mayo."

"She wouldn't know."

Eddie settled himself in a visitor's chair. "Nah, she'd smell it on my breath."

Charlie raised his eyebrows slightly and put his sandwich back onto a sheet of plastic wrap so Eddie wouldn't feel tempted. "Cholesterol?"

"Poly fats. She says eating arsenic is safer."

Charlie tried to look concerned. "So what brings you here?" He realized that Eddie looked embarrassed, a rare event considering the thickness of Eddie's skin.

Eddie shifted in his chair and stared at the photograph of Jesse James. "I thought you were getting rid of that picture."

"Sometime next week. I'm getting another picture framed up the street: a painting of Saint Jerome."

"You Catholic?"

"No, but I like lions. You going to say what's on your mind?"

Eddie looked embarrassed again and began fiddling with the zipper on his leather jacket. "I heard about Mickey Martin."

"You knew him?"

"Like anyone else, I guess. We'd talk now and then. He had that breath."

Charlie waited.

"You got to see that with Mickey, how he looked, I mean like his expression, it had nothing to do with what was happening inside his head. Like, he had this big smile, he could be a real charmer, but, I don't know, he was mean as a snake."

"I'd heard something like that."

"Yeah. Especially if he'd been drinking."

"Is that what you came to tell me?"

Again there was the embarrassment as Eddie inspected a liver spot on the back of his left hand. "I bumped into him Monday after work at Home Depot. My grandkid tossed a ball through the kitchen window and the wife said I had to fix it. You know how it is. A window's a window, right?"

"I thought the boy was about fifteen months."

"He's got a good arm. He's going to be a pitcher. I was teaching him how to pitch."

"You have any more to say about Mickey Martin?"

"Yeah, we talked a little."

"And?"

Eddie went back to inspecting the liver spot, which, he was sure, had appeared overnight. "He asked about you."

The office was warm, the radiator clanking, and Charlie had begun to feel drowsy. Now he perked up. "Me?"

"That's right. We'd been talking about this and that and Mickey asked if you'd moved away. I guess he'd driven by your place on the lake and seen some other people living in it."

"What did you tell him?"

"Nothing really, I mean, I said you and Janey had gotten married and you were living at her place."

"So you told him where I lived."

"Not directly, but I guess someone might interpret it like that. All I said was, she had an old house on the west side."

"She's in the phone book."

"That's what I told him. Me and the wife are unlisted. She says it's crazy to put your name in the phone book where anybody, like serial killers, can find you."

"What else did Mickey ask?"

"Not much. It was very casual, but later I felt bad about it. I felt I shouldn't have said anything. Like he had a big mouth, right? He asked if you were still a PI and I said you'd retired. Mickey, he just smiled, but with his mouth shut on account of the breath. Know what I mean?"

"Was there more?"

"I said you'd wanted more time to read and he said he'd heard you had a big stash of dirty books. That was Mickey all over."

"I guess so." Actually, Charlie was thinking of Dave Parlucci. He had assumed that Parlucci had told Mickey Martin where he lived, but instead Mickey had learned it from Eddie. So then why had Parlucci asked Victor where Charlie could be found? "Do you know Dave Parlucci?"

"We've crossed paths. He tossed me out of a bar about five years ago. Believe me, I'd hardly had a drop. After that we were never close."

"Do you know if he and Mickey Martin knew each other?"

"They must have seen each other around, but neither of them were guys that had a lot of friends. Why?"

Once again Charlie realized he was no longer a private investigator. "No real reason, I guess."

The knife was an old bowie knife with a twelve-inch blade and a handle carved from an antelope's horn. It wasn't good for delicate work but it was sharp. His dad had bought it from Herter's back in the 1950s and his mother had let him have it when he'd left home at sixteen. Now it was the only thing he had of his dad's. He didn't even have a picture. And he hadn't seen his mother for years.

But the man had kept the knife with him, sometimes in a trunk for safekeeping, sometimes in a stiff leather sheath shoved down over his butt with a jacket to cover the handle. The army had taught him to do tricks with it, had taught him to make it dance. But mostly he didn't need to use it. He just showed it. A knife like that was like a whole brass band. There was nothing subtle about it.

Next to the knife on the table was a long whetstone on which the man had been sharpening the blade. Now it could split a hair in half. Lifting the knife, he balanced it on his palm, then ran his thumb lightly across the blade. It made a noise like a kitchen match dragged across a rough surface, but softer, barely a whisper. He slipped the blade into the sheath and tucked it into his pants behind his back. It felt comfortable there, like everything was ready.

Also on the table were six cardboard figures cut from a shoe box, each about six inches tall and set into a slot on a circle of wood the size of an orange slice so they'd stand up. The man had decorated them with a ballpoint pen, giving them clothes, faces and hair. Two were heavyset, two were thin and two were in between: five men and one woman. One of the in-between figures was lying facedown. The man picked it up. He didn't quite smile, but his lips bent upward a fraction. A red X was drawn across its neck and a smaller X over its mouth. At least that bad business was over. The man set the figure back on the table, laying it down on its face. Then he picked up one of the thin figures. It had a nose made from a bit of twig stuck to the face with Elmer's glue. The man put it to one side of the table, away from the others. "That's limbo," the man said to the empty room. "You're in limbo." Then he got to his feet.

The room was a small efficiency apartment in a motel on Route 9 on the way to Glens Falls. In the summer it would rent by the day, but in the off-season you could rent by the week or longer. It had the appearance of a room last decorated in the 1960s, with faded green walls and a painting of a racehorse over the double bed, a racehorse painted by someone who'd probably never seen a racehorse. The man had rented the room for a week, hoping he wouldn't need it any longer, but already he knew he'd need it for a second week, if not more. The room was neat and the man's few clothes had been carefully put away. A pair of shiny black shoes stood side by side, half under the edge of the bed. On a table by an armchair was a stack of *Saratogians*. The man went to the small refrigerator, poured himself a glass of milk, and then walked to the window and looked out at the parking lot. It was raining and the wind whipped the tree branches back and forth. Now and then a car hissed by, but there wasn't much traffic.

The man felt if he wanted, he could finish his work in a week, ten days at most. But that had always been his problem. He tended to rush things, which got him into trouble. Planning and patience, that's what it took; so even two months would be okay if that's what the job required. Yet he wanted to be done with it; he wanted to be gone. He just had to make sure that what he called "patience" wasn't a matter of being scared. But he knew he wasn't scared; he wasn't scared of anything.

Four

The packed shelves rose up twenty feet on either side of Charlie, bringing to mind the Valley of Death in the Twenty-third Psalm or the walls of the Red Sea towering over Moses and the Jews, but it was only Charlie's local Home Depot. Yet the very narrowness of the aisles and ascending mountain of merchandise gave him a mild sense of peril, as if the whole business might collapse. But maybe his sense of danger came from his talk with Eddie Gillespie and Charlie's realization that it hadn't been Parlucci who had told Mickey Martin where he lived. Possibly Parlucci's question to Victor had been innocent and in some dim moment years before, Charlie had actually lent him a hundred dollars. Perhaps Parlucci had joined some twelve-step program—there were at least half a dozen for which he qualified—and was making amends by trying to return forgotten money.

On the other hand, maybe Parlucci had wanted Charlie's address in order to give it to someone else. What if he had given it to the murderer who had wanted to intercept Mickey Martin before he had a chance to talk to Charlie? Was this possible? And so the Home

Depot's high shelves took on a morbid quality: the high walls of the Valley of Death, even prison walls.

As for Charlie's presence in Home Depot, that, too, was a result of Eddie's visit. Eddie had inserted the idea of Home Depot in his head and Charlie had decided this afternoon was a good time to buy that screwdriver he'd been thinking about, along with an assortment of screws. There were chores at home he had been avoiding—a bookcase to put together, a table to dismantle. It was another result of Charlie's advancing age, or so it seemed, that each day he fell a little further behind in doing what needed to be done, so that greater and more heroic efforts were required to catch up with life's minutiae. The screwdriver fell into this category. But today, in a very small way, he had triumphed.

For nearly sixty years Charlie had struggled with screwdrivers, panting, puffing, twisting and getting blisters on his palms. These were what he now saw as old-fashioned manual jobbies only fit for the garbage dump. What he presently carried under his right arm was a blue plastic case containing an 18-volt cordless drill-and-driver combo—Japanese and flashy—while under his left arm he held a 90-piece drill accessory kit, including nut setters, titanium nitride twist drills, hex shank spade bits, masonry bits, brad-point drills, Phillips and slot insert bits, and five round saw-like things whose purpose Charlie couldn't imagine. But they were bright red and he liked them.

Charlie felt if he were suddenly called upon to take apart his entire house, he was ready for the job. He itched to unscrew something and he glanced at the surrounding shelves, seeking out the bolts and screws that kept them in place. Surely the removal of a single screw would do no harm.

It was then that his name was called, leading his guilty desires to scatter to their cheerless inner caverns.

"Aren't you Charlie Bradshaw? I must say, you've aged."

The woman standing before him had aged as well, which is why it took Charlie a moment to recognize her. She was thin and below-medium height, with dark hair streaked with gray, dark eyes and sculpted cheekbones. Her hands were on the hips of her calf-length burgundy coat and her determined chin pointed directly at him. "Artemis?" he asked.

"At least you're still capable of acts of memory. When I saw you no longer occupied that cute little house on the lake, I worried that one of your desperadoes had plunked you with a bullet."

"Not yet. Actually, I'm no longer a detective. I've retired. Not only that, I'm married."

Artemis raised an eyebrow. "Do you plan to raise a family?"

"Nope, the children came in the marital package: three daughters mostly grown."

"Well, that was intelligent at least."

Charlie and Artemis continued to talk. It had been nearly eight years since he had seen her last and she bore the passage of time with more grace than he did, or this was his opinion, and retained such beauty as was available in late middle age. For many years she had been an equestrienne in Vienna, renowned for her acrobatics on a series of horses as they galloped madly about the ring while she cartwheeled and flung herself from horse to horse as easily as a lumberjack hopping across river-borne logs. Her off-season—a four-month period in summer—she'd spent on her farm outside of Saratoga, developing routines of greater complexity until gravity seemed something she could flick away as easily as a pebble. Then, about seven and a half years ago, Charlie learned that Artemis had decided to stay in Austria year-round, and her farm had been rented to a young couple who raised llamas. She had sent Charlie a postcard detailing the nuisance of transporting horses across the Atlantic and that she had rented a small farm in an idyllic alpine valley. There had been a return address, but Charlie had been unable to make it out. Now, as she explained, she had been back several months.

"As a matter of fact," said Artemis, "I've retired as well."

"You still look very fit."

"Perhaps, but at sixty I feel too long in the tooth to be hurling myself dressed in sequined halter top and tights across the backs of vigorous quadrupeds. I've come back to Saratoga to write my autobiography or memoirs, I can't decide which."

"Is there a difference?"

"Well, in an autobiography one reveals all one's indiscretions, and in a memoir one can pick and choose, allowing me to focus on the crème de la crème of sin."

"And how far have you gotten?"

"I'm still dealing with the virginity question. Such a bother. Losing it was like purposefully leaving a pair of ugly gloves behind on a bus."

"But do you have horses?"

"Three codgers, and I spend some time each day doing flips on their backs. The exercise is useful. I also give lessons to several local girls consumed with foolish ambition. Those will continue till one of them breaks her neck."

Charlie tried to remember her farm. "Don't you live near Fletcher Campbell?"

"He's a neighbor. I've known him for years and I met him again shortly after I returned. He said he was glad to 'reconnect.' I found the word moderately salacious and intend to keep the connection at arm's length. But we've had tea several times and one evening there were cocktails with local folk. He's a trifle hearty for my taste. Can't carry on a conversation without breaking into shouts. But he has some lovely horses and he was kind enough to recommend a vet when Larry was sick."

Charlie looked blank.

"Larry, the horse," Artemis added.

"I was surprised when you left and sorry I didn't have your address."

Artemis brushed back a wave of hair that had fallen at an angle across her brow. "Yes, you might have visited. That would have been a treat. But I'd been having trouble here getting adequate help for the horses. One fellow broke into my house and took various articles, including some pieces of jewelry, the gift of a departed great-grandmother. I had to fire him."

"You didn't call the police?"

"Well, he was an addict. I didn't want to get him into further trouble."

"What was his name? Maybe I know him."

"I've been trying to remember. Matthew something. I think his last name was Perkins, or at least it was something *like* Perkins."

"Anyway, you should have called me."

"I did, but you were away at the time. Then, when I returned to Vienna, I decided to stay the year, and, inevitably, one year stretched into another. People over there may be mean, but they're always very polite about it."

They talked for a little longer, discussing dinner invitations and exchanging telephone numbers. "I don't e-mail," said Artemis. "It's like the remark by that French Symbolist, Villiers de l'Isle-Adam: 'Living? Our servants can do that for us.' I feel that way about e-mail."

Shortly, as Charlie made his way to the checkout line, he thought of the coincidence that Artemis should live near Campbell. Next he thought he was forgetting something. Was it another tool, a wireless saw or power hammer? But he'd already walked five miles within the vast store and his feet hurt. If a power hammer turned out to be necessary for a good life, he'd come back another day.

It was now midafternoon and the rain had settled into a steady drizzle. Men and women sprinted for their cars across Home Depot's ten-acre parking lot. Charlie was no longer at an age where his knees would let him sprint with style, but he had a respectable hurry. Reaching his green Golf, he flung open the door and maneuvered himself inside.

He had meant to go home and begin the chores that would benefit from his 18-volt cordless drill-and-driver combo, but instead he decided to visit Victor. After all, the very act of purchasing the tool was equivalent to half finishing whatever job needed to be done. It made sense to take a break. In addition, he wanted to ask Victor more about Parlucci. Before starting his car, he checked to see if his cell phone was on or if he had inadvertently pushed the silent or vibrate button. No telling when Campbell would call about his kidnapped horse.

The wind shook the trees on either side of Route 29 as Charlie drove out toward Rosemary's diner. Another day of such wind and the leaves would be gone. Then, in another week or so, the time would change and soon it would be dark by four o'clock. Maybe Eddie Gillespie was right with his dreams of a condo in Tampa, but Charlie felt the social life of self-satisfied septuagenarians held little charm.

The grave or a nursing home would put him in their company soon enough. Besides, he didn't play golf.

He found Victor relaxed in a large semicircular booth, not quite like resident royalty but almost. This booth, as well as the others, was upholstered in gold plastic decorated with black squiggles. Victor was thoughtfully chewing a pencil stub and studying the day's *Racing Form*. In front of him on the Formica was a pad on which to take notes. The Wurlitzer jukebox was playing Roy Orbison—*Uptown, in penthouse number three / Uptown, just my baby and me*. Nothing was unusual about this. Victor had packed the jukebox with thirty Roy Orbison numbers, causing some dissension among Rosemary's regular customers. As for Charlie, he sometimes felt that if he ever again heard the five ascending guitar notes that began "Pretty Woman," he would, as his stepdaughter Emma liked to say, lose it.

Seeing Charlie, Victor asked, "You hear of a filly named Jamaica Lady?"

"You know I don't pay much attention to that stuff."

"Hope springs eternal. Coffee?"

Moments later Charlie had a cup of coffee, a slab of blueberry pie and a bright red lipstick smudge on his cheek where Rosemary had kissed him hello. "I want to ask you about Dave Parlucci," said Charlie.

Victor took the pencil stub from his mouth. "Do we have to discuss that again?"

"It's different now."

"Hey, I already said I was sorry. I got a clean slate."

So Charlie told him of his visit from Eddie Gillespie. "The point is that Mickey Martin probably never talked to Parlucci."

"And you want to know who he talked to, if anyone."

"That's about it."

"I thought you'd quit the detective racket."

"I'm not investigating anything. You said he was looking for me."

"Why don't you tell the cops what Eddie said?"

"He's worried about his job with the city and doesn't want the attention."

Victor gave Charlie a sardonic look from under his eyebrows. "You're sly. You've got as many answers as a toad has warts. Tell me, does Eddie's hair still look like the prow of the *Titanic*?"

"Just about." Charlie took a bite of blueberry pie. At the counter a couple of men were talking about football. The wind blew leaves against the windows.

"So what d'you want from me?" asked Victor. "Remember, I'm retired as well."

"Anything else you can tell me about when you spoke to him?"

"Yeah, he said he could tie a maraschino cherry stem into a knot with his tongue."

Charlie lifted his cup and blew across the surface of his coffee. "Anything of substance."

"I don't think so. At first he didn't want to say what he wanted to see you about, but it didn't seem like any big thing, at least nothing to make me suspicious."

"And you wanted to get back to studying the waitress's breasts."

Victor shot a glance toward the cash register to see if the Queen of Softness was settled into her usual spot and not close enough to overhear Charlie's remark. "Cleavage," said Victor. "Not breasts, cleavage. Vast and deep with her tits rising up on either side like mountaintops."

"That reminds me," said Charlie, "I ran into Artemis about an hour ago at the Home Depot. She's moved back to her horse farm."

"The last I saw Artemis, she had a somewhat shallow cleavage. A nice lady, but more of a snack than a meal."

"She's come back to write a book. And she's a neighbor of Fletcher Campbell." Charlie didn't plan to say anything about Campbell hiring him to deliver the money to the horse-nappers. Trusting Victor with a secret was like trusting water to a sieve.

"I don't know, Charlie, you're getting a little deep for me. Oh yeah, I told Parlucci you were opening a bar."

Charlie paused with his fork upraised. "I'd never dream of such a thing."

"Well, I had to tell him something and I'd run out of regular conversation."

"Do you know where Parlucci lives?"

"No idea. Didn't Eddie know?"

"I didn't ask him."

"He drives that big city truck all over; he probably knows where everyone lives."

"I'll find him." Charlie took a sip of coffee and got to his feet. "I expect he's still at work." He set his cup on the table. "Tell me, why was Mickey coming to my house?"

"Hey, what am I, a mind reader? Maybe he wanted to borrow a cup of sugar."

"Really, I want to hear what you think about it. What was he after?"

"Well, if he's coming to see you after midnight, it says he's afraid of something or he's got something to hide. Like he learned where you lived earlier in the day, so why wait till after midnight to visit? And if he's going to you instead of the police, it's maybe about something illegal or at least questionable. He liked to call you a sleazy detective; maybe he wanted a sleazy detective. It's not like you were friends or anything. But he must have thought you could help and he must have been desperate. Most likely he was also scared and, you figure what happened, he had good reason."

"That's a start," said Charlie. "I'll give you a call if I learn anything."

"Anything you want, you got it. And if you come back later, I've a movie you'll like. I picked up the video of my colonoscopy at the hospital. On Rosemary's sixty-five-inch plasma TV, my guts look like the insides of an anaconda in heat."

It took Charlie an hour to find Eddie. First he'd called the maintenance department, and because Eddie wasn't supposed to consort with shifty characters like Charlie and Victor, he identified himself as an insurance agent, Henry Notley, who had to clear up a problem with Eddie's home insurance by five o'clock or else Eddie's policy would be canceled. He was told that Eddie was picking up leaves and lawn debris on the north side near Skidmore. As Charlie drove up Broadway, he took comfort in his falsehood. It was the sort of deception he'd practiced as a private detective. Lying to the clerk in the maintenance office had touched his heart with a little fillip of nostalgia.

After fifteen minutes of crisscrossing the north side of town, Charlie spotted the city's orange truck parked at a curb as Eddie and two other men loaded piles of leaves into the hopper. It was still drizzling and the men wore yellow slickers and rain hats. They worked slowly and methodically, like robots running out of juice. Charlie pulled up and called Eddie over to his car.

"How'd you know where to find me?" asked Eddie, and when Charlie told him, Eddie grew upset. "Jesus, I'm not supposed to know you. They've warned me about that. For Pete's sake, Charlie, a job's a job." Eddie's rain hat was perched on his pompadour like a soup plate on a baked apple.

"I didn't say who it was. I'm trying to find Dave Parlucci. You know where he lives?"

"Like I said, we wasn't close. Anyway, he moves a lot. He told me it was cheaper than paying rent. He pays first and last month, then stays till he's booted out."

They talked about how Charlie might find Parlucci as Eddie leaned on his rake. "It could be anywhere. Now, if you wanted to know where he *worked*, that I could help you with."

"Tell me."

"He's day bartender at the Greasy Mattress, a biker bar over by the harness track."

It wasn't Dave Parlucci who stood behind the bar of the Greasy Mattress, but a barrel-shaped woman in an army camouflage T-shirt and a black leather vest with silver studs placed at close intervals along the seams. A black leather cap with "Harley-Davidson" printed in red across the brow was wedged on her tomato-shaped head. If she had hair, none showed, and Charlie suspected that her head was shaved. Snake tattoos traveled the length of her arms, disappearing beneath her short sleeves, and as the woman washed and dried a row of beer mugs, the snakes seemed to dance. Two long-haired men in jeans and T-shirts were playing mumblety-peg nearby and their knives made dull thuds as they stuck point-first into the wooden floor. All three paused when Charlie entered and stared at him as if he were compost.

Charlie knew the bartender as a woman known as Bad Maud,

which led him to wonder if another bar, or maybe a pastry shop, employed someone called Good Maud. As for the men, Charlie thought it likely that he'd jailed their grandfathers thirty years before. No one spoke as he walked to the bar. There was another *thunk* as a knife hit the floor, and one of the men extended his leg to touch the mark, then drew the knife from the wood. Both men wore black boots with chains across the instep.

Charlie sat down on a stool and tried to sound agreeable. "I thought Dave might be working today. You know where I might find him?"

Bad Maud studied Charlie's face. "Dave?"

"Dave Parlucci, he works here. I thought I might be able to find him."

There was another *thunk*, but this time the knife struck the floor by Charlie's stool. He glanced at it quivering in the wood, scratched his head and turned back to the woman. "I heard he was looking for me about a business deal."

"I don't know where the fuck he is. He didn't show up today."

One of the men retrieved the knife. "You know where he lives?" asked Charlie. The knife once again hit the floor by Charlie's stool and he ignored it. "Dave moves around a lot and I don't have his present address."

Bad Maud kept washing the mugs. "What makes you think I know?"

"This is your bar, right?"

"I guess."

"And Dave works for you, right?"

"What of it?"

"Then you should know where he lives, not just for tax purposes, but he serves alcohol and so the police must have his address."

"Then talk to them."

Again there was a *thunk* as the knife hit the wood. Even though Charlie's feet were resting on the bottom rung, the knife had still stuck in the wood about five inches from his shoe. Shifting his weight, he dropped down so his foot pressed against the hilt. There was a snap as the blade broke.

"Whups," said Charlie.

"Jesus fuckin' Christ!" said one of the young men. "What'd you do that for?"

"It's a game," said Charlie. "I thought we were playing a game."

"We'll show you a game," said the other man. The men moved toward him.

Nearby on the bar were several empty Budweiser bottles. Charlie grabbed one by the neck, smashed it on the edge of the bar and raised its jagged edge toward the men. "Don't," he said. Even as he engaged in this bit of melodrama, a voice in his head told him he was still being motivated by nostalgia and a hankering for old times. It had been years since he'd pretended to be a tough guy.

The response, to Charlie, was unexpected. "Damn!" said Bad Maud. "You're our kind of people." Though she spoke with more irony than sincerity, the two men paused. Bad Maud waved them away. "You made your move. Now back off and let the man tend to his business."

"Dave Parlucci," said Charlie, turning partly away from the men behind him.

"You're not a cop, right." It wasn't a question. Bad Maud filled a mug with Bud Light and pushed it toward Charlie. "I seem to remember you're a private dick."

"Retired. This is no legal thing. Dave and I go way back." He took a mouthful of beer to be polite.

"Dave has a room over on Van Dam. Second floor." Bad Maud

gave him the address. "He said his last place didn't allow pets. He's got a python."

"I appreciate it." Charlie put a twenty on the bar and headed toward the door.

"Hey," said one of the young men, "what about my knife?"

Charlie gave him a friendly smile. "Think of it this way, just the experience was worth the price."

D ave Parlucci no longer lived in the room on Van Dam. He had moved two weeks before, taking his python with him. Now the room was rented by a middle-aged woman with a nose as red as a caboose lantern. She sipped a little glass of something as she spoke to Charlie in the doorway.

"I tell you, when I think of that python creeping around under my bed, it gives me the shakes. Twenty-five feet some of them are. I read it in a book." The woman's name was Lucy. She wore a blue terry-cloth robe and her bleached blond hair rose up from her scalp as if she'd stuck a bobby pin into a wall socket. "Sometimes when people move, they say they're taking their snakes, but they really leave them behind. My girlfriend found a six-foot corn snake in her sock drawer. If that creature's still here, he'll try to squeeze me in the night."

Charlie shook his head sympathetically. "D'you know where Dave moved to?"

"He bailed on his rent and left no forwarding address. I guess I'm lucky to get a place with windows on two sides. Some people will die for cross-ventilation."

"Any mail come for him?"

She shrugged. "I gather he wasn't a big letter writer."

"There're bills."

"Hell, d'you think he'd pay them? I bet the companies gave up trying. You want to come in for a snoot? You look like a jolly kind of guy."

Charlie stepped back into the hall. "No thanks, I think I'm coming down with a cold. You watch out for that snake."

As Charlie descended to the first floor, he heard a lock turn, and a door opened about two inches. "Hey," said a voice.

Charlie paused.

"What you want to see Dave for?"

"He owes me some money," said Charlie.

The door opened another two inches, revealing a face like waxed paper in need of a shave. "How much?"

Charlie took a step toward the door. "Hundred bucks."

"You give me ten and I'll go get it for you."

"Don't give me that," said Charlie. "You don't even know where he lives."

"Sure I do, sure I do, it's not so far." The man opened the door a little more. He looked about seventy, thin as a fence post and with gray hairs poking out above the top of his T-shirt. From inside came the smell of cigarettes and an overloaded cat box.

"I don't believe you. It's hard work renting a room when you've got a python."

"He keeps it in a trunk. Landlords never know."

"Yeah, so you say." Charlie turned away toward the front door.

"I'm telling you, he's just over on Adams Street."

Charlie took ten dollars from his wallet. "What's the address on Adams Street?"

"You think I'll tell you for a measly ten bucks?" said the man.

"Then forget it." Charlie again turned toward the front door.

"Hey, hey, can't you take a joke? What about twenty?"

It was five o'clock when Charlie left the rooming house. The drizzle showed no signs of stopping, a fine gray mist that filmed over his glasses. Once in his Golf, he drew out his cell phone and then stared at it, trying to make up his mind. At last he punched in a number that he knew better than his own. After two rings, a voice said, "Saratoga Police Department."

"May I speak to Lieutenant Hutchins, please?"

"Who shall I say is calling?"

"Charlie Bradshaw."

The woman's voice gave no sign of recognition. "And this is a police matter?"

"You could call it that." It struck Charlie that everyone he'd known on the police force when he was a sergeant was either dead or retired. There was no reason for the secretary to recognize his name. He was history.

Hutchins came on the line a moment later. "So have you decided to talk?"

"I already told you: I know nothing. I just wondered if you'd made any arrests."

"This is police business, Charlie. Just tell me how it concerns you."

Charlie watched a yellow dog dash across Van Dam in front of a UPS truck. "A man gets his throat slashed on my front walk and I want to know if you've caught the killer. Of course it concerns me."

"No arrests have been made, if that makes you happy. You sure you're staying out of this?"

"I retired," said Charlie. "Concern for me and my family is as far as I go."

"Actually," said Hutchins, "there's one detail that might interest you. It'll become public knowledge pretty soon anyway."

"What's that?" He expected another bad joke, but he was wrong.

"Mickey's tongue was cut out. There was no trace of it at the scene. The perp probably drew it out with a hook and sliced it. You know why someone might do that?"

To himself Charlie said, Because Mickey talked too much. To Hutchins he said, "Your guess is as good as mine, Lieutenant. Anyway, I'm out of the business. I don't ask that sort of question anymore."

"That's what I like to hear, Charlie."

Charlie closed his cell phone and started his car. The thought of a man slicing out Mickey's tongue made him queasy. It suggested something about the nature of the killer, something about anger and ferocity that made Charlie hope he was done with his work. Parlucci's address was three blocks away on Adams Street. The gray day was drawing to a close; streetlights were coming on.

Five

The house on Adams was similar to the one on Van Dam, an oversized white Victorian in need of paint, which had been broken up into rooms and efficiency apartments. During the summer it was full of men and women who worked at the track, grooms and maintenance people. During the winter there were probably a few students, older women who worked at Walmart or Lowe's, people down on their luck traveling through town, people getting by on Social Security. It seemed to Charlie that he'd prowled the hallways of a hundred such buildings, seeking people who never wanted to be found. Even this building was one he knew he'd visited, though he couldn't recall the circumstances or when it had been.

On the porch by the front door were ten mailboxes with names beside half: Rodriguez, Overbeck, Lucini, Skoyles and Gerstenburger. Any of them could be Parlucci. The front door was unlocked and Charlie entered into a long hall with yellow walls. On a card table were envelopes marked "Forward" or "Moved." The hall didn't so much smell of food as of vague organic substances of a semi-edible nature. Antique food and Lysol. Charlie had once thought he'd end up in such a place with his books, old records and old-guy clothes. He'd said as much to Janey, who had given him an angry poke in the ribs, saying, "You kidding? I'm going to hang on to you till it's time for you to be stuffed. And if I go first, you belong to the girls." Since then Charlie had sometimes wondered how he'd look stuffed and what he'd be wearing. Perhaps he'd have his own glass case in the museum in Congress Park, sitting at his old oak desk or peering from behind a plastic tree wearing a deerstalker hat.

Charlie approached a door with the numeral 1 painted in black on the upper panel and gave the door a jaunty knock: shave and a haircut, two bits. Then he listened as a pair of slippers slid and scratched their way across the linoleum.

"Who is it?" It was an old woman's voice—hopeful and anxious—someone so lonely that even a robbery might be seen as credible human contact to reduce the emotional murk.

"Hi, my name's Charlie. I'm looking for a pal a mine who moved in last week. Can't remember if he's on the first or second floor. Name's Dave."

"Dave?"

"Yeah, a young guy, midthirties—we go way back. But he's footloose, know what I mean? Always packing his bags."

There was no answer. Charlie thought he heard the mutter of a TV. The sadness in such buildings felt like the damp found in old cellars. "You still there, ma'am?"

"Try Room Seven," came the voice. Then the slippers shuffled away across the linoleum.

Duplicity, thought Charlie, thy name is I don't know what. Did I get this from Victor or have I always had it? But he didn't have to articulate the answer; he'd been born with it.

Charlie climbed the stairs to the second floor—rubber treads and a wobbly handrail. Room Seven was at the end of another yellow hall, looking out on whatever passed for a backyard. Charlie gave the door another jaunty knock and listened. There was no sound. He knocked again. Could he hear anything? He didn't think so. A minute passed. There was a gap at the bottom of the door and Charlie got down on his knees to look. Although he could only see about two inches, it was enough to tell that a light was on. He got up and knocked again. "Dave?" Another minute passed.

Charlie tried the doorknob. The door was locked but it rattled in a way that indicated the dead bolt hadn't been set, while the lock on the knob was a simple button jobby. Charlie took a Visa card from his wallet and slid it through the crack. After fiddling for a moment, he pushed the door open. He stepped forward, then came to an abrupt stop and put out his hands to protect himself.

Whether it was the blood he saw first or the python, he never knew for sure. Nor was he aware of the noise he made—a rasping groan as the ten-foot python slid toward him across Parlucci's blood-splattered body so that the snake's golden patches were wet with it; so it seemed not just the snake, but the blood itself was sliding toward him. As for Parlucci, his throat had been cut, the blade going so deep as to reach the bone. Worse, but not worse of course, only visually worse, his nose had been sliced from his face. Dressed in jeans and what had been a white T-shirt, he lay in his blood like a canoe in a narrow stream as the python shivered its way across Parlucci's chest to the floor, till its tongue-flicking head was five feet from where Charlie stood and its tail was just sliding off the bed. Charlie leapt back and slammed the door. He drew out his cell phone, but it took a moment before he caught his breath. Then he double-clicked the send button to call the last person he'd spoken to.

Lieutenant Hutchins picked up on the second ring. "What is it now, Bradshaw?"

Charlie told him where he was. "You need to get over here. There's a guy dead with his throat cut. And bring a snake handler."

Hutchins had arrived in ten minutes, followed by two patrol cars. "Where's the snake handler?" asked Charlie. But Hutchins hadn't brought a snake handler. He had assumed Charlie was joking. As a result, when he opened the door to Parlucci's room, the python slid swiftly into the hall.

Later, when sufficient time had passed and Charlie's own sense of horror had diminished, he was able to describe the scene to Janey with a certain levity.

"Hutch had six cops with him. He yanked open the door and the python must have been waiting on the other side. Do you know they can almost leap? Every one of those cops let out a bellow. And move? I've never seen cops move that fast, but it wasn't to anyplace in particular. They jumped up or back or banged into the wall; two fell down. And right away ten feet of blood-smeared snake was in the middle of them. One cop drew his weapon and waved it around. He didn't fire, but it kept everyone hopping. Hutch was shouting, 'Put up your weapon, put up your weapon!' Then the snake disappeared. It hadn't been attacking them; it was just passing through. It got behind the wall somehow or into the attic. They still haven't found it."

"And what did you do?"

"I told Hutch he should have brought the snake handler."

But on that particular evening, the awfulness had filled Charlie's mind as he stood in the hall with Hutchins, staring through the doorway at Parlucci's corpse. His red hair seemed part of the blood and his eyes were slightly open. "Too close together," Victor had said. "Lobster eyes." Hutchins shouted into his phone. "I need backup. We got to close down the area!"

Time went by. Charlie sat down on the stairs to the third floor as police came and went. Crime scene guys from the sheriff's department set up lights, took pictures, snooped around, put little bits in plastic bags, dusted for prints. The narrow hall was jammed with men coming and going. People in the building began to be questioned. Cops searched the rooms for the snake, and stamped or plodded through the attic, upsetting boxes. Other men looked for the snake outside. Yellow tape appeared everyplace. More time passed. Every so often Charlie was asked rather gruffly what he was doing sitting on the stairs.

"Lieutenant Hutchins planted me here," he said, which was true enough. Hutch had warned him not to move an inch from that spot. But now the rubber treads were digging into his butt, his stomach was growling and his legs were stiff. He called Janey to say where he was and briefly told her what had happened. It wasn't until Parlucci's body was removed that Charlie was taken back to police headquarters. By then it was past ten o'clock.

There he was kept in a windowless interview room with the heat cranked up to about ninety degrees. The gray walls were bare except for a few sets of scratched initials. Sweat beaded on his brow and damp half circles formed around the armpits of his shirt. The mirror built into the wall indicated a sheet of one-way glass, making Charlie think that his smallest gesture was being noted and written down. By the time someone came to get him forty-five minutes later, he was down to his T-shirt, with his shirt, sport coat and raincoat folded neatly on the table in front of him.

A patrolman took him to Chief Novak's office and he was told where to sit. Charlie held his folded clothes on his lap. No-Neck Novak was seated behind his desk, and in an armchair by the window sat Lieutenant Hutchins, who glanced at Charlie's clothes, or lack of them, as if they formed one more example of Charlie's degeneracy. The black T-shirt had been a gift from his oldest stepdaughter, a souvenir from a hip-hop concert at the Saratoga Performing Arts Center. On the front were the words "Public Enemy" in yellow and on the back "Fear of a Black Planet."

The only articles in the office that suggested the sort of man who inhabited it were half a dozen weight-lifting trophies—small golden men hoisting free weights over their heads. The walls were bare except for a 9/11 tribute poster with three firefighters raising a flag before the wreckage of the World Trade Center, and a poster of former president Reagan sitting at his desk in the Oval Office above the words "Gone But Not Forgotten."

Novak stared down at a legal pad on which he was making notes. He seemed unaware of Charlie's presence. Hutchins studied his nails with an appreciation that suggested they'd been trimmed by Michelangelo himself. Charlie knew this was supposed to make him nervous. Instead, he tried not to lose his temper. There was no point, at the moment, to shout at them and demand to see his lawyer. They were, to the best of their abilities, doing their job. His only regret was that he hadn't worn some other T-shirt.

After a few minutes, Charlie turned to Hutchins. "Catch the snake?"

Hutchins looked up as if seeing Charlie for the first time and grunted.

"Boy, I've never seen anyone move as fast," said Charlie appreciatively. "You know, pythons aren't poisonous, if that's what you were afraid of. They just squeeze you to death."

"You're on thin ice here, Bradshaw," said Novak. The police chief had very large, pink hands that were folded before him on the desk. They resembled a small pagan temple.

Charlie tried a mildly curious tone. "Why's that?"

"You've got no license anymore, remember? You could get two years in the clink if it turns out you're working. To tell you the truth, I'd love to see that happen." Novak affected a slight southern drawl. Though raised in Connecticut, he'd spent a year stationed at Fort Benning, Georgia, some thirty years before.

"Look, I found a corpse and immediately called the lieutenant. What's your problem with that?"

"You broke in," said Hutchins.

"Prove it."

"Your prints were on the doorknob and faceplate," said Hutchins.

"That doesn't prove I got the door open."

"Then how'd you know that Parlucci had his throat cut? How'd you know to tell me to bring a snake handler?"

"Maybe I looked under the door."

"Give me a break," said Hutchins.

"What were you doing there anyway?" asked Novak.

"I heard Parlucci was looking for me."

"Who'd you hear it from?"

By now the police had surely talked to the old woman on the first floor, who would have told them that Charlie had knocked on her door. Either tonight or tomorrow they would talk to the woman who lived in Parlucci's old room on Van Dam. They'd even find their way to the Greasy Mattress and talk to Bad Maud. If Charlie refused to answer Novak's question, he had no doubt he'd be locked up in a holding cell within the next five minutes. And he could easily be prosecuted for doing PI work without a license. Even if Charlie were acquitted, he'd have to pay his lawyer, which could be a substantial amount of money.

"My friend Vic Plotz told me. Parlucci talked to him last night at the Parting Glass and Vic gave him my address. Parlucci said he had a hundred bucks of mine he wanted to repay. Instead of waiting for Parlucci to find me, I went to look for him."

Novak nodded to Hutchins, who got up and left the room. It was eleven thirty. Charlie hoped that Victor hadn't gone to bed or wasn't in the hot tub or seeing his colonoscopy movie, because very soon he'd hear a heavy knock on his door.

"So how long you been friends with Parlucci?" asked Novak.

"We weren't friends. He was just somebody I'd seen around town for years. Sometimes we'd talk."

"You lent him a hundred bucks, that seems pretty friendly."

"That's what he told Vic, but I had absolutely no memory of it. He wasn't the sort of person you'd lend money to."

"Why not?"

"He'd either drink it or put it up his nose."

Hutchins reentered the room, walked to the armchair and nodded at Novak.

"So Parlucci wanted to know where you lived and then he didn't come by?"

"Well, I was out for much of the day, so he might have come by without my knowing. My stepdaughter got home from school around three thirty; my wife got home at five. They didn't see him."

There was a pause as the two policemen ran through their repertoire of skeptical expressions. Then Hutchins said, "I want to know exactly what you did from when I left you around six a.m. till when you called about Parlucci. Give it to me in detail and don't leave anything out."

So Charlie began with his inability to get to sleep the previous morning, to Victor waking him up to tell him about Parlucci and then on to his visit to the Home Depot, enumerating the contents of the accessory kit that he'd bought to accompany his 18-volt drill-and-driver combo—nut setters, titanium nitride twist drills, hex shank spade bits, masonry bits, brad-point drills and so on. He talked about the pork chops Janey had cooked the previous evening and what he'd seen on TV. He didn't mention Fletcher Campbell, Artemis or Eddie Gillespie, but he mentioned going to his office for a while.

"You still have that private slum?" said Hutchins. "You're retired. I thought you'd have given it up."

"Friends drop by," said Charlie.

He continued to detail what he had done during the day and had just reached the point when he had arrived at the rooming house on Adams Street when a patrolman pushed open the door and there was Victor, his royal purple pajama bottoms poking out from under his overcoat.

Victor was unhappy. "You know how fuckin' much I dislike this?" he shouted. "I know right where you live, you no-neck monster; you wait till I come pounding on your door some midnight!"

"Parlucci's been murdered," said Charlie. "His throat was cut." Charlie knew that Hutchins had no reason to bring Victor to police headquarters when he could have questioned him at Rosemary's diner. But Hutchins disliked Victor and had done it only out of meanness.

"Yeah, that's a shame," said Victor. "Couldn't it have waited till morning?"

"Bradshaw found the body," said Hutchins. "He said you told him Parlucci was looking for him and you gave him Bradshaw's address."

Victor gave Charlie an exaggerated disappointed look and turned back to Hutchins. "Well, maybe I did, maybe I didn't. What the fuck business is it of yours?"

"Take him downstairs and put him in a cell," said Novak.

"Wait, wait," said Victor in a milder tone. "I seem to remember something like that after all. Would it have been at the Parting Glass?"

Novak rubbed his forehead as if suddenly tired. "Just tell us what happened."

So Victor retold his story as he stood before Novak's desk, only leaving out the part about the waitress and her cleavage.

At the end Hutchins turned to Charlie. "You really thinking of opening a bar? You'll never get a license."

"No," said Charlie, "he was just saying it."

Novak slapped a hand down on his desk. "Don't you people ever tell the truth?"

Just then Charlie's cell phone began to play the jaunty staccato notes of "The Mickey Mouse Club March." Conversation ceased. It seemed to Charlie that if he'd farted, Novak and Hutchins couldn't look at him with any greater disgust. As for Victor, he appeared smugly superior. "My daughter . . ." Charlie began, and then stopped. He'd started to say that his stepdaughter gave him different rings as a joke—last week it had been "Whistle While You Work"—but he didn't want to blame her and he disliked excuses. Instead, he put the phone to his ear. "Hello?"

It was Fletcher Campbell. He had heard from the horse thieves. He needed to talk to Charlie right away. "Did I wake you up?"

"I'm afraid I can't talk right now. I'm over at the police station."

Campbell grew concerned. Did it have anything to do with his horses?

"No, no, it's just a small thing. I should be home soon." But glancing at Novak, Charlie saw he'd made the wrong remark. In Novak's world, there was no such creature as a "small thing," especially if Charlie was being questioned about a murder.

"On the other hand," Charlie continued, "Novak might lock me up till I turn to dust. I'll let you know one way or the other when I'm free. I mean, when I get the chance." He closed his phone before Campbell could respond, then he turned it off. He glanced at the three faces staring at him. "The wife," he said.

"Cute phone, Charlie," said Victor. "Mine plays 'Stars and Stripes Forever.' What does yours play, Chief?"

Novak ignored him. "What you don't seem to realize, Bradshaw, is that Parlucci was most likely murdered by the same person who killed Mickey Martin. The modus operandi is virtually identical. Both had their throats cut, while in the first case the tongue was excised and in the second the nose was removed. In each case the amputations were performed by a sharp instrument, presumably the same one responsible for their throat wounds, maybe a bayonet or hunting knife—"

Victor interrupted, "Are you saying Mickey had his tongue sliced out and Parlucci had his nose lopped off?" He seemed appalled. "Jesus, Novak, what kind of nutcase are you dealing with?"

"That's what I thought you could help us with."

"Don't give me that. I got some weird friends, but none are nut jobs. Did you know about this, Charlie?"

"I just learned this evening."

"Well, you should've let me know right away. These jerks haven't taken away my pistol permit yet. I should have greased that sucker and loaded up. It's probably not even safe here in the cop station. Bring out the fuckin' shotguns, is what I say."

Charlie was the only one who knew Victor was having a little joke. Novak waited for Victor to calm down and then asked, "What makes you think you'd be in danger?"

"You got a madman slashing throats and excising body parts, and you got some amateur cops waving their Glocks at a harmless snake. Believe me, innocent people can get hurt. I know what I'm talking about. I seen it happen."

It went on. Victor had to explain his movements over the past two days, while both Charlie and Victor had to describe their contacts with Mickey Martin and Parlucci going back to the third Ice Age. Neither mentioned that Eddie Gillespie had talked to Mickey in Home Depot. Novak would have given another nod and Eddie would have been dragged from bed and brought to the police station. He'd have no time to do his hair.

"Why should Mickey have been going to your house?" asked Novak.

"I've no idea."

"Why'd you go to Parlucci's? Do you have a client?"

"I'm not investigating anything. Victor said Parlucci was looking for me."

Novak again slammed his large, pink hand down on his desk. "You really want to be locked up, Bradshaw? We've got two murders here."

"And I tell you, I know nothing about them."

It went on for another half hour and the only information Charlie concealed, or almost, was about Eddie Gillespie and Fletcher Campbell. It seemed that Parlucci had been killed to keep him quiet; that he had been the one to tell the killer where Charlie lived and the killer was shutting him up. And the nose? Perhaps it meant Parlucci had been sticking his nose in other people's business, or maybe, like Pinocchio, he'd been lying. But Charlie expected it was more than that.

"Tell me," said Charlie, interrupting another of Hutchins's repeated questions about Parlucci, "had either Mickey or Parlucci been in prison?"

"They both had."

"Why're you telling him that?" said Novak. "It's police business."

Hutchins shrugged. "What harm does it do? It'll be in the paper."

"Were they in prison together?" asked Charlie. "I mean, did they know each other?"

"Don't answer him," said Novak. "Don't you see you can't trust him? How many times has he made you look like a jerk in the papers? Neither of them have a lick of truth or integrity. Get out of here, Bradshaw, and take your friend with you! If I find you playing detective, it's prison. Don't forget it."

Charlie started to ask, "What have I ever done to you?" But he already knew the answer. He'd solved cases the police couldn't solve, which had led to unfriendly editorials in *The Saratogian*.

Once out on the street, Victor asked, "Why'd you keep quiet about Eddie?"

Charlie was buttoning his shirt. The drizzle had stopped but it was cold. "The same reason as you."

"Yeah, he'd lose his job for sure. Consorting with lowlifes and known murder victims. But it means the guy who Parlucci gave your address to was the same guy who killed him."

"That's what I figure."

"Was that really Janey who called a while ago?"

Charlie paused a second too long. "Yeah."

"Hey, Charlie, you got to practice your lying. Stand in front of the mirror five minutes every morning and say, 'I am a very truthful person.' That should do it."

It was about one o'clock. Charlie's car was still over on Adams

Street and Victor had been brought into town by a patrolman. Charlie called Janey, waking her up, and explained their predicament. Closing his phone, he said, "She's coming."

"You're sure lucky you've got a nice wife. The Queen of Softness would guffaw and hang up."

"I can't believe that."

"Nah, I like them tough. And you're not going to tell me who called you?"

"Maybe some other time."

By two o'clock, Victor had been delivered back to Rosemary's diner, Charlie's car was again parked in front of the house and he and Janey were in the kitchen as Charlie made himself a salami and cheese sandwich and a cup of chamomile tea.

"I've always liked snakes," said Janey, sitting at the table with a cup of warm milk and honey. "It was probably lonely over there, lonely and scared."

"Ten feet long is too long to cuddle." Charlie brought his sandwich and tea over to the table and pulled out a chair.

"I suppose it would be silly to try to find the poor thing. It'd probably eat the dog. A Chihuahua would be no more than a gumdrop for a python." Janey had exchanged her coat for a white terry-cloth robe and was in the process of cleaning out the clogged holes of a saltcellar with a pin. "That man who was killed out in front, Mickey Martin, I remember when he made that scene at Lillian's last spring, how nasty he was to the woman. What was her name?"

"He called her Lizzie. I don't know who she was."

"He tore her up like bits of paper. Why was he coming here?"

"That's what everybody wants to know. I don't think I'd seen him since that night at the restaurant, so I doubt he wanted to do me a good turn."

"But he must've been killed to keep him from telling you something. Wouldn't cutting out his tongue suggest that? What could he tell you that was so important? And Dave Parlucci getting his nose cut off, as if he had been interfering with someone else's business . . ."

"Both Mickey and Parlucci had been in prison. I don't know the details. But sometimes a man makes an enemy in prison, then years later, when the other man is released, he comes to take revenge."

"Payback," said Janey.

"That's right." Charlie hadn't peeled the skin from the salami and a piece of it was stuck between his teeth. He was picking at it.

"I suppose someone might also want to get even with the person who put him in prison, like the man who arrested him or testified against him or fingered him in some way. You must have put a lot of people in prison, Charlie."

He grinned. "A few. And I expect some get paroled or released every year."

"Does it worry you?"

"No. I mean, I might wonder about someone, but that's about it. I was doing my job, that's all. I wasn't mean or sadistic; I didn't make fun of them. I don't expect them to like me, but I was just doing my job. It was nothing personal."

"When people learn how Mickey and Parlucci were killed, they're going to be terrified. It's bound to be in the paper tomorrow."

"I'm pretty terrified myself." He paused to sip his tea. "It makes the act of just plain shooting someone in the head seem almost wholesome."

At that moment the house phone rang. Both Charlie and Janey jumped.

"Oh, a man's been calling you," said Janey, getting the phone. "I bet that's him."

Campbell, thought Charlie.

Fletcher Campbell was angry. "What the hell were you doing at the police station, Charlie? I hope you didn't say anything."

Charlie was always impressed by egoists who believed that other people's undefined actions must have something to do with them. It seemed too much to worry about. "Dave Parlucci was murdered. His throat was cut, just like Mickey Martin. I happened to find the body."

"Don't get yourself in trouble, Charlie! I need your help right now."

Campbell had shouted into the phone and Charlie held the receiver six inches away from his head to protect his eardrums. Glancing at Janey, he saw she could hear quite easily. "Didn't you say you knew Parlucci?"

"No, I told you I'd never heard of the guy. Don't play games with me, Charlie."

"That's right, it was Mickey Martin you knew."

"We'd had run-ins, that's all, just a few run-ins. Come on, Charlie, I want to talk business. I heard from the guys that got Bengal Lancer."

Charlie saw Janey raise an eyebrow. "So what's up?"

Campbell lowered his voice slightly. "They want the money tomorrow and they want it delivered in Albany at noon. I said I had a guy who'd do it. They want it done in front of the statehouse. You're to stand at the curb with the money in a briefcase; there's a spot by a row of newspaper machines."

"The place's going to be jammed with people going to lunch."

"That's what they want. They'll watch to make sure no cops are around; then they'll grab the money. If everything goes to plan, I'll get the horse a week later. Maybe sooner. You still have that porkpie hat? It was brown plaid or something. Looked like a dog had been chewing it."

My good hat, thought Charlie. "It's in the attic someplace."

"Wear it. That's how they'll recognize you. Be at my place at nine and I'll give you the money."

Campbell hung up before Charlie had a chance to ask any questions. Glancing at Janey, he saw her staring at him quizzically.

"Charlie," she said, "I believe there's something you haven't told me."

Six

Friday morning was cold but the sky clear. This was just as well because Charlie had a scratchy feeling in the back of his throat, which he blamed on getting wet the day before, probably when hurrying across Home Depot's vast parking lot. Now he was in Albany, standing in front of the capitol building by the row of newspaper boxes, wearing his heavy winter overcoat, his porkpie hat and trying to look businesslike. In his right hand, he carried the old leather briefcase that Campbell had given him that morning, saying, "No point in losing a new briefcase on the deal, is there? They're lucky it's not a plastic bag."

Charlie attributed Campbell's remarks to the bravado of the defeated, but he'd dutifully laughed. Within the briefcase was a hundred thousand dollars, a mixture of older bills that Campbell had spent the previous day accumulating. The hurry of this had surprised Charlie, but Campbell said the crooks were afraid that the more time that went by, the more likely the police would get into the business and set up a trap.

"But do guys, even rich guys, have that much money lying around?" Charlie had asked that morning.

"Of course not, I had some people drive it up from the City."

By "the City" Campbell had meant New York City, since he belonged to one of those byzantine financial networks where the rest of the country was just a suburb of Manhattan. "Remember, Charlie, don't do any funny stuff. Just stand at the curb and let them grab the money."

"How will I know it's them?"

"The guy will say the horse's name. You remember what it is?"

"Sure. Bengal Lancer."

Now it was shortly past noon, and hungry civil servants intent on lunch hurried down the capitol steps. A steady stream of cars passed the newspaper boxes in metallic indifference. Charlie tried to assume a relaxed demeanor, not shifting his feet or looking around. He guessed he was being watched, maybe by several people.

When he had told Janey about Fletcher Campbell and his missing horse, she had not been pleased. "I thought you'd retired."

"It's a thousand bucks."

"You sound like Victor. We don't need the money."

"We can go on a cheap vacation."

"Like where?"

"Like Utica."

"Is that a nice place?"

"No, but it has cheap hotels."

Janey gave Charlie an exasperated look. "You said you were just going to sit around the house and read and tinker."

"I've done that. I've been reading and tinkering, and now I'm bored. It's not as if I'm really working. I'm just making a delivery for an old acquaintance. It's getting me out of the house, that's all."

"Charlie, this is how it always begins. There's some small thing and a few days later, people are shooting at you. What's the connection between Fletcher Campbell and Mickey Martin?"

"Nothing, nothing at all."

When the driver of the yellow cab honked at him, Charlie at first didn't attribute it to anything important. The driver maybe wanted directions or wanted Charlie to grab him a newspaper. So Charlie only shook his head and looked away.

When the driver honked again, Charlie saw someone sitting in the backseat. His adrenaline gave a little hop. The cab was drawn up at the curb to his left beyond the newspaper boxes. Charlie strolled to the cab, trying to look calm, but his foot slipped on the curb and he had to catch himself on the cab's fender. He straightened up again and proceeded to the rear window. Inside was a man in a charcoal-gray overcoat, dark glasses and a Yankees cap with the brim covering his forehead.

"Bengal Lancer."

It pained Charlie to give up the money, but he could think of no options. He passed the briefcase through the window.

"Go back to where you were standing," said the man. "Stay there for fifteen minutes. If you reach into your pocket or use a cell phone, the deal's off."

The cab pulled away from the curb and slid into traffic. Was it only out of habit that Charlie memorized the license plate and hack number? It was twelve fifteen. Returning to his position by the newspaper boxes, he watched the cab proceed down the street. People streamed past, oblivious that a hundred thousand dollars had just changed hands. That's as it should be, Charlie thought. Who knew how much nasty business occurred only a centimeter or two beneath the surface of daily intercourse? The best idea, Charlie thought, was not to think about it. Brooding on unpleasant truths only led to cynicism and a fondness for conspiracy theories.

The cab was now out of sight; either it had turned or had seamlessly blended in with other cabs. Charlie thought about the man with the cap. The bulky overcoat had concealed his shape, but he appeared to be of average height and any age between thirty and fifty. He had no rings on his fingers and no watch was visible. On one cheek were traces of old acne scars. The skin was pale, parchment-colored, as if rarely exposed to sunlight. Charlie hadn't seen his forehead or eyebrows. The hair on the side of his head had been dark brown. His one visible ear had been small, almost without a lobe, and reminded Charlie of a cat's ear. His nose had been short with a slight thickening at the end and nostrils like olive pits. Thin lips, a pointed chin and no chain visible around his neck. His voice had a nasal quality and he hadn't pronounced the "g" in "standing." Did Charlie find the face familiar? There was something he couldn't put his finger on.

By now fifteen minutes had passed. Charlie turned to his left and strolled to the corner. He wanted a cab, but not any cab, he wanted a cab from the same company that his contact had used: Veterans Cab. At first it seemed that every company except Veterans was visible, and then the only Veterans cab that went by had several business-suited men in the backseat. But within five more minutes Charlie found the cab he wanted and he flagged it down.

"Where to?" The driver had an Eastern European accent and a saucer-sized bald spot. He looked at Charlie in the rearview mirror.

"It depends. Another Veterans cab passed here about half an hour ago. He probably picked up his fare from someplace nearby a little after twelve-oh-five and dropped him off around twelve twenty-five, maybe at the same place. How do I find out where he was picked up and dropped off?"

"You a cop?"

"Retired," said Charlie. "I'm not anything."

"You gotta be something." The driver squinted at Charlie. "Everybody's something."

"Let's say I'm a concerned citizen."

"That not good enough."

"Okay, it's a husband-and-wife thing. I'm sorry, it's embarrassing."

"I know all about that," said the driver. "I could write a book. I touch your pain, is that what they say? I touch your pain?"

"Feel."

"That's right, I feel your pain."

"So how do I find out?" Perhaps, thought Charlie, I'm too old to be ashamed of these lies.

"A coupla ways. I take you back to the office and you talk to the dispatcher. He's, what you say, hard as tacks. Or you give me twenty bucks and I find out for you. Sorry, even though I feel your pain, I gotta eat."

Ten minutes later the cab pulled up to the Downtown Hilton four blocks from the capitol building. "It's been a gladness," said the driver as Charlie got out.

Charlie paid his fare, a two-dollar tip and the twenty bucks. "Likewise."

A doorman in a dark burgundy uniform stood by the entrance to the hotel. Charlie approached him. "You been on duty long?"

"Since ten this morning, why?" The doorman glanced at Charlie and glanced away, scanning the traffic.

"A man caught a cab here at twelve-oh-seven and returned at twelve twenty-three. He wore a charcoal-gray overcoat, a Yankees cap and dark glasses."

"I'm a Red Sox fan. I don't remember the dark glasses."

"Do you remember his eyes?"

"They were just regular eyes. He had two of them." He focused on Charlie for the first time and lowered his voice. "What's this about, anyway—you a cop? You'll have to see the manager."

"It's a husband-and-wife thing. How old would you say he was? How tall?"

"Maybe thirty-five or forty. I'm not good with heights. He was taller than me and I'm five-ten."

"Was he staying at the hotel?"

"I can't say. He came out of the lobby and took the cab that was standing here. I opened the door and he gave me a buck. Then he was back, I don't know, ten minutes later. I opened the door and he gave me another buck."

"Did he have a briefcase?"

"This is Albany; everybody's got briefcases. He went through the revolving door and that was that."

"Did he go toward the front desk or toward the elevator?"

"Once they go through the door, I'm no longer interested."

Charlie gave the man a ten-dollar bill, passed through the revolving door and walked to the front desk, where a young woman was staring at a computer screen. She looked up when Charlie lightly tapped on the desk with a knuckle.

"I'm late for a business meeting in the coffee shop. The man I'm supposed to meet got dropped off by a cab about thirty minutes ago: gray overcoat and a Yankees cap, six feet tall, about forty. He was probably carrying a briefcase. I've misplaced his name. Do you know if he's staying here?"

"I noticed him, that's all. He's not a guest. My boyfriend's got an overcoat just like it. Barneys' January sale. Armani. He saved a bundle on it. I looked to see if this guy's was an Armani, but it wasn't. You can always tell, can't you? A cashmere blend at best, just a little cashmere. And too big for him, a forty-eight when it should have been a forty-four. My boyfriend—really, my ex-boyfriend—was a perfect forty-six regular." The woman looked away. She was around twenty-five and pretty.

"And what about the man thirty minutes ago?" asked Charlie gently.

"Oh, him? He walked down that hallway to the men's room."

T wenty minutes later Charlie was on the Northway, driving back to Saratoga. He felt sure that the man with the Yankees cap had simply walked through the hotel to the rear entrance, where he had been picked up by an accomplice. Now they were a hundred thousand dollars richer. Even though it wasn't Charlie's money, it stuck in his craw. He thought again of the man, the acne scars and small ears, the nasal voice. Had there really been something familiar about him or was it just that he wanted to find him familiar, wanted some clue? And was he doing this only because he was bored?

As for the time he'd spent in Chief Novak's office the previous night, its effect hadn't been to dissuade Charlie to butt out, as Novak said, more or less, but the reverse, though he wasn't sure what he'd do. But the looks he had gotten from Novak and Hutchins when his cell phone began playing "The Mickey Mouse Club March" remained vivid in his memory. It wasn't that he was angry, but he disliked being seen as a trifler. And if he poked around in this business a little more, he wouldn't be investigating like a PI investigates. No, that sort of investigation required that Charlie have a client and, of course, he had no client. What he was doing was merely interfering in police business, which, he told himself with a grim smile, would be a lesser charge and add up to no more than six months in the county slammer.

Charlie got back to Campbell's farm at two o'clock. A wind was blowing and the day, which had started out clear, had grown overcast. There was even a chance of snow later in the evening. Charlie found Campbell in his office in front of a fire, finishing his lunch and glancing through a horse breeders' magazine. On the walls were paintings of Campbell's prize-winning horses, some in fields sniffing the breeze, others in winner's circles. A seven-unit floor-to-ceiling bookcase covered one wall, though only the center unit contained books. The others held trophies.

"No problem?"

"The man came by in a cab at twelve fifteen. He had dark glasses and a Yankees cap. I gave him the briefcase, then waited fifteen more minutes. He'd taken the cab from the Downtown Hilton and then went back to the same place, but he wasn't a guest. He just walked through the building and out the back."

"How d'you know that?" Campbell had paused with a sandwich quarter lifted halfway to his mouth.

"I found out. I thought you'd be interested."

"Charlie, I'm not interested. Your job ended when you handed over the bag. You're not working for me. Everything's finished. And let me tell you," said Campbell, raising his voice, "if you've done anything to screw up this deal, I'll take it out of your hide. Maybe worse. Do I make myself clear?"

A variety of angry words began to form in Charlie's brain, but he said nothing. Campbell, of course, was right. He should have left well enough alone. He had no business following the cab. It was just old habits, he told himself. But even that answer was unsatisfactory. It was as if he were trying to show himself that he was capable of action, of doing something.

"It's clear."

Campbell gestured toward an envelope on the table. "Then take your money and get outta here."

Charlie stayed where he was. "Listen, Campbell, I did what you told me to do. I don't like being talked to like this."

"And what the fuck are you going to do about it?" Campbell shoved the sandwich quarter into his mouth and returned to his magazine.

Charlie continued standing, but Campbell didn't look up. Charlie took the envelope and left.

He tried to let go of his anger as he drove back to Saratoga. Campbell was a rich guy and could do what he wanted. But he'd also been right. Charlie shouldn't have dug out the information about the cab and the rest of it. On the other hand, Campbell shouldn't have been rude. But that was Campbell's problem, not his. Charlie's problem was plain nosiness. In fact, his mother used to say he'd been born nosy, always sticking his nose into what didn't concern him. No, all that he regretted was having made himself smaller in Campbell's eyes, and even that wouldn't mean much after Campbell got his horse back.

Charlie drove home, intending to get busy with his 18-volt drill-and-driver combo and make repairs. He had to spend a few hours being a good citizen. In any case, he had Campbell's money—not a check but ten one-hundred-dollar bills. It would more than make up for the money he'd been passing around. As that thought crossed his mind, he remembered the old fellow on Van Dam to whom he'd paid twenty bucks for Parlucci's address. What else did he know? Surely, if

Charlie talked to him, it would only delay the repairs by ten or fifteen minutes. It'd be foolish not to take advantage of the opportunity.

The sky was solidly overcast when Charlie parked his Golf on Van Dam; the day had gotten darker, even though the sun wouldn't set for several hours. As he walked to the rooming house, he noticed a single snowflake zigzag downward toward the street. An advance scout, he thought.

The old man lived in Apartment Three, but there was no name on the mailbox. Charlie knocked and waited.

"Who is it?"

Charlie heard fear in the man's voice. "Charlie."

"What's that?"

"I gave you twenty dollars last night."

"You can't get it back. I spent it."

"I don't want it back. You were right about the address. I saw Dave."

There was a scuffling behind the door and the lock turned. The door opened about three inches and an unshaven face looked out.

"The only problem was that Dave had his throat cut."

His eyes widening, the man shoved at the door, but it was blocked by Charlie's shoe. After a moment Charlie gave a hard push and the door opened. He stepped inside and closed the door behind him.

"Who else did you give Dave's address to?"

The man had stumbled back. He was nearly bald, rheumy-eyed and as thin as a fat broom. His gray T-shirt and jeans hung on him loosely. Two black cats watched Charlie from a tattered couch, next to which were a half-dozen empty wine bottles. Not French.

"I didn't tell anybody else, I swear it."

"Sure you did. You told the guy who killed him. How much did he give you?"

"No I didn't, I swear."

"So who killed him?"

"I've no idea."

"It was the same guy who killed Mickey Martin, except Mickey got his tongue cut out and Dave got his nose sliced off."

"I tell you, I don't know nothing about it. I don't even know Mickey Martin."

Charlie took out his cell phone. "Okay, I'm calling the cops. You can tell them instead." He began punching in a number.

"Wait!"

Charlie waited. He didn't like being a bully; he didn't like the small pleasure it gave him.

"I don't know who killed them, really. But I knew Mickey; I was lying about that. I known him about ten, twelve years."

"You knew him in prison?"

"Yeah, up in Adirondack."

"What was he in for?"

"Maybe for some kind of insurance fraud. You know how it is, he said he'd been framed."

"Is that where he met Parlucci?"

"No, Parlucci was down in Albany. The county jail. He got fifteen months for hanging paper. Mickey was brought down there a few months before his release. They knew each other." He spoke haltingly, as if fishhooks were dragging the words from his gut. He hardly looked at Charlie when he spoke.

"You were there as well?"

"Both places, at least some of the time. I was getting out, too."

"What were you in for?"

"Robbery, mostly. Convenience stores. Couldn't do it anymore. Takes too much running. You're not goin' to tell anyone we talked, are you?"

Charlie glanced around the room. A TV was on, the sound turned down to a mutter. Piles of clothes, some dirty, some clean, covered most of the surfaces. The bed had no sheets, just two cheap baby-blue blankets. There was one wooden chair that looked fairly sturdy. "Let's sit down," said Charlie, trying to make his voice less threatening. He took the chair.

The man sat down next to his cats. His hands were shaking, maybe from palsy or alcohol, maybe from fear. The room had two windows, each covered by a drawn yellow shade. The windows were shut and the room had a sour smell.

"What's your name?" asked Charlie.

"Milo Rutkowski."

"What're you doing in Saratoga?"

"I get some work in the backstretch, mostly in the summer. Some of the grooms know me. And I work a little at the harness track."

"Were you friends with Mickey and Parlucci?"

"I'd done them favors. Running errands, picking up bits and pieces of stuff."

"What kind of stuff?"

"Information. Who people were, what they're saying."

"You're a snitch?"

"No, nothing like that, I mean, not really. It's just information. Anyway, you need people to look out for you. They looked out for me." Milo picked up a wine bottle and checked if anything was left. He sighed and set it back on the floor.

"Did you know that Mickey had wanted to see me?"

"No way. I don't even know who you are."

"Charlie Bradshaw."

There was no look of recognition on Milo's face. "All I know is something was bothering him. Like he saw somebody or heard about somebody, I don't know."

"When did this start?"

"Last week sometime."

"Do you know Lizzie?"

"Lizzie? Never heard of her."

"Did Parlucci seem scared too?"

"Not so much. But he was concerned. I gotta say he was concerned. That's why he moved. The landlord don't give a fuck if he had a snake or not. It kept down the mice."

"Did Mickey have any enemies up in Adirondack?"

Milo thought about it. "He was never a popular guy. I mean, we knew each other, like there were those favors, but we didn't hang out. Some guys said he was a snitch. Like there was a drug bust they said he'd snitched on. And he had money. Nobody trusted him, but then in prison, trust isn't a big thing. There might have been guys who hated him, I mean white guys, but I couldn't put a name to them. Colored guys didn't seem to like much of anybody 'cept other coloreds. Then the Ricans were a whole 'nother story. For that matter, Mickey had some coloreds working for him. You know, protection, and he paid them."

"And this person that Mickey saw or heard about that frightened him, what can you tell me about him?"

"Nothing, except Mickey didn't know him personally."

"How d'you know?"

"'Cause I heard him talking to Dave. He said he didn't know how to recognize him. 'How'll I know his face?' he said."

"Mickey was killed on my sidewalk; he was coming to see me. And you know who told the killer where Mickey could find me?"

"Who?"

"Parlucci did."

Charlie saw he'd said the wrong thing. Milo seemed to take a breath he couldn't release. His waxed-paper skin grew waxier.

"What's wrong?" asked Charlie.

"I gotta get out of here." Milo got to his feet.

"You know something, don't you?"

"I don't know nothing; I just need to get moving."

"You know who Parlucci talked to, don't you?"

"I tell you, I don't know nothing." Milo took a torn plastic travel bag from under the couch and began putting clothes in it.

"I can still call the police."

"Go ahead. I'll be safer in jail." Milo hurried back and forth across the room, grabbing a few things, dropping others on the floor.

"Who'd Parlucci talk to?"

"Nobody, nobody, I tell you, I don't know nothing."

Charlie asked a few more questions but it didn't make any difference. Milo was too frightened. At last Charlie gave Milo two twenties and his card with his phone number. It was a card to match his stepdaughter's joke on his office door: "Charles F. Bradshaw, Consultant, Legal and Otherwise."

"Call me if you change your mind. I can make it worth your while."

"Believe me, you can't make anything worth my while."

This time Bad Maud's only customers were two middle-aged women in leather jackets and pants watching Jerry Springer on the TV. They kept clapping and hooting when somebody said something embarrassing, which was often.

"My pal," said Bad Maud. She stood at the bar with a deck of cards, playing solitaire. She still wore her black vest, but instead of a cap, she wore a red bandanna wrapped around her head like a bit of rope. The top of her head had a sprinkling of black bristles like Wooly Willy.

"Not quite." Charlie sat down at the bar. "Let me have a draft, will you? And do you have any chips or peanuts? I missed lunch."

"I got some jerky a friend made. It's moose."

"I guess it'll have to do."

"I read about Dave getting cut. Some people, right? I gave him that python when he came to town five years ago. I wouldn't of done it if I'd known he wasn't going to treat it right. I'm like a snake-type person." Bad Maud raised her arms, and her snake tattoos appeared to wiggle.

"How'd he mistreat the snake?"

"He went and got killed and now the snake is on the loose, terrorizing the neighborhood, though nobody's seen it. I call that mistreatment."

"You can't blame Dave for getting killed."

"He was a fuck-up. He wouldn't of gotten killed if he wasn't a fuck-up."

"How long did he work here?"

"'Bout a year. But it was hardly work. He used the place as his private clubhouse. Gave away beer. I had to dock his pay. Said he used to have a Norton, but it was bullshit. Fell over the first time he got on a bike. 'Course, he was drunk, but he didn't know the brakes from the gas. That's the sort of fuck-up he was. I'd have fired his ass if he hadn't gotten sliced."

"Still," said Charlie, searching for some sympathy, "he's dead."

"You're right, I gotta count my blessings."

Charlie chewed on the moose jerky. Its taste and texture were like the tongue of a shoe but with a smoky flavor. "Any idea who killed him?"

Bad Maud looked philosophical. "Now, that's a question I make a point not to ask. Who're you going to make happy asking questions like that? Like I won't even speculate about who didn't kill him. Let bygones be bygones, it's safer."

"What about Mickey Martin?"

"Same thing, 'cept Mickey was an even bigger fuck-up. Piss-breath. I've known guys who'd of killed Mickey just because he breathed on him. Guy came in here with a fresh carnation in his buttonhole and Mickey breathed on it. Carnation curled up like a dead baby's fist. How's that not going to get you in trouble?"

"Maybe he had a gum disease."

"Then they should've been amputated. Thing is, Mickey didn't just get in another guy's space, he stamped on it. So the other day somebody stamped back."

"Do you know a girlfriend of Mickey's named Lizzie?"

"I seen her but not for some time. Scared little thing. Mickey'd pick her apart like the wings off a fly."

"You know anything about her? Like where she lives or anything?"

"Nope, like I say, it's been a while. She used to work in one of those stores on Broadway that sells smelly candles." Bad Maud turned to stare at the door. A tightness crossed her face like a mask. Charlie knew who she'd seen even before he turned.

"I wouldn't have thought this was your kind of place, Bradshaw."

Lieutenant Hutchins walked toward the bar as if he meant to buy it. He was accompanied by an overweight plainclothesman whom Charlie knew only by the name of Goofball Godfrey.

"Maud and I go way back," said Charlie.

"Yeah, you both crawled out of the sea together."

"Hey," said Bad Maud, "I pay my taxes . . ."

"What are you doing here, Charlie?"

"I told you, Maud and I—"

"Just beat it. I want to talk to Maud without your help."

Charlie moved toward the door. He'd been trying to decide whether to tell Hutchins about Milo Rutkowski. Now it seemed a bad idea.

T he man sat at the table with a square of cardboard cut from a box on which he'd drawn a figure. He had stuck his knife into the cardboard and was easing the blade along the black line of his drawing, chewing slightly on the inside of his cheek as he cut. The figure represented another man, but thin, very thin. On one side of the table, four figures were still standing; on the other side, two lay facedown.

This is what the man didn't like. He was modifying his plans; he was adding another figure. It would just make more trouble for himself. And the other figures, well, everything wasn't ready yet. One of his figures was missing; that is, he had the figure right there on the table, but the man was missing. It meant he'd have to wait.

But for the guy he was cutting out of the box, there'd be no waiting. In fact, he'd have to hurry. And what would he stick on his face? He'd give him ears, two big red ears. The kind of ears you've got if you're a snitch.

Seven

L ater that Saturday, when he thought about it, Charlie realized
that even in his dream he'd known the increased thumping
had been a policeman's heavy feet ascending the stairs to his bedroom. It didn't matter that the policeman in question wasn't wearing
standard-issue duty boots, but regular black oxfords. The man had
worn duty boots as a rookie and for many years afterward. Even
walking barefoot he'd have a heavy tread. This was a man who had
been trained to stomp. Moments later, as Charlie opened his eyes,
Lieutenant Frank Hutchins opened the bedroom door.

"You're a real prick, Charlie," said Hutchins.

Charlie sat up in bed. His blue pajamas had a pattern of red and
blue Red Sox logos—a birthday gift from his stepdaughter. "Aren't you
breaking and entering?" The clock on the dresser said seven fifteen.

"Your daughter let me in." Hutchins reached into the pocket of
his suit coat, wadded something up, something small, and threw it at
Charlie.

It landed on the comforter in the area of Charlie's lap. He didn't
need to unwad it to know that it read, "Charles F. Bradshaw,

Consultant, Legal and Otherwise." Since he'd given out few cards in the past six months, it required little thought to know that this one had been given to Milo Rutkowski.

Charlie got out of bed and reached for his robe. "What happened?"

"This old guy was found behind the bus station with his throat cut. He had your card in his pocket. Milo Rutkowski. Why didn't you tell me about him? It could have saved his life."

Briefly, it seemed to Charlie that he could see Milo's rheumy and frightened eyes in the air in front of him. Then he thought, He wasn't an "old guy," he was my age. And lastly he thought: Hutchins is right.

"You must have talked to him, too."

Hutchins still stood in the door. "Yeah, but I didn't know he was connected to Dave Parlucci. You did."

It occurred to Charlie to lie, which, he knew, would require another lie and another after that. It was too early in the morning to conjure up the intricate twists and turns of drawn-out deception.

"Milo knew both Parlucci and Mickey Martin," said Charlie. "He knew Mickey up in Adirondack and he'd met Parlucci in the Albany county jail. You must have all the information on one of your computers."

This made the lieutenant angrier. By now Charlie had put on his slippers and robe, and felt reasonably respectable, not that he felt better about Milo. It would have been wiser to bring the "old guy" back to his house and put him in the spare bedroom.

"And why the fuck didn't you tell me?" asked Hutchins.

Charlie knew it was because Hutchins had been rude to him at the Greasy Mattress, and the foolishness of this had struck him only seconds after leaving the bar. "Would you have paid any attention? Anyway, you kicked me out of the bar before I had a chance to."

Hutchins didn't bother to answer this.

"I thought he wasn't in real danger. Obviously, I was wrong. Parlucci told somebody where I lived. That was the person who killed him and killed Mickey Martin. And probably Milo, too, for that matter." Charlie went on to describe what he had learned from Milo Rutkowski.

"I should lock you up right now." Hutchins pushed his hand up across his forehead, his anger changing to apparent fatigue.

"I'm not investigating anything," Charlie insisted. "I just wanted to find out why Mickey'd been looking for me. Can't you see that?"

"Cut the crap, Charlie."

They talked some more, or rather Hutchins talked and Charlie listened. Mostly it was about keeping out of police business, but also there was more about the deaths of Parlucci and Milo Rutkowski and how they might have been avoided. Again Hutchins said he was sure that Charlie knew what Mickey Martin wanted to see him about and to refuse to reveal it was an obstruction of justice. As for Hutchins's own liability in the matter, he probably knew he should have spent more time looking for Parlucci and more time talking to Milo. And, as Charlie said, he could have checked out their prison history online. But he had other cases he was working on and most likely he had court appearances to make as well.

"Charlie, I've been up since three this morning about this business. I won't lie to you; I know you've helped us in the past. But things have changed. You're still back in the seventies. You're a fucking romantic, for God's sake. This is the twenty-first century and you're an antique." Hutchins made a noise in his throat resembling laughter. "Besides, Novak hates you."

Charlie tried to think of something to say. He was touched by Hutchins's trace of concern, but he disliked what he heard. He even

disliked that Hutchins was straying from the two-dimensional stereotype that Charlie had created for him.

"You got one more chance, Charlie," said Hutchins, his anger re-
asserting itself. "If you fuck up, we'll put you away."

Charlie nodded somberly. The stereotype had been reestablished.
"Maybe so, but I'll be out on bail pretty quick. And then there'll have
to be a trial, which will be months away. Nothing's certain, Hutch.
You know that." Then he thought of something. "Was Milo muti-
lated like the other two?"

Hutchins gave him an angry look. "Yeah, both his ears were cut
off." Then he tromped back down the stairs.

After Charlie dressed, he sat down in the small chintz-covered
armchair by the bedroom window. It was snowing: wet, fat flakes
that clung to the branches and few remaining leaves, the kind of
snow that cracked limbs and bent bushes to the ground. The small
Victorian house across the street, which its owners had painted purple with yellow trim, was a ghostly configuration of color in a white
and gray landscape.

Charlie watched the snowflakes coat the lawn and wondered
what was wrong with him. It was more than eccentricity; it was a
form of sickness. When Hutchins had told him to forget about
Mickey and Parlucci, to leave the case alone or go to jail, it only encouraged him to dig deeper. He disliked being told he was out of
date, that he was a romantic. He tried to justify his interference in the
case: Mickey had been coming to see him; Parlucci had wanted to
talk to him and Milo perhaps could explain why. But now Milo was
dead and Charlie bore some responsibility. He also felt he'd been
more interested in questions than in answers. It was the *process* of
investigating more than the results that he enjoyed. He liked talking
to people and poking around. But his modest explanation of his

behavior—"I'm just poking around"—was a falsehood. It disguised his passion. And he'd used the phrase for years to minimize his intrusion in police affairs. Its very appearance of humility seemed to render his actions innocent, at least in his own mind.

No, Charlie was investigating; he wanted to know what had taken place and why. He was a professional Nosey Parker, a practiced meddler. "I must be sick," he said to himself, knowing this was a description he'd never share with Janey or Victor. Maybe he'd tell a psychiatrist, but he doubted it. It wasn't that he felt he'd succeed where the police might fail, though that was part of it. He was a snoop. He thought how he had disobeyed Campbell's orders and traced the cab to the Hilton. "I'm worse than sick," he said as he got to his feet. "Maybe it's a psychosis."

When he reached the bottom of the stairs, Bruiser was waiting for him, wagging his tail. Charlie scratched the Chihuahua's ears. "I'm a bad person," he told the puppy, "I might kick you." Bruiser kept wagging his tail.

As he drank his coffee at the kitchen table, Charlie considered what he'd learned. Milo and Mickey Martin had known each other at Adirondack, where Mickey had a reputation for being a snitch. Then the two men had met Parlucci at the Albany county jail just prior to release. A bigger piece of information was that Mickey had known someone might be after him, though he said he wouldn't be able to recognize him. Had the man been hired to kill Mickey? What was the connection? But Parlucci and Milo could recognize the man. After all, they'd talked to him. But it wasn't clear if they had known the killer before he came to Saratoga.

Of course, Mickey might have been killed because of something that had happened quite recently. Perhaps a blackmail victim, even someone who'd only been the victim of Mickey's gossip, had finally reached the point of anger when he'd made up his mind to do something. But Charlie didn't think so. The mutilations didn't fit the anger theory. He believed that Mickey had been killed because of something that happened years before, and Parlucci and Milo had been killed to keep them quiet. "Do I only think that because I'm living in the past?" Charlie asked himself. And in a moment of near panic, he admitted that he didn't know.

But if Mickey's death was the result of something in the past, then the killer possibly had only an indirect link to Mickey. So either he'd been hired to do the job or had been motivated by a wish for revenge or something else. It was always the "something else" that caused the most trouble. Charlie pondered the awful intimacy of killing a man with a knife, and this was what the killer wanted: intimacy and brutality. And slicing off the tongue, the nose and ears suggested a specific and personal motivation.

So was it over? If the killer had a connection to Mickey's past and wasn't from Saratoga, then had he finished what he'd come to do and left town? Maybe. And there was another inference Charlie could draw: Mickey came to him rather than the police because Mickey had something to hide. Something he didn't want the police to know. But it seemed again that Charlie's argument was based on the fact that he himself was living in the past, that he wanted to believe the murders' origins lay years ago, not in Hutchins's and Novak's time of computers and flashy technology. And this had led to Charlie's wish "to poke around," as if the past were his particular business. "I really must be completely nuts," he said aloud to himself, but now his attitude wasn't one of censure, but bemusement.

Charlie got up to pour himself another cup of coffee. The snow was still coming down hard and several inches had fallen, but the temperature was slightly above freezing; the street was nearly bare.

Charlie got a bagel from the refrigerator and sliced it in half. Then, by the toaster, he saw a copy of *The Saratogian* carefully folded to one of the back pages where a short article had been circled with a green highlighter: Mickey's funeral was set for ten o'clock that morning out of Fogerty's Funeral Home with interment in Maplewood Cemetery on the other side of the Northway. Charlie had guessed the funeral would be soon, but he hadn't decided what to do about it. Janey must have seen the article before leaving for work and circled it for him. Glancing at his watch, Charlie saw he just had time to shower, shave, put on a presentable suit and drive across town.

A lthough it couldn't be said that Charlie enjoyed funerals, in the past few years he'd come to face them with increasing trepidation. First his mother had died in Florida five years before, then four years ago the oldest of his three cousins, James, had died of prostate cancer, only to be followed a year later by his middle cousin, Robert, who'd dropped dead on Broadway from a massive coronary. Then in May his youngest cousin, Jack—a year older than Charlie—had a quintuple bypass. Though Charlie loved his cousins, he'd never liked them. They were too full of advice and disapproval. Visiting one of them was like visiting the dentist. Yet he had sat with Jack in the hospital and offered to bring him whatever he wanted. Not that Jack had wanted much; he had been too appalled by the knowledge of his mortality to take any pleasure in the living artifacts of ongoing life.

Then there were Charlie's friends and acquaintances, who seemed to slip away too soon from life's party, as if they had babysitters at home whom they'd promised to relieve at an early hour. Several had been men and women he'd known since first grade; others had been more recent, relatively—men and women he'd worked with in the police department, people from the track, from local restaurants and bars, even people he had put in prison.

Charlie's trepidation had little to do with a fear of his own eventual demise; rather, he was losing the people who could corroborate his recollections of the distant past. Although he'd never been chummy with his cousins, they had shared similar memories of his grandparents, his many aunts and uncles who had now been gone for at least a dozen years. They could remember Christmases in the 1950s and the time when Uncle Rupert on his eightieth birthday had blown out the candles on his cake so forcefully that his false teeth shot from his mouth and lodged in the pink frosting. With whom could he now share this memory except his cousin Jack, who was too concerned with his own fragility to take an interest in anything else? Two cousins, a number of friends and his teachers in school were gone. Many had attended the same church as Charlie as a kid. Many would recall the day when the vast Grand Union Hotel had been demolished in the 1950s. This wasn't a matter of nostalgia, but a wish to avoid revisionism, to make sure that his memories remained accurate, or pretty much. And there had been times late in the evening when Charlie was tempted to call his first wife, Marge, who now lived in Phoenix, and ask, "Did this really happen or am I imagining it?"

So when Charlie entered Fogerty's Funeral Home on West Avenue—a building more resembling an oversized ranch house than a funeral home—he felt a weight, like a heavy wooden ox yoke he'd seen in a historical museum, being lowered onto his shoulders. The service was in a kind of secular chapel—religion-like but with no specific religious reference to cause offense. An inexpensive casket stood at the front of the room; there were few flowers and those, Charlie guessed, had been supplied by the funeral home. The casket was closed and the mourners were made up of two plainclothesmen who appeared on the very cusp of sleep, and a man and a woman in their fifties whom Charlie found elusively familiar. He'd hoped that Mickey Martin's girlfriend, Lizzie, might make an appearance, but there was no sign of her. Charlie wiped the snow from his shoes and walked quietly across the somber carpet to the man and woman. Vague organ music played in the background, not quite a tune, more like the linking together of melancholy chords.

Charlie introduced himself. There was a shared timidity about the couple, like a family resemblance. "Awfully early for snow, don't you think?" said Charlie as he sat down. Despite his innocuous remark and smile, the couple's apprehension increased. They seemed unwilling to commit themselves to his comment on snow one way or another. "I haven't seen a weather report," Charlie continued. "Is it supposed to stick?"

The man and woman rustled in their chairs. They still hadn't offered their names, and the man's handshake was even limper than Mickey's must have been inside his casket. "I haven't seen the paper," said the man slowly. "I'm Lewis Penfield, this is my wife, Laura. She was Mr. Martin's secretary."

Laura Penfield glanced at her husband as if he had given too much away.

"It's a sad occasion," said Charlie, looking briefly down at the carpet. "Mickey was on his way to my house when he . . . died." Could he say "passed," he wondered, if someone had his throat cut?

"So I read in the paper," said Penfield. A note of mild dissatisfaction crept into his voice. "Mr. Martin owed my wife three months' back salary. Were you his friend?"

"I rather doubt that Mickey had any friends," said Charlie, "though that seems a harsh thing to say of a person. I gather he'd had a girlfriend."

Laura Penfield abruptly spoke up. Her staccato voice reminded Charlie of an ice pick attacking a block of ice. "If you mean Lizzie Whitaker, she wouldn't come here if you offered her a million dollars. Mr. Martin was terrible to her."

"So she still lives in Saratoga?" asked Charlie.

"I should say not. She moved to Glens Falls just to get away from him."

Charlie nodded his head sagely. "I'm certainly glad of that. Is she in sales again?"

"No, she took a position at the Hyde. It was a real step up for her." Mrs. Penfield quickly glanced at her husband, who pursed his lips and stared at the floor.

The Hyde Collection was a small art museum situated in an Italian Renaissance–style mansion once belonging to Louis and Charlotte Hyde. The couple had collected works of art with the profits from their paper mill.

"That's great," said Charlie. "Does she have a background in art?"

Before either could answer, a middle-aged man in a black suit entered through a side door. He seemed to carry silence with him like a smell. He positioned himself in front of Mickey's coffin and nodded to the visitors.

The best Charlie could say of the service was it was short and the plainclothesmen managed to stay awake. The prayers seemed addressed to the concept of a benevolent idea or a questionable but well-meant premise, about which the man in black was vaguely approving but otherwise noncommittal. About Mickey, he had little to say, though what he said was conveyed in a whisper indicative of grief. Mickey had moved to Saratoga a little more than six years before and had opened an insurance agency. He had also been a Realtor. Although Mickey had neither wife nor children, he had become a figure in the business community and now he had been taken from us prematurely. There was no word whether he would be missed. Lastly, he read a prayer to the effect that wherever Mickey had gone, if indeed he'd gone anywhere, we all, he was sure, wished him well. The moment he finished, four brawny men entered to hurry the casket to a waiting hearse.

Charlie stood up. "Do you plan to go to the cemetery?" he asked the Penfields.

"We think not," said the husband. "The weather, you know."

"And what about Mickey's insurance agency, will you be keeping it open?"

Mrs. Penfield squinched her eyes as if suffering a little pain. "His sister in Troy asked me to close it up. Accounts need to be transferred to other agencies; papers need to be put in order. At least I'll be paid. Although to tell the truth, I hate to spend another day in that awful place."

Charlie didn't ask why; he planned to speak to Mrs. Penfield again. "And was it the sister who took care of the funeral arrangements?"

"She said she felt it was her duty, though she felt no obligation to attend."

With that, Mr. Penfield drew his wife toward the door. The casket and plainclothesmen were already gone. A moment or two later, the organ music stopped midnote. Charlie scratched the back of his head. He tried to think of a good reason why he shouldn't go to the cemetery, other than the weather and his own disinclination, but none sprang to mind.

Before leaving, Charlie stopped by the office of the funeral home to get the address of Mickey's sister. "I'd like to write her a sympathy note," he explained.

Fogerty's was a family-run funeral home and the youngest

Fogerty—Larry—was seated behind the desk. He had thinning red hair, very white hands and, though in his midtwenties, he'd already acquired the look of generalized commiseration that went with the trade. "Sympathy!" said Fogerty. "You'd think I was telling her the price of potatoes or that we were talking about a complete stranger. At least she paid for his funeral, though between you and me, it was the cheapest available."

"I'd still like to write a note," said Charlie. "And how d'you spell her name?"

Larry Fogerty gave Charlie an ironic look. "Joan Miller, the usual spelling."

"Who gave the . . . homily?" Charlie couldn't think what to call it.

"Oh, that was my cousin Bob. Public speaking is a hobby of his. He fills in when we don't use a minister."

Shortly, Charlie left the funeral home with Joan Miller's address in Troy.

By the time Charlie got to Maplewood Cemetery, the black hearse was driving away and Mickey's casket was being lowered into the ground. It was still snowing, but at any moment the big wet flakes would turn to rain. Still, it was pretty, with the snowcapped tombstones poking up through an unruffled expanse of white. A single plainclothesman in a dark overcoat was glancing around rather gloomily. A yellow backhoe stood waiting about fifty yards away. Charlie parked his car and got out. He had forgotten to wear boots and the snow slopped into his shoes. It was twenty yards to Mickey's grave and he tried to place his feet in the footprints of the men who had walked ahead of him, with little success.

He approached the plainclothesman, who was blowing his nose. "So, did Novak send you," asked Charlie, "or was it Hutch?"

Charlie hadn't meant to startle the man, but he turned so quickly that he nearly fell. Charlie put out a hand to steady him and the man batted it away. He was about forty and his face had the shape and pasty, pockmarked appearance of an English muffin. "I don't know who you're talking about," he said.

"No-Neck Novak, your boss. You must have noticed him around the station."

"You're mixing me up with someone else." The plainclothesman trudged off through the snow toward his car, or rather the department's car.

Charlie watched him go. Their brief exchange had exemplified what he'd disliked about being a cop. A simple yes or no was almost always rejected in favor of the ambiguous or evasive. There was a roar from the backhoe as it rumbled toward the grave. Charlie pushed forward through the snow, wanting to catch a glimpse of Mickey's coffin before Mickey was tucked away for the long night. If asked why the glimpse was important to him, he wouldn't have been able to answer.

The coffin was covered with a smattering of snow and Charlie stared down at it. Although he'd disliked Mickey, the moment bore a certain solemnity. All the turmoil and animosity, envy and deception, gossip and slander that had described the man in the cheap coffin had been swept away and here he was with no one to grieve for him. In fact, most of his acquaintances were glad.

"You fucked up, Mickey," said Charlie. He tried to think of something else to say, but nothing came to mind. It occurred to him, however, that Mickey hadn't always been bad. Most likely his first year or so had been relatively innocent, maybe even his second and third years, though those might be open to question. On the other hand, it was something he could ask Mickey's sister. The yellow backhoe had nearly reached Mickey's grave. Charlie headed toward his car.

He'd walked about halfway when his eyes fixed upon an impos-ing granite headstone and he came to a stop so quickly that he almost slipped. The name read "Harvey L. Peterson." Beneath his dates were the words "Protector of the People."

Peterson had died six years earlier and retired ten years before that, but for more than thirty years, he had been Saratoga's police chief, or, to use Peterson's preferred title, Commissioner of Public Safety. More important, he'd been police chief during most of the time Charlie had been a cop, as well as chief during Charlie's years as a private investigator. A large man, except in his last years, Peterson had been pompous, vain and a stickler for bureaucratic formality. The only creatures for which he showed affection were his show dogs, two glossy Irish setters practiced in striking noble attitudes, but which probably shared half a brain between them.

Charlie and Peterson had sometimes worked together, but they never got along. Charlie was too intuitive and hunch-driven, while Peterson, as he liked to say, did things by the book, uttering the word as if he meant the Bible itself. Nevertheless, Peterson had occupied space in Charlie's head for more than thirty years. Looking at his tombstone, Charlie couldn't say he missed him, but it was hard to imagine life without him, as if Peterson's absence were a kind of am-putation. In fact, Charlie wasn't exactly sure what he felt. Instead, it felt like a hole in his emotional self, which made it seem significant. Not that it made him consider his own mortality, but it was like seeing half of his life encapsulated in one spot. All the shouting and quarrel-ing and threatening, even the venomous rivalry to solve a forgotten case—where was it now except in his memory? "It made me feel a little philosophical" was what he told Janey later, and that was the best he could do. But now, as he stared at Peterson's stone, the snow began to turn to rain, and he hurried to his car, glad for any excuse to get away.

Eight

The Northway was almost free of snow as Charlie drove south toward Troy, though big trucks threw buckets of mush and salty water onto his windshield. He drove barefooted with the defroster on full blast and his shoes and socks drying out on the dashboard. His feet were icy. He tried to tuck his left foot under his right thigh, but his car swerved threateningly. James Bond had never had such problems. That, too, made Charlie philosophical.

Downtown Troy had gone through a period of near urban collapse, with the once handsome brownstones becoming shabby and poor. But over the past ten years gentrification had begun—bricks had been repointed, stone steps had been repaired and the wood trim shone. The poor were gone, wherever they went, to some shabbier place, as if there had been a concerted effort to have them repopulate a crumbling ghost town in the middle of the country.

Joan Miller lived in such a brownstone on Second Street about two blocks from Russell Sage College, where, as it turned out, she worked as a secretary in the dean's office. She was in her forties and reminded Charlie of a large suitcase—solid, squarish and difficult to move. Her graying hair was cut short and she wore a thick blue terry-cloth bathrobe. She held a tissue to her nose and snuffled into it. Charlie noticed she wore no wedding ring.

"And why should I talk to you?" she asked, closing the door a little. "I've already talked to the police."

Charlie had given her one of his cards, which she studied without enthusiasm. "I've just come from Mickey's funeral and I wanted to ask you a few questions. It won't take a minute."

The woman pointed to his card. "What does this mean? 'Consultant, Legal and Otherwise.' Are you a crook?"

"No, no, it means advice. You know, suggestions. Ideas. My daughter made them up for me. She's sixteen. Not that I'm blaming her; she's a wonderful girl." What in the world am I dithering about? thought Charlie. Only old farts dither.

Joan Miller looked skeptical. "You were a friend of Mickey's?"

Charlie shrugged. "I don't believe Mickey had any friends in Saratoga. That's not to insult him, or you either for that matter, but most people couldn't stand him. It's just a statement of fact. But he was killed on my sidewalk and I want to know why." Charlie tried to look harmless but sympathetic. If it turned out that Joan Miller doted on her brother, then Charlie guessed he'd be walking back to his car in about two seconds. He waited.

"Well, I'll catch pneumonia if I keep standing here. You might as well come in. But don't expect to learn anything from me. I hadn't seen Mickey for fifteen years and I counted that as a blessing. And don't get too close, I've got a nasty cold."

Joan Miller's living room was as tidy and self-contained as Joan Miller herself. The couch, two armchairs, TV, several small tables and bookcase were all exactly parallel or exactly perpendicular to one another. The rug had a pattern of small blue squares; even the two pictures were square and set in the exact middle of two white walls. Both were black-and-white photographs of wilderness scenes from a western national park, scenes in which nothing was square or symmetrical.

Charlie had quickly put his shoes and socks back on in the car. The socks were still wet and the left sock bunched beneath his instep so he limped. Joan Miller watched him move with mild sympathy, as if Charlie suffered from an old war wound.

After Charlie had taken off his overcoat and was seated in an armchair, he said, "I wonder if you could tell me, Mrs. Miller—"

Joan Miller was seated across from him in the second armchair with a box of tissues in her lap. She held up one hand like a traffic policeman. "You may call me Joan or you may call me Miller. I haven't been Mrs. Miller for twenty years. Good riddance to bad rubbish, is what I say."

"You paid for Mickey's funeral. Are you his heir?" It was the sort of question Charlie often asked late in an interview, but he wanted to see if he could ruffle her.

"What would I inherit, a pair of old socks? I don't think Mickey ever had an extra dime to his name. He was a spender, not a saver. That was one of his problems. As for paying for his funeral, it was something that had to be done. He might have been bad family, but he was still family." She blew her nose, making a noise that geese make in cartoons. She shook her head. "I should have taken the ten dollars I paid for my flu shot and just thrown it in the street."

"You bought a coffin and burial plot. Presumably you'll put up a stone. You could have cremated him for a lot less."

Joan Miller's eyes narrowed. "I wanted him to lie in his cheap coffin and brood about what a bastard he was. I wanted him to brood till he had rotted away."

Charlie started to speak, but then thought better of it. He scratched the back of his neck. "Why'd he been sent to prison?"

"Embezzlement and extortion. He had a job at State Farm and submitted false claims. He got ten to fifteen years."

"That's pretty stiff."

"It was his second conviction. He'd been caught embezzling money from a bank in Cohoes about a dozen years ago. And there'd been other arrests without convictions."

"How much of that second sentence did he serve?"

"I hadn't seen him for fifteen years. He'd stolen money from me, and it wasn't the first time. I decided enough was enough. He got out of prison after serving a small part of his sentence. I told him I was sorry to hear it. He said he'd been working personally for the warden. He found it funny. He said he'd been a real hero so they'd paroled him. He asked for money to get on his feet. I said I'd give him two hundred and fifty dollars. He got huffy, said he needed at least a thousand. Fat chance, I told him. My partner at the time said I shouldn't give him a dime. But he took the two fifty when he saw he wouldn't get more. 'Aren't you going to thank me?' I asked. On the phone, of course. 'Yeah, thanks,' he said. Of course he never paid it back."

"Did he have a parole officer in Albany?"

"I couldn't say. We weren't chatty."

"When did you last hear from him?"

"About a year ago. He called whenever he was feeling smug and had had a few drinks. He said he was making good money, though he didn't tell me how he made it. I asked if he meant to pay back the money I'd lent him. That made him hang up fast enough."

"But you've no idea how he got the money?"

"No idea. But he had that insurance business up in Saratoga. He had to have it registered under somebody else's name because of his record. But the money he was talking about wasn't the kind you make from an insurance business. I guessed it was some scam. Mickey loved scams." Again she blew her nose.

"Which of you was older, you or him?"

Joan Miller narrowed her eyes again. "I'm two years older. What's that got to do with anything?"

"I was curious about when Mickey began to go, you know, crooked."

"As far as I'm concerned he was born crooked—crooked and sneaky." She paused and looked at her hands, first the backs, then turned them over to see the fronts. She had square palms and clear nail polish on the nails. "Our dad was killed in Vietnam. That probably didn't help. And my mom was one of those weak women, always complaining and sneaking pints of vodka. She was afraid of Mickey, afraid he'd do something nasty. So she let him do what he wanted."

"But he couldn't have been born bad," Charlie insisted. "There must have been some times he was okay."

The woman shrugged. "He cried a lot. My mom'd say, 'Listen to him singing.' I'd look at him in his crib and his face would be all red. Later I had some stuffed animals and he liked playing with those, bears and rabbits and a sheep. He must have been two and a half or three. He'd have them talking to each other and doing tricks. Pretty stupid really."

"What about his insurance business? Won't you inherit money from that?"

"Bills," said Joan. "He hadn't paid his rent for months and he owed money to Mrs. Penfield. Mickey made her life a living hell."

"How so?"

"He baited her. Made fun of how she dressed. I know for a fact she was looking for another job. Home Depot would hire her and she told me she'd been getting desperate enough to take it. At least it would have meant health insurance."

"Do you know who worked for Mickey before Mrs. Penfield?"

"I've no idea. Some poor soul Mickey never paid—at least that's my educated opinion. No, I'll sell the tables and chairs—his office furnishings—and whatever's in his apartment, then divide up the money between the landlord and Mrs. Penfield. As for the others Mickey owed money to, that's not my business. Can I get you a cup of chamomile tea? My throat's scratchy."

Charlie said that would be nice and Joan went to the kitchen. The water tap was turned on, cupboards banged, the refrigerator door opened, the microwave hummed. At one point, Charlie had thought that Mickey wanted to borrow money from him, that it might have been the reason for his late-night visit, but Charlie knew he was one of the last people Mickey would ask. Then he thought Mickey might want to sell him something—not an object, but something along the lines of information. But what could it be? Just the fact that Mickey had shown up after midnight suggested he was desperate, unless he was drunk, which was doubtful. But Mickey had been afraid of something, afraid of someone who might be looking for him, someone he wouldn't recognize. So he wanted to get out of town, but he was broke. Maybe he had a piece of information he couldn't tell the police about. But why would Charlie be interested? Why would he pay money for it?

Joan stuck her head out of the kitchen. "Honey?"

"Sure."

A moment later, Joan returned with a tray on which there were two mugs, a small cream pitcher and a plate of rust-colored cookies. She nodded toward the cookies as she set the tray on the table. "They're organic."

Charlie poured a little milk into his tea and bit into a cookie. It was hard, as if made from ground-up rocks, and had a muddy taste. "Good," he said.

Joan looked pleased. "I make them myself."

"I sometimes make cookies as well." Charlie paused, as if engaged in cookie thoughts, cookie memories. He sipped his tea. Looking down at the tea's surface, he thought he saw little bee legs and bee wings from the honey. He set his cup carefully on the table.

Joan bit into a cookie. The steady crunching was the only sound in the room. "You think I cooked them too long?"

"They're just right."

Ten minutes later Charlie was driving back to Saratoga. It was still raining, and by dark the rain would turn to ice. He thought of Mickey playing with stuffed bears and rabbits. Then he decided he was being sentimental and concentrated on his driving. After a minute, he remembered a stuffed bear he had as a child. He tried to recall its name. Jo Jo the Dancing Bear, that was it. What had become of it? Tossed in the trash most likely. Oh yes, it had a red beret.

He drove to Mickey's insurance office on Henry Street, three blocks east of Broadway: a two-story white clapboard building next to a garage. Mickey's office took up about half of one story. The sign above the door said "Michael Martin, Insurance and Real Estate." Charlie was surprised by the sign. He'd never thought of Mickey as a Michael, as if he lacked the gravitas to be called anything but Mickey. And is that why I'm called Charlie? he thought. But "Charles" was on his business cards and Janey sometimes called him Charles when she was irritated with him. It was still raining slightly and he hurried to the front door.

It was locked, but a light was on inside. Charlie knocked, and after a moment Laura Penfield appeared. She had a worried look and

Charlie supposed she almost always had a worried look, as if it were her default expression, the expression her face returned to when she relaxed.

She pursed her lips and then unlocked the front door and opened it slightly.

"May I come in?" asked Charlie.

"The police won't like it." She spoke very exactly, putting a tiny space between each word.

Charlie looked over his shoulder and then back. "We don't have to tell them."

Mrs. Penfield opened the door just enough for Charlie to enter. "If you're sure it's all right . . ."

The office was very plain, with two gray metal desks, five or six chairs and two file cabinets with their drawers open. Other doors led to an inner office, a closet and a lavatory. Three-quarters of the way up the lavatory door were silhouettes of a pudgy man and pudgy woman holding hands. The office, Charlie thought, was nearly as plain and shabby as his own, but at least he had a computer.

"Don't you have a computer?" asked Charlie.

"We had two; the police took them. They took most of the files as well. I don't know how I can close the accounts if I don't have my computer. The policeman said it would only be a few days, but I don't know."

Mrs. Penfield was a thin, gray woman. Her white blouse and light-colored slacks made a statement about the unlikelihood that she might be in mourning.

"So the police searched the whole building?"

"Just about."

"Is there a basement and attic?"

"There's another office above us, and downstairs there's a half-basement and a furnace that isn't used. Mr. Martin turned everything over to electric long before I got here. But the policemen looked in the basement. One got stuck in the space behind the furnace, it's so small. Other men had to help him out. He was so . . ." Here she paused and seemed a bit flustered.

"Fat?" asked Charlie.

"Certainly overweight."

"Sorry I missed it."

They stood in the middle of the room on a dark carpet. Mrs. Penfield kept glancing through the window, as if expecting the police to burst in at any moment.

"And how long did you say you'd worked here?" Charlie continued.

"Six months, though it seems longer. I should never have taken the job, but Mr. Martin promised me health insurance, as well as a raise after a certain time. Of course, he never mentioned them again after I came here. Then at the Stop and Shop, I ran into the woman who'd worked for Mr. Martin before me. She lasted eight months and said she'd never gotten a raise or health insurance either, though Mr. Martin had promised them to her as well. Nor had she been paid for her last weeks of work."

"Could you tell me her name?"

"Margaret Ross. She works over at the high school now, lucky woman."

"You handled all the secretarial business, all the accounts and billing?"

"Pretty much, though, as I said, Mr. Martin had his own computer. Even his own printer. He was quite private about it, not that I would have looked into it, and he always locked his office door when he left for lunch or an appointment. And he made sure to be in the office when the cleaning woman was here."

Charlie saw the office door had a dead-bolt lock. "How'd the police get in?"

"They had to get a locksmith."

Charlie tried the door, but it was locked. "So Mickey might have had accounts you knew nothing about?"

"My husband, Mr. Penfield, thought so. Many times Mr. Penfield told me that Mr. Martin was an absolute crook. Those were his words. But I tried to make it my business to pay as little attention to Mr. Martin as possible. He didn't even like me to look at him, and more than once he asked what I was staring at."

Charlie imagined being shut up in a small space with Mickey Martin day after day. It didn't make a pleasant picture. He considered asking Mrs. Penfield about Mickey's urinous breath, but decided against it. "Did he act any differently in the few days before he was killed?"

"Yes, he did, and I told the police the same thing." Mrs. Penfield crossed her arms and again pursed her lips. "He was less brash, quieter, and at first I thought he was coming down with something. He spent more time in his office with the door shut, even locked. Sometimes I heard his printer. He didn't come in on Monday at all, but I know for a fact he'd been here over the weekend, because he used the coffeemaker. He always left it dirty. He said it was my job to care for it and make sure that we never ran out of coffee and to buy half-and-half. And several drawers in the file cabinets weren't entirely closed."

"Had anything been removed?"

"I couldn't tell, but Mr. Penfield said he was trying to cover his tracks, that he probably meant to leave town and was getting rid of files that might be 'incriminating'; that was Mr. Penfield's word."

"Did he have any reason to think that?"

"Not really, but he, well, he hated Mr. Martin. He always said bad things about him. In any case, Mr. Martin kept his most important files in his office."

"And I gather you've been talking to Joan Miller. How'd you meet her?"

Mrs. Penfield looked embarrassed. "Margaret Ross had told me that Mr. Martin had a sister who lived in Troy. Then, three months ago, Mr. Martin didn't come to the office for two weeks, a little longer. There were bills to sign and clients had been calling. I was nearly frantic. So I called Joan and asked if she'd seen him. She just laughed. But we had a long talk. She knew exactly what her brother was like and was quite sympathetic. After that she called several times to see how I was doing and I called her, I think twice, when I felt low. Mr. Martin had a dirty tongue and could be quite insulting. I called her the first time out of desperation and Joan told me to quit. I said I couldn't, that we had too many bills; so she said I must ignore him and make sure that I didn't weep again, at least where he could see me."

"Did Mickey ever mention her?"

"Only once." Mrs. Penfield reddened slightly. "He called her 'that dyke bitch.'"

Charlie talked to Mrs. Penfield for a few more minutes, then gave her his card and urged her to call if she discovered anything. "I don't know why he was coming to see me," he said. "I'd hate to think my family was in danger." Saying this made him feel like a hypocrite, but he wanted to offer an excuse for being there if the police asked about him. Mrs. Penfield nodded sympathetically. Then, after getting the name of the landlord, Charlie hurried back to his car. He wasn't wearing a hat and he hated cold drops of rain striking his bald spot.

Next, Charlie drove to Mickey's apartment on Grove Street, which occupied the second floor of a house built at the turn of the nineteenth century. Charlie had never been inside, but he knew the building, admired the slate roof and the single turret on the southeast corner.

Mickey's apartment had its own entrance, a door right off the driveway that opened onto a set of stairs to the second floor. But as Charlie walked along the driveway, he saw the yellow police tape and a police seal on Mickey's door. As he studied it, he considered what he'd need to do to break in. The thought shocked him, not because of the danger of being found out, but because of how quickly his mind had turned to the illegal and foolish. As he walked back to his car, he thought of talking to Mickey's landlord, a man he knew slightly and had seen at the Y. But he knew there was a line he couldn't cross. It was one thing to talk to Joan Miller, but it would be hard to justify his conversation with Mrs. Penfield. If he talked to Mickey's two landlords, then Hutch and Chief Novak would, as they had told him with one of their favorite clichés, "come down on him like a ton of bricks."

So Charlie went home. It was getting late anyway, he told himself. Janey and Emma would be home and there was dinner to think of.

Victor Plotz's old Mercedes diesel was parked in front of Charlie's house, half blocking the driveway. Its original cream color had turned to a jaundiced yellow mixed with rust, while black smudges on the trunk attested to billowing diesel exhaust; because Victor didn't simply drive away, he vanished in a cloud of smoke.

Entering the front door, Charlie heard Victor's laughter, followed by Emma's. Charlie hung up his wet coat and then went into the kitchen to find Victor with a glass of milk and a plate of oatmeal cookies that Emma had just baked. This was not uncommon. Victor often enjoyed a range of snacks at Charlie's that the Queen of

Softness didn't let him eat at home. Soon Charlie joined them with a smaller glass of milk and a single cookie. He glanced at it with a touch of regret. Would James Bond eat oatmeal cookies? Then he wondered how many pleasures he reduced with second thoughts, like adding a teaspoon of salt to a bowl of ice cream.

"What's so funny?" he asked.

Emma laughed again. She was sixteen, had short blond hair and the lanky body of a long-distance runner. "Victor was saying how Mickey Martin was buried in one place and his tongue must be buried someplace else."

"Like turkey parts," said Victor. "You buy a turkey and get the body, but the neck, liver, heart and lungs belong to other birds. It's the opposite of twins being separated at birth; it's turkeys separated at death. Like Mickey. Who knows where his tongue wound up? And Parlucci and that old guy, for that matter."

Charlie nodded. He wasn't sure how he felt about Victor corrupting his stepdaughter with black humor.

"Is there any news about the snake?" asked Emma, still laughing.

"Nervous sightings," said Victor. "There've been so many you'd think there'd been fifty snakes."

They continued to talk about snakes. Then Charlie told Emma that he'd have to order new calling cards. "That phrase 'Consultant, Legal and Otherwise' is going to get me in trouble."

Victor and Emma remained amused. "What about 'Charlie Bradshaw, A Good Guy'?" said Victor.

"Or 'Charles Bradshaw: Friend to the People,'" suggested Emma.

Charlie got to his feet, leaving his cookie half eaten. It was obvious he could expect no serious advice. Sugar rush, he said to himself.

As he stepped away from the table, his cell phone began to play the Mickey Mouse march. Again there was laughter. Charlie dug the phone out of his pocket.

His caller was Joan Miller; she spoke with breathy excitement. "I've just heard from Mickey's lawyer. I'm going to inherit about seventy-five thousand dollars. And that's *after* the bills have been paid. Maybe I should have bought him a better stone."

Nine

It was Charlie's intention to sleep late that Sunday morning, but when he got up at five thirty to take his second pee of the night, he'd been unable to fall back to dreamy unconsciousness. This he blamed on what he called "nervous brain syndrome," which had begun when he asked himself, Where did Mickey get all the money? Once the question was lodged in his head, he could kiss his pillow good-bye.

Was there any chance that Mickey had come upon the money legally? Charlie would swear on a stack of Bibles that he hadn't. But if the net amount to be given to Joan Miller was seventy-five thousand dollars, then the gross must have been huge. And who knew who else, if anyone, had received money. "A healthy chunk of change," Victor would say. Where did Mickey get it and how come it was so much? Charlie had heard nothing about Mickey's good fortune or sudden change of lifestyle, and this indicated that he wanted to keep the money secret, either because he had obtained it illegally or to hide it from the IRS, or both. On the other hand, Mickey wasn't someone to offer information. He was secretive by nature. It was in his genes, an overdeveloped secretive gene.

Charlie eased himself out of bed so as not to wake Janey, tried to find socks, shoes and clothes in the darkness, then quietly made his way to the hall. Here he discovered he'd picked up mismatched shoes and a bright red shirt, so he tiptoed back into the bedroom.

"Are you wandering around for any good reason?" asked Janey sleepily.

"Shoes don't match."

There was a long silence and Charlie thought she'd gone back to sleep. Then he heard a whisper, "Go barefoot."

Once dressed, Charlie drove out to Rosemary's diner to organize his thoughts with the help of his notebook and a stack of blueberry pancakes. It was still dark when he arrived, but the parking lot was nearly full. Several semis hummed peacefully at the far end. Glancing upward, he could see no stars.

Rosemary sat in her usual place behind the register with her large breasts looming above the cash drawer. She wore a lavender silk blouse and her red hair had been recently hennaed. Thick golden hoops dangled from her substantial lobes. Though definitely large and soft, she gave no sense of being overweight; rather, she called to mind a great pink peony just beginning to turn.

Rosemary slowly batted her eyelashes at him. "How's my number two boy?"

"Ready for some pancakes."

"You want 'em, we got 'em."

Charlie made his way through the crowded tables to a semicircular booth with golden plastic. Rosemary always kept the booth available for special friends, and a small "Reserved" sign stood on the table.

That and his private locker at the Y were about the only perks in Charlie's life and he appreciated both. A waitress brought him coffee.

Charlie had decided to drive up to the Hyde Collection in Glens Falls as soon as the museum opened and talk to Lizzie Whitaker. Perhaps she knew something about Mickey's money and where it came from. He guessed that, wherever it had come from, Mickey probably had nothing to fear from the IRS, since it had been Mickey's lawyer who called Joan Miller. No way was the lawyer going to risk an accessory charge. So either he had gotten it legally or it had been laundered.

Taking a notebook from his back pocket, he began to jot down the sequence of events and what he knew. The very act of writing seemed to validate his thoughts. This, he suspected, was a placebo effect. It gave him credibility, or ersatz credibility, in his own eyes. But the more he wrote, the more he felt he was hitting a dead end. No matter where Mickey's money had come from, Charlie doubted it had anything to do with his murder. The connection to Parlucci and Milo Rutkowski suggested the cause was something that happened before Mickey moved to Saratoga and it was that event, or events, that had led Mickey to Charlie's house Monday night or early Tuesday morning. Maybe Mickey's parole officer could give him a lead, but there was absolutely no reason the parole officer should talk to him. In any case, Hutchins had surely talked to him already.

Charlie was halfway through his stack of blueberry pancakes when Rosemary slipped into the booth beside him. Her perfume struck him like a blast from an open furnace. "Are you bored?" she asked.

"No, of course not, why do you say that?"

"You have a wonderful wife and daughter, a nice house and money in your pocket and you're bored."

"Why d'you keep saying that? I'm not bored at all." Am I bored? Charlie asked himself.

"Victor says you've gone back to being a private detective even though you could end up in jail. You wouldn't like jail, Charlie."

"I'm not investigating, I'm just—"

"Please don't say you're 'poking around.'" Rosemary's black eyelashes—surely they were false—extended from her heavy lids like a cowcatcher from a steam locomotive. "You don't believe it and I don't believe it. You're investigating."

"Mickey was murdered on my sidewalk and I'm trying to find out why." Despite his defense, Charlie knew he was engaged in a losing argument. "Anyway, I'm not bored."

Rosemary put a be-ringed hand gently on his wrist. "Charlie, do you have enough sex in your life?"

He was just taking a sip of coffee and he spilled a little on his shirt. "Really, Rosemary, how can you expect me—"

"Just make sure that Victor doesn't go to jail with you. The food wouldn't sit well with him." With that, Rosemary slid gracefully out of the booth and returned to her cash register.

Is everything I'm doing a lie? Charlie asked himself. Am I only trying to prove to myself that I'm not old? But he'd gone too far to stop now. Anyway, he'd already decided to talk to Lizzie, and after that he'd only talk to a few more people and then call it quits, or try to.

L izzie Whitaker had short black hair and probably weighed one hundred pounds. She wore a gray turtleneck sweater, an ankle-length skirt of a darker gray and a black leather belt. All she needed was an iron ring to make her look like a granite hitching post, or such was Charlie's thought. Standing behind the counter in the Hyde's small museum shop, she had looked at Charlie with increasing alarm as he approached. Then, when he introduced himself, she'd seemed ready to sprint for the door. Skittish, he thought.

"Have the police been to speak to you?" Charlie asked.

"Several times." Her voice fell between a whisper and a repressed scream.

Lizzie avoided his eyes and Charlie wondered if she treated her customers with the same degree of apprehension. He decided to be avuncular. "Well, I bet you're wondering why I'm disturbing you if you've already talked to the police." He paused to see if she'd respond, but she continued to look away. She had pale skin and her ears looked like small porcelain shells. She wore no earrings. "That's easy to answer," Charlie continued. "Mickey was killed on my sidewalk. I've no idea why he was coming to my house, but I've a wife and young daughter. I'd like to make sure they're safe. That's why I've come to you. I'm worried." Someday I'm going to be punished for this sort of folderol, thought Charlie.

Lizzie quickly glanced at him and looked away. "I don't see how I can help."

"Didn't I see you with Mickey at Lillian's last spring?" Charlie persisted. "He'd been drinking and was rude to you. To my mind, he was way out of line."

Lizzie gave him a longer look. "Yes, I remember you." Her nervousness seemed to decrease slightly. "Mickey said awful things about you."

"I expect he said awful things about everyone. How long had you been dating him?" And why? Charlie wanted to add.

"About four months. I broke it off soon after that time in Lillian's. I couldn't stand it anymore."

Charlie pursed his lips and nodded kindly. "How'd you happen to meet?"

Lizzie hesitated and then plunged ahead. "It was an online dating service. It was the first time I'd tried it. The first and only time, I should say. I'll never do it again. Our profiles matched."

"And how'd they match?" Charlie asked himself how his own profile would read: nosy and secretive, a compulsive liar.

"We both liked books and long walks. We'd both suffered from heartache in the past. But he said he was younger than he really was, only in his midthirties. That should have warned me. But he was nice at the beginning. At least he didn't seem *unnice*. He could even be charming."

"Did he tell you he'd been in prison?"

"No, never."

"But it doesn't surprise you?"

"I read it in the paper in the article about his . . . passing." She glanced up at him again, pressing her fingertips against the glass top of the display case so the tips turned white. "After I broke it off, he kept calling, saying awful things, personal things. He didn't stop calling till I threatened to get a restraining order."

"He had that breath," Charlie offered.

The glance she gave him was almost angry. "He was very sensitive about it. He said it was the cross he had to bear. It made me quite sympathetic, at least at first. We all have crosses to bear. Some more than others."

Charlie wondered about her own cross. Timidity, shyness, or was it bigger? "And then what happened?"

Lizzie pressed her fingertips more firmly against the glass. "But after we'd become . . . intimate. That's what he became especially mean about, the sort of things he said about me. He was never gentle; I don't think he knew *how* to be gentle."

Her eyes grew moist and Charlie was afraid she would weep. They had been talking quietly as four or five other visitors inspected the postcards and leafed through display books.

"Mickey was known for his meanness. That and gossip."

"Slander is more like it." She looked at Charlie directly, as if taking courage from her anger. "I should have stopped seeing him right away, I mean as soon as I saw what he was like. At first, the things he told me about myself, I thought they might be true. I thought things were my fault and I tried to make it up to him. That night you spoke to him, he criticized my clothes, my 'mousiness,' he called it. When I stopped seeing him, I decided he'd never been interested in dating. He was just looking for someone to hurt."

Lizzie was as slender as an adolescent boy—the very opposite of the Queen of Softness. Charlie found her pretty, in a watery sort of way, with delicate features and light blue eyes. Mickey had been good at seeing someone's weaknesses. Once identified, he could pop a person open like an oyster. "Did Mickey talk about money or of having some sort of good fortune?"

"He'd brag, but he wasn't truthful. In his profile, he said he liked art and music. He said he was a retired investment banker who'd left Wall Street to pursue his own creative impulses."

"And what did you find out?"

"That he sold insurance and a little real estate; that he was mean to his secretary, just as he was mean to me."

"So he *did* talk about money?"

They were interrupted by a young man with a handful of postcards. Charlie stepped back to study a framed reproduction of a yellow painting with black lines and curves. It didn't seem to be about anything. He decided it was unfinished.

When the man left, Charlie returned to the counter. He wanted to ask Lizzie about the picture, but he didn't wish to seem ignorant. Maybe he'd come back and look at it another time. He could bring Janey.

"Money was the one thing he didn't seem mean about," said Lizzie when Charlie repeated his question. "Not that he liked to spend it. He liked to carry a large roll of bills and show it off. Actually, it was mostly made up of paper with a few large bills wrapped around the outside."

"Did he seem well-off?"

Lizzie thought for a moment. "I don't know. He certainly didn't throw his money around. But he said he meant to retire soon. He wanted to move to the Caribbean and get away from the snow. He said he'd already been to some island to look at property. I thought it was another of his stories."

"Did he ever seem afraid?"

Lizzie looked thoughtful. "Cautious, perhaps. He liked to say he had a million enemies. It was a source of pride. Really, apart from the meanness, I've no idea what he was like. Once I understood that he lied, then even the true things seemed untrue. Even his apartment was secretive. It could have been a room in a motel."

"And you moved up here after you broke up with him?"

"I moved here in June. He wouldn't let me alone."

Charlie asked her if she knew the names of any of his other girl-friends, but she didn't. "He knew lots of people, but none that he ever said anything nice about."

"How did you meet his secretary?"

"He'd broken a date and I didn't hear from him for a week. It was during the time he was still being nice. I stopped by his office to see if he was all right, but Mrs. Penfield hadn't seen him either. About a month later, I ran into her at the post office and we talked. By then, very little that she said about Mickey surprised me."

"But something did?"

"No, nothing surprised me. She wanted to quit her job; I couldn't blame her."

Charlie had driven halfway back to Saratoga when he decided to call Lieutenant Hutchins. He didn't expect to tell the lieutenant anything he didn't know, but he hoped to get a little more information. He was "going fishing," as Victor liked to say. After reaching the desk sergeant, Charlie had to wait about two more minutes before Hutchins came on the line. His tone was angry.

"What's it now, Charlie? You going to say why Mickey went to your house?"

"I wanted to tell you that Mickey's sister inherited a whole lot of money from her brother. I just learned about it."

"You think we didn't know about it? How come you were talking to her?"

"I thought I could help her out; you know, winding up Mickey's affairs."

"And what business is it of yours? No, don't tell me. You're just a Good Samaritan spreading goodness wherever you go."

"I was interested, that's all. Remember, he was killed on my doorstep. Somehow his death was connected to me. Did Parlucci have any money?"

"Not a dime."

"And you talked to Mickey's parole officer? Maybe he was killed because of something in prison."

Hutchins groaned. "Maybe yes, maybe no." Then he hung up.

I'm sick of acting like an idiot, thought Charlie. It was clear he wasn't getting anywhere. Maybe he should quit being foolish and leave it to the police. Yet, five minutes later, when Hutchins called back, his first thought was that the lieutenant was going to ask for help after all.

"I just wanted to warn you again about jail, Charlie. You're getting pretty close to getting locked up."

"But I don't have a client."

The connection, however, had been cut.

Okay, I'm an idiot, thought Charlie. Having gotten that off his chest, he called Mickey's office, hoping to reach Mrs. Penfield. She picked up on the second ring. After identifying himself, Charlie said, "I heard from Joan Miller last night. Mickey's lawyer had called to say she stood to inherit about seventy-five thousand dollars. And I gather there's other money to be used for Mickey's debts."

"Really," she said eagerly. "Does that mean I'll be paid as well?"

"I expect so, but you should call Joan and get the lawyer's number. I'd think he'd put you at the top of the list."

Back in Saratoga, Charlie grabbed a ham and cheese sandwich at Bruegger's and went to his office. It was dusty and gray, filled with ghosts from thirty years. Faces floated up toward him and he wondered, not for the first time, how many were dead. At home he had chores to finish, leaves to rake, storm windows to lower, but he didn't want to tackle them just yet. He sat at his desk, eating his sandwich and staring at his photograph of Jesse James. What a jerk he was. A bushwhacking sadist and slave owner. Charlie couldn't imagine why he'd ever romanticized him. He should replace Jesse with a picture of Sing Sing to remind himself of the trouble he was getting into. The trouble with retirement was it made him claustrophobic. The walls were narrowing and he could only go forward, like a cow entering the slaughterhouse. Even before the thought was finished, he remembered Chief Peterson's gravestone rising out of the wet snow. I should give up this cop stuff, he told himself, I should take classes in yoga.

Then, once he had sufficiently berated himself, he left his office to drive over to the Greasy Mattress to talk to Bad Maud.

At least twenty Harleys were parked outside the bar, each at a forty-five-degree angle from the curb in a display of biker obsessive-compulsive disorder. The chrome was polished and the colors ranged from turquoise to red to baby blue, with only one or two black bikes. Charlie approached the door, expecting raucous cries of "Show your tits!" Instead he found the bikers watching the New York Jets play the Buffalo Bills. Would Marlon Brando have ridden a turquoise Harley? Would he have cared two cents about football? Charlie doubted it.

Bad Maud waved to him from the bar. "If you're going to hang out here, you gotta get a leather jacket. It's like the dress code. You ever find Dave's snake? I'd like it back. It's got sentimental value."

"If someone finds it, I'll make sure you get it." Charlie climbed up on a stool and ordered a beer. "Tell me, were you ever Good Maud?"

"Yeah, before I lost my looks. First I was Good Maud, then I was So-So Maud, now I'm Bad Maud. I'm serious about the leather jacket."

Bad Maud's head was as round as a bowling ball and she maybe outweighed Charlie by twenty pounds. Today she wore neither a motorcycle cap nor a bandanna, and her short black bristles reminded him of a hedgehog. Her eyes were of the sort that Charlie called "flinty" and her nose had been broken more than once.

"You must have been pretty," he said.

"Nah, I wouldn't go that far. But I was a good fighter."

"It's nice to have a skill. You mind if I ask a little more about Mickey?"

"You saying I could stop you?"

"Maybe not, but I like to be polite. It turns out that Mickey had quite a lot of money, could be over a hundred thousand or more. D'you know where it might have come from?" He reached for a bowl of unshelled peanuts a little to his right.

"The fuck I know. Maybe real estate."

"Neither of us believes that."

"Yeah, given the choice between straight and crooked, Mickey always chose crooked." A sudden roaring erupted behind Charlie like big cats at feeding time. Somebody had scored a touchdown.

"He ever talk about money?"

"He didn't talk about shit, as far as I could see. He just complained and gossiped. Why was he so cheap if he had money?"

"Maybe he was a miser; maybe it was a recent acquisition, maybe he was scared someone would try to take it."

"You ever catch up with that girlfriend of his?"

"She's up in Glens Falls." Charlie described talking to her.

"I'm glad she's okay. I liked her. Of course, she's so small I could throw her over my shoulder and run around the building ten times without breaking a sweat."

Charlie contemplated the image. "What I'd really like is to talk to someone who knew Mickey in prison. You know anyone?"

"Just Dave, and he got sliced and diced. Anyway, he wasn't in Adirondack."

"You think you could find someone, maybe make a few phone calls?"

Maud patted her lips in an artificial yawn. "Sounds like work to me."

Charlie put a twenty on the bar. Maud looked at it and looked away. Charlie put another twenty on the bar. "It's not like I've got a rich client; I'm doing this on my own."

Maud scooped up the twenties and tucked them in the pocket of her leather vest. "I'd only do this for a friend, but if I find someone, you'll have to cough up fifty more. This here"—she touched her pocket—"is just a deposit."

Ten

Charlie was driving back to his office when his cell phone rang. He had returned it to a basic ring, like the telephone ring he'd known in the past, an antique ring, but he expected Emma would change it again when she had the chance.

"Mr. Bradshaw? This is Laura Penfield. I've found something you might be interested in. I'm in the office."

"What sort of thing?"

"You better come over and see."

Charlie continued on to Broadway and then turned right, trying to restrain his speed. He wasn't sure how to view his excitement. It was like how he used to feel when he'd found a break in a case or discovered a major clue. Excitement like that would only get him in trouble with the police, who, unfortunately, wanted to keep his life sleepy and law-abiding.

Mrs. Penfield was waiting at the door.

"It was just luck I found it. Really, it was the footprints that got me thinking."

Charlie tossed his coat over a chair. "Footprints?"

"Yes, sometimes I'd come back from lunch and see dirty foot-prints on the rug. After I saw the first, I kept my eye out for them. I saw them three or four times, but it wasn't mud. It was dust." She looked at him significantly.

Briefly, Charlie wondered if the woman was losing her wits. Apart from her strange talk, she also had a smudge of soot on her cheek, filthy hands and her blue blouse partially untucked from her skirt. "I don't get it."

"The furnace." Mrs. Penfield opened a drawer in her desk and withdrew a black notebook. "I realized Mr. Martin had been going down into the cellar and I wondered why. There seemed no reason for it. After you called me about his money, I went down with a flash-light." She blushed. "I thought I might find some money, but I'd only take what Mr. Martin owed me. The last place I looked was the fur-nace. I found this in a pipe." She handed the notebook to Charlie.

"Why give it to me? Why didn't you call the police?"

Mrs. Penfield blushed again. "Lieutenant Hutchins was rude to me. He suggested I was lying. It was bad enough when Mr. Martin was rude to me. I always hated it. Anyway, it's not as if the notebook makes any sense."

Charlie started to say that Hutchins was rude to everyone, but then, opening the notebook, it didn't make any sense to him either. On the first page, he read: *Ink in igloo except voles mickey mouse voila idiot in Iowa gap charming-details.* And on the second page: *Vaccinated axel money maker virgin iffy in Illinois rift clover-bugs interstice zip.* And the third: *Vacuumed insects idealistic vampires magic matters vampire iambics in Idaho lacuna axis vacant.* The fourth: *Xanax kitty kats zany zealous zebras old oxen xmas Kaiser kaftans kale recess ever-finger stop-page egg.* The next six pages had further entries.

Mrs. Penfield leaned over Charlie's shoulder. In a hushed voice, she asked, "Is it poetry?"

"I expect it's code. Will you show me where you found it?"

"It's too dirty. Just look at my blouse. I don't want to go back there again."

So Charlie took the flashlight and descended the cellar stairs. The ceiling beams were hardly six feet above the floor. A low-watt bulb hanging from a black wire threw the corners into shadow. When he bumped it with his head, the shadows swung back and forth. The floor was covered with dust mixed with the powder from crumbling cement and pockets of dirt. It was also crisscrossed with footprints: Mrs. Penfield's and the larger footprints of men. The air smelt of damp paper. Charlie made his way to the furnace as he tried to quiet his claustrophobia.

It was an old gravity furnace that had been converted from coal to oil. Now it probably hadn't been used for about five years, or for as long as Mickey had had the office. Six fat ducts rose up to grates in the ceiling. Charlie bent to open the door. He had a memory of being a child and watching his oldest cousin shovel coal into a similar furnace or carry the ashes out to the ashbin. An "octopus furnace," his cousin had called it, which, to Charlie, had made it especially sinister.

Charlie shone his light around the inside. It, too, was dusty and spotted with rust. The dust around the ducts and exhaust flue had been disturbed. One of them might have been the hiding place for Mickey's notebook, probably the exhaust duct to the chimney. He sneezed and closed the door; it made a metallic clang. He tapped his knuckles on an oil tank and it responded like a brass gong. Empty. Then he stumbled over a shovel, which clattered to the floor. I could make a whole band down here, he thought: Charlie and the Clumsy Rhythm Cats. He retraced his steps to the stairs.

Mrs. Penfield was coming out of the bathroom, wiping her face with a paper towel. "I must have looked a sight. Now you've a sooty face as well." She turned back to the bathroom. Charlie heard water running. A moment later she brought him a wet paper towel. Charlie dabbed his face.

Mrs. Penfield nodded to the notebook on the desk. She lowered her voice. "What do you think it means?"

"I don't know, but it was clearly important to him and it was something he didn't want anyone to see."

Her voice grew more hushed, hardly more than a whisper. "Do you think it's why he was killed?"

"I've no idea. Anyway, you should call the police. Do you have a copier here? I'd like to make a copy." Charlie had already seen an all-in-one printer against the wall, but he'd thought it best to ask.

"I'll do it right away."

"And don't tell the police about giving me a copy. They'd have a fit."

As Charlie drove home, he guessed that the case was about to get active. The black notebook, Mickey's unexpected money, his link to Parlucci and whatever had happened in prison, these pieces would come together and the police would make an arrest. Whatever Charlie's disappointment, he knew it was best that way. Poking around, as he called it, would only get him in trouble. Surely he told himself this one hundred times a day. It was a paradox. How could he tell himself something over and over, and still not be listening?

But his expectations of sudden police activity turned out to be wrong, because nothing happened. Or almost nothing. For instance, later on Sunday, Charlie went over to the Y to swim his mile, something he did three or four times a week, or tried to. In the locker room, he bumped into the fellow who owned the building where Mickey lived, Frank Pisasale, whom Charlie had hoped to talk to. Pisasale said it was a shame about Mickey.

"Was he a friend of yours?" asked Charlie.

Frank shrugged. "As a matter of fact, I couldn't stand him. But it's a terrible thing to get your throat cut on a nice quiet street in a nice quiet neighborhood. It fucks up the real estate. I just thank my lucky stars he didn't get his throat cut in his apartment. I'd never be able to rent the place. It's bad enough with the police tape everywhere. When can I get Mickey's shit outta there and find a new tenant, that's what I want to know? And who's going to pay the rent during that time? Nobody!"

Charlie said that it turned out that Mickey had quite a lot of money in the bank and maybe Frank would get a piece of it, which cheered him. But about Mickey's life and how he made his money, Frank knew little and he'd never been disposed to learn more.

"Sometimes he'd take off for a few weeks or so and I'd be afraid he was bailing on the rent, but he always came back. Actually, my big hope was he'd move out; I'm just sorry it had to happen *this* way."

And over the next few days, Charlie bumped into other people who had known Mickey or Parlucci, but none knew them well, nor had they been tempted to know them better. As for Mickey's un-expected wealth, it seemed a surprise to everyone.

Twice Charlie had gone back to the Greasy Mattress to see Bad Maud.

"Hey, let me tell you two things. One, I haven't dug up any ex-cons who knew Mickey, and two, when I do, you'll be the first to know. At this rate you'll owe me another hundred bucks."

Then, for a few hours each day, Charlie brooded about the black notebook, going over the ten entries until he knew them by heart, even muttering them as he wandered around the house: "Ink in igloo except voles mickey mouse voila idiot in Iowa gap charming-details," and "Vaccinated axel money maker virgin iffy in Illinois rift clover-bugs interstice zip."

One morning when Charlie was washing the dishes, Janey came into the kitchen. He hadn't heard her because of the noise he'd been making with the pots and when she spoke it startled him.

"Charlie, what in the world are you talking about: ink and igloos and idiots?"

He wiped his hands on the dishtowel. "Oh, it's just a poem I was reading."

Janey stood with her hands on her hips. "It doesn't sound like a poem to me. You've been muttering that stuff all week. Just promise you won't go crazy on me, Charlie, it'd put a dent in our relationship."

The trouble was that Charlie had promised Janey not to do any more detective work and he swore he'd hardly thought of Mickey for days. If she knew about the notebook, she'd have given him one of those looks that made his stomach knot. So Charlie set the notebook aside for a while. Instead, he concentrated on being a good home-owner, or co-owner, and sought out tasks that would require his 18-volt cordless drill-and-driver combo. He fixed a rickety bookcase, and then built a three-shelf bookcase for Emma's bedroom. Both required painting, which required another trip to the Home Depot for brushes, paint, a drop cloth, turpentine and other odds and ends. However, before he painted, he realized he had to clean up the basement so he'd have a place to put his new purchases. This meant building more shelves, a workbench and hanging up several new lights. During this flurry of activity, he almost forgot about Mickey's notebook, but not quite.

Friday night, Artemis was coming over to dinner. Charlie had invited her the previous Monday and she had gladly accepted. Janey wasn't sure how she felt about this. "You were never mixed up with her, were you? Kissing and hugging?"

"No, no, nothing like that. She's . . . not my type." He'd been about to say that Artemis was too classy for him, but he knew Janey would take it the wrong way.

"And what am I," she'd ask, "sliced carrots?"

Friday afternoon Janey asked, "So what's this woman's last name?"

Charlie scratched his head. "I don't remember. Maybe she doesn't have one."

"Come on, Charlie, everyone's got a last name."

"Not necessarily. She's got one of those old Greek or Roman names. They only came in ones, not twos or threes. I mean, you wouldn't say Zeus McCarthy or Apollo Schmidt."

Despite Janey's uncertainty, she and Artemis liked each other right away. She couldn't quite explain it afterward, but it had to do with the fact that Artemis said exactly what she felt, without exaggeration or softening the edges. She wasn't rude or abrasive, but she said what she meant. "You can believe her," said Janey, "even if you don't agree with her. But mostly I do. We've the same ideas about stuff. I like that. And I see why you weren't involved with her. She's too classy for you."

Janey had served baked salmon with a dill sauce, rice pilaf and a green salad. Artemis brought a bottle of white wine—some Austrian thing. They talked about their lives over the past years before Charlie had run into her at Home Depot; Artemis asked Janey about her daughters and her job as a nurse. They both agreed that Charlie could be difficult. It wasn't that he was deceptive, but he could be less than forthright. They laughed about this; they also laughed about his porkpie hat.

"Hey," said Charlie, "do you have to say this stuff in front of me? I'd prefer you talked behind my back."

Artemis also talked about the difficulties of having a riding school. "I hate surrounding myself with dull and unimaginative horses. A horse with any gumption would pitch one of these children to the other side of the barn, but that wouldn't further the professional career I've been forced to choose for myself. Perhaps I should buy lottery tickets, but until I win my millions, I have to entertain these slowpokes—the horses, not the children."

"Do you take care of them by yourself?" asked Janey.

"That's another bother. I've had to hire hands: men and women with every virtue except reliability. They never seem to stay long. I no sooner train one than he or she leaves for parts unknown."

"How many do you have?" asked Charlie.

"Two men at the moment. Fortunately, one I've known for many years." She turned to Janey. "The other is brand-new and I hold out hopes for him. He's energetic, efficient and doesn't chat. But you must bring your daughter to the stable. Riding's so good for a girl's posture. I'd be glad to give her free lessons, just because of how Charlie helped me years ago."

They talked about when Emma got out of school each day and when she might be free. "She loves riding," said Janey, "but we haven't found the right place for her."

Charlie enjoyed dinners like this. They were a notch above being dull. No tension, no fighting. He liked to think they were the sort of dinners most people had, which gave him, falsely he knew, a sense of community.

Janey had made an apple pie for dessert. She was just cutting it when there was a knock at the door. Charlie answered. Their visitor was Lieutenant Hutchins. Charlie winced. He assumed he was going to be yelled at and he didn't want to be yelled at in front of Artemis. But Hutchins seemed calm, even subdued, as if he'd been taking tranquilizers. He wore a blue suit, not a uniform, but uniform-like.

"Can I talk to you alone, Charlie? It's important."

After Hutch turned down an offer of apple pie, coffee or a glass of wine, Charlie took him into the TV room. He was ill at ease and wouldn't sit down.

"I wanted to say something about these killings. I thought you should know."

If Charlie had been surprised by the lieutenant's mood, he was even more surprised by his offer to share information.

"I'd be glad to help any way I can."

"It's not your help I want," said Hutchins, with a touch of his old manner. "Just listen to what I've got to say."

Hutchins described their hunt for the killer. Two people in Parlucci's building had seen a dark-haired man entering shortly before Parlucci was killed, while a third person had seen the man, or someone like him, hurrying down the back steps and across the yard. Then two people had seen a dark-haired man near the bus station around the time of Milo's murder. Both agreed he was relatively young—between twenty and thirty-five, depending on which one you talked to—and all agreed he was dressed in black. And he was in good shape, or at least he was thin and moved quickly. They couldn't say anything about his face.

Then phone calls to local motels had turned up a man who seemed to match the vague description. He'd been staying at the Tea Kettle Motel for the previous ten days. It was up on Route 9, on the way to Glens Falls. Hutchins and a sheriff's investigator had taken eight men in four unmarked cars, but the man was gone. In fact, he'd probably left hurriedly in the past ten minutes. A saucepan with a little soup on the stove was still hot. A chair had been overturned. The man had registered under the name of Tad Browning and had given a home address in Rochester. His car was a tan Toyota Corolla with New York plates. Browning had told the owner, Gene McCarthy, that he was in the area because of a divorce case and was hiding out to avoid being served further papers. Hutchins guessed that McCarthy had told him about the call from the police, that Browning had paid the clerk to notify him if anyone called. Hutchins told McCarthy that Browning was the primary suspect in three murder cases. He also warned him that if he had protected Browning, he'd be charged as an accessory.

"The nosy fuck nearly shit his pants." Hutchins found this very funny and Charlie managed a smile.

"But the most troubling business," the lieutenant continued, "or almost, were these little cardboard things McCarthy found in a bag in the dumpster about a week later. He and his wife were closing up the motel to go south for the winter. It was a plastic Walmart bag and McCarthy recalled that Browning had had a Walmart bag. So McCarthy dragged it out. He'd only had a couple of customers since Browning had fled, so the dumpster was pretty empty. Inside the bag were little figures cut out of a shoe box and colored with different-colored pens. So he called us.

"Each figure was about six inches tall and stuck into a little piece of wood so they'd stand up. I first thought they were like voodoo dolls, but that was wrong.

"They were meant to resemble specific people—six men and a woman. The guy had gone to a lot of trouble with them. One had a red X across his throat and a smaller X across his mouth. It was meant to be Mickey. I mean, it even looked like Mickey. Two of the others also had Xs across their throats, one had two little Xs over his ears, and one had an X across his nose. Those were meant to be Parlucci and the Milo guy. The other four had no Xs, like he still meant to get to them but hadn't done it yet. One of them was a little overweight, like you are, Charlie. And he had a round face like yours. He even wore a little plaid hat, a little porkpie hat. It was you, Charlie. This guy means to kill you."

Charlie's shock swept through him like ice water. None of it seemed credible. "Me? Why'd he want to kill me?"

"That's the big question, Charlie, but there's no doubt he plans to do it. And the problem is we don't know where he's gone. He could still be around here or he could be in Nebraska, but we'll catch him eventually, I expect."

"You expect!"

"You know how it is, Charlie. Nothing's certain. We can't put a guard outside your house, but we'll have patrol cars cruising up and down your street. You can trust me on that. Maybe you could hire a bodyguard. It could come off your taxes."

Charlie felt less than reassured. "So if these cardboard figures weren't the most disturbing thing, what was?"

Hutchins glanced around the room, avoiding Charlie's eyes. In the past, Hutchins's primary emotions had been anger and indignation; now he showed hesitation, even fear. "I found these jars in the closet of Browning's room, canning jars. Each was filled with alcohol. One had Mickey's tongue floating in it like some kind of pink fish. In another was Parlucci's nose. The third had a pair of ears.

They looked like those white mushrooms. Let me tell you, it wasn't pretty."

Again Charlie felt a rush of fear. Then he said: "Can I have my pistol license back?"

Hutch shook his head. "Chief Novak says it'd set a bad precedent. I mean, if everybody demanded a pistol license, think of the trouble we'd be in. Downtown would become like the O.K. Corral."

"It's my life." This guy's still an asshole, thought Charlie.

"And we'll take care of it for you. You can trust us on that." But Hutchins was still avoiding Charlie's eyes.

"Thanks, Lieutenant. I'll make sure you get a front-row seat at my funeral. And never mind the flowers. Just send twenty bucks to the retarded cops' fund."

"You don't have to talk like that, Charlie. I'm trying to do my best here."

Charlie gave himself a moment to settle down. "Do you have any idea why Mickey was murdered?"

"Novak says he has a few ideas, but I think he's totally in the dark. So, well, it's a mystery."

"Great," said Charlie. "That's just great. What about the other figures, did you recognize them?"

"The other heavyset guy had a colorful vest. It might be Campbell. Some sheriff's deputies are going to talk to him."

"And the woman, could she have been Janey?"

"I doubt it. Is there any reason it might be Janey?"

"How the hell would I know? If the man wants to kill me, he might also want to kill my wife."

"We've been thinking it might be your friend Artemis, but we're not sure yet. The woman's wearing a little skirt, like a ballerina."

"Good grief, I've got to tell her!"

"Let us handle that. Sheriff's investigators will talk to them in the morning."

"But she's right in the other room!"

"We're the professionals, Charlie. Stay out of it."

Charlie didn't like that and thought of a few insulting remarks. But he hoped to keep Hutchins talking. "What about fingerprints? There must have been prints."

"A few smudges. He'd cleaned up pretty good. In the trash were a bunch of those thin latex gloves that food servers wear. I bet he wore them even when he slept. But the crime scene guys think they'll find something. They've already turned up a few hairs. It takes time."

"Maybe I don't have time."

After Hutchins left, Charlie returned to the dining room. A slice of apple pie was on his plate, but he didn't feel hungry anymore.

Both Janey and Artemis were staring at him with question mark expressions. "What was that all about?" asked Janey. "You're pale."

Charlie touched his face as if he could feel his pallor, feel his fear. "Nothing," he said. "Nothing at all." His face felt clammy.

Eleven

Charlie fretted through the night about being unable to get his pistol license reinstated. The next day, Saturday, he stayed around the house. Even raking the leaves seemed dangerous. He felt frail and this surprised him. This wasn't the first time a threat had been made against his life, but he thought how he couldn't run fast anymore and he couldn't hear as well and his muscles were flabby. He told himself he'd go to the Y and start lifting weights on Sunday; that is, if he lived that long.

Janey watched him uncertainly. She'd stopped asking what was wrong, but she wouldn't let him get too far from sight. In the afternoon, he watched football on the upstairs TV. He kept the sound off and turned the chair so his back wasn't to the door. No way was he going to make Wild Bill Hickok's mistake.

"Don't you want me to turn up the sound?" asked Janey.

"It's not important. They always say the same thing."

Janey focused on something on the floor by Charlie's chair. "What's that doing here?" She picked up the carving knife: part of her two-piece Wüsthof carving set that had been a wedding present from her former husband thirty years earlier.

"I was going to cut myself some cheese," said Charlie.

T he first thing Monday morning, Charlie drove down to a gun shop near the Albany airport and bought a Benelli M4 Super 90: a 12-gauge semi-automatic shotgun with an 18.5-inch barrel and a regular stock. It held five rounds and a sixth in the chamber. It could fire as fast as Charlie could pull the trigger. To buy it, all he needed was the money—no permit, no registration, no license. It was as simple as buying a birthday cake.

The salesman had gray skin, a constant smile and was thin enough to slip through a picket fence. "Home defense system?" he asked.

Charlie nodded.

He then drove to another gun shop two miles away and bought a factory collapsible buttstock and a pistol grip. It was illegal to sell the Benelli with these attached, but there was no law against buying them separately. To change stocks took about a minute. But Charlie wasn't done.

He continued along Central Avenue to Schenectady, getting caught up in stop-and-go traffic that made him impatient, as if the murderer with the knife would try to leap into his car. A silly idea, he thought, but he kept the doors locked. It was a bright fall morning with leaves blowing across the highway.

Charlie went to a third gun shop where he'd done business for the past twenty years after helping the owner, Larry Wisniewski, with a divorce. Charlie had phoned him earlier and Wisniewski was waiting behind the counter. He was a middle-aged, average-sized man with

Coke-bottle glasses and a blue and somewhat greasy Patriots cap that he never seemed to take off.

"I hope you know what you're doing, Charlie." On the glass case was a 14.5-inch barrel. "It's illegal for a civilian to use this."

"I can deal with it. Can you put it on? I'll look the other way."

"You ask a lot, Charlie." His worried expression deepened the nickel slot between his eyebrows.

"Who'll know? Anyway, I need the favor."

Wisniewski looked down at the box with the Benelli. Charlie could almost hear the heated conversation rattling between his ears.

"It will take a few minutes. Watch the shop, will you?"

Wisniewski disappeared behind a purple velvet curtain with the short barrel in one hand and the box with the Benelli in the other. Charlie heard him bumping around and the scrape of a chair being moved.

"Can you get a magazine extension with those?" called Charlie.

Wisniewski stuck his head around the curtain. "With one of these shorties, it'd only add one more round. It's also illegal. Have you thought this over, Charlie?"

"All night long." He'd always found something exhilarating about buying a gun. It was almost sexual. He disapproved of the feeling, but he also liked it. "Let me have the extension. One more round's one more round, right?"

Wisniewski took off his cap, looked inside it, and then put it back on his head. "Can't be done, Charlie. First of all, I'd have to order one, which would take time. Second, it could cost me my license. Shit, if you can't take care of your business with six rounds, you might as well quit right now."

In his disappointment, Charlie wanted to ask Wisniewski where he could get a bagful of grenades, but the foolishness of the thought embarrassed him. He was struck by how fast he could change from a rational human being to a fanatic eager for explosives. He shrugged and nodded, not trusting himself to speak.

Wisniewski watched him and then said, "I got something else you'll want." He again disappeared into the back. Time passed. Charlie pondered the dangerous seesawing of his emotions. Wisniewski returned ten minutes later carrying the Benelli in one hand and a black Boyt Harness hard case in the other. "You'll need this. You can't just carry it around in a plastic bag. I put the long barrel inside. And there's something else you'll need." From the glass case, he removed a Beretta shotgun cleaning kit with a cleaning-rod handle, aluminum rods, a three-piece bronze brush, cotton patches, lubricant oil and a few other odds and ends. "Now get out of here. You can pay me another time as long as it's soon." The crease between his eyebrows deepened.

Charlie hefted the hard case. He figured he could drive back and forth over it with his Golf and it would hardly scratch. He put the case on the counter. "Can you give me four boxes of two-and-three-quarter-inch shells?"

"Jesus, Charlie." Wisniewski dug out the shells and slid the boxes across the counter. "I'll throw a bag in for free as long as you get outta here." He went into the other room and returned shortly with a small black backpack. "This is a Boyt Tactical backpack. It'll hold your stuff. Now beat it."

Charlie put the shells and cleaning kit into the backpack, and then opened the hard case and set the shotgun into its foam bed as gently as he might set a baby in a cradle. Closing the case, he took comfort in the decisive snapping sounds of its latches. "Give my greetings to the wife."

———

Charlie then drove to a rod-and-gun club north of Troy that had an outdoor range. He'd been there years before with his cousin Jack, but he wasn't a member. He'd never been a hunter and saw his reluctance to prowl through the woods as caused by a hopeless streak of sentimentality: He was fond of animals. The idea of shooting grouse, pheasants, ducks, geese, turkeys, rabbits and deer was disagreeable to him. Little creatures with big families. If he was starving, he might reconsider, but otherwise, what was the point? No, the only creatures he'd shot had been human beings, and once a pit bull.

But these feelings embarrassed him. Every fall during deer hunting season, part of him, a small part, felt he should be out there too. He'd put on heavy, high-top boots, clomp around the house and sigh. Only Janey and Victor knew about Charlie's sentimental streak and it was rarely mentioned. Not that Charlie hid the fact that he didn't hunt, but if anyone asked he'd say, "Not recently." In fact, his previous hunting experience had been popping a squirrel with a slingshot when he was ten. It fell to the ground twisting and writhing and then lay still. He'd been surprised to hit it, and he never tried again.

Charlie drove east on Route 2 toward Cropseyville. The countryside was mostly trees and farmland, but small subdivisions were creeping out from Troy. The gun club was down a dead-end gravel road and he parked by the clubhouse, a long one-story building. Four pickups were parked outside. Charlie walked to the door, wondering what little story he'd make up.

Fifteen minutes later he was out at the rifle range taking the shotgun out of its case. He stood under a long, roofed structure without walls. Five targets were placed at different intervals to about seventy-five yards up a slight incline. The target backers were made of railroad ties and straw, with a red post on either side.

Six men had been in the clubhouse; four were playing cards. Charlie explained he was a former cop and he wanted to try out a new shotgun. He gave them the names of five men he knew who used to belong to the club. All turned out to be dead. Charlie was so stunned by this fact that the man in charge waved him toward the door, calling out, "Go on, go on. Do your best!"

The act of sliding the shells into the magazine gave him a slightly carnal buzz. Curbing his annoyance, he inserted the sixth shell in the chamber and took his position at the barrier. He raised the Benelli, tucked it against his shoulder, peered along the sight at the twenty-five-yard target and fired. The sound was more of a crack than an explosion. Actually, it seemed like one longish sound, because the six shots took about six seconds. The spent cases darted away like speedy finches. The recoil wasn't as soft as he was told it would be, but he could deal with it. Only two of his shots had hit the target, and neither in the center. His feelings at this point were high adrenaline and fear, not focused fear, but a fear, it seemed, of everything encircling his life, as if fear were the air he breathed.

He fired thirty-six more rounds and his aim improved. Then he held the shotgun out horizontally in his outstretched arm. The short barrel and collapsible stock made the weapon about ten inches shorter than the unmodified Benelli—under thirty inches—not much in the natural scheme of things, but short enough to put it under a sport coat. Charlie returned everything to the case and headed back to his car. This had been the easy part. The hard part would be when he got home.

———

"Y ou moving in or out?"

Janey had seen Charlie come through the back door to the kitchen carrying the black hard case and backpack.

Charlie laughed, but Janey could see it was a false laugh, one of those little laughs that take up space while you're figuring out what to say. "No, no," he said. "I'm just doing some work. I've been at my office." That was technically true, but he hadn't been in his office on that particular Monday. It was now early afternoon.

"What's in the suitcase? It looks new."

So Charlie gave up his plan to sneak the Benelli into the house. He set the case on the yellow Formica table, snapped the clasps and opened it up. The black shotgun made the whole room smaller. It sucked up the light from the ceiling fixture and reflected nothing back. Charlie heard the wall clock tick.

"Is it loaded?"

"No."

"Get rid of it," said Janey flatly.

"It's a home defense system." Charlie closed the case. The kitchen got bigger again. One might even imagine, with hard work, that the gun case contained no more than dirty socks.

"I want you to get rid of it."

"I think I need it."

"Damn it, Charlie, you've got to tell me what's going on! I'm your wife! Ever since that policeman was here on Friday night you've been sneaking around the house peeking out the windows and now I find you with this monster rifle."

"Shotgun."

"Charlie, can't you be truthful with me?"

"Okay, let's sit down and talk about it."

So Charlie told her about the three murders in more detail. Then he told her what Hutchins had said and described the little cardboard figures. "I called him about an hour ago. He said that Campbell and Artemis had been 'notified.' So that's a relief." He spent a minute describing the figure with the little porkpie hat. He told her about Mickey's sister and his trip to Glens Falls to talk to Lizzie Whitaker, and told her of Mrs. Penfield and Mickey's office. Charlie even showed her his copy of Mickey's secret notebook: *Vaccinated axel money maker virgin iffy in Illinois rift clover-bugs interstice zip.* Lastly, he explained that the police refused to give him a pistol license, so he'd bought the shotgun, which had no restrictions. He didn't say that the short barrel and collapsible stock made its legality problematic.

Janey sat across the table with her arms folded. "Aren't the police looking out for us? It's their job."

"Hutchins said the police would keep an eye on the house, but it's a now-and-then sort of thing. Like they'll drive by. Nothing steady. I got chills listening to him. So I got this. Have you ever fired a gun?"

"You kidding? I'm a nurse. I'm a patcher-upper, not a shooter-upper. Who's the man who wants to kill you, or maybe us?"

"That's the trouble, I don't know and neither do the police. They almost caught him at the motel, but he got away. And they don't know what he looks like, except generally. They know nothing about him. There weren't even fingerprints."

"What did Lieutenant Hutchins mean by saying the police would drive by now and then? What's 'now and then'? Did you tell him about Emma?"

"Of course."

Janey stood up with a scraping of her chair. She stepped away from Charlie and looked down at her shoes, the white clogs she wore in the hospital. "I've got to talk to this guy."

And with that she left the house.

L ieutenant Hutchins was a man who never felt at a loss for words, never thought he could be surprised, never expected to have his authority questioned except by his boss, No-Neck Novak. None of that interested Janey. She blew past the dispatcher, as she told Charlie later, and barged into Hutchins's office, where he was joking with two men in plainclothes. "I ripped him a new asshole. I called him an incompetent fuck and when he threatened to throw me out of his office, I told him I'd rip his balls off, then I'd take him to court for assault. Here he's fucked up catching the maniac who killed Mickey and those other guys, and instead of putting cops in our house twenty-four/seven, he's going to drive up and down the goddamn street a couple of times a day."

For years Charlie had been impressed by how Janey could drop her pleasant demeanor and take on the abusive language of a gutter ruffian. Had she learned this as a nurse? Charlie felt she had. He was sure that at times she was forced to draw a line around things about which there could be no doubt, times when the business of healing was about to go haywire due to someone's meddling and Mr. Hyde had to be called in to deal with the shortcomings of Dr. Jekyll. Charlie himself had been a victim of these transformations and they frightened him.

"And what did he say to that?" asked Charlie, keeping his voice mildly pleasant. He'd been in the living room, once again studying Mickey's notebook.

"He jumped on his high horse and said I couldn't speak to him like that. I told him to take a flying fuck and if he didn't do his fucking job, I'd go to the mayor. He said the department lacked sufficient manpower to keep someone at our house twenty-four hours a day, and after all we could always call 9-1-1. So I said he had to do fucking better or the next time he showed up in the ICU, I'd rip out his tubes."

"That was nice of you."

"You bet it was nice. I mean, I didn't have to give him the warning."

"Did Hutchins say anything about the investigation?"

"Not a word. He said he couldn't be expected to talk about police business. I thought he'd explode, but instead he tried to stay calm and sensible. Maybe it was because those other cops were watching. He said he'd increase the patrols and keep someone parked outside at night, though he wouldn't be there till around midnight. Then I said if anything happened to Artemis, I'd seriously hurt him. He said she wasn't his business. She was the sheriff's business. I said I'd hurt him anyway."

"Did you tell him about the Benelli?"

"I didn't want to upset him again. Just keep the case locked, okay? I don't want to see the damn thing. It scares me."

Charlie was glad about the increased patrols, if they actually happened, but he was also glad he had the shotgun.

Twelve

Tuesday morning there was sun, but Charlie had felt a chill blowing through the slightly open bedroom window. Faded leaves flew past the glass. After breakfast, he left the house with the Benelli, drove downtown to a sporting goods store and bought six boxes of 2¾-inch shells of 12-gauge buckshot. Then he drove out Route 29 toward Schuylerville. He knew of another rifle range in the hills north of Greenwich that belonged to the Washington County Gun Club. He felt he needed more practice, that he could never have too much practice. But he also worried that he wanted to reexperience the thrill of firing off six rounds in a few seconds.

Charlie parked in the gravel by the small clubhouse. Two SUVs were parked there as well; smoke was puffing up from the chimney. Charlie had been to the gun club before and he knew people who were members, even people he thought were still alive, youngsters about his age. Four men were leaning back in their chairs around a table, drinking coffee. After Charlie had signed several forms promising not to hold the gun club responsible if he shot himself in the foot, he went back outside to his car and retrieved the Benelli in its case. A minute later he was walking up the dirt track toward the rifle range with a rolled-up target under his arm.

Here, too, was a roofed structure or firing point without walls with stations for five shooters. Six targets had been placed at intervals along the small incline toward the trees. Each was set against a dirt backstop held in place by railway ties and bracketed by two six-by-six red posts. On a stanchion under the roof was a sign reading, "Do Not Shoot the Red Posts" with underlinings and exclamation marks, and printed in a schoolboy's block letters. Charlie carried his roll of paper out to the 25-yard target and tacked it in place. It showed the silhouette of a Western gunslinger slightly crouched and drawing his six-gun. A target was printed on the gunslinger with the bull's-eye situated over his heart.

Returning to the firing point, Charlie at first thought he had forgotten the key to the hard case, but then he found it in his back pocket. He mildly felt he was doing something illegal, not because of the Benelli's modifications, but in a larger sense, and he felt somewhat silly firing at the paper gunslinger. This time he had earplugs. He stuck them in his ears and began sliding the rounds into the magazine.

Once again, the Benelli seemed to shoot all by itself, as if it needed Charlie only as a steady platform upon which to be situated, rather than needing Charlie's finger on the trigger. He kept a tight grip on the barrel to prevent the gun from riding up, and as a result the six-inch spread obliterated the gunslinger's right foot.

He stayed till he had finished the sixty shells, and it hadn't taken him long to center the spread around the gunslinger's chest. But what interested him most was how quickly he could make himself load the shotgun, and next how quickly he could unlock the case, remove the shotgun and pack in six shells. If he stayed calm, he could do it in thirty seconds, which meant taking the key from his pocket, unlocking the case and so on till he fired his first shot. But if the shotgun was already loaded it took about ten seconds. That left him in a quandary. He'd told Janey he would keep the shotgun unloaded. But what was the harm in keeping it loaded if it was locked in its case? Why, no harm at all. But he wouldn't tell her about it.

F ifteen minutes later, Charlie was parked just off the side of the road on a hilltop, admiring the blue autumn sky and looking east over the fields and stands of trees toward Vermont's Green Mountains. The yellow-leaved birch trees along the top of the embankment to his left swayed as gracefully as antique ladies dancing a minuet. He'd always loved fall, but now that he was sixty-seven he found that spring offered more uplifting pleasures. Autumn's metaphors were metaphors he cared not to dwell upon. He thought, not for the first time, that few actions in life come to tidy conclusions, while occasionally their outcomes could be like tsunamis wreaking havoc a thousand miles from the earthquake that had set them on their destructive rush. This, he suspected, was also the answer to Mickey's murder: It was the playing out of a story begun many years before, a story in which Charlie may have played a part, but for the life of him he couldn't think what it had been. For the life of me indeed, he thought as he again recalled Mickey sprawled dead on his sidewalk and Parlucci's noseless corpse with the python slithering through the blood.

O f the two plainclothesmen Janey had seen in Hutchins's office, one turned out to be an investigator with the Criminal Investigations Unit of the Saratoga County Sheriff's Office and the other was a state police sergeant with the Bureau of Criminal Investigation attached to Troop G. The Tea Kettle Motel, where the suspect had stayed, was in Gansevoort and out of the jurisdiction of the Saratoga cops. But the city police had already turned the crime scenes over to the county sheriff's office for crime scene processing, and some of the evidence had been sent down to the state police lab, or Forensic Information Center, in Albany. This pleased Novak. Given the choice, he'd have liked to turn the whole business over to the sheriff's office and the troopers, but it wasn't possible. However, as he had told *The Saratogian*, "I been liaising with sheriff's boys and the troopers since the git-go."

This reduced Novak's and Hutchins's role to little more than spectators, or so it seemed to Charlie, though he knew that Hutchins was still investigating within the city. But to Charlie—irrationally, as he told himself that morning—it felt like a rejection, as if in dropping the case, they'd dropped him as well. The thought caused him to laugh out loud—his first good laugh since he'd bought the Benelli. Even so, Novak and Hutchins still knew him, though they disliked him; but Charlie knew no one in the sheriff's office, while the men he'd once known in the state police were probably retired and gone to Florida. Just to make sure, he made some calls and found he was more or less right: Two had died and two were working out of state as security consultants. Then, when he called the sheriff's office to ask who was running the Mickey Martin investigation, he was told the information wasn't available to the public.

Hanging up, Charlie thought, Public? Who's public? And he had a sudden impulse to grab the Benelli, crawl into the back of the bedroom closet and stay there till the murderer had been caught. Maybe Janey could toss in a sandwich now and then. This wasn't garden-variety cowardice, in Charlie's opinion. Plenty of bad guys in the past had wanted him dead. But none had wanted to put his tongue or nose or ears into a little jar of alcohol. If Charlie had to be dead and buried—an inevitability in any case—he wanted all his little bits and pieces buried with him.

Next he called Fletcher Campbell.

"I've beefed up security," said Campbell, "and some of my stable hands know how to shoot. I don't want to go into details. The sheriff's had a few men out here. We're pretty well covered."

Then he called Artemis.

"Such a nuisance, Charlie. There's a police officer in the driveway, a sheriff's deputy. I looked out the front window this morning and saw him urinating on a fence post. So I informed him that if he had to use the bathroom, he could come into the house. Now I'm making him a sandwich. I wish I could just send him away. I'm sure I'm in no danger. Why should anyone hurt me? I've been in Europe for years."

A little later, standing by the living room window, Charlie saw a Saratoga police car drive slowly down the street. Inside were two uniformed cops, while the one closest to Charlie had his head back and was guffawing so loudly that Charlie thought he heard a distant spluttering noise. Neither took the briefest glance at his house. Great, he thought, that's just great.

Over the next few days, Charlie stayed inside the house. He didn't surrender to the temptation of crawling into the closet, but he kept the Benelli nearby without leaving it around on the furniture. Like a big box of condoms, it wasn't something to be left on the coffee table. He tried to get Janey and Emma to stay in the house as well, but they said they had more important stuff to do.

"More important than living? Come on, give me a break."

At least a dozen times Charlie saw a police car drive past the house, but the men inside never seemed to be paying attention.

"Get a dog," said Victor. "It'll bark and carry on."

"There's Bruiser. He yaps."

"You mean that Chihuahua puppy? That's not a dog; it's a snack. You need a dog like a junkyard dog. I bet you can get one from the pound."

"Even a dog from the pound would have to be trained."

"Then rent one. There's got to be a place that rents multifunctional pit bulls. It stands to reason. It'll save you money in the long run, like funeral money."

By Friday afternoon, Charlie was bored silly with skulking about the house. He also felt guilty. Parlucci's funeral had been on Wednesday and Charlie missed it because he didn't want to go out in public. He'd heard nothing about Milo's funeral, but he doubted he'd have gone in any case. He was suspicious of everyone who drove down the street, even the cops. Once, when the doorbell rang, Charlie ran to get the Benelli and then forgot where he had put it. Looking through the glass, he saw it was the postman. But how do I know it's a *real* postman? he had asked himself. Why does he look familiar?

The postman turned out to be one of Charlie's ex-wife's nephews.

"You forgot to put a stamp on this one to Verizon, Charlie. One of those senior moments, right?"

Charlie began to say his wife took care of the bills and then said nothing.

When Victor came through the back door unannounced around four on Friday afternoon, he heard a kitchen chair tip over and found Charlie by the refrigerator fumbling with the latches on the Boyt hard case.

"You're a little jumpy, Charlie. You'd be upset if you shot me. It'd weigh on your conscience. Let's grab a coupla beers and chill, as the kiddies say. The Parting Glass?"

Charlie put the case on the Formica table. "Too many people."

"That never bothered Wild Bill Hickok. You think you might be overdoing the Nervous Nellie business? We could grab a six-pack and drink it in the park."

Charlie disliked the allusion to Nervous Nellie. "The Parting Glass is okay."

As they walked to the door, Victor saw that Charlie was carrying the hard case. "You better leave your blankie here in the closet or something."

Charlie put the case behind the couch and felt his sense of fragility increase.

They arrived shortly before five and Charlie got a booth opposite the door, where he could sit with his back to the wall. He figured that a dozen of the men in the bar roughly fit Hutchins's description of the murderer. This has got to stop, thought Charlie. He ordered a Jack Daniel's Manhattan and a bowl of cashews.

Victor nodded to the nuts, which Charlie had said some weeks before that he could never eat again because of the calories and fats. "I take it this is your last meal. Me, I'd choose surf and turf."

Charlie stirred his Manhattan with his little finger and gave Victor an apologetic look. "I guess I've been getting frazzled."

Victor was drinking an Amstel Light. "Imminent death has that effect on people. You still been working on Mickey's secret code?"

"I look at it all the time, but I haven't made any headway, or not really." He pulled a piece of paper from his back pocket on which he had written out the ten nonsense sentences.

Victor leaned over the table. "What d'you mean, 'not really'?"

"Look at this." Charlie flattened out the paper on the table. "You see these next-to-last words or next-to-next-last words?"

"Penultimate and antepenultimate, what of them?"

Charlie read them out. "Gap, rift, lacuna, recess, gulch, hiatus, cleft, lapse, hitch and breather."

Victor leaned back, passed his hand over his shaved head, glanced around to see which waitresses were working and then looked at Charlie. "So? It sounds like a hip-hop song."

"They're synonyms more or less. They might signify a pause between the first part of the sentences and the last one or two words. Then there're these words starting with Z. But I don't see why Mickey should go to all that trouble to hide his notebook when what was inside was already in code. It's like hiding it twice."

Victor thought about it for a moment and then gave a slight start and nodded toward the door. "Why don't you ask Mr. Professional?"

Looking up, Charlie saw Lieutenant Hutchins making his way through a group of young women at the door. He was at least a head taller than the tallest of them. Seeing Charlie and Victor, Hutchins turned in their direction. Charlie stuck the piece of paper back in his pocket and took a restorative sip of his Manhattan.

"Sit down, Lieutenant," said Victor. "Have some cashews before Charlie eats them all."

Hutchins hesitated, afraid to be seen in bad company, and then sat down. He blinked and squinched his eyes shut as if something was caught in one of them. Charlie thought the lieutenant looked not only tired, but balanced on the edge of some inner crisis. He was also surprised Hutchins had joined them, though he guessed it wasn't for social reasons.

Victor pushed the bowl of nuts across the table. "Hey, Hutch, you look like your dog just died. Maybe this police stuff is taking its toll.

I've seen it happen before—a fine, upstanding officer suddenly crushed by a conviction of the world's wickedness. Believe me, it's nothing that whiskey can't cure."

Hutchins ignored him and nodded to Charlie. "I ran into your friend Gillespie at City Hall. He told me he was the one who told Mickey where you lived. Why didn't you say that earlier?"

"I didn't want to get him in trouble. He has a lot of anxieties . . ."

"Like his hair's falling out," said Victor. "I told him to shave his head like me so we could look like matching cue balls."

Hutchins waited for Victor to finish. "You still should have told me, Charlie."

"Eddie's afraid of losing his job with the city. No offense, Lieutenant, you've got no subtlety."

Hutchins picked up a cashew, studied it and then set it back in the bowl. "That's what the sheriff's investigator told me."

"Is that what's bothering you?"

"Partly that, partly other things." He paused, gave the waitress a wave and asked for a Bud Light. "I don't suppose it matters if I tell you. It'll be in the paper tomorrow. My son was arrested for shoplifting down at the mall in Cohoes—a pricey pair of sunglasses at Macy's."

"Hey, hey, hey! Ouch!" yelped Victor. "Charlie, you kicked me!"

"So be quiet." Charlie turned to Hutchins. "Couldn't Novak squash it?"

"The security guy down there's an ex-cop. I guess he'd had some run-ins with Novak. And Macy's wants it to go to court. Those sunglasses, they cost about two hundred bucks, so it's a felony. Then somebody down there called *The Saratogian*."

Hutchins's son, Bobby, was in the same eleventh-grade class as Emma at the high school. She'd described him as loud and obnoxious. But since Emma was class secretary, president of the French

Club and militantly bookish, she found many boys loud and obnoxious. Her particular boyfriend was Cecil, a freshman at Skidmore from New York City who liked to talk about Derrida, which Charlie had first thought was a square dance term, like do-si-do.

"It's still his first offense, correct? He'll probably get a warning and be banned from the mall."

"I don't know. My lawyer says they want to make an example of him. And Novak says the Cohoes cops are jealous because we run a tight ship up here."

"Tight jockstrap is more like it," said Victor. "Don't kick me, Charlie."

"What kind of kid is he?"

"He's fine, maybe a little loud. I was worse at that age. All I cared about was pussy, gin fizzes and fast cars."

Charlie laughed. "I was too shy to get in much trouble, though I'd have loved the chance. Anyway, my cousins would have smacked me around if I'd been bad."

"So, Hutch, tell me," said Victor, "why're you cozying up to us?"

Hutchins leaned violently back in the booth. "Not you, fuckhead. You're the same asshole you've always been. I just wanted to say something about Gillespie—"

"And then one thing led to another—"

"Be quiet, Victor."

Hutchins glanced around the room, which had gotten crowded and noisy. He looked uncertain. "That trooper, Sergeant Evans, who was in my office when your wife barged in, he said a teacher of his at the academy had talked about you, Charlie. He said you could be clumsy, but you were also clearheaded and stubborn. And he said you had sharp eyes. I've never liked you, Charlie, maybe I still don't, but it doesn't mean you're stupid. Anyway, forget what I said about

Bobby. He'll straighten out or I'll beat the shit out of him. It's been on my mind, that's all."

Hutchins still looked uncomfortable, though his voice had regained a bit of its old truculence. Charlie decided he needed to be distracted from his personal problems. He took the paper with Mickey's nonsense sentences and set it again on the table. "I happened to look at Mickey's black notebook when I was in his office last week. What I wonder about is why hide the notebook if it's already in code?"

Hutchins looked at Charlie in exasperation. "Jesus, Charlie, you shouldn't have done that. You're incorrigible."

"Yes, I guess I am. Sorry about it." Charlie glanced at Victor, who was grinning; then he turned back to Hutchins. "Well, why should he hide it?"

Hutchins didn't answer at first. He looked around the room and then, when he spoke, his voice was so low that Charlie had to lean forward to hear him. "Maybe he thought it was something someone else would recognize, or maybe he didn't trust the complexity of the code."

"Have you figured it out yet?"

Hutchins put some money on the table for his beer. "Not so far, but we're getting close. The troopers turned it over to the professionals. But, Charlie, you shouldn't be asking me this shit. It's none of your business. And if you're working as a PI without a license, I'll have to slap your ass in jail."

Victor laughed. "That's the Hutchins we know and love."

When Charlie got home an hour later, Janey was in the kitchen. Sometimes Charlie cooked, but decades of bachelor cooking had crippled any culinary skills he might have had, making his attempts, in Janey's view, unfit for polite society. His last attempt had been a Spam roast with prune slices, which he'd had to eat by himself. Janey felt he'd made it just so she wouldn't let him cook again.

"Artemis invited us for tea for Sunday afternoon," Janey called from the kitchen. "Do you want to go?"

"Tea?" Holding the Benelli's hard case loosely in his right hand, Charlie entered the kitchen and gave his wife a kiss on the cheek.

"Not tea, *a* tea. I gather other people are invited. But if you don't leave that thing at home, I'm not going."

"I'll keep it in the trunk of the car." He got a Heineken from the refrigerator, a handful of pretzels from the cupboard and headed back to the living room.

"Don't ruin your dinner."

"No way."

Emma was sitting at the end of the couch reading a book for her civics class: *Sexual Harassment in the Workplace.* Charlie ruffled her hair, which was still damp from her shower. She was on the high school cross-country team and had gotten home half an hour earlier. Her short dark blond hair smelled of raspberry junket. She wore an extra-large Irish fisherman's sweater that had been passed down by her older sisters, a mixture of off-white, dirt and a catalog of stains. It fit Emma as a large mitten might fit a monkey's paw.

"Hi, Pop."

Charlie sat down at the other end of the couch and put the hard case on the floor. Once again he began to study the ten nonsense sentences. Not nonsense, he thought, it's code. But what if it really *was* nonsense, what if Mickey had left it in the furnace as a joke designed to drive people—people like me, thought Charlie—absolutely nuts? The fourth sentence read: *Xanax kitty kats zany zealous zebras old oxen xmas Kaiser kaftans kale recess ever-finger stoppage egg.*

"Absolutely nuts," said Charlie out loud.

"Problems?" asked Emma. She'd raised an eyebrow and her pretty face had an aggressively adult expression, slightly condescending and bemused.

"This guy who was murdered out front had a notebook in which he'd written these ten crazy sentences and then he hid it in a furnace that wasn't working. I'm sorry it was ever found. 'Ink in igloo except voles mickey mouse voila idiot in Iowa gap charming-details.' How's that going to do anything but drive me crazy?"

Emma held out her hand. "May I see?"

Charlie hesitated, and then decided it couldn't do any harm. "Sure."

Emma settled back in her corner. "'Vaccinated axel money maker virgin iffy in Illinois rift clover-bugs interstice zip.' Cool!"

"I bet Mickey's looking down or up from wherever he is," said Charlie, "and laughing his guts out. He always had a sadistic sense of humor."

Charlie worked on his Heineken and chewed pretzels as Emma muttered to herself. After a few minutes, she took a pencil from behind her ear and began writing in her notebook.

She's just showing off, thought Charlie. But then why shouldn't she get it as well as anyone else? After all, she had young brains, limber synapses.

After several more minutes she put her pencil back behind her ear. "They're Roman numerals."

"What!?" Charlie felt he'd been thumped in the stomach.

Emma scooted across the couch. "Look at all the Is and Vs and Xs in the first four. 'Ink in igloo except voles mickey mouse voila idiot in Iowa gap charming-details.' That's 'IIIXVMMVIII.' If it's a date, it could be three, fifteen, two thousand eight. Then 'gap' simply means space. See how the synonyms figure in more or less the same position: rift, lacuna, recess and the rest? While 'charming-details' might be C with a bar over it, which would be a hundred thousand."

"I guessed that part about the spaces," said Charlie.

"See? You're not so bad. The second one—'Vaccinated axel money maker virgin iffy in Illinois rift clover-bugs interstice zip.' That's VXMMVIII, space C with a bar over it, another space: zip. So that's five, ten, two thousand eight, then a hundred thousand and then 'zip.' The hundred thousand might refer to money."

"What are these Ks in the fourth one: 'Xanax kitty kats zany zealous zebras old oxen xmas Kaiser kaftans kale recess ever-finger stoppage egg'?"

"He's moved up two letters from I to K. Instead of VIIXXX, it's XKKZZZ. 'Old oxen' is two thousand, 'xmas Kaiser kaftans kale' is eight. So the date is seven, thirty, two thousand eight. Then there's a gap and probably another hundred thousand with 'ever-finger,' and then another gap and 'egg.' I expect that 'egg' is like 'zip.' And he's got two more later on: 'vacuity' and 'null.' Then on the ninth entry, he's moved up again. So the last entry is 'Babies' breath bother mother quit queens zowie matches make messes breather gravy-horn' and he's using Bs where he'd used Zs before and Xs before that. It translates into ten, twenty-one, two thousand eight, then a space and another hundred thousand. That's about two weeks ago. But there's nothing after 'gravy-horn.' Isn't that when Mickey was killed? Maybe he didn't have the chance to write down the final words."

"Sure, but it's unlikely he was writing down the date of his own death." Charlie asked himself what else had happened on the twenty-first. Right away, he thought of the theft of Fletcher Campbell's horse. But wasn't that too much of a coincidence? But perhaps the one hundred thousand referred to the amount of money Campbell paid to get his horse back. Charlie sighed. "Maybe you're right."

Janey knocked on the woodwork between the dining room and living room. "If you two don't stop whispering and come to dinner, I'll give your food to the dog."

Thirteen

Charlie pulled his Golf up to the curb across the street from Mickey's office at eight thirty Saturday morning. A light rain was falling and the wet leaves stuck to the pavement like polished mahogany. He saw no car that might have been Mrs. Penfield's, nor did he see a light inside the building. Maybe she'd finished her work in closing up Mickey's business affairs. If that were so, he'd go to her house. But he would prefer to see her without the interference of her husband.

The case with the Benelli was in the backseat covered with an old blanket. He was tired of lugging it around, but the chance of being caught without it when attacked by a man with a knife convinced him that he could put up with it for a while longer. Surely its presence made him feel more relaxed, or sort of relaxed.

Mrs. Penfield arrived in front of the office at nine o'clock in a yellow Toyota Corolla, punctual even though her boss was cold in the ground. As she climbed the front steps, Charlie got out of the car and crossed the street.

Mrs. Penfield heard him as she was opening the door and turned. At first her face was blank, even anxious, and then she broke into a smile. "I've wonderful news. Mr. Martin left me fifteen thousand dollars. That's more than double what he owed me."

"That's great!" said Charlie, joining her on the top step. "Shall we go inside?"

Mrs. Penfield wrinkled her brow and then smiled again. She wore a gray raincoat and slacks of a lighter gray. Her brown hair was tied up in a ponytail. It, too, was getting gray.

"I was afraid you might be finished here." Charlie shut the door behind him and removed his hat.

"The police brought back the files they took, though they kept the computers. I hope to be done by Wednesday at the latest. Anyway, I can't stand it here. It's too quiet. Shall I make coffee?"

"That would be nice." It struck Charlie that she hadn't asked what he wanted. Maybe that was just as well. He took off his raincoat and put it over a chair.

After hanging up her coat, she filled a carafe from the bathroom tap and went to the coffeemaker on top of a file cabinet.

Charlie cleared his throat. "You've disappointed me, Mrs. Penfield."

She turned quickly, spilling a little of the water. "What do you mean?"

"I think you know what I mean." When Mrs. Penfield didn't speak, Charlie continued. "It wasn't Mickey who hid the notebook in the furnace. It was you, and you did it after the police searched his office."

Mrs. Penfield's face grew more pinched. "I don't understand."

"There was no reason for Mickey to go to all that trouble to hide it. So it must have been you."

"That's a silly idea."

"Would you prefer to talk to Lieutenant Hutchins?"

Mrs. Penfield still held the carafe. Her eyes began to tear up.

"My guess is the notebook wasn't here when the police searched the place. You probably had it at home and were trying to figure out the code. Where'd you originally find it? In a desk drawer? But you were afraid other people might know about it, and if they came forward, the police would wonder where it'd gone. So you did all this foolishness with the furnace. You wanted me to find it and turn it over to the police. Am I right?"

"Mr. Penfield said we couldn't keep it."

"But you made a copy."

She nodded and wiped her eyes with a handkerchief with tiny red and blue flowers. Charlie remembered that his grandmother had had one exactly like it.

"What do you think those sentences mean?"

"I've no idea. That's why I took the notebook. I thought Mr. Penfield might make sense of it."

"Did he?"

"He said they might include some dates, but he wasn't sure. The next day I put the notebook in my purse and went to the office at my usual time. Mr. Martin always came two or three hours later. The office was full of policemen searching everything and I learned that Mr. Martin had been murdered. I thought of leaving the notebook in a drawer, but the police had already searched the desk. I was afraid they'd guess I had it. So I waited till they'd left and put the notebook someplace they hadn't searched."

"The furnace."

"Yes."

"What about the footprints?"

"Mr. Martin had a spare pair of shoes in his office. I had to stuff them with paper to keep them from falling off."

"Very clever of you."

Mrs. Penfield looked as pleased as if she had won third place in a cake-baking contest: a grudging smile. "Then I called you because I thought you'd be easier to deal with than Lieutenant Hutchins."

"Didn't you say Mickey kept the inner office locked when he wasn't here?"

Mrs. Penfield pursed her lips.

"So I assume you had a key. Did Mickey know you had a key?"

Mrs. Penfield shook her head. "No."

"What a sneaky creature you are, Mrs. Penfield."

The secretary colored slightly, but she didn't seem to mind the accusation.

"Did you take any other stuff out of Mickey's office?"

"Of course not! Sometimes someone would call with a question about their policy. House insurance mostly. But the file would be in Mr. Martin's office and he might show up that day or he might not. So I got a key."

"And how'd you do that?"

"Mr. Penfield made it for me. He can do all sorts of things."

"Are you sure you didn't take anything else from his office?"

"Of course I'm sure!"

Charlie thought it might be true or it might not be true. But he didn't think it worth pressing her to find out. She stood in front of him, still holding the carafe, with an annoyed, birdlike expression.

"Why don't you finish making the coffee? I'll have a quick cup, then leave you in peace."

Charlie prowled around the office, opening a drawer, looking in the closet. He didn't think it was necessary; it was just an automatic response to the situation: detective mode. An old tan raincoat hung in the closet and he searched the pockets, though he knew the police had searched them as well.

When the coffee was ready, Charlie took a cup and sipped it. It occurred to him that Mickey had probably put his lips on the very same spot.

"Good coffee," said Charlie.

Mrs. Penfield smiled. "That's what Mr. Penfield always says."

"Tell me, did Mickey insure horses by any chance?"

"Not while I worked for him."

"Did he ever talk about horses? Maybe said something to you."

"All he said to me were complaints, criticism and orders. Other than that, he rarely spoke."

"So he never talked about horses or showed any interest in them?" Charlie put on his raincoat.

Mrs. Penfield held her chin between her thumb and two fingers and looked thoughtful. "He'd read the *Racing Form* sometimes."

Charlie felt a pinprick of alertness. "How often?"

"I really can't say. Several times a month he'd have it in his pocket when he came in. And it looked as if he'd already read it, you know, rumpled."

"So he might have read it every day."

"Yes, that's possible."

The Greasy Mattress was empty when Charlie reached it around ten thirty that morning. Maud was sitting at the bar watching a soap opera reruns on TV. She turned the stool when Charlie entered.

"You again? I'll have to start charging you rent."

"My mother used to watch *Guiding Light*." In point of fact, his mother never watched soap operas. What she liked best was wrestling, boxing and *Gunsmoke*.

"That doesn't mean squat. Everyone watches *The Guiding Light*. It's like McDonald's for the eyes. What I want is a soap about motorcycle gangs and white slaving. And if you're here to ask if I've found a guy who knew Mickey, you're sniffing the wrong bike seat."

Charlie sat down on a nearby stool, not too close. "Maybe I just came to see your pretty eyes."

"Fuck you, I keep my pretty eyes for my friends, and I don't mean guy friends." Maud gulped a mouthful of beer. "There's got to be some crooks you put in the clink who'd tell you what you wanted."

"Maybe so, but they're spread through the state and don't tend to be chatty, least not with me. I'm the one who stuck them there."

"The guys I been talking to don't like me asking. And if I say it's for a friend, it's even worse. They think I want them to snitch. You ever notice you never see an old guy who's a snitch. They don't last long."

"But you'll keep trying?"

"You keep paying, I'll keep trying. You can trust me on that."

Charlie questioned whether she'd spoken to anyone. Maybe she was collecting the money just for sitting on the barstool.

"You play pool by any chance?" asked Maud, climbing off her stool.

"Not since I was in my twenties." A well-used, eight-foot table stood over by the restrooms.

"I'll play you, ten bucks a game."

"Make it one buck and you're on."

"Jesus, Charlie, why are law-abiding people such cheapskates?"

———

On Sunday afternoon, Charlie was delicately lifting a cucumber sandwich from a silver tray held by a blond server whom Artemis had hired for her tea. He eyed the sandwich with doubt. It wasn't a real sandwich, nowhere near it. First of all, it was only a quarter of a sandwich: a triangle of two slices of white bread, with a dab of mayonnaise and a silver dollar–sized chunk of cucumber. "'Real' mayonnaise," Janey said. But it had no weight, no heft. Making a meal of cucumber sandwiches would be like getting drunk on nonalcoholic beer—a lot of work.

"You're not supposed to make a meal of them," hissed Janey. "Have a deviled egg if you're hungry."

"They're not much better." In fact, Charlie hadn't been hungry till he'd seen the cucumber sandwiches. They were a culinary tease, the concept of food rather than food itself. Now he was starving and ready to call out for a pizza.

"And how would Artemis feel about that?" demanded Janey.

Charlie sipped his tea. His cup was small and as delicate as a flower blossom. Tiny red flowers formed a spiral pattern inside and out. The handle was a fragile question mark. Charlie preferred mugs—the heavy white mugs found in diners that you could bounce six feet off the floor. He didn't like a cup he had to worry about.

Twenty men and women, separated into half a dozen groups, stood about Artemis's sunroom. A huge window overlooked the fields to the south where horses were nibbling grass. The sky was a dark blue; the sun was an hour from setting. Faraway birds swirled in flocks like organized confetti.

Most of Artemis's guests held teacups or glasses of sherry as they chatted affably and nibbled cucumber sandwiches. They were people who—in Charlie's mind—had grown up with cucumber sandwiches. The beauty of the sunny autumn afternoon figured largely in their conversations. "It can't last" was a remark Charlie heard more than once. On a buffet table by the window, a brass cornucopia flanked by pumpkins spewed forth apples, pears and grapes.

Charlie and Janey had arrived ten minutes earlier and had been welcomed by Artemis with a kiss on the cheek and the injunction "to go meet people." Once they had shed their coats, a young woman offered them tea and another came by with a tray of cucumber sandwiches and deviled eggs. There were also square crackers slathered with a pink fishy spread that Charlie didn't like the look of. Now he and Janey were making their way into the room.

Charlie acknowledged his discomfort. Porsche, Cadillac and Lexus SUVs were parked in the turnaround in front of the house, and his elderly Golf felt out of place. But a sense of not belonging was new for him. In the past, he'd never questioned his right to chitchat with whomever he wished—rich or poor, educated or ignorant. The fact that something had changed interested him. Perhaps, he decided, it's because I no longer see myself on the upward curve of life; rather, I'm gaining speed on the long slide. The result was to make him feel apologetic, as if he were taking up too much space and should be shunted aside.

But he knew that was foolish. After all, Artemis had invited them and they had as much right to be there as anyone else. And seeing someone he knew by the fireplace, Charlie firmly gripped Janey's arm and practically dragged her forward. "There's Fletcher Campbell. Let me introduce you to him."

With his thick white hair, white moustache and red complexion,

Campbell was particularly conspicuous. Or perhaps it was his tweed shooting coat, tweed hunting breeks and knee-length tartan socks. Equally conspicuous was his voice, which was hearty and booming, as if accustomed only to outdoor use.

He hadn't seen Campbell since he'd spoken rudely to Charlie and thrown him out of his house—telling him, "What the fuck are you going to do about it?" when he protested Campbell's rudeness. Their only communication had been earlier in the week when Charlie had called to ask about his security arrangements now that Campbell knew that his life might be in danger. In fact, until Emma's discovery of the code, Charlie had thought his dealings with Campbell were done. Now, however, came the chance that the last date on Mickey's list referred to the theft of Bengal Lancer, and Charlie wanted to know the meaning of some of the other dates. If Janey had asked, as he led her across the room, what business it was of his, he'd have been surprised. Curiosity seemed its own justification. In any case, Janey didn't get a chance to say more than a muttered "Are you sure . . . ?" because Charlie was moving too quickly.

Coming up behind Campbell, Charlie put a hand on his shoulder. "Fletcher, I bet you're glad to have those deputies at your place. I was happy to hear about them. Better safe than sorry, right?"

Campbell stepped back and broke off his conversation with another tweedy couple. "Let me introduce you to my wife, Janey," Charlie continued. "She's heard a lot about you."

Campbell shot Charlie a wary look and then nodded to Janey, who seemed equally skeptical. But a moment later he reached out his hand as his gentlemanly instincts clicked into gear. Janey wore a red dress with high-heeled black boots and a gold necklace, making her one of the few splashes of color in a field of tweed.

"Mostly they sleep," said Campbell scornfully. "I got my own security."

"Too bad you didn't have them when Bengal Lancer was stolen. You must be relieved he's safe in his stall. No one's been arrested, I gather. Whoops, Artemis is waving to me. I'll be right back." Charlie stepped away, but it was a lie that Artemis had waved to him. She was nowhere in sight. Charlie guessed she was either at the front door or in the kitchen, so he aimed toward the kitchen. He was ashamed by his sudden surge of passive-aggressiveness, and he needed a minute or so to bedevil himself in peace. He also felt Janey would be best at dealing with Campbell, soothing whatever residual irritation he might have, so when Charlie returned all would be smooth sailing. Of course, Janey would be furious, but he'd explain it later. And it would do no harm for Campbell to see that Artemis was their good friend, that they were all equal in the eyes of their hostess. But was it necessary? Charlie asked himself. Why was he making it as complicated as a chess game? Still, he wanted those dates, especially the ones on which horses had been killed. And he wanted to jar Campbell from his customary self-assurance. Again Charlie felt his very desire justified his action. After all, he was "working." But as he thought this, another voice whispered: "Idiot."

Artemis was in the kitchen giving directions to the caterer as two young women in blue pantsuits unpacked further goodies from large plastic containers. She waved to him: "Charlie, I need your opinion about horseradish." Then she turned back to the caterer, a willowy young man with thick blond hair held in a ponytail. "Mr. Bradshaw's an expert on all kinds of equine matters."

Charlie joined them and shook the caterer's hand. "Including horseradish?"

"You must know something about it."

"It tarnishes silver."

"See," Artemis told the caterer, "I *told* you he'd know something."

The young man curled a lip. "I knew that perfectly well myself."

"I've a friend," said Charlie, speaking of Victor, "who makes homemade vanilla ice cream with a touch of horseradish."

Artemis beamed at him. "I should have hired you instead of Cecil. He forgot the shrimp."

Artemis looked severe; Cecil looked abashed. Charlie thought, Aren't such problems preferable to murder and the harm we do one another? "Would you like me to get another log or two for the fire?" he asked Artemis.

But she didn't. She'd been wondering if a bit of horseradish should be added to the potato salad. Charlie told her it was a great idea.

"How's your deputy working out?"

Artemis raised an eyebrow. "So far he's eaten fourteen deviled eggs, but he isn't drawn to cucumber sandwiches. He told me that he's allergic to cucumber. I only hope I don't run out of eggs. Do you think we have enough sherry?"

This was briefly discussed and moments later Charlie picked up two more bottles of shooting sherry for the buffet. He'd lacked the nerve to ask Artemis if she had any beer.

When he reentered the sunroom, he saw Janey and Fletcher Campbell chuckling together as if they had known each other since birth.

Campbell was relating horrible hospital stories, near calamities experienced by friends, relations, employees and himself. Once Charlie had joined them, he saw that Janey's laughter didn't reach above her lips. Her eyes had the steely quality that, when directed at him, usually led to apology and reparation. But Campbell didn't see it.

"And the next thing he knew, they'd cut out his appendix. The nurse had mixed up the charts . . ."

Charlie took Campbell's arm and turned him toward the fireplace, taking a step away from Janey. "Sorry to interrupt, but I think I've partly solved your little problem with Bengal Lancer. Do you know the dates of the other thefts?"

Campbell pulled away. "Are you still messing with that? I thought I said to leave it alone."

"It's on my time, not yours. What about the dates?"

Campbell gave Charlie an angry look. "It's stuff I heard about. I couldn't tell you exactly when they happened, even if I wanted to." Campbell watched Janey make her way to the buffet. He looked sorry that he couldn't follow her.

"What about the horses that were killed? I thought you knew the owners."

"Just one of them and he had the photos of the other dead horses, but I don't know the exact date. Why're you doing this? Did someone hire you?"

"I'm planning to write a book. Bengal Lancer would finish it nicely."

"I didn't know you wrote."

"It's just for my own consumption, and my family's, of course." Charlie felt that one half of him was standing back and eyeing the other half with disapproval. This was not a new feeling. "Could you give me the name of the owner?"

"It's public knowledge. Just Google it under 'equine beheadings.'"

"Google it?" Charlie could only think of goo-goo-googly eyes.

"You got a teenage daughter, right? She'll help you." Campbell began to move away, and then turned back. "Charlie, if you learn who took my horse, I want to know."

"It might cost you."

"That can be arranged."

When Charlie and Janey got home two hours later, they found Emma in the living room, sitting in a corner of the couch with her laptop beside her. Again she wore her oversized Irish fisherman's sweater. It was as if she'd never left that spot since he had talked to her there several days before, though he'd just seen her at breakfast that morning. She was reading a book on gender issues called *The You Behind the You*. On the drive back, Janey had explained to Charlie what it meant "to Google it," but Emma was the computer pro in the house and so he'd decided to go directly to the boss.

In addition, Janey had been a little cool with Charlie; well, more than cool. "If you ever again stick me with a sexist pig like Fletcher Campbell, I'll give you a very significant kick in a very significant spot."

"You did me a big favor. It's for a case I'm working on."

"You've retired, remember? And where's that awful gun of yours?"

"In the trunk."

"Why don't you volunteer for Meals on Wheels instead? That's what people your age are supposed to do. You could at least bring me dinner."

Janey kissed Emma on the cheek. "Charlie needs your help in Googling unpleasant things. Have you eaten? Artemis sent you a care package—cucumber sandwiches, deviled eggs and some other delicacies. Oh, yes, fudge brownies." Janey held up a small paper bag.

Emma supposed she might be able to force down a brownie; Janey went to get her a plate and napkin. The head of Bruiser, the

Chihuahua puppy, poked out from the sweater's loose collar like a canine Siamese twin. "Did you have a good time?" Emma asked Charlie.

He took a seat at the other end of the couch. "I enjoyed seeing Artemis and I was glad to see a sheriff's deputy parked out in front. Some of the guests were nice. Artemis told me you're welcome to come riding anytime you'd like."

While Charlie had always admired his stepdaughter, the way she had instantly—or so it seemed—deciphered Mickey's secret code still filled him with awe. Her mind had fixed on the ridiculous strings of words and had found a pattern as quickly as a magnet can order a handful of iron fillings. Now Charlie had all ten dates, from March 15, 2008, to the present, the last being the date when Bengal Lancer had been stolen, a fact that might be a coincidence or might not.

Janey brought back a plate with a brownie. "Please don't give any to the dog; it'll make him throw up."

After Janey had left, Emma said, "So what's this Googling business?"

Charlie explained about the kidnapped horses as Emma ate her brownie, giving the last quarter to Bruiser. "Three of the owners contacted the police, and their horses were killed. I need to know when they were killed and the names of their owners. Can Googling do that?"

Emma began clicking the keys of her laptop. "If they were written about anywhere, they'd be in here. Did you eat any of those cucumber sandwiches?"

"I ate one; I didn't like it much. You could never make a meal out of them."

"Here's one of the stories. They cut off the horse's head? How awful!"

"You found it already?"

"The owners live over in Hyde Park, near where the Roosevelts lived."

Charlie wrote down the names of the owners and the date on which the horse was slaughtered. He'd hardly finished, when Emma spoke again: "Here's a second one. They put the poor horse's head on a flagpole! Who *are* these people?"

"I don't know."

The farm was west of Poughkeepsie, across the Hudson. Charlie again jotted down the names of the owners and the date of the killing. The deaths of the two horses matched two of the dates. One sentence had ended "interstice zip." The kidnappers had demanded a hundred thousand dollars and hadn't gotten it. The last words of the sentence referring to the second horse were "stoppage egg." Here the kidnappers had wanted a hundred and fifty thousand, but had also received no money.

"Those words mean the horses were killed? 'Zip' and 'egg'? Such little words for such a terrible thing?"

"That's how it seems."

Monday morning shortly after eight o'clock, Charlie entered the high school, on the southwest side of town and across from St. Peter's Cemetery. The location pleased Charlie as a metaphor for the beginning and end of life: school and cemetery, suitable bookends for all the confusion between. The school was a brick and glass building of the sort called "modern" in the 1960s. Possibly some of its earliest students were already buried across the street, making the arrangement a model of convenience.

Charlie was looking for Margaret Ross, who had worked for

Mickey as secretary before Mrs. Penfield. Being in the high school reminded Charlie of the old high school he'd attended on Lake Avenue. He hadn't liked it. When his tenth-grade English teacher said that someday he'd look back on this period as being the best time of his life, it had given him self-destructive thoughts.

He asked for Margaret Ross at the front desk and was told that she worked in the dean's office. After she'd been called and permission was granted to see her, an aide showed Charlie the way. Five students, boys with glum faces, were sitting in straight chairs against a wall. Do-badders, thought Charlie.

Mrs. Ross was in her early fifties and a few inches taller than Charlie, with a rectangular and muscular body. She wore a maroon pantsuit with knife-like lapels and she stared at him, as if thinking: Prove it to me, little man. Her dark hair was cut in a pageboy, and Charlie guessed it had been that way for thirty years. Her wedding ring was very thin.

"Yes?" she said.

When Charlie said that he was trying to gather information about Mickey Martin, her eyes narrowed.

"I hated him. I had to quit before I threw him across the room."

Charlie nodded, admitting this was a common response to Mickey. He explained that he was a retired private investigator and Mickey was murdered on his sidewalk. The killer hadn't been found and Charlie wanted to know if he and his family were in danger. Although the police were watching his house on an occasional basis, he wanted to see if he could learn more.

Margaret Ross didn't unstiffen; rather, she seemed to change from iron to bronze: a hint of flexibility.

"Many people must have been happy to hear he was dead. Personally, it made my day."

Charlie explained that he'd already talked to Mrs. Penfield. Had

Mickey ever talked about horse racing or showed any interest in the subject?

"We never talked unless it was about business. A few times I saw a copy of the *Daily Racing Form* on his desk. I tried to know as little about him as possible. If I could have found another job, I'd have left in a shot."

A boy of about fifteen came into the office. Mrs. Ross gave him a dagger-laden glance and he backed away. She's the enforcer, thought Charlie.

Charlie's questions to Mrs. Ross elicited answers like "No," "No way," "Never," as she kept looking at the clock on the wall.

"Did any friends or acquaintances ever come to visit him?"

She shook her head. "Never . . ." Mrs. Ross stopped and reconsidered. "I remember one time, after all. A man came in, ignored me and knocked on Mr. Martin's door. He remained inside for ten or fifteen minutes. I could hear them muttering and several times the man raised his voice and called Mr. Martin names."

"What sort of names?"

"Bad names."

"What did he look like?"

"Average looking, around forty, dark hair and balding. He wasn't wearing a suit, just slacks and a shirt."

"What did his face look like?"

"It was a regular face. No glasses."

"Pink, tanned, pale?"

"Pale, his face was very pale. I was struck by that."

"Was it smooth? Had his nose ever been broken? Were there scars?"

Mrs. Ross looked down at the floor. A moment passed. "He had acne scars."

Charlie recalled the man in the cab in Albany, the one who had gotten Campbell's money. He experienced a small surge of pleasure, a glissando of gratification. "Did he have very small ears, without lobes, a little like a cat's ears?"

"Yes, he did. No lobes at all and very flat to his head. That's one thing I remember well. Cat's ears."

Charlie's next appointment came as the result of a certain amount of soul-searching. He had to admit that in claiming to be "investigating," he was fooling himself. Could he talk to the people who'd had their horses stolen? Could he search for some commonality among them? Had they known Mickey Martin? Oh, he'd have lots of questions. Then he'd have to learn about those years when Mickey was in prison; also Dave Parlucci. Even if he were still a private investigator, it would take time. He had imagined he knew a lot, but he knew little, a few effects from a few causes. Basically, he knew nothing. He was in over his head.

His first thought was to tell what he'd learned to Lieutenant Hutchins. But since Hutchins had no authority outside of Saratoga and couldn't travel around the state, this would be pointless. Or perhaps he could turn the whole business over to the FBI, who could easily find the hidden causes of visible effects. They were good at that. They would learn, for instance, that Charlie had been playing at being a PI, which could result in being charged with meddling in a police investigation. They also might learn about the modified Benelli. All told, they could gather enough information to put him in prison. No, it would be a bad idea to talk to the FBI.

Instead, Charlie made some other calls. The result was a scheduled meeting in the food court of the Albany airport at three o'clock that afternoon.

Although it was barely thirty miles, Charlie left at one in case of heavy traffic or he had a flat tire or was hit by a truck. He was meeting an investigator with the Thoroughbred Racing Protective Bureau, or TRPB, who was flying up from Philadelphia and would presumably return later in the afternoon. Charlie felt sure the bureau already knew about the horse-nappings, but wouldn't know about Mickey's involvement. Years before, Charlie had known several investigators from TRPB, but they had retired. This man's name was Shawn Smith. When Charlie asked how he'd recognize him, the man said: "I'm big, bald and black."

The result of Charlie's haste was that he arrived at the designated table in the food court an hour before his meeting. He ate a green salad, and when that turned out not to be sufficiently filling, he got two slices of pizza.

It took Charlie about a nanosecond to recognize Shawn Smith. He looked like a retired wrestler and his head was shaved, somewhat like Victor's, but his head was much bigger. Big chin, big mouth, big nose, big forehead—he could have been an escapee from Mount Rushmore. Charlie stood up, took a step forward, stretched out his hand and then saw his own hand disappear into the paw of the other.

"I need to see some identification before we go any further," said Smith. He took out a white handkerchief and wiped his forehead.

Charlie handed him a bunch of cards and Smith handed him back his Saratoga Springs library card. "I don't need this."

Smith had already talked to a retired investigator for TRPB whom Charlie had known years before: John Serphos, who now lived in Phoenix.

He gave Charlie the rest of his cards. "Serphos says you're dependable, impulsive but dependable. He also says you're obstinate. You want a slice of pizza before we start? I'm getting one."

"No thanks."

"On a diet?"

"I already ate one, actually two."

Smith grinned. "That's what I like to hear!" A few people at nearby tables looked over at him.

Charlie told the story from the beginning, right from when he'd woken in the night and remembered the garbage. He described finding Mickey and a little about his relationship with the Saratoga police.

"That's not a relationship. That's called *no* relationship."

Charlie spoke of the other murders and the discovery of the little cardboard figures. He described Fletcher Campbell and the man with the little ears. He described Mickey's office and the discovery of the notebook. He gave Smith a copy of the page with the sentences and the translated dates next to each entry.

"Did you figure that out? That's good work."

Charlie hesitated and then said, "My daughter did."

Smith had been taking notes and compared the dates to a list of his own.

"Campbell never contacted us. We know the three instances when the horses were killed and three of the others. So that's four we never heard of. Whoever's doing it is after small operations. They'd never get away with it at a big farm. Why d'you think the horsenapping is separate from Mickey's murder?"

"I thought if it had something to do with the horses, then Mickey's apartment and office would have been searched and they weren't."

"That's not sufficient proof. I'll keep the question open. But we'd come to a brick wall in this investigation. Now we can start moving again. You expecting some kind of reward out of this?"

"Just keep my name out of it," said Charlie. "I don't want the cops or FBI to know I ever spoke to you."

Fourteen

Time passed: a day, several days, a week, several weeks, a month, six weeks. Thanksgiving and Christmas came and went. Throughout that time there was no trace of the man who had camped out in the Tea Kettle Motel and made those unpleasant little figures. The killer: That's what he's called, thought Charlie, there's been no trace of the killer. Because this was a fact that Charlie wanted to keep in the forefront of his brain. The second fact was the man was still on the loose, meaning, in all likelihood, he still wanted to cut Charlie's throat. These were the last things Charlie thought at night and the first he thought on waking in the morning. All in all, it made for restless nights.

With security guards, a private bodyguard and visits from sheriff's deputies and troopers, Fletcher Campbell claimed to be ready for anything. Artemis still brushed off the threat and went on as ever, though deputies and troopers dropped by regularly. Police cars drifted past Charlie's house several times a day, and several times a week Charlie called Lieutenant Hutchins to see if there'd been any "developments." Hutchins would answer with barely concealed impatience: "No." For that matter, not even the snake had been found.

However, when a few weeks had gone by, only a short time after Thanksgiving, Charlie had gotten a call from Shawn Smith at the Thoroughbred Racing Protective Bureau.

"We've matched all the dates and talked to the owners of the horses. The last horse was taken on the night that Mickey Martin was murdered."

"You know who took them?"

"We're working on it."

"How about Mickey's killer?"

"We've talked to the FBI, state police and sheriff's department. Nothing's turned up, but they say they've got some leads."

"So I'm still in danger?"

"I'd say so."

Despite this, the Benelli in its hard case had slowly migrated from the living room couch to the hall closet to the upstairs bedroom to the bedroom closet and was on the very cusp of being moved to the attic.

"Why don't you sell it?" said Janey.

"I'm not going to sell it till this guy's been caught."

"He's probably in California."

"No, I think he's looking for his fourth person, before he gets busy with me."

"You've no proof of that."

"It's a gut feeling."

Then Janey sighed.

When Victor learned about the Benelli, he nagged Charlie about going out someplace "and blasting some targets." This went on for a month.

Charlie didn't want to.

"It'll get all rusty and then where will you be?"

But Charlie oiled it every week. He took it apart—which he learned to do online—rubbed the inside of the barrel with cleaning patches and the moving parts with Ballistol, which had a licorice smell. Soon the whole house had a licorice smell.

"Can't you do that out in the garage?" asked Janey.

"I don't feel safe in the garage."

After the sixth time that Victor said they should go out and shoot up some targets, Charlie agreed.

It was two weeks before Christmas and the leaves had fallen from all but the most tenacious oaks. Charlie drove out through Schuyler-ville and over the Hudson into the hills north of Greenwich to the Washington County Gun Club. He and Victor signed their waivers, paid their money and walked out the dirt track to the rifle range. Victor carried the rolled-up target and kept blowing down the tube to make depressed cow noises, until Charlie asked him to stop. A red-and-black-plaid Stormy Kromer cap covered Victor's shaved head. The air was crisp and the day clear. Just carrying the hard case in his right hand made Charlie feel stronger.

How foolish, he thought.

He chose the firing point in the middle of the long shelter and tacked up the target with the Western gunslinger drawing his .45. Then he opened the hard case. Once more he experienced a little thrill when his eyes focused on the black semi-automatic shotgun.

Victor rubbed his hands together. "Hot damn!"

He'd been talking nonstop about guns in general, the chances of Charlie getting his throat cut, his love life with the Queen of Softness and about a New York sirloin that she'd broiled the previous evening. He nodded to the sign on the stanchion. "Why can't you shoot the red posts?"

Charlie was sliding five rounds into the magazine and putting a sixth in the chamber. "Because it'd break them down."

"You really think you could shoot a guy running at you with a knife with that pretty chunk of metal?"

Charlie didn't answer. It was a question he had asked himself before.

"Personally," said Victor, "if I was in your shoes, I'd take the family to Costa Rica for sixth months. By the time you got back, this guy would've been caught."

Again Charlie didn't answer. He handed Victor a set of earplugs, then inserted two into his own ears. Raising the shotgun, he aimed at the gunslinger's heart twenty-five yards away and began squeezing the trigger. The six shots, so close together, were more of a rattle than individual discharges. The empty red shells leapt from the magazine. Again Charlie had obliterated the gunslinger's right foot.

"That's one way to do it," said Victor calmly. "You don't kill him, but you turn him into a cripple. Good plan."

Because of Charlie's earplugs, Victor's voice reached him as a whisper. He wondered what his life would be like if he always wore earplugs. Restful, most likely. He inserted another five rounds into the magazine and a sixth in the chamber. He was fairly sure he wouldn't be able to shoot someone attacking him with a knife unless he carried the Benelli twenty-four hours a day. It would mean putting the shotgun in a small duffel bag with his swimming stuff. But the shotgun still gave him confidence, irrational confidence. It helped him sleep at night. It gave him a sense of comfort more than a sense of safety. It was like money in the bank.

Charlie aimed again, squeezed the trigger and put six rounds in the center of the target.

"Atta boy. Is it my turn now?"

But Charlie held on to the shotgun till he had fired twenty-four more rounds. He didn't really want to hand Victor the Benelli. He wasn't sure what would happen. But he had no alternative: A promise was a promise. So he showed Victor how to load the shotgun, how to aim, how to squeeze the trigger.

"Come on, Charlie, I've fired guns before."

"Not a gun like this, you haven't."

"A gun's a gun. I'll fuckin' mow 'im down."

The six shots rattled from the Benelli. All six struck the red post on the left.

"At least I hit something, right? Let me do it again. I got the hang of it now."

Again the six shots struck the red post, which leaned forward, bending in the middle. Only the backing on the target kept it from falling. Charlie had an empty feeling in his stomach that wasn't hunger.

"Think of it this way," said Victor, "at least I'd put a scare into him. Should I blast the other post so they're symmetrical?"

"No, we're going."

Charlie left Victor in the car as he went into the clubhouse. Four men in red-and-black mackinaws were playing cards. They gave him blank looks.

"One of the red posts was knocked down," said Charlie.

"Did you do it?" asked one of the men.

Charlie considered blaming Victor. Then he shrugged. "Let's just say it was done. Do I make the check out to the Washington County Gun Club?"

Shortly, as he got into the Golf, he told Victor, "You owe me a hundred bucks."

"Hey," said Victor, "you were the one that brought me out here."

The result of this display of recreational shooting was that this became the day when Charlie asked himself: What's the point of living like a mouse? It was also the day he moved the Benelli from the downstairs closet to the bedroom closet. And he'd also stopped obsessively cleaning it, unless he'd been target practicing, though he felt that particular activity was over and done with. No more red posts.

Sitting at home that afternoon, he told himself that seeing the Benelli as a source of strength was a pretext. The main reason he kept the shotgun was that its potency made up for Charlie's growing sense of decrepitude, or was supposed to. His knees sometimes ached; his back was often sore; he had bursitis in both shoulders from swimming; he was increasingly forgetful; his reaction time was getting longer; he needed glasses. Good grief, he was even getting shorter. But the Benelli wouldn't cure any of that.

After several weeks of not hearing from Bad Maud, Charlie made a list of the men he had sent to prison over twenty-five years. He'd done this before in his head and no one stood out. He also knew he must be missing someone, surely more than one. So after a few more days he wrote out the names on paper, trying to go over each year, each season and month, and just when he thought he'd gotten them all, he recalled another. But he was only interested in men from the Adirondack Correctional Facility between Lake Placid and Saranac Lake. On the other hand, some might have been transferred to Adirondack from someplace else. And all had originally received sentences for specific periods of times, which would have been added to or reduced depending on their behavior.

Eventually, Charlie came up with a list of twenty men who had overlapped with Mickey, or just about. Three he knew were dead, so he crossed them out. And others might be dead he didn't know about. He tried to think of ways to find out if they were still in prison without having to use the telephone.

Once again his stepdaughter helped him. The Department of Corrections had a website for "inmate search." From there Charlie went to Inmate Population Information Search, where he could enter the inmate's name, year of birth and department ID number, or DIN. The only birth year he knew right off the bat was Mickey's, so he typed it in. This led to the name search results page and up popped Mickey and the date of his release. Charlie clicked on Mickey's name, which took him to the inmate information page, where he learned when Mickey entered prison, when he was released and the length of time he'd spent on parole. It also listed three crimes for which he had been convicted, the most recent being extortion. The aggregate maximum sentence was fifteen years. The aggregate minimum was ten. Mickey had served three years; then he'd spent two years on parole.

"Do they always let people out so quickly?" asked Emma.

Charlie thought about it. "Not to my knowledge."

"He must have been an awfully good prisoner."

For a moment Charlie considered what to say; then he said nothing at all.

So Charlie had seventeen names and for a week he typed them into the Inmate Population Information Search. What took time was he mostly didn't know the years of their births, so he had to guess, typing in one year after another only to draw a blank. He would sit at the computer with his elbows on the table and his head in his hands and think: Jimmy Delancy, was he born in the 1950s or

'60s? It turned out he was born in 1948 and had died seven years ago. Charlie tried to bring him to mind. Was he that affable con man who had talked Mrs. What's-her-name out of thirty thousand dollars? Charlie didn't think so, but he spent about a minute feeling sorry that Delancy was dead, not that he'd been especially fond of Delancy, whoever he was; rather, he regretted anyone's death.

What sped up the process was looking through back issues of *The Saratogian* at the library to find news of the crimes and arrests of the men on his list. He found seven. At last, by the evening of the fifth day, he had finished, or almost finished, because there were three guys he found no trace of.

All he knew at the end was that three more were dead and five were still in prison. That left him with nine, including the ones he couldn't find. Three of the nine lived in Florida and one lived in Arizona. These were old guys; they liked warm weather. The website didn't supply their phone numbers.

Of the remaining five, only three who'd been released had overlapped with Mickey Martin, including one he couldn't find. But Charlie thought that meant little, since he was sure there were men he'd forgotten. All that last day, his mind was full of question marks.

"Are you coming to bed?" Janey called out at about eleven.

"Right away."

Not that he was doing much. He'd only been staring at a blank computer screen, as his mind full of question marks turned to a mind full of zeros.

After he was in bed and told Janey that he'd wound up with two names, she said, "I don't suppose it makes any difference for me to tell you that you're no longer a private investigator?"

"You've told me that before."

"Yes, but you keep forgetting."

The light was off and Charlie lay on his back staring up at an invisible ceiling. "It's some kind of awful compulsion. I tell myself it's pointless, that it's a dumb thing to do, but I keep right on doing it, like I'm schizophrenic or something. That Benelli and hard case and other stuff cost a lot of money."

"Then stop," said Janey. "Sell that awful gun and we can go on a trip. I'll take off a couple of weeks. We can spend Valentine's Day in the Bahamas."

"I can't. Like I say, it's a fixation and I got to keep going till the end. It's like being a robot."

The room was silent for a bit; then Janey said: "Turn over and let me rub your back. You're all tense."

The next morning Charlie set off to find the last two men on his list. They were no longer on parole and could be anywhere, despite the fact that Charlie had their addresses. One, Frankie Lomax, lived in Albany, and the other, Kentay Benson, lived in Utica. The address in Albany was forty miles away; the address in Utica was a hundred. The whole business, Charlie knew, would take all day, if he was lucky.

He went to the bedroom closet to look at the Benelli. Not to take it, he told himself, just to look at it. Then he took it after all.

It was eight thirty and traffic was fairly heavy. Charlie usually drove faster than he should, but with the Benelli in the trunk he kept it right at sixty-five. He was sure he was passed by every car on the road.

The address he was looking for in Albany was on Van Vechten just off Second Avenue. It turned out to be a small apartment house with eight units. Charlie parked and went up the front steps. A row of eight buzzers was next to the front door. Only four were labeled with names and none were Lomax. Charlie pushed one of the unmarked buzzers. Nothing. He kept pushing it on and off for about thirty seconds. No answer.

Charlie pushed another buzzer and shortly there was a click. A woman's voice said: "Is that you, Jimmy?"

"I'm looking for Frankie Lomax," said Charlie.

"Not here."

"Does he live in the building?"

No answer. Charlie pushed the button again.

After a few more seconds there was a click and the same woman said: "You want I should call the cops?"

"I *am* a cop," said Charlie. "D'you know which is Lomax's apartment?"

"Never heard of him. I only been here a month."

"Okay, thanks."

So one after another Charlie pushed the remaining two unmarked buttons and then the four labeled buttons. In two apartments, no one seemed at home. From another, a man shouted, "I work nights! I don't give a fuck what you want!"

Charlie kept trying and the man got angrier, but at last he said he'd never heard of Frankie Lomax.

From another apartment, a heavily accented voice answered with a series of sounds that might have been Chinese.

Charlie asked about Frankie Lomax.

"What you say, what you say?" shouted the voice.

Again Charlie asked his question and again the voice responded: "What you say?" They went back and forth for a few rounds and then Charlie gave it up.

The final two tenants were moderately polite, though they made it clear that Charlie was asking a great deal of them. In any case, neither had heard of Lomax.

Charlie sat down on the front steps. Maybe Lomax had one of the apartments where no one seemed to be home; maybe he lived in one of the others and either the people were lying or they themselves were Lomax. Charlie felt this never happened in movies. Filming was too pricey to waste on empty apartments. Usually the bad guy skedaddled out the back door, jumped over a fence and the detective gave chase. Sometimes he was successful, sometimes not. In any case, Charlie knew he couldn't run after anyone. At best he might manage a slow-motion rush as the bad guy got farther and farther away. He got up and walked to his car. After he was done in Utica, he'd come back to the Van Vechten address and try all the buzzers again.

By the time Charlie reached Utica, it was two o'clock and he hadn't had lunch. He stopped for a beer and corned beef sandwich at a bar on Genesee Street. As he ate, he asked himself just what in the hell he was doing. It was a thought he was having so often that he felt he should have it printed on a T-shirt.

The second man, Kentay Benson, lived on Blandina Street and Charlie asked the woman behind the bar for directions. She pointed over Charlie's shoulder and opined it was half a mile. Charlie thanked her and walked back to his Golf, which, he discovered, he'd left unlocked. He hurried to the back and lifted the hatch. The hard case was where he'd left it. Shaking his head, he climbed into the car.

Most of the small houses on Blandina were covered with old

siding and all had big yards with brown December grass that could still benefit from cutting. A few lots had been covered with macadam long before and now had a chewed look, with almost as much grass pushing through the cracks as in the unpaved lots. Some had rusted junkers that would never be driven again. Small apartment houses and double-deckers, a body shop, a mom-and-pop store mixed with the houses.

The address Charlie wanted was near Albany Street: a small two-story with old mustard-colored siding. Two front doors stood side by side on the porch, with a single rusty mailbox by each. Neither had a name. The door on the left led to a flight of stairs; the one on the right was for the first-floor apartment.

Charlie knocked on the right-hand door and listened. Nothing. He knocked louder. This time Charlie thought he heard a rustling. He hammered on the door with the soft part of his fist. Seemingly in response, a side door banged opened, and by the time Charlie managed to get a look, he saw a guy in jean overalls hightailing it down the driveway toward an empty lot.

This was so similar to Charlie's imagined movie scenario that he paused before hurrying down the steps and down the driveway. But, after all, it was only a hurry, and with each jarring step it seemed that a nail was being driven through his knee. Ahead, he saw the running man reach the far end of the lot. Then, when he disappeared around a house on the next street, Charlie took three more steps and stopped. There was a siren in the distance, but otherwise everything was silent. As he walked back up the driveway, he heard another door slam, this one on the front porch. He hurried a few more steps. A big-bellied man in a Yankees cap was waiting for him.

"Was that Kentay Benson?" asked Charlie, still catching his breath.

The man turned away from Charlie and spat. "He was a white guy, right?"

Charlie nodded.

"How many white guys you know named Kentay?"

"Then why was he running?"

The man leaned back against the wall. He'd remained on the front porch, several feet above Charlie. "Child support. He thought you had papers. You aren't much of a runner, are you?"

Charlie thought of three or four answers, none of them polite. "So does Kentay Benson live here?"

The man spat again. "He used to live downstairs, but he took off about two months ago still owing rent. You a cop? He's had a bunch of cops looking for him."

Charlie decided not to answer. "You know any of his friends, or family?"

"A guy like Kentay don't generally have friends. He only spoke to me once. It was like a growl. His family lives downstate. They sent postcards now and then."

"Which you read."

The man shrugged. "So arrest me. It's no crime. His mother sent them; she was worrying about him. So what else is new, right? As I see it, that's a mother's business: worrying, shouting and burning the biscuits."

"Was there a return address?"

"Not that I noticed."

"Do you remember the town on the postmark?"

"Nope."

Five minutes later Charlie was back on the turnpike driving east. He'd wasted the whole day. But he was a retired guy, sort of. What used to be a waste of time was now time well spent, or so he told himself. He wanted to go back to the apartment house in Albany to ask again about Frankie Lomax. It would be after five o'clock when he got there and more people should be home. And what have I learned in my travels? he asked himself. Almost nothing, and the whole time he kept thinking there were other names he couldn't remember.

Fifteen

At three thirty the next morning, Charlie woke from a sound sleep as if he'd been kicked. This time, however, his sudden wakefulness had nothing to do with forgetting to put out the garbage. He sat up straight and stared at the window, where there was a faint glow from the streetlight. "Petey LaBarca!" he said.

Janey rolled over. "Are you doing a recitation or is that it for now?"

"That's it for now." Charlie got out of bed and found his robe and slippers. Having thought of the name, he knew he'd get no more sleep that night.

Charlie had collared Petey LaBarca eighteen years earlier. Someone had been selling cocaine to Skidmore students, and after the police came up empty-handed, the college hired Charlie to see if he could do better. He was supposed to be a custodian, wore a gray uniform and wandered around with a push broom.

Three days later, about four o'clock in the morning, he caught Petey LaBarca halfway through a dormitory window. Charlie had grabbed his feet and pulled. After a certain amount of tugging, Petey slid out like a splinter from a thumb, fell onto his stomach and had the wind knocked out of him. By the time he recovered, the police were on their way. Petey's pockets were filled with little bags of cocaine.

Unfortunately, Petey had served time for selling weed some years before. This time he was sentenced to twenty years. People said he was lucky the judge was so lenient. He was sent to the Adirondack medium-security prison. But what had seemed bad luck for Petey turned into good luck. Right away he began a twelve-step program to kick his drug habit and then he passed his GED. And every time something good happened to Petey, kicking drugs, getting his GED and being assigned to the prison library—oh, lots of stuff—he wrote Charlie to say it was all due to him and if he'd continued selling and using, he'd be dead. Charlie, himself, didn't feel he'd done anything special, but he was glad of the praise and mostly he wrote back to tell Petey he was pleased things were going well.

After two years, Petey began taking distance-learning classes in acupuncture from a school in New York City. Charlie felt this was karmicly fitting for a former junkie, as if Petey were fated for acupuncture all along but had been sidetracked by the dark side of needledom. In time, he finished the classwork for his bachelor's and needed only two semesters of clinical work till he got his degree. He then began to take classes toward a master's degree and practiced acupuncture on other inmates. He seemed particularly skilled in dealing with stress, anxiety and penile dysfunction.

Petey served ten years of his sentence and moved to Queens. He finished his clinical requirement, got his master's and branched out into energy work, medical intuition and Reiki. Every six months, he sent Charlie a note saying what he was doing and how much he owed him. Then, three years earlier, he moved to New Paltz and started a practice, sharing office space with several other holistic workers. He also began to teach tai chi.

It was now seven years since Petey had been in prison, and Charlie thought that if he hadn't overlapped with Mickey, he must know people who did. He made coffee, ate some raisin toast and kept looking at his watch. New Paltz was a hundred miles south. If Charlie shaved, showered, dressed and left right away, he'd be knocking on Petey's door around six a.m. He tried to convince himself that Petey would surely be up by that time. In this he wasn't successful.

He got ready in any case, then moped around the house for an hour, cleaning the kitchen and feeding the dog and cat. By six o'clock, he was on the road. It was still dark, but to the east a bit of dark was fading to gray. As he drove, he continued to think about Petey. Charlie had last seen him after he'd been in prison for nearly a year. Petey had been lifting weights and had his hair in a greasy pompadour. He was Charlie's height and had a wrinkle in his nose where someone had once decked him. They spoke in the visitors' room.

"I owe you one, Charlie. That's God's truth. I'd take a bullet for you."

Charlie had been embarrassed. "Hey, if I hadn't caught you, someone else would've pretty soon. You were getting sloppy."

"Yeah, but you're the one who did it, so you're the one I got to thank. This place is like the Ritz compared to what my life was like outside. You dragged me up out of the grave, Charlie. That sloppiness, as you called it, that was my cry for help." Then Petey had begun to weep.

———

Charlie reached New Paltz at seven thirty. It was an artsy little town with a lot of Victorian second homes owned by New Yorkers. A few stone houses formed part of a museum for the Huguenot settlers who'd bought the land from the Indians more than three hundred years before. Charlie knew this because Petey lived on Huguenot Street, across from one of these houses, and Charlie read an informative sign out in front, because he disliked bothering Petey so early. Petey's house was a square Victorian, white with black shutters. Crystals twinkled in the windows.

The man who answered the doorbell wore a heavy red robe with golden stars. He had a thick gray beard, a thick moustache and long gray hair in a ponytail. His glasses were round and tinted blue. In one ear was a silver earring of a unicorn.

"Is Petey around?"

The man's eyes widened and he leapt forward, grabbing Charlie in a bear hug, lifting him off the porch and kissing his cheek. Charlie didn't care for embraces from strangers. Firm handshakes were as far as he'd go. "Personal space" was a term he liked and he now thought: This guy's fucking with my personal space.

In the meantime, the man—Charlie knew it was Petey—had his mouth pressed to Charlie's ear and was saying, "Charlie-Charlie-Charlie."

Charlie felt he'd made a mistake and his only wish was to hurry back to his car. He struggled to free himself. Petey squeezed him tighter and his moustache tickled Charlie. Charlie hoped no one he knew would see him.

Giving Petey a push and kicking at his shins, Charlie shouted, "Cut it out!" Then he stumbled back and nearly fell off the porch.

Petey stared at him beatifically and waved one hand in a circle over his head. "I owe this all to you!" He wore rings with different-colored stones on eight fingers; they twinkled in the morning light. Then he reached for Charlie to hug him again.

Charlie jumped from the porch. "Quit it, Petey! If you don't quit it, I'm leaving right away."

Petey joined his hands in front of his chest. "I'm feeling an inner hum."

"I'm warning you. Calm down or I'm gone. And stop trying to touch me!"

It took more than this. It took additional threats. And Charlie said he'd only driven down to get a little information and would soon be leaving. Fat chance he was going to hang around. It wasn't a social visit. Petey responded in a hushed voice, as if he had congenital laryngitis. "Whatever you say, Charlie. Your words are gold to me." Then the two men entered the house in search of coffee.

Once he'd accepted Petey's red robe with golden stars, unicorn earring and gray ponytail, the house and its ornamental embellishments seemed, to Charlie, cut from the same cloth. He saw more gold stars and bright red and blue walls, Navaho rugs and heavy Victorian furniture. Hanging from the ceiling were little wooden angels with blond hair and white robes. Oversized, fluffy cats rubbed against Charlie's legs. Every step of the staircase rising to the second floor was painted a different bright color.

As they entered the kitchen, Petey whispered, "Can I look at your feet?"

"No. Why'd you want to do such a thing?"

"To bring you inner peace."

"Jesus, Petey, I don't want any inner peace. I'm a plain, white-bread kind of guy and you've moved up to twelve-grain. I came down here because somebody wants to kill me and I don't know who it is. I thought you might be able to help."

Petey threw out his arms toward Charlie, who said: "No more hugs, Petey."

Soon they were sitting in the living room drinking coffee as Charlie described what had happened, starting with finding Mickey dead on his sidewalk. Petey hung on every word, often saying, "I don't believe it!" Like a pond's surface on a windy day, his face moved through a variety of expressions. His coffee grew cold.

"Move in here with me," said Petey. "I'll keep you hidden."

"That would be great, except there's Janey and our daughter, and I have a lot to do at home." Charlie thought he'd rather lose his left foot than live with Petey.

"I think there's a link between something that happened with Mickey in prison and these murders in Saratoga. Did you know him in prison?"

"I don't like to think about that time, Charlie. I've moved on."

"Well, move back a little just to humor me. Did you know him?"

"No. He got there about a year after I left."

"But you heard of him?"

"A friend was there when he was there. He wasn't popular. These are bad memories, Charlie."

"You remember any stories?"

"If I did, I've forgotten them. It was over seven years ago."

"D'you know the name Dave Parlucci?"

Petey pressed a hand to his forehead. "No, I've never heard it."

"D'you think I could talk to this man who knew Mickey?"

Petey thought a moment and fussed with his many rings. "He

doesn't like talking about that time either. I'd have to ask him and that means finding him."

"Where does he live?"

"Well, he lives in Tupper Lake, but he doesn't spend much time there. Mostly he lives in the woods. He's a bow hunter and traps some. He says that since he's gone straight, it's his only chance to shoot something. And he likes camping. 'Playing savage,' he calls it. Of course I disapprove. Did I tell you I'm a raw vegan, Charlie? Nuts, berries and grains have changed my life."

Charlie ignored the question. "So right this moment he might be camping?"

"That's about it. He tries to live off the land, but he packs some dried food just in case."

Charlie's frustration grew with each of Petey's answers. "Does he stick to any particular part of the park?"

"No, he goes to a different section each year. Like last year, he stuck to Adirondack State Park. This year he might be around Five Ponds or the High Peaks, but, on the other hand, it might be some-place else, like West Canada Lake."

"Does he have a cell phone?"

"Not with him." As Petey spoke, his hands made swooping ges-tures, raising above his head and then zooming down to his belly. Charlie started to ask what he was doing and then decided against it. He pretended not to notice.

"Does he have a wife who might know where he is?"

"He never married."

"What's his name?"

"Cracker Johnson—Cracker's a nickname. I've never known his real name."

"Is he southern?"

"No, he's a little nuts."

Briefly, Charlie contemplated life's injustice. "So he could be anywhere within six or seven million acres?"

Petey's hands zoomed down again. "He's a great walker. A few years ago he hiked the Appalachian Trail."

"And nobody knows where he is?"

"There're little stores he might check into every two weeks or so."

"So how can I find him?" Why have I gotten mixed up in this? thought Charlie.

"That's a problem, he doesn't want to be found. I taught him how to meditate and he sits outside his tent and meditates. Do you meditate, Charlie?"

Charlie ignored the question. "What was he in prison for?"

"He had a bunch of assault charges, but most of his time up there was for manslaughter. He broke a man's neck with his hands. That's why I was teaching him meditation. He's got a terrible temper. But he's not a crook; he'd never steal anything. He's very honest. It's just that temper."

"Great, that's just great."

Charlie drove home around noon, staying longer than he intended, because, not to hurt Petey's feelings, he'd asked Petey what sort of work he did. The answer, or part of it, took about three hours and then Charlie called it quits. One more word and he'd either start screaming or weeping. He understood little of what Petey was talking about, and questions led to twenty-minute answers. Basically, Petey was an acupuncturist with a mix of confusing sidelines, though Petey wouldn't call them sidelines. He spoke of biofield energy healing, channeling universal energy into the sick and suffering, and qigong with various theories of body, breath and mind alignment. He seemed good at what he did and Charlie's doubts made him feel guilty. He didn't have time for this new age stuff when he was still trying to figure out the previous age, his own age, his old age.

"May I give you a massage, Charlie?" asked Petey in his hushed voice. "For free? It will make you forget everything."

But Charlie didn't want to forget everything.

Before Charlie left, Petey agreed to call if he heard from Cracker Johnson. Charlie felt this was the best he could hope for and he walked back to his car. Getting home about two, he sat down at his computer, went to the Department of Corrections website and clicked on "inmate search." Soon he gave it up. Cracker Johnson wasn't listed, most likely because the Department of Corrections had listed him by his real first name, which could be anything from Joey to Nebuchadnezzar. Later, when Charlie told Janey about his day, her response was "I can't believe you gave up a free massage."

Time passed; the new year began. Some days it snowed and the snow accumulated. Charlie waited for the phone to ring. It was even hard to go to the Y for fear he'd get a call while he was swimming. Twice he called Petey, but Petey's protestations of devotion were so awkward that Charlie decided not to call again. Instead, he'd wait.

The Benelli was in the bedroom closet and Janey kept urging Charlie to put it in the attic. Another week of inactivity and the shotgun would disappear upstairs among boxes of mementos, empty birdcages and dusty suitcases. Charlie guessed if he heard someone breaking into the house at night, it would take him ten minutes to rush up to the attic, unlock the case, find the shells, load them into the magazine and then go downstairs again. A lot of bad things could happen in ten minutes.

Charlie called Lieutenant Hutchins to see if anything new had turned up. It hadn't and Hutchins told Charlie not to call again. Actually, he shouted it. He shouted it was none of Charlie's business. He also called Shawn Smith, the investigator with the Racing Protective Bureau. He, too, had no news. Although he was politer than Hutchins, he made it clear that he didn't want Charlie to call. "I'll call you the first I hear anything," he said. Charlie also visited Bad Maud, but he was barely through the door when she yelled: "I haven't learned fuckin' squat. Didn't I say I'd call you?"

So Charlie was waiting for four phone calls. He was even hesitant to take a shower in case someone called. He slept with his cell phone under his pillow, and might wake up once or twice to see if it was working. During the day he'd stand silently in the middle of the living room waiting for something to happen. Police cars drove past his house more infrequently. Sheriff's deputies visited Artemis and Fletcher Campbell only two or three times a day.

"Charlie, you've got to *do* something," said Janey. "You've got to keep busy."

So Charlie fixed a leaky bathroom faucet; he replaced a cracked pane of glass in an upstairs window; he shoveled snow and scattered sand on the sidewalk; he tidied up the garage; he washed dishes even when they were clean. He didn't feel like reading; he didn't want to watch TV; he didn't play backgammon with Emma. He was the first to admit he was being pathetic. "I'm pathetic," he said. Every so often he took his cell phone from his pocket and shook it.

"Why don't you go for a walk?" suggested Janey.

"There's nothing I want to look at."

"You could try to find the snake."

"Be reasonable."

"Charlie, it would be *something*. That's all that matters. You've got to keep busy. Go see Victor."

"Cell phone reception's not so good out there."

In truth, Charlie didn't want to leave the property, as if even going next door would make him miss a call.

And if he received a call from anyone else, he'd say: "I'm sorry, I'm expecting an important call." And hang up. Several weeks passed like this. Janey and Emma no longer gave him sympathetic looks.

In early February, Petey LaBarca finally called late in the morning. Charlie was polishing Janey's great-grandmother's silver tea set to pass the time.

"Cracker doesn't want to talk to you, Charlie. He hates cops. I said you were a retired PI and very sweet. He said that PIs were cop-like and that cop-like was too much like cop for him. I told him all you'd done for me. I mean, Charlie, you saved my life! So he wants to know exactly what you want to know."

Charlie explained what he wanted to learn about Mickey Martin. "But make sure he understands that Mickey is dead, and Parlucci too, if it makes any difference. Explain this has nothing to do with him. Just Mickey. I want to know why Mickey served only three years of a fifteen-year sentence."

"Okay, Charlie, I'll get back to you."

"D'you know when?"

"Hopefully today."

It turned out to be the next morning.

"He'll see you, but he doesn't like it. He'll meet you at this little pizza place in Long Lake. He loves pizza. It's one of the few foods he hasn't shot or fished for. He's camping near there. He'll hang around from between one and two o'clock."

"Where the heck is Long Lake?"

"It's a little dimple of a place about twenty miles south of Tupper Lake. You better hurry if you expect to get there between one and two."

The Long Lake pizza place was about ninety miles north of Saratoga, with the first third on the Northway. The day was clear but it had snowed earlier in the week and the snow grew deeper as Charlie got farther north. The temperature was in the midteens. At Warrensburg, he turned north on Route 28. Plows had shaped high banks of snow along the verge of the road that at times rose above Charlie's Golf. Snow-covered trees poked out of the landscape, mostly pine and leafless maples and birch, interspersed with frozen marshland. He passed frozen lakes and a few villages with a dozen or so houses, but mostly he looked out at a white landscape of snowy trees. He pictured Cracker Johnson prowling through the snow with one of those compound bows that looks like a Transformer robot, with a draw weight of seventy pounds and a quiver full of carbon arrows, as he tried to control his temper. Cracker had already been prowling around the woods for several months and by now, thought Charlie, he's probably barely human; he's probably reverted to wolf or catamount, creatures that would laugh at his Benelli.

The village of Long Lake was divided by a bridge that separated two parts of the lake, which was fourteen miles long and shaped like the blade of a sword. It was frozen and snow-covered; snowmobile tracks zigzagged across the ice. Snowy pines edged the shore. The pizza place was one of those log cabins that arrives as numbered pieces on the back of a flatbed truck. Inside, the logs were golden with polyurethane. Milk, bread, eggs, canned food, beer and soft drinks made up the grocery section. The restaurant section had six tables. Only one was occupied.

Cracker Johnson was in his midforties. He wore paint-spotted jeans and a green-and-black-plaid shirt. White thermal underwear poked through his worn elbows and knees. He might have been five-foot-eight, but because he was sitting it was hard to tell. Ten-inch insulated boots stuck out from under the table. His brown hair was cut short and his pencil-thin lips were barely visible within a straggly beard. He called to mind a fisher, that smaller cousin of the wolverine, known for its ferocity. His eyes were dark brown like a fisher's, with large pupils as cool as cubes of ice. He had a triangular face with a pointy chin and high cheekbones. A green down jacket hung over the back of his chair.

Cracker stared at Charlie without expression. He was a type that Charlie labeled "small-scale bully": small but very strong men who loved to thrash muscular and much bigger men. They attacked and attacked until their adversary fled, or formed a pulpy mass on the floor, or was saved by the police.

Charlie approached with some uncertainty. On the table were the remains of a large pizza and an empty bottle of Budweiser. He held out his hand. "You're Cracker Johnson; I'm Charlie Bradshaw."

Cracker stared at the hand, but made no other movement. Charlie withdrew his hand, pulled out a chair and sat down. The dirt beneath Cracker's untrimmed nails made dark semicircles. A sour, unwashed smell clung to him like fog.

"Petey LaBarca said you could give me some information."

"What's in it for me?" His voice was a whisper.

"What do you want?"

Cracker folded one hand over the other. "A hundred bucks."

"Twenty-five."

They settled on fifty. Cracker never looked away from Charlie's eyes. Charlie understood that he was meant to feel intimidated.

"You're a friend of Petey's?" asked Charlie.

"We know each other."

"What about Mickey Martin?"

"I knew him too." The ceiling's fluorescent lights made Cracker's head look slightly green.

A radio was on in the kitchen, a talk show. Charlie couldn't hear what was being said, just an angry mutter. He tried to make his expression appear indifferent and sleepy, as if what he really wanted was a nap. Actually, he wished he were someplace else. A coiled spring, a cocked revolver, a drawn bowstring: all the usual clichés that might describe Cracker Johnson came to his mind.

"I want to know how Mickey got out of Adirondack after three years when he was sentenced to fifteen."

"He snitched."

Charlie could barely hear what Cracker said. A man behind the counter asked if he could get Charlie anything. He and Cracker were his only customers.

"You want another beer?" said Charlie.

Cracker didn't respond and Charlie ordered a Budweiser for himself.

Accepting the beer from the counterman, Charlie took a slow drink and considered what to say next. But Cracker spoke first.

"You're a scaredy-cat, ain't you."

At first Charlie didn't answer, and then he said, "Look, I'm here to ask you a few questions. When we're done, I'll give you fifty bucks. Let's leave it at that."

Cracker grinned. His knuckles were oversized, as if arthritic.

"Okay, tell me about the snitching. What happened?"

Charlie wasn't sure that Cracker would speak, but then, slowly, he uttered several scattered words. Then he began to speak more easily.

"Drugs, a whole operation. A guard was bribed. Pills, mostly, some cocaine."

"Were you involved in it?"

"Not me. I don't use that shit. I got mixed up later."

What Cracker meant was that he'd become Mickey's bodyguard after the business was broken up and ten guys were busted. Mickey had gotten drugs from the outside and sold them on the inside, delivering them with the help of another inmate. After six months, Mickey went to the superintendent and told him about the drug use. He said he'd give him the names of the men involved if the superintendent would make a deal. But Mickey didn't say he'd been running the operation himself; hardly anybody knew that. So he'd both started it and ended it. And he didn't snitch on his accomplice or the crooked guard. Mickey was a good talker. After all, he was a con man. He sounded plausible.

From then on, Mickey wore a wire, and after his last delivery, he gave the names of the drug users to the superintendent, who called for a full lockdown. Cells were searched; arrests were made. The big question was who had told.

Before suspicion could land on Mickey, he accused another man: Matthew Durkin, a small-time user and dealer in prison for larceny. For two days Durkin scurried around like a chased rabbit. Then he was found dead.

Charlie repeated Durkin's name to himself. It seemed familiar. "Where was Durkin from?" he asked.

"I don't know, maybe around Saratoga. He'd worked at the track."

"You ever talk to him? You know what he did?"

Cracker shook his head. "I never talked to him. I never talked to nobody if I could help it."

After Matthew Durkin had been killed, Mickey hired Cracker Johnson to protect him, as well as his accomplice. Cracker couldn't remember his name.

"And did you have to do anything?" asked Charlie.

"I hung around. I'd been in fights at Adirondack. Guys knew me. A few guys blamed Mickey, but they didn't think it worth doing anything. It wasn't worth the hurt I'd hand out. And Mickey kept talking about Durkin; he sold them a whole package. His friend talked about it too. Two or three guys thought Mickey and his friend killed Durkin. He'd been knifed in the laundry. I convinced them they were wrong. Want to know how I did it?"

A little smile hovered over Cracker's lips like a butterfly over a flower.

"Not particularly." Charlie drank some beer and worked on his sleepy look.

Cracker seemed disappointed. In any case, Durkin's killers weren't found. The men who'd been busted were transferred to other prisons. Cracker got paid. A month later Mickey was sent to the Albany County Correctional Facility.

"What about the guy who helped him?"

"He went down a few months after that, but he'd almost finished his sentence anyway. Albany's where they try to civilize you, get you ready for the outside."

"Who were the men who were busted?"

"Just guys. Losers." Cracker stared at Charlie's eyes. He never seemed to blink.

"You see Mickey once you got out?"

Cracker shook his head. "Our business was done."

"What did you think when you heard Mickey was dead?"

"One of those guys must've caught up with him. Getting his tongue cut out, that's what you do to a snitch."

"And Mickey's friend in Adirondack, the accomplice?"

"They weren't real friends, they were business friends."

"What was his name?"

"I don't recollect, like I said. It had something to do with cemeteries: graves or coffins. Something like that."

"Could he have killed Mickey?"

Cracker shrugged. "Dunno. Mickey might've tried to blackmail him."

"What did he look like?"

"He was about forty, just regular looking." Cracker paused. "He had little ears, ears like pink silver dollars stuck to the side of his head."

Charlie left about five minutes later. Cracker turned down his offer of a ride, which Charlie was glad of. A compound bow, a quiver full of arrows and a small backpack had been leaning against the wall. Cracker had picked them up, opened the door and disappeared without looking back at Charlie. The door banged shut.

Driving back down south, Charlie was sweating as if he'd run five miles. Sociopaths gave him the creeps. As for who killed Mickey, it must have been one of the guys who'd been busted, or maybe Mickey's accomplice, the one with little ears.

It was past five and the sun was beginning to set. Charlie called Shawn Smith at the Racing Protective Bureau, wanting to catch him before he left the office.

"So what have you got to tell me?" said Smith, after cool greetings had been exchanged. "And, no, I don't know anything new."

"I've got some information about Mickey, about how he got out of prison. I thought you'd want to know." The cell phone reception was weak with brief lapses in service, voices reduced to a crackling. Charlie told Smith what he'd learned from Cracker Johnson, though he didn't tell him his source of information. Because of the poor reception, he had to raise his voice. He was a little hoarse when he was done.

"As a matter of fact," said Smith, "a dozen guys got busted. So far we've tracked down eight. And the guy you said was Coffin or Graves, his name's Toombs, Rodger Toombs. He's around Albany someplace. We've been looking for him."

Charlie stared out at the darkening pines. The sun must have set, but Charlie couldn't tell. The sky was uniformly gray—light gray to the west, dark to the east. He considered what to say, but he didn't feel like saying much of anything.

"No offense, Charlie," said Smith, "you put a lot of legwork into this. But why spend time finding out what we already know? Who's the guy that told you this?"

But Charlie, who wished to retain a smidgen of self-respect, said: "I'm sorry, Shawn, that's confidential information."

After hanging up, Charlie thought of Coffin, Graves and Toombs. For some reason, it reminded him of Artemis. Then he realized why. He called her as he was entering Saratoga. "That groom you fired for stealing eight years ago, you thought his name was Matthew Perkins. Could it have been Durkin, Matthew Durkin?"

"Oh, Charlie, of course it was: Matthew Durkin. How clever you are. Where is he now? I hope he's all right."

"He's dead, I'm afraid."

"Oh, no, what a shame. How did he die?"

"Cancer, I think."

Next Charlie called Fletcher Campbell. Had it been Matthew Durkin who was arrested eight years ago for stealing tack from Campbell's barn? But Campbell was in Miami and wouldn't be home until the weekend.

Sixteen

In early February, Artemis decided to have a small dinner party to celebrate having escaped the burdens of Thanksgiving, Christmas and New Year's. She invited Charlie, Janey and Emma. Emma, who was mad about horses, could ride Artemis's safest horse: a gelding called Feather-Foot that she had ridden before. Other people were coming as well, including Fletcher Campbell.

"I didn't know you cooked," said Charlie over the phone.

"I don't," said Artemis. "I'm having it catered."

Friday evening, Janey asked: "You're not taking that gun, are you?"

"I thought I'd pop it in the back of the car."

They sat at the kitchen table waiting for Emma, who was upstairs getting ready. Freezing rain spattered against the window. Soon it would turn to snow.

"If it goes," said Janey, "I'm not."

"I might need it. Anything could happen." His disquiet about future dangers had increased after having met Cracker Johnson.

Janey sipped her coffee and looked at the rain. "Charlie, did you have a favorite doll you dragged around when you were a kid?"

"A Raggedy Andy." Charlie distrusted Janey's abrupt change of topic. "He had bright blue eyes on one side, closed eyes on the other and a fringe of red yarn for the hair—I took it everyplace."

"That shotgun's your Raggedy Andy, isn't it? And you want to take it everywhere. Think about it, Charlie: If it goes, I don't."

"I think you're being overdramatic."

"Charlie, I'm not the one carrying the shotgun."

"I keep telling you we're still in danger. It makes sense to keep it nearby."

"Nothing's happened for months."

Charlie was unhappy with the conversation. He felt hurt and misunderstood. First Victor had called the Benelli his "blankie" and now this. But he left the hard case in the bedroom closet.

Because he was annoyed, Charlie said little to Janey on the way over. Instead, he and Emma discussed horses. She had ridden horses at Artemis's stable six or seven times and wanted to take lessons. Though Charlie had ridden, he'd never felt comfortable on a horse. There was something about him that horses didn't like. Maybe a smell, or perhaps they could sense his discomfort. They exuded antipathy; they rolled their eyes in an unfriendly manner. He wasn't disappointed by this; rather, he understood that some relationships weren't meant to blossom. But for Emma the opposite was true. She now knew all the horses in Artemis's stable, knew their names and favorite treats, knew their little idiosyncrasies, how one would nuzzle a pocket in search of a carrot, how another might try to step on her foot.

Victor came with Rosemary, who wore a red satin dress cut so low that Charlie guessed he could lob hot rolls into her cleavage. She was a woman composed entirely of curves, hence the name the Queen of Softness. Sometimes she was blond, sometimes a brunette, but today her hair was red. She had long red fingernails and on the tip of each was painted a miniature heart in light pink, which everyone was called upon to inspect. "Cool," said Emma.

Fletcher Campbell came with his wife, Ursula, twenty years younger than her husband, with blond hair that didn't come from a bottle. She had a slight accent, which Charlie guessed was German. They had flown in from their condo in Miami Beach earlier that day and their skin was golden. Campbell spoke loudly as always, as if speaking into a stiff wind. He wore tweeds and a dark leather vest. At some point, Charlie meant to talk to him.

Three other couples, whom Charlie had never met, had also been invited: middle-aged horse lovers who lived nearby. And there was also a man visiting from Vienna: a horse trainer whom Artemis had worked with for many years. He was about sixty, wore a dark gray suit with a bright red vest and was very thin. Had he been a dog, he'd have been a whippet. Servers wound through the large living room with drinks and interesting tidbits on silver trays.

"You seem subdued," said Charlie to Victor, who stood by the fireplace with a bacon-wrapped scallop in either hand.

"I've been warned."

"How so?"

"If I raise my voice or don't behave myself, I sleep on the couch till Valentine's Day. She's squashed my natural exuberance; she's tied a string around my balls and wound me in like a trout. I'm only lucky she doesn't make me take Valium. I like a little abuse in my sexual life, but this is excessive."

Shortly before they sat down at the table, Campbell approached Charlie. "Well, have you learned who stole my horse?" When Campbell chuckled, his heavy white moustache moved up and down.

"You know about Mickey Martin's involvement, of course," said

Charlie, who hated being patronized. "The man who picked up the money in Albany was Rodger Toombs. Do you recognize the name? He and Mickey were in prison together."

Campbell tilted his head. "No, I don't think I do."

"A third guy was in prison with them who you might recall: Matthew Durkin."

Campbell was silent a moment as he tried to remember. "It rings a bell, but I can't place him. Was he also mixed up with stealing Bengal Lancer?"

Charlie shook his head. "No, he died in prison. But he's the guy I caught stealing tack from your barn eight years ago."

Campbell grinned. "Damn it, Charlie, you're a hotshot. Yeah, Durkin, that's right. He would have been out by now. I wonder what happened to him."

"Heart attack, I think." Charlie decided not to say that Durkin had been stabbed to death in the prison laundry.

"Well, at least he won't be stealing shit from my barn anymore. What about this Toombs character?"

"I've been looking for him in the Albany area. If we hadn't come here today, I'd have found him this afternoon or tomorrow at the latest."

This was a complete lie. Ever since Shawn Smith had told him about Toombs, Charlie hadn't felt like leaving the house. He was divided between resignation and chagrin. Why had he thought he could make the least bit of difference in learning who had killed Mickey? Even so, he kept thinking of Matthew Durkin's murder in the Adirondack Correctional Facility. Mickey was responsible for that and so Mickey's death might be the result of Durkin's murder, but Charlie couldn't imagine the connection.

His conversation with Campbell was interrupted by Emma, who

came hurrying over. Her face shone. "Artemis said she'd give me lessons for free if I worked two afternoons a week after school. Isn't that wonderful?"

Whenever one of his stepdaughters announced some future undertaking, Charlie imagined the worst: broken bones, loitering sex-crazed deviants, car crashes. Now he pictured Emma being trampled by a horse in the dark stable, or maybe a fire, or a deadly germ picked up from the manure. He considered her eager expression. "That's great," he said. "When do you start?"

"As soon as I want."

"Doesn't she have some guys already working for her?"

"She has two, but she said there'd be work for me as well."

"Do you know these guys?"

"I've seen them, but I haven't met them."

Charlie wondered if he should run a check on them. Then he told himself he was being foolish. Moments later, Artemis called them to dinner.

Years before, Charlie had had three or four dinners at Artemis's house before she moved to Europe. He was living out at the lake at that time and hadn't met Janey. Recalling those occasions, he thought of who had been there, what they'd eaten, who was still living and who, more likely, was dead. For a moment he felt caught up in a swirl of multiple occasions, but then the present moment reasserted itself and he got ready to enjoy the evening.

Campbell Fletcher wanted to say grace and recited the Lord's Prayer taken from the Massachusetts Indian Bible: "*Nooshun kesukqut, wunneetupantamuch koowesuounk. Peyamooutch kukkeitasootamounk . . .*"

"Give me a fucking break," whispered Victor.

"It's one of the Algonquin languages," continued Fletcher. "In point of fact, the Mohawks were the Indians who lived in our own neighborhood. I can recite a bit of their language, if you'd like . . ."

Campbell's young wife touched a hand to his wrist. "Darling, the food will get cold."

"You ever noticed," whispered Victor to Charlie, "that women like to begin a complaint with an endearment?"

The fifteen people at the table alternated man, woman, man, woman, but Charlie had been placed next to Victor. It made him realize that his job was to keep Victor under control. He nudged Victor's arm. "Lower your voice."

The Viennese horse trainer, Heinrich Bernhardt, was seated next to Ursula Campbell and they spoke quietly to each other in German. Victor said they were criticizing the manners of the American guests, and again Charlie shushed him. There was roast lamb with mint jelly, small red potatoes, a spinach soufflé and a green salad. Victor spilled a splop of mint jelly on his burlesque-dancer necktie: turn to the right she was clothed; turn to the left she was naked. Now she had a large green spot where her face should be.

"Can someone please pass me some of that spinach stuff," said Victor, raising his voice, "and a couple of those toy potatoes?"

Inevitably, horses were the main topic of conversation, though movies came in for their share of chat. Victor tried to introduce the subject of Jane Russell's blouse, or the lack of it, in *The Outlaw*: a movie in which there'd been plenty of horses. Rosemary elbowed him in the ribs. Because she was blessed, as Victor liked to say, with "considerable heft," he lurched to his left into Charlie's shoulder.

"You see," said Victor, "if I keep my trap shut, I get ignored. It's better to be noisy and disliked than silent and overlooked. For fuck's sake, Charlie, other than tits, crime and getting rich, what's there to talk about?"

"Do you ever worry about all the Americans suffering from food insecurities?" said a young woman to Victor, rather coolly. Charlie thought she meant people who were gluten sensitive.

Victor said to Charlie in a stage whisper, "She means hungry." And then, to the young woman: "Every frigging waking hour!" Again Rosemary nudged Victor, this time harder, and he grunted.

Fletcher Campbell leaned across the table toward Emma. "I hear you took a job with Artemis. You watch out for the young guys she has working for her."

"One of those 'young guys' is Stanley," said Artemis. "He's been with for me for thirty years. The other's a man I hired this fall, but he seems to take no interest in anything but horses. He's certainly not chatty, but he's strong and hardworking."

Campbell began talking about the difficulty in getting qualified stable help. "The lazy beggars like to work in places where it's warm or near a city."

One of the other men at the table, a middle-aged doctor named Buchanan, said, "Maybe you don't treat them well enough."

Charlie glanced at the man, who seemed to be suggesting more than he was saying. Besides being a doctor, Buchanan owned a couple of horses.

"Ridiculous. I treat them as they should be treated. Charlie just remembered one he caught stealing years ago. He was selling my tack to buy drugs. Charlie had to act like a stable hand and do real work. That's probably why he caught him so fast. I suspected the guy from the start. He just didn't look right."

"You mean Matthew Durkin?" asked Artemis. "He was quite nice apart from his addiction, and a good worker. I was sorry when he was sent to prison."

"I didn't know he'd worked for you," said Campbell.

"It was only for a month. Things started to disappear. It wasn't difficult to realize he was the culprit, since I had only one other employee. I had to fire him, though I offered to help with his addiction and send him to one of those rehab places. Unfortunately, he didn't want my help."

"What did he take?" asked Dr. Buchanan.

"A saddle, some tack, and some jewelry. I also once found him in my living room. We were both embarrassed."

"Why didn't you tell me he was a crook?" said Campbell, growing red.

"I didn't realize you had hired him until I read that he'd been arrested. After that I saw no reason to mention it. Charlie said he'd died of cancer."

"I heard it was a heart attack," said Campbell.

Charlie studied his empty plate as Victor and Janey shot him quick looks.

"Perhaps it was both," said Dr. Buchanan, glancing at Charlie. "I've known it to happen. The chemo can get them. By the way, Campbell, how did Bengal Lancer act after he'd been returned?"

"A little skittish, maybe, but he's fine now. He looked a wreck when I got him back: knots in his tail and mane, the hair matted on his fetlocks. And he was hungry. Those shits hardly fed him." Campbell glanced at Artemis. "Pardon my French."

More wine was drunk; guests took seconds and some took thirds; the doctor's wife asked the caterer for his recipe for the spinach soufflé. The salad had avocados that Victor pushed to the edge of his plate. Shaking her head, Rosemary scooped them up. Eventually, the dishes were cleared; then came a variety of desserts: several pies, vanilla ice cream and a flourless chocolate cake.

Through dinner a steady drone-like noise resonated low down in Charlie's ears, which was his memory of the murders and threat to his life. This wasn't fear, exactly, but recognition tinged with dread, and he regretted the shotgun being foolishly tucked away in his bedroom closet. No way could he depend on the police to protect his safety and the safety of his family. He also kept thinking of Matthew Durkin and the coincidence that he'd worked for both Artemis and Campbell.

"What about the movie *And God Created Woman?*" said Victor to the table at large. "I'm sure I remember horses. You know, Brigitte Bardot, sitting up on a horse with her bosom pushed out."

"So you like bosoms, do you, Vic?" Campbell pronounced it *BahZOOMS.*

"The name's Victor. I stopped being Vic when I got into my sixties. It adds a bit of gravitas. Speaking of bosoms, I'd a friend who made up his own American flag, but instead of fifty stars it had fifty little tits. It's the only time I've felt patriotic."

"Did you salute?" asked Campbell. When Campbell made what he thought was a little joke, he looked around at the others at the table and bobbed his head.

"Only where it didn't show," said Victor.

It was about five minutes later, as Charlie was lifting his first forkful of apple pie to his lips, that his cell phone began to vibrate. He meant to ignore it, but saw the call came from Lieutenant Hutchins. He excused himself, got up from the table and walked to the living room slowly enough to attract no attention.

"Sorry to bother you," said Hutchins, sounding as if he didn't care one way or the other, "but Shawn Smith said I should call you."

"Oh?" Charlie's interior drone grew louder.

"They found the guy you asked about, Rodger Toombs, down in Albany."

"Dead?"

"That's right. He was in an Econo Lodge. His throat was cut, just like the others." Hutchins paused.

"What else?"

"His cock and balls were stuck in his jacket pocket. Shawn Smith said the guy who'd killed Mickey must've been looking for him all this time. The maid found him in the morning when she came to make up the room. It didn't make her happy."

"So you'll give me back my pistol permit?"

"Can't do it, Charlie. But we'll keep an eye on you. Just like before."

At two o'clock the next morning, Charlie flopped over for the twentieth time, resituated his pillow and kicked one foot free of the down comforter. Beside him, Janey slept so peacefully that Charlie had an urge to give her a poke. By the light of the streetlight, he saw the bare branches of the maple in the front yard heave and twist. That's what I feel like, he thought.

Beneath his side of the bed lay his fully loaded Benelli M4 Super 90, 12-gauge shotgun. Half a dozen times he'd timed himself in reaching for it and swinging it up. The first time he'd nearly fallen out of bed, but now he could do it smoothly, almost.

Earlier, as he'd practiced grabbing the shotgun, Janey had watched from her side of the bed. She hadn't been happy. "Let's go visit my sister in Denver. I can take time off and Emma needs a break from school. There's skiing."

But Charlie felt that skiing would be more dangerous than facing a killer with a knife. And it wouldn't do any good. The man would be waiting when they got back. Charlie might be terrified, but he wasn't a coward, at least that's what he told himself. He'd stay in Saratoga with his Benelli. But he couldn't sleep.

When Rodger Toombs was found, no evidence suggested who his killer might be. On the other hand, Toombs had opened the door for him, which suggested he might have known him. Forensics showed that Toombs died early in the evening. The Albany police tracked down the guests in the surrounding rooms, but if Toombs had made any noise, no one had heard it.

In the drawer on the bedside night table had been a 9mm Kahr with a three-inch barrel and a laser sight.

"Right on top of the Gideon Bible," said Hutchins. "He never touched it."

Charlie had asked if Toombs had looked like any of the cardboard figures.

"I guess so. There's one with little ears. We didn't even realize they were ears. I mean, they're just tiny circles."

"And the remaining figures?"

"Well, there's the one with the porkpie hat and we know who that is, don't we? Then there's a man with a plaid vest and a woman in a white dancer's skirt."

"Fletcher Campbell and Artemis."

"Most likely. So there seems to be a horsey connection here. At least that's what the sheriff's deputies think. I just called Campbell, but he's not home."

Charlie explained where he was, and that Campbell and Artemis were in the next room. "Call them later tonight or in the morning. Telling them now would upset people. Campbell would probably start shouting."

"Okay, Charlie, I'll do it first thing," said Hutchins. "But the sheriff's sending deputies out to their places right now."

When Charlie had gotten back to the dinner table, Janey had whispered, "What's wrong. You look awful."

Charlie tried to shake it off. "Just a little cramp in my leg." He bent over to massage his calf; then he sat down.

"Maybe it's giardia," said Victor. "I had that once. Beaver fever. Fucked up my insides for months. You don't want to hear about it."

The only virtue in Victor's remarks was that it drew attention away from Charlie. Then Fletcher Campbell said he'd had giardia twice. It impressed Charlie to see that Campbell was competitive even about his ailments. When attention returned to Charlie, he'd composed himself. But he didn't eat any pie.

Later, when they left Artemis's house, Janey again asked what was wrong.

"We can talk about it when we get home." Emma watched with concern and interest from the backseat, but Charlie didn't want her to know about Rodger Toombs. If the killer had indeed been delayed by his inability to find Toombs, then he could be back in Saratoga by now.

It wasn't until they were alone in the bedroom that Charlie told Janey about the phone call. But she'd had a general idea of what was wrong when Charlie fetched the Benelli from the closet directly after closing the bedroom door.

"So he could be anywhere."

Charlie heard the fear in her voice. "That's what Hutchins said."

"What are you going to do?"

Charlie sat on the bed, sliding shells into the shotgun. Janey hardly glanced at the Benelli. This, too, scared him: the fact that Janey didn't complain about the gun, that she accepted its presence. It showed what she was thinking.

"Wait," said Charlie. "Just wait."

"That's all? I don't want to wait!" Her words seemed to rush from her mouth.

"I'll hire a security guy to spend the night downstairs on the couch."

This was when Janey said they should go visit her sister in Denver.

Seventeen

Charlie climbed out of bed the next morning when the night sky began to lighten. It was six o'clock. He'd slept only two hours and spent the last hour staring at the ceiling, telling himself he was just about to fall back to sleep. But it hadn't been true.

He washed, brushed his teeth, took his various old-fart pills and went downstairs for coffee, bringing the Benelli with him. He had come to hate it, even though he still admired it. But he admired it as someone might admire a three-hundred-pound slave driver. Instead of it belonging to him, he belonged to it. And he was chained to it till the end, whatever that might be. Then, in a moment of bravado, he considered sticking it up in the attic or even selling it. The thought unsettled him to the degree that his coffee sloshed over the rim of his cup. It wasn't that he thought "Uh-oh" or "Better not"; rather, he'd a sudden image of Mickey lying on the sidewalk with his throat cut. Next he saw Parlucci's bloody body with the python sliding across his belly. Then he imagined Mickey again.

At seven, he backed his Golf out the driveway and headed east to Fletcher Campbell's horse farm. Was he worried about waking him?

Not a bit. Horse guys made a point of getting up around four, and if that didn't include Campbell, then it should. By the time the sun crested the farther hills, Charlie was crossing the Hudson. The shotgun lay on the passenger's seat, riding shotgun, as it were.

Charlie found Campbell in the barn with Bengal Lancer tethered outside of his stall. A stable hand was using a hoof pick to go over the horse's rear left hoof, which he held between his legs.

"General maintenance?" said Charlie.

Campbell hadn't heard Charlie approach and turned quickly. His surprise faded as his face settled itself into its customary look of smug certainty. But for a nanosecond Charlie had seen fear in his eyes.

"You're up early, Bradshaw." Campbell smoothed his white moustache with his thumb and forefinger.

"You've got a deputy parked out front. The police call you?" Charlie glanced at the stable hand, who was focused on the hoof. He wore a green work shirt with the name of Campbell's farm—Tartan Stables—embroidered in gold on the pocket.

Campbell seemed to shrink a little as his fear returned. "Not yet. What's going on?" He took Charlie's arm and they walked toward the sliding barn door. The concrete floor had been swept clean, not clean enough to eat off of, but almost. Three horses poked their necks over their stall doors with "What's up?" expressions. There was the slightly sweet smell of manure.

"What do you know about Rodger Toombs?" asked Charlie.

"I know that he was one of the scumbags who stole Bengal Lancer and that he worked with Mickey Martin."

"The police found him yesterday in a motel room by the turnpike, south of Albany. His throat had been cut and his genitals were shoved into his jacket pocket. Lieutenant Hutchins called me last night at Artemis's. He said he'd call you this morning."

"I've heard nothing," Campbell said softly. "They catch who did it?"

"No. The maid found Toombs yesterday morning. There was no sign of the killer, except he must have been the guy who killed Mickey. Toombs had been in prison with Mickey." Charlie hesitated. "What do you know about these murders?"

The fear stayed in Campbell's eyes, a narrowing of the lids as if he faced a bright light. "I know three guys got their throats cut. And with Toombs getting the same treatment, it has to be connected to these horses being stolen."

"You know the police have you down as one of the suspects." This wasn't true, as far as Charlie knew, but he wanted to see how Campbell would respond. And maybe there was a touch of malice in Charlie's remark.

"You must be joking!" barked Campbell.

"Not at all. You might have known the people who had their horses taken and arranged to have Bengal Lancer stolen to take attention away from you. Then Mickey might have tried blackmailing you. He was good at blackmail. The other murders were just cleaning up. As for Toombs, he was working with Mickey and also knew about the blackmail. I'm surprised the police haven't questioned you." All this was conjecture, though Charlie guessed the police might have wondered something like this and dismissed it.

"That's ridiculous!" A horse stamped nervously in its stall.

"Hey, Campbell, it's nothing I think myself. But the police must look into every possibility."

It annoyed Charlie that he took pleasure in saying this, as if it were more important that Campbell was frightened than in danger. And Charlie knew that his pleasure was the pleasure of getting even with a bully. But, of course, Campbell *was* in danger. This time,

however, Charlie saw no fear in the other man's eyes: just indignation and the startled look of imperiled honor. They stood in the doorway of the barn. It was cold, and bits of hay corkscrewed across the
gravel drive. There was no one in sight apart from the sheriff's deputy's white-and-red Impala parked farther down the drive. The rising
sun lit up the house so the windows turned golden.

"You know about these little cardboard figures?"

"Only what Hutchins told me. I gather one's supposed to be me.
That's why I've got this." Campbell pulled back his coat to reveal a
revolver in a small holster. "I've also got three security guys doing
eight-hour shifts."

Charlie nodded. "That makes sense. Anyway, Toombs was also
one of them. The police know that now. That leaves three: you, me
and Artemis. The police think the killer was waiting till he killed
Toombs before he moved on to the rest of us, but they don't
know why."

Charlie was impressed by his own composure, as if Campbell's
fear had sucked up his as well. But of course the Benelli was
just twenty feet away, near enough for Charlie to imagine that he
was safe.

Instead of responding, Campbell looked back over his shoulder.
Charlie heard a crunching in the gravel. Lieutenant Hutchins was
coming up the drive in a black unmarked Chevy from the detectives
unit. Charlie's first thought was that he didn't want Hutchins to see
the shotgun on the front seat of his Golf.

Hutchins stopped to say a few words to the sheriff's deputy; then
he got out of his car and walked toward Charlie and Campbell. A
police radio squawked in the background.

"Doing our work again for us, Bradshaw, or is this a social visit?"

"I was telling him what you told me last night. And I wanted to see how you were going to protect Campbell and Artemis."

"Well, despite those little figures, the sheriff wasn't sure that Campbell and Artemis were involved until Toombs was killed. That was positive evidence that the murders were linked to the horse-nappings. But we don't know how Artemis fits into this, unless one of her horses would've been taken next."

"You're sure it's connected to the horse-nappings?"

Hutchins looked critically at Charlie. "What else can it be?"

"I think there're other possibilities. And you'll 'keep an eye' on Campbell and Artemis like you keep an eye on me?"

Hutchins's confident manner turned to irritation and he spoke in a clipped voice. "The sheriff's department and the troopers are taking care of that. But, Charlie, as I've said often, you're butting into police business. Now, if you don't mind, I'd like to talk to Mr. Campbell in private."

The morning sun was still low in the sky when Charlie turned up the long driveway to Artemis's house and parked in front of a metal structure large enough to contain a full-sized dressage arena. Climbing out of his Golf, he walked toward the wide sliding door behind which he heard voices and the faint galloping sounds of horses' hooves. He'd left the shotgun on the front seat and already missed it.

The first person Charlie saw was Emma wearing riding pants and boots. In her left hand dangled a riding helmet covered with black velveteen.

"How'd you get here?" said Charlie. His immediate thought was that she might be in danger.

"I'm doing work for Artemis today." She said this proudly. "She had some errands in town, so she picked me up."

"You don't seem dressed for work."

"First I ride, then I work, then, if there's time, I ride again. And I get to do the same thing on Sunday. Isn't that great?"

"Shoveling manure?"

"I'll do that and grooming and horse-walking. It's awesome. I'll totally do anything she wants."

"Your mother know you're here?"

"She was out, so I left her a note."

Charlie opened his mouth to protest, but decided to say nothing. His first image on seeing Emma dressed in riding pants and boots had been of Emma being thrown over the horse's head. Then he'd visualized other dangers—she might be stepped on, or a girth would break and send her flying. But the memory of the little figure in the dancer's skirt conjured up more realistic dangers. That was what scared him most. Despite the sheriff's deputy parked out front, someone wanted to murder Artemis, and Emma might be in the way.

"Call your mother right now. And when I leave, you're coming with me."

"But that's not fair," she said indignantly. "I want to stay. I'm certainly old enough to stay here by myself."

"It's not a matter of your age. I'm taking you home." Seeing Emma's face redden with anger, he added: "Look, it's police business. People have been killed. It's not safe here."

Artemis was walking toward them from her small office. "How do you like my new assistant? She's perfect on a horse, quite natural. I'll have her standing on its back in no time."

Again Charlie had an image of Emma falling. "Great, that's just great."

Emma was still angry. "Charlie wants me to go home with him. He says it's not safe here."

"Not safe?" Artemis turned to Charlie. "Oh, you mean those murders. But why would someone want to hurt anyone here? It's ridiculous. Anyway, policemen are strolling around all over the place."

Charlie shook his head. "I don't care. When I go, Emma comes with me."

Shortly, he and Artemis were in her office in a corner of the barn. Charlie wanted to know more about Matthew Durkin, and he also wanted to convince Artemis that she was in danger. He was leaning against the door frame, while she sat at her desk.

"I don't know what to say. He was a small, nervous man. Polite, inoffensive, relatively clean. I don't think he had much experience with horses, but he caught on quickly. If he weren't a thief, he might still be here. I felt sorry for him. As I said, I tried to offer him help with his addiction, but either he didn't want it or he wasn't able to take it. So I let him go. He was quite angry about it, which surprised me, since after all I was the victim. But how could I employ him if I didn't trust him?"

Artemis wore a khaki shirt with a red scarf at the neck, khaki pants and black boots. A small wave of hair fell across her forehead and she brushed it away. She looked at Charlie with a mix of expectancy and good cheer.

"Did he live in town?"

"He lived here. There's a small room with a cot at the other end of the barn. He said he couldn't afford a room, much less an apartment. He only had one duffel bag and a box with tools. He also did carpentry work, which was useful. He drove a very old Datsun pickup that kept breaking down. He was always tinkering with it."

"Married?"

"Divorced."

"Children?"

"He never mentioned any."

"Where was he from?"

"Someplace downstate. Perhaps Kingston, or nearby. I think he still had family in the area."

"Did he talk about anything that you remember?"

"I've been thinking about that. He wasn't interested in the races. He had a small radio with which he listened to baseball games in the evening. The Yankees, most likely." This last was said with the slight scorn of a committed Red Sox fan.

"He wasn't a reader and had no off-color magazines. He was fond of solitaire and didn't drink. I've known heroin addicts who take a daily fix or two and just move along with life. Matthew seemed like that. I wouldn't have minded if he hadn't been stealing. He also took a dressage saddle when he left. It was a Devoucoux, which was expensive. They're quite light. Even a used Devoucoux can cost three thousand dollars."

"And you didn't contact the police?"

"I wasn't interested in punishing him. I was sorry when I heard Campbell had him arrested. Campbell's always liked forceful solutions to small problems."

Charlie pushed himself away from the door and glanced at the photographs of horses that covered the walls. "Do you have a dog?"

Artemis raised her eyebrows. "I have half a dozen cats, if that's any help."

"Dogs bark."

"Yes, I've known them to do so."

Charlie was sure that Hutchins would arrive at any minute, but he wanted to convince Artemis of her danger.

"I was talking about guard dogs. Do you remember those murders in Saratoga in October?"

Artemis nodded. "Very unpleasant. Cutting a man's throat is such an intimate crime. Personally, I'd rather be shot."

"Another man had his throat cut in Albany the day before yesterday: Rodger Toombs. He was one of the men who stole Fletcher Campbell's horse." Slowly, he told her the story of the murders, speaking of his own connection and what he'd found out. He again repeated that she was in grave danger.

"Lieutenant Hutchins described the cardboard figures," said Artemis. "I was rather offended to learn that mine wore a tutu. When I perform, I've always worn tights."

Charlie went on to talk about Matthew Durkin in prison, describing Mickey's accusations that Durkin was a snitch and had told the warden about the buying and selling of drugs, which had led to Durkin's murder.

"But why would Mickey Martin have done that? It was so cruel. Matthew was absolutely harmless."

"It cut his sentence by two-thirds and got him out of prison."

She listened with her head lowered and her hands folded together on the surface of the walnut desk.

"What disturbs me most," she said at last, "is the knowledge that Matthew was murdered in prison. I bear some responsibility in sending him there. I should have done more to help him with his addiction."

"You did what you could."

Artemis slightly raised one shoulder as if to suggest she didn't quite agree.

"In any case," continued Charlie, "you're in danger. Of course, I may be wrong, but you should leave here for a while."

"Dear Charlie, there's no way that I can leave here. You must have been a mother hen in a former life."

Charlie smiled. "Is that meant to be an insult?"

"Only a little. I'm extremely busy for the next few weeks and I simply don't have time to have my life threatened. I'm not sure I like it that you told me. I would have preferred ignorance."

Charlie was impressed and annoyed by her unconcern. "Come on, Artemis, Hutchins will be here at any moment. Why can't you stay at my house for a few days, or until this is over? We've a very nice guest room."

"That's impossible. You may have a nice house, but you lack a stable. Those deputies will just have to stay awake, that's all. Anyway, I thought the deaths were connected to the horse-napping and I had no involvement with that."

"No, I think they're connected to Matthew Durkin and you *are* involved with that. The people who were killed all knew him, with one exception."

Charlie heard heavy footsteps and guessed their source. In a few seconds, Lieutenant Hutchins appeared at the door. "I saw your little car outside, Charlie. I figured you'd be hurrying over here. Now you gotta go."

"Aren't you going to tell me this is police business and how important it is?"

Hutchins wasn't amused. "Just get lost."

"At least try to convince Artemis that she's in serious danger."

Charlie and Emma had just driven back to Saratoga and were waiting at the light by city hall. Emma hadn't spoken to Charlie the whole way and exuded disapproval and unhappiness like sweat in an August heat wave. Charlie was about to apologize for the tenth time when he saw a familiar figure entering Adirondack Trust across the street on Broadway: Eddie Gillespie. As soon as the light changed, he pulled to the curb and jumped out.

"Put the car someplace," he told Emma. "I need to speak to Eddie. I'll call you in five minutes. No later."

Emma began to protest, but then she hurried around the car and got behind the wheel. "It better be no more than five minutes," she called.

But crossing the street, Charlie didn't hear her as he hurried toward the bank. Broadway had changed in the many years he'd known it. Now it was crowded with stores mostly found in malls. As Artemis might have said, they lacked charm. It was still early, not quite eleven o'clock.

Entering the lobby of Adirondack Trust, Charlie saw Eddie's black pompadour bobbing in front of a cash machine.

"Eddie, my friend." Charlie put a hand lightly on Eddie's shoulder.

Eddie didn't cringe so much as to become smaller. He sucked himself into himself, bent his knees and glanced around to see if anyone was watching. He was one of several people waiting in line.

"Jesus, Charlie, I told you I can't talk to you in public," he said in a whisper. "What if the wife found out?"

"Eddie, you hurt my feelings. I wanted to buy you breakfast."

"I've already had breakfast."

"Then lunch."

"It's too early for lunch."

"Eddie," Charlie hissed, "if you don't come with me now for at least a cup of coffee, I'll make a scene."

Soon the two men were sitting at the back of the Common

Ground, a coffee shop on Broadway close to the bank. Eddie sat hunched over with his back to the room. Even his pompadour seemed to deflate.

"You're just lucky the wife's in Tampa seeing her folks or I'd never come with you."

"I'm honored, Eddie. So you're home by yourself? It must be lonely."

Eddie was picking the paper off a blueberry muffin that he'd condescended to have with the coffee. "It's just another week but I gotta eat frozen, you know, frozen pizzas, frozen mac and cheese, frozen chicken dinners. That shit's a whole lot smaller than its picture on the box. Like you gotta eat two just to have one. I been starving most of the time."

"Why don't you come to my house for dinner?"

Eddie looked up. "What're you having?"

Charlie arranged his features into a benevolent expression. "Whatever you want: chicken, spaghetti, steak, fish . . ."

"I never been a fish person. They're too slippery. You talkin' porterhouse?"

"Of course! You like it with mushrooms?"

"I never been a mushroom person either. Like they grow them in horseshit from the track. Anyway, I like my porterhouse straight, maybe a baked potato on the side. The wife won't cook steaks. She says they're too fatty. Jesus, Charlie, I thought *fatty* was the point of steak."

"What about a green veg?"

"Does it have to be green?"

Charlie's benevolent expression had begun to ache. He worried about getting a cramp in his cheeks. "What would you prefer?"

"I like a nice yellow veg, like corn."

"Corn it is. Seven o'clock okay?"

"You serious? You really think you could sneak me in somehow?"

"Sneak?"

"People talk. If the wife hears I been hanging with you, my balls are gone."

"I'll slip you through the back." Charlie paused and looked concerned. "You been doing Valentine's Day shopping?"

Eddie wrinkled his brow. "What's that got to do with anything?"

"Valentine's the day we husbands get a chance to make up for a year's worth of little mistakes."

"I never thought of it like that."

"Wouldn't it be nice if you could give the wife something really big? It'd make up for a lot."

Eddie shook his head. "A big box of candy's about all I can afford. I still got bills from Christmas."

"That's the trouble with holidays," said Charlie. "They cost money. When I was a cop, I'd have to take a second job just to buy presents for my nephews and nieces. As for Valentine's Day, Marge didn't want just candy. She liked big presents, like fancy handbags. You going to take a second job or d'you already have one?"

"For Valentine's Day?"

"You don't want to seem cheap."

Eddie leaned back in his chair and stared at his left hand as if an interesting jingle were written across the palm. "Yeah, she calls me cheap sometimes."

"Well, then, there you are." Charlie gave a friendly grin.

"I looked around for a part-time job at Christmas, but I couldn't get anything. I went all over. All I could find were day jobs and those'd mess up my real job."

Charlie plucked a large crumb off Eddie's blueberry muffin.

Popping it in his mouth, he chewed slowly and smiled. "So, Eddie, I've got some work for you: one hundred for the night and no heavy lifting. You can even sleep on the job."

Eddie narrowed his eyes. He'd been burned by Charlie's generous offers in the past. "What is it?"

"Simple. You sit on the couch. Maybe watch some TV. Eat some cookies. You a light sleeper, Eddie? You sit there from eleven till seven in the morning and I'll give you a hundred bucks for each night you do it."

When Eddie spoke, there was a hiss to his voice. "What's the catch, Charlie?"

"Catch, Eddie? Why d'you think there's a catch?" Charlie got to his feet. "And don't forget dinner tonight!" Then he slapped his head. "Good grief, I've forgotten Emma." Nearly three-quarters of an hour had passed since he'd promised to be gone only five minutes. Worse, he'd left her alone with the Benelli.

Charlie hurried out to the sidewalk and punched in her number. Emma answered immediately. "You're really lucky I love you or I'd never forgive you. Anyway, I'm home now. I suppose you want to be picked up."

"How'd you guess? Is the shotgun still in the car?"

Eighteen

I t had often seemed to Charlie that just when he needed sleep the most, events conspired to keep it from him. Shortly after midnight on Sunday morning, his cell phone rang. Removing his head from under the pillow, he reached for it on the bedside table only to knock it to the floor. Now he had to climb from bed to retrieve it, patting the rug with his palms till he found it. Flicking it on, he heard discordant music. It was Bad Maud calling from the Greasy Mattress.

"You still looking for an ex-con from Adirondack? I got one for you."

Charlie heard shouting in the background, and glass breaking. "Can't this wait till tomorrow?"

"Not if you want to talk to him. I mean like now."

So Charlie began getting dressed.

Janey grunted. "What time is it?"

"Twelve thirty. I've got to talk to Bad Maud."

"Give her my best." She puffed up her pillow a few times, rolled over and went back to sleep.

Charlie tiptoed downstairs in order not to wake Eddie Gillespie, who was snoring on the couch. Eddie had had no wish to spend seven nights on Charlie's couch, but the offer of seven hundred dollars was too much for him. Charlie, however, didn't tell him he'd be waiting for a murderer. Nor did he know where he'd get the money to pay him. It seemed unfair that he should have to get an equity loan from Adirondack Trust just to keep himself from being killed.

"There've been break-ins in the neighborhood," Charlie had told him, "and I thought I heard the back door rattling the other night. If someone sneaks in, just shout a few times. I got the cops on speed dial."

"He might shoot me."

"That only happens in movies."

Eddie wasn't armed, but he had a baseball bat.

Looking at him now in the light from the streetlight, Charlie saw that Eddie wore a hairnet to protect his pompadour. That in itself, thought Charlie, would frighten away any intruder. He tiptoed toward the kitchen and back door and then stopped. Eddie was snoring softly. Charlie returned to the living room and lightly stamped on the floor, but Eddie remained asleep. He stamped hard several times. No reaction.

Emma appeared on the stairs. "What's all this racket?" she asked sleepily.

"I'm conducting an experiment."

Emma went back upstairs. "You're weird," she said.

A s feeding time is the best time to hear lions at their noisiest, so Saturday nights were the best time to see the Greasy Mattress at its most colorful. As he made his way through the parking lot toward the door, Charlie heard shouting and a local band play-ing "Stairway to Heaven." He wore jeans, a flannel shirt and a moss-green barn coat, all of which made him think he was over-dressed. His attire should have been ripped, paint-stained and dirty. Two bouncers at the front door wanted to see his ID. Each out-weighed Charlie by a hundred pounds. Their angry expressions, thought Charlie, must have been a vital part of their wardrobes since birth, as if they'd broken out of the womb like breaking out of jail.

"Maud wants to see me," Charlie shouted over the noise.

One of the bad guys gestured with his thumb over his shoul-der and seemed sorry he couldn't give Charlie a smack in the nose.

He elbowed his way through the crowd and toward the bar. The customers were mostly biker types with Harley-Davidson parapher-nalia and club names written on the back of their jackets: The Zom-bies, Devil-Lovers, Wrath of God.

Bad Maud handed him a Budweiser. "Great, isn't it," she shouted. "This is where we get to howl."

"Charming. So who did you find?"

"Give me the money first."

Charlie gave her a hundred-dollar bill.

"More."

He gave her another.

"More."

"No more, and this better be worth it."

Bad Maud inspected her fingernails, which were chipped and needed cutting. "I don't guarantee the merchandise. He's over there in the booth by the potty. He's the one with the black motorcy-cle cap."

"What's his name?"

"You can call him Sharkie."

Again Charlie pushed his way through the crowd. Someone tromped on his foot; someone else elbowed him in the back. Sharkie watched him approach with a grin. He had black hair down past his collar and seemed thin all over; even his nose was narrow. He looked about forty. A man and two women were also in the booth. Tattoos and motorcycle gear gave them a family resemblance.

"Can we talk in private?" said Charlie, raising his voice over the noise. The band was like a semi-melodic traffic accident: all crashes and screams.

A dark-haired woman with a facial landscape of piercings snickered. She was pretty except for the missing teeth. "Don't you like us, Pops?"

Sharkie jerked his thumb toward the room. After looking briefly defiant, the man and two women picked up their drinks and headed for the bar.

Charlie sat down. He felt he'd already had too much of the Greasy Mattress. "What do you know about Matthew Durkin?"

Sharkie stretched out his hand and brushed his thumb over his fingers a few times. Charlie put a hundred-dollar bill on the table and Sharkie reached for it.

Charlie drew it back. "Not till you tell me."

Sharkie's face tightened and slackened in a mix of defiance and desire, both wanting the money and wanting to keep silent. At last, he said, "We were cellmates for a while. He was a chump. Guys took his food, cigarettes, made him run errands. If he whined, they slapped him around."

"You help him?"

"It wasn't my business."

"What were you in for?"

"They said I'd swiped some bikes. It was just bullshit, all bullshit."

Charlie nodded sagely. "Were you there when Durkin was murdered?"

"I'd been transferred downstate about two months before." Sharkie's voice had the wavering buzz of an electric razor.

"You think he was dealing drugs?"

"Shit, no. If Durkin had drugs, who'd buy 'em? They'd just take 'em. They even took his shoes once."

"You think he snitched on guys who sold drugs?"

"That's what they said, but he didn't have the guts. He just wanted to keep his trap shut, serve his time and get out."

"What about Mickey Martin, was he dealing?"

Sharkie rubbed a thumb across his scarred knuckles, as if feeling nostalgic for battles gone by. "Maybe. Or that's what I heard later, but Mickey was out by then."

"How long after Durkin had been killed?"

"A few months. Guys said a deal'd been made."

"You knew he was murdered last fall?"

"Who the fuck didn't? It was about time, wasn't it?"

"What about Rodger Toombs?"

"He hung out with Mickey. They looked out for each other, you know? I never talked to Toombs. I'm not a big talker. Open your mouth and flies get in."

A waiter brought two beers as a treat from Bad Maud. Charlie took a drink; Sharkie let his stand. Other than rubbing his knuckles, he was totally still. There was more broken glass and shouting. A bouncer dragged a guy out of the bar by his feet. The laughter made Charlie think of dogs barking.

"What did you and Durkin talk about?"

Sharkie looked scornful. "Like fuckin' discussions? We didn't have any."

"Well, what did *he* talk about?"

Sharkie cracked his knuckles and studied them some more. "He talked about horses; he liked horses. Not the racing part, the stable part. He said there were all different types: some friendly, some not; some stupid, some not; some high-strung, some not. Shit like that. He said if you looked hard, you could tell what they were thinking. I told him to shut up more'n once. What the fuck do I care about horses?"

"Anything else?"

"He was angry at the people who fired him. The last place beat him up and called the cops. I mean, he'd been stealing stuff to buy dope. What'd he expect? His head wasn't straight. At least he didn't snore."

"You know where he was from?"

"South of Kingston—Port Ewen, on the river. He worked on boats down there as a kid. So'd his old man. He'd jabber about it. Sometimes I'd shake my fist in his face to make him shut up."

"He still have family down there?"

"Maybe. His folks were born there, but they were dead. Maybe he had some uncles and cousins. His ex-wife was out west. He mentioned some kids, but none were nearby. I forget."

"Anything else about him?"

Sharkie stared down at the hundred-dollar bill. "He had a temper, the slow-boil kind. A crazy thing for a wimp to have. It got him beat up more'n once. He lost it with me one time. I smacked him around till he quit. He said it ran in his family."

First thing Monday morning, Charlie took the Northway down-state. It was rush hour and cars streamed toward Albany. Piles of old snow bordered the road. It always amazed Charlie to see these people he'd never see again. To his left, a gray-haired guy was shout-ing into a cell phone; to his right, a young woman was saying some-thing to the guy next to her and laughing. Then they disappeared. Often their likes and dislikes were spread across their trunks and bumpers. This one was a Christian; that one believed in Darwin. This woman's son was an honor student in Milton High School; that man said something about peeling his .45 from his dead fingers. Team insignias, names of politicians, names of vacation spots and the news that this particular Jeep had climbed Mount Washington—the vital minutiae of people he'd never know.

It wasn't that Charlie wanted to meet them. It was the size of it. Over the years he'd seen hundreds of thousands of people pursuing their separate paths with different degrees of passion. Some were crooks, some not; some were truthful, some not. Somebody once said that if you knew the deepest, darkest secrets of the strangers around you, you'd hate them all. But Charlie didn't believe that.

One of his pleasures as an investigator had been going into a strange place, finding a person he'd never met, like Sharkie, and ask-ing questions. And surely some of these people rushing toward Al-bany were people he'd seen before, seen so briefly that he couldn't recall them, as if he were surrounded by the swirls of overlapping currents of air. Maybe it wasn't a pleasure, maybe it was only inter-esting; but maybe it made him feel more alive, maybe it made him feel lonelier.

Port Ewen was on a triangular poke of land wedged between the Hudson on the right and Rondout Creek on the left, with the Kingston lighthouse at the tip. It was a small town, a hamlet in the town of Esopus about five miles to the south. Charlie knew the distance because he had driven down to the Esopus Library on Canal Street to get help in finding anyone named Durkin. The librarian had located two, a man and a woman at separate addresses. "You could have easily found these on the Internet," said the librarian.

"Hmm," said Charlie.

Janet Durkin lived on Browne Street, just past Broadway and half a mile west of the river. Some houses were from the turn of the century, some older: simple, house-like houses, like the miniature houses in Monopoly sets. It wasn't a rich place, though along the river rows of contemporary condos faced the water.

One of those Monopoly houses belonged to Janet Durkin. A chest-high chain-link fence surrounded the small, snow-covered front yard. There was no car in the drive; the curtains were drawn.

Charlie opened the gate, climbed the steps and rang the bell. He heard no noise from inside. He knocked on the door and waited. After a moment, he knocked harder. The door rattled in its frame. He walked around the house on the crusty snow, trying to see around the curtains. He knocked on the back door. Nothing. As he walked back up the drive, he glimpsed a face in the window of a house next door. The image came and went so quickly that he couldn't tell if it was a man or woman.

He walked over to the neighboring house and knocked on the front door. The door opened a crack. In the shadow, he still couldn't tell if it was a man or woman.

"Do you know anything about Janet Durkin?"

"She dead, been dead since May." The person had either a low voice for a woman or a high voice for a man.

"What happened?"

"She lived eighty-five years and dropped dead in her driveway; lay there over an hour before the cops showed up."

"She have family around here?"

"I make a point of not knowing stuff like that." The door closed.

Charlie considered knocking again just to see if the person was male or female. Instead, he walked back to his car.

The other Durkin, Robert Durkin, lived two blocks west of the river in a more prosperous area of small Victorians. The yard was neat and a car was parked in the drive, but here, too, the curtains were drawn. Charlie rang the bell.

He was about to walk to the back, when a voice called, "Bobby's not home."

Charlie turned to see a heavyset man bundled up in a red parka taking down Christmas lights from a small spruce. "You know when he's coming back?"

Before the man could answer, a barking dog jumped up with its paws on the window. It was a low bark; a big dog's bark. Its jaw was open so wide that Charlie could count its teeth from ten feet away. The dog scratched at the glass as if it meant to break through.

"Don't mind him; he's a sweetie. Anyway, Bobby won't be back till April first, leastways that's how it was last year. Him and his wife's got a trailer in Sarasota. Me, I love snow, as long as it behaves itself and I don't need to plow, you hear me?"

Charlie walked to the fence separating the two yards. The dog's barking increased. "Is Bobby related to Matthew Durkin?"

The man held a string of colored lights. In his red down jacket, he looked like a tomato. "Yeah, they're brothers. That used to be Matty's house till he passed. Then Bobby got it. Matty's wife moved out west a long time ago. I don't want to tell tales, but Matty and his wife fought like cats and dogs. Once I was mowing the lawn and a frying pan came flying right through that window." He pointed at the window and Charlie turned. It was just a regular window.

"Wow," said Charlie. "They have kids?"

"Three—two sons and a daughter. The girl married a guy in the City and moved down there. I don't know what he did; I wasn't invited to the wedding. And I don't know much about the boys: One moved west like his mom, and one joined the army right outta high school. Then he re-upped. He went to the ranger school, his uncle told me. Probably the army was the best thing for him. He could be wild."

"How so?"

"Fights, mostly. And he stole a car or two, though it didn't get to court. He wasn't someone you'd want to testify against. He's got his dad's temper, but he's not a bad guy. Helped me paint my house once and he'd take care of the dog if we went someplace."

The dog kept barking with its paws on the window. Spittle dribbled down the glass. Its only wish was to turn Charlie into pulled pork.

"What are their names?"

"Luke and Paulie. Paulie was the soldier. I haven't laid eyes on him since before his dad passed."

"They have relatives around here?"

"Nope, that's it as far as I know. A great-aunt died last May."

Charlie could hardly take his eyes off the dog. "What do they look like?"

"You know, just regular guys, neither this way or that. Both have light brown hair. Both about six feet, a little over."

"Any obvious scars, missing teeth, broken bones?"

"Oh yeah, Luke got his nose busted in high school football. So his nose's got a wiggle; Paulie's is straight."

"Anything else?"

"Not really, just regular-looking guys."

"What d'you mean 'not really'?"

"I mean 'not at all.'"

"The boys have friends around here?"

The man thought a moment. "Luke might of, though I don't recall any names. Paulie was pretty much of a loner."

Charlie wanted to ask more about the fights, but he let it go. He felt he had all the information he needed. Once he was back on the turnpike heading toward Saratoga, he called Shawn Smith's cell phone.

"Matthew Durkin had two sons, both are in their late twenties. The older son, Paulie, has been in the army and maybe still is." Charlie heard a sigh.

"Tell me, Charlie, what have these guys got to do with the horses?"

"One of them might have killed Mickey, Parlucci and Toombs. They were all involved with horses. Not the boys though, as far as I know. But their dad worked with horses. He was murdered up in Adirondack and—"

"Hey, Charlie," interrupted Smith, "I'm interested in the stealing part of horses. Any of these guys involved with that?"

"I don't think so, but—"

"So call that cop in Saratoga, Hutchins. He's the guy to deal with.

Or call the sheriff's department. On the other hand, if it turns out it's really tied to the horse-nappings, then call back. But right now I got too much on my plate."

Smith hung up before Charlie could say anything else.

One of the dubious benefits of living in a small city was that Charlie knew where Lieutenant Frank Hutchins lived, a modest Cape Cod in the northwest part of town. But knowing the house's location and being invited inside were very different, and midafternoon on Monday, Charlie stood on the small front porch, while from the other side of the storm door Hutchins shook a finger at him.

"I already said," shouted Hutchins through the glass, "Mickey and Toombs had to be killed by their partners. The other two guys just got in the way. And the troopers already got a line on these partners. They'll pick them up sometime this week. I don't like you coming over here, Charlie. I got a bad cold and I need some sleep." Hutchins wiped his nose on the sleeve of his white terry-cloth bathrobe.

Charlie recalled Hutchins stamping up the stairs to his bedroom at seven fifteen in the morning back in October. He decided not to mention it. It was cold on the porch and the wind was blowing. Charlie smiled and pretended to enjoy it. "Can't you try and get a photo of Paulie Durkin? The army must have one. All you need is to show it to the clerk at the motel and we'll know one way or the other."

"Hey, Charlie, we're not your personal helpers. We got jobs to do."

"So you're refusing to help just because I'm the person who asked?"

"Jesus, Charlie, I already told you. I'm out sick today. I'd say no to anybody."

Charlie was tired of shouting through the glass. "I'm sure you would." He returned to his car, scuffing his feet through patches of snow in a little display of futile anger.

He was cold and hungry. His main wish was to drive out to Rosemary's diner and have a big, unhealthy, hot pastrami sandwich. Instead, he drove to the Tea Kettle Motel—a large and shiny brass teakettle hung over the front door—to talk to the man who'd talked to Mickey's killer. Unfortunately, a sign out in front read: "Closed for the Season. See You in May—Gene and Mary Lou McCarthy."

It took another hour to learn that Gene and Mary Lou had another motel in Saint Petersburg—the Tea Kettle, Too—which they closed during the summer months. Sitting in his car, he got the number from information and called. It was now five thirty and almost dark. The woman who answered had the high voice of a child. Charlie asked if he could speak to Gene or Mary Lou.

"They're around here someplace," said the woman with the child's voice. "I'll look for them. Is it important?"

"Yes."

Charlie was afraid he'd run out of battery before someone again picked up the phone. The wind was strong enough to shake his car. Me too, thought Charlie, I'm cold too. After ten minutes Gene answered. He apologized; he'd been in the pool. Charlie explained what he was doing and asked his question. Was the nose straight or crooked?

"Straight," said Gene. "Straight, and he had cold eyes, a killer's eyes, but I don't recall the color. You caught him yet?"

Charlie said they hadn't.

"Then I'm sure glad I'm down here than up there. You got snow yet?"

Charlie said they'd had some.

"I hate snow."

Charlie opined that some people did and some didn't. He knew that once Gene rang off he'd go back for another splash in the pool before cocktail hour. Then he and his wife might toss a couple of T-bones on the charcoal grill. Charlie glanced out at the highway. Flurries swirled in the lights of passing cars.

"What's the weather down there like?"

"Quadruple glorious!"

As he drove back to Saratoga, Charlie wondered why he was here in the cold, rather than someplace where it was warm. Then he wondered how many men in the country between the ages of twenty-five and thirty-five had formerly broken noses. Maybe twenty million. Mentally, Charlie crossed them off his list of suspects.

B efore he reached town, Charlie called Janey to ask if she needed anything.

"Can you pick up Emma? She's out at Artemis's. Be a dear, will you? I've got dinner in the oven."

"Jesus, she can't be out there! It's dangerous. I already told her that."

"I talked to Artemis earlier. She said the danger was exaggerated."

"She doesn't know the first thing about it. Like she's in denial or something. I'm telling you, the killer is still loose! How could you be so foolish?"

"Watch your tone, Charles Bradshaw." Janey cut the connection.

So Charlie turned the Golf east on Route 129. Wind buffeted the car and large flakes of snow rushed recklessly across the windshield and sparkled in his headlights. He saw that it was beginning to collect along the side of the road.

Turning into Artemis's long driveway, Charlie was relieved to see the deputy's patrol car still in place. He parked by the large metal barn, expecting to find Emma inside. But the only person in sight was a young man in the process of attaching a hinge to a wooden door. Charlie had seen him before, but couldn't recall his name: tall, with the angular shoulders of a weightlifter. Charlie walked toward him.

"Have you seen Artemis or Emma?" Charlie thought the man might not know who Emma was. "Emma's a teenager, slight with blond hair."

The man's blank expression was neither indifferent nor patient; rather, he seemed to have no expression at all, like people in nineteenth-century tintypes.

"They left a while ago. Maybe they're at the house."

"My name's Charlie Bradshaw. You the new guy?"

"I been here a few months. I'm Richie."

They stood about twenty feet apart and neither made any move to shake hands. Richie kept looking at him.

"You from around here?" asked Charlie.

"Other part of the state. Fredonia area."

Charlie realized he couldn't grill the man without being rude and there seemed no reason for that. "Okay, thanks, I'll check the house."

As Charlie walked back into the wind, he wondered if there was anything slightly odd about Richie, but other than his lack of expression, nothing struck him as unusual. I'm being completely paranoid, he thought.

Artemis and Emma were drinking hot chocolate in the living

room. Emma looked quite ladylike, sitting toward the edge of her chair with her back straight. At home she didn't so much sit in a chair as drape herself over it.

"Richie said where you were," said Charlie. "He's fixing a door in the barn."

Artemis got up to kiss Charlie's cheek, which he thought of as a European gesture. "He always seems to be working. What did you think of him?"

What *did* I think of him? thought Charlie. "He seems civilized. We only exchanged a few words."

"He's not conversational, but I prefer that in someone who works for me. Random chat can be quite exhausting."

"Does Emma inflict random chat on you?"

"Don't start, Daddy." Emma spoke with seeming anger, and then grinned.

"Emma is full of interesting conversation. Will I see you tomorrow, Emma?"

"Right after school, I hope." She put on her green jacket. It was old and she needed a new one, but considering the money that had been recently flying out of Charlie's pockets, he'd be lucky if he could buy her a new toothbrush. He wanted to say that Emma wouldn't be coming tomorrow, that it was too dangerous, but that could wait until later. Anyway, he'd feel better once he got her back in the car.

On the way home, he asked, "What sort of interesting conversation are you full of?"

"I don't think I talked much, just about the horses and a little about school. And she tells me about Vienna. Oh, I really want to go there! It sounds magical, full of coffee shops and pastries!"

———

Charlie meant to drive straight past Rosemary's diner, but it had been a long time since breakfast and he heard the muffins calling. Maybe he'd get a bran muffin and imagine it was good for his health. He also had a question for Victor.

"We'll only stop a moment," he said.

Emma groaned. "It's already dinnertime. It'll be just like when you left me outside the bank."

Charlie laughed. "Maybe so, but this time you'll be with me."

Ten minutes later Charlie sat in a corner booth facing a large bran muffin and a cup of hot chocolate. He realized that ever since he'd known about the threat on his life, he'd stopped paying attention to his weight. Emma had a small green salad with dressing on the side. Victor, who had recently eaten, was picking his teeth with a silver toothpick: a present from the Queen of Softness.

"So tell me, Victor," said Charlie with his mouth half full, "do you still have that pistol you used to have? What was it, a Smith and Wesson?"

Victor looked up at the ceiling where nothing was happening. "Yeah, a Chief's Special. Rosemary hid it. She said I wasn't mature enough for it. Can you imagine?"

Emma giggled. Charlie's expression was mildly curious. He stared down at his muffin. "Could you get it from her if you really needed it?"

Victor slid the toothpick into a silver box that resembled a tiny coffin. He put it back in his shirt pocket and patted the pocket. "*Do I need it?*"

"You never know."

"That's the trouble, Charlie, I like to know. I like to know exactly. Are you planning to risk my life again? I'm too old for it."

Charlie laughed. He had a false laugh, more of a chuckle, that he imagined put people off their guard. But for those who knew him, it caused instant alarm. "Don't think of it as risk. Think of all I've done for you. I just want you to sit in your car for a while with the gun beside you on the seat, and maybe keeping your head down. The chance of any trouble is like five hundred to one." He took another bite of his muffin and dabbed his mouth with a napkin.

Victor winced. "Those odds are closer than I like. My life's important to me. What am I supposed to be doing?"

"You'll be like a private guard over at Artemis's; well, more like a sentry than a guard, more like an interested observer. If you see anything suspicious, you make a phone call. You still got your cell phone?"

Victor ignored the question. He looked again up at the ceiling. "As I said, Rosemary's got the gun. It's her call, so talk to her. But I don't like it, Charlie. I hate to think how many times you've nearly got me killed."

Charlie started to say that Rosemary didn't entirely trust him, when Emma spoke up: "I'll do it. I'll talk to her."

Victor smiled a happy smile. No way would Rosemary allow this. Emma scooted out of the booth.

"If she gets the gun," said Victor, "I'll consider going with you."

"You really think you can do it?" Charlie asked Emma. His words gave him a pain, which he realized was guilt.

"I can try. She likes me. We had a good time at Artemis's on Friday."

Victor sat back, getting comfortable. He figured he was safe about the gun.

He and Charlie watched Emma hurry toward the cash register, where Rosemary was established on her small throne.

"Well," said Victor, "at least Rosemary won't hit her if she gets angry."

Charlie smiled comfortably and finished the last of his hot chocolate. He was betting on Emma.

Nineteen

The metallic clashing and banging filled the house as fully as air fills a balloon. Charlie found himself rising up in bed, unaware even of waking. He swung his legs to the floor. The clashing continued.

"Charlie, help!" It was Eddie Gillespie, who had been downstairs asleep on the couch.

"What's going on?" asked Janey, rolling over.

"It's an intruder. Go back to sleep." The bedside clock said three thirty. Charlie scooped up the shotgun and headed for the door. Still in bed, Janey was making noises of protest, which Charlie ignored. Is it really an intruder? he asked himself. The crashing noise stopped, but Eddie kept shouting for Charlie. Barefoot, he headed for the stairs through the dark hall.

"Charlie, someone's breaking in!"

The descending stairs made an L-shape, turning right three-fourths of the way down at the wall of the hall closet. In the dark, Charlie miscalculated and slipped on the top step, falling back and landing on his butt. Startled, he squeezed the trigger of the shotgun. It fired, kicked up, fell from his hand and rattled down the stairs. The back door slammed open, breaking the glass.

In the enclosed space, the discharge had the force of a blow. Charlie thought of neighbors on either side of the house leaping from bed. The Benelli had come to a stop somewhere near the bottom of the stairs, but Charlie couldn't see it. His tailbone hurt and he dreaded that something might have happened to Eddie. And the intruder, where was he? Bruiser's high bark made a steady stream of noise.

Charlie slipped down a few more steps, grabbed the bannister and pulled himself up. Abruptly, the hall light flicked on. The Benelli lay by the front door. Charlie hurried downstairs and snatched it up. Bits of broken plaster dug into his feet. The wall of the hall closet, hardly more than fiberboard, was in dozens of pieces; the coats on the other side were peppered with shot.

Eddie, in his boxers and Rolling Stones T-shirt, stood hunched by the couch gripping his baseball bat. His hairnet had slipped and his shark fin of glossy black hair tilted jauntily to the left. No one else was in the room. By the entrance to the kitchen was a long string of beer cans. Another string of cans lay by the front door. Glancing up, Charlie saw Janey and Emma staring fearfully over the railing. It was Janey who had flicked on the light.

Charlie threw open the front door and ran onto the porch. Nearly all the surrounding houses were dark and he saw no movement in either direction. He hurried down the steps toward the street, but the frozen chunks of snow along the walk jabbed his instep, causing him to hop back. He again peered up and down the street. Whoever had broken into the kitchen could be anywhere, could even be standing someplace nearby. He went back inside and locked the door.

By now Eddie had put down the bat, but he remained scared. "It was a big guy. He jimmied the back door."

"Did he have anything in his hands?"

"I couldn't see. I didn't sign on for this, Charlie. You said you were sure no one'd show!"

"Well, it's a good thing you strung together those beer cans."

"What's happening?" said Janey, still at the upstairs railing.

"Somebody tried to break in. Eddie scared him."

"I scared him? Your fuckin' gun scared him. And me, too; I thought you'd shot me."

"Is that what happened to the wall?" asked Emma, standing a little behind her mother. "Why'd you shoot at the wall?"

"I slipped." Charlie's butt still hurt, but he chose not to mention it. He knew that under the circumstances, he could expect no sympathy. He'd wait a few days till the black-and-blue marks showed up.

Janey's arms were crossed over her nightgown and she looked worried.

Emma opened the door to the closet and took out Charlie's raincoat. She held it up to the light. Bright spots flickered through twenty little holes. It was almost pretty.

"Call the police," said Janey.

"There's no point. By the time they get here, the guy'll be miles away." But the real reason he didn't call the police was he was afraid they'd take the Benelli.

He did, however, make other calls. The first was to Fletcher Campbell. It rang six times and then the voicemail clicked on. Charlie waited about ten seconds and tried again. Again voicemail picked up after six rings. Charlie tried a third time and this time Campbell picked up.

"Who the hell are you!? You know what time it is!?"

Charlie identified himself and described the scene with the intruder. "I think it was Paulie Durkin, the son of Matthew Durkin, who you beat up and had arrested years ago."

Campbell was silent a moment. "What are you talking about? What's that have to do with stealing my horse?"

"It's got nothing to do with your horse. Paulie wants to get even for his dad." Charlie explained how Mickey and Parlucci had framed Matthew Durkin, accusing him of snitching, and how this led to Durkin's murder. He realized he was talking too fast and making it too complicated. Campbell was still half asleep. Besides, Campbell hated it when someone else was right and he wasn't.

"I don't get it. That's not what Lieutenant Hutchins has been telling me."

"Look, Campbell, even if you think I'm wrong, it'd be reckless not to protect yourself till this is settled."

"I am protecting myself. Did you call the police?"

"I thought I should call you first."

"Well, call them, for Pete's sake!"

But the next person Charlie called was Artemis. She picked up on the third ring and he again described what had happened. "I think the same person will attempt to get to you as well. After all, you fired Matthew Durkin. Victor's in a car in your driveway, but that may not be enough. Is a sheriff's deputy there?"

"I think he's parked over by the barn, but he might be on his break."

"Do you have a gun?"

"Only an old musket that a relative used in the Revolutionary War, I'm sorry to say." Though her tone remained faintly ironic, she spoke hurriedly.

"Nothing else?"

"A dressage whip and a crop, of course."

"A knife?"

"My best is part of my grandmother's silver. I'd hate to use it."

"Can you lock yourself in a room with your cell phone?"

"Yes, I can manage that. Perhaps I should call Richie as well. He seems muscular. Have you called the police?"

"I was just going to."

B ut Charlie didn't call the police, until Janey made him. Ten minutes later, two patrolmen showed up. At least they hadn't used the siren. Shortly after that, Hutchins arrived. He, too, had been woken from sleep and his shirt was buttoned improperly, making him seem slanted. He kept sneezing and blowing his nose on a tissue. Soon two more Saratoga patrolmen arrived and two detectives, and not long after that came two crime scene investigators from the sheriff's department. All the policemen, including Hutchins, studied the mess Charlie had made of the wall and the damage to the coats. Several chuckled, looked at Charlie and shook their heads. As each new person arrived, Charlie saw sleep getting further away.

"I told you," Eddie repeated, "the guy was big, that's all I saw."

Patrolmen kept getting caught up in the string of beer cans and, with every jarring rattle, the others jumped.

As Hutchins questioned Charlie, Eddie kept interrupting to say he was going home. The job was too dangerous. Hutchins told him to wait.

Janey made coffee and passed out cups to the policemen. Other policemen were searching the neighborhood. There was talk of getting a dog.

"You're letting me down, Eddie."

Eddie touched his hands to his pompadour. "I could of been killed."

"But you weren't, that's the main thing. You were a great success."

"Then why am I terrified?"

"But those beer cans worked brilliantly. That was a great job, Eddie!"

"They were Emma's idea."

Hutchins gave Charlie a bump on the shoulder. "Where the hell'd that shotgun come from?"

The Benelli lay on the coffee table: short, black and lethal. Charlie looked at it as if seeing it for the first time. "It's winter hunting season."

Hutchins looked doubtful. "And you hunt?"

"I thought I needed a new hobby. I'm going out this weekend." He described the area around Long Lake where he had talked to Cracker Johnson.

Hutchins gingerly picked up the Benelli and removed the remaining shells. Then he balanced it in his hand, weighing it. Then he lifted the sight and fiddled with the collapsible stock. He seemed to have forgotten Charlie's intruder.

"Is this legal?" Hutchins asked.

Charlie nodded. "And I belong to a gun club."

"What d'you hunt with it?"

Charlie made an exasperated noise. "Sparrows and the occasional cow. Come on, Hutchins. If I hadn't had it nearby, we'd probably be dead."

He turned back to Eddie, who was putting on his coat. "You're really leaving?"

Eddie nodded somewhat guiltily and then touched his hair.

"You'd feel terrible if you heard tomorrow I was dead," said Charlie, "that Emma and Janey were dead."

"Yeah, but it would be a lot worse if I heard *I* was dead. I mean, I wouldn't hear anything. Ever."

More policemen brushed past them.

"We've been friends a long time, Eddie."

"And you've gotten me in a lot of trouble. I don't like being arrested, I don't like being beaten up, and I don't like getting killed."

Charlie rubbed his hands together thoughtfully. "Well, you know, I can't pay you as much as I said, since you're leaving me in the lurch like this. And I'll have to find someone to take your place. How's fifty bucks sound?"

Eddie's face crinkled. "You said one hundred a night."

"But that was before, Eddie. Now I'll need it for some new guy."

Hutchins bumped Charlie again in the shoulder. "Are you really sure this is legal?" The Benelli lay balanced across his two hands like a baby.

"Absolutely. They've freed up the laws." Lies, lies, lies, thought Charlie.

Hutchins weighed the shotgun again in his palm. "This is lighter than my laptop and riskier than a pistol. But you can hang on to it till I check the regs."

Charlie didn't get any more sleep that night. He got dressed and sat on the living room couch with the Benelli on his lap. He stayed away from the windows and remained focused on the back door, even though he was sure the intruder wouldn't return. It was windy and branches swayed back and forth. Snow flurries rushed in circles. The only good news, as he saw it, was that Hutchins hadn't taken the Benelli. Luckily, the sheriff's crime scene investigators had found scratches on the back-door lock. If it wasn't for that, Hutchins might have doubted the existence of an intruder. A patrol car had been assigned to stay by the curb till daylight.

Around eight, Charlie called Fletcher Campbell. He'd gone out, his wife said.

"D'you know when he might come back?"

"I've no idea. I'm always the last to know what he's doing."

"Ask him to call me. It's important. Doesn't he have a cell phone?"

"It's in the kitchen. He always forgets it when his mind's on something else."

Like me, Charlie thought. "Did Lieutenant Hutchins from Saratoga contact him?"

"Not that I know of."

Charlie couldn't think of the woman's name, but her worry began to sound like irritation. "Is the sheriff's patrol car still in the driveway?" asked Charlie.

There was a pause. "Yes, it's still there."

At least that's something, thought Charlie. Next he again called Artemis. A man answered and it took a while for Artemis to get to the phone.

"I was jumping." She was out of breath.

It took a second for Charlie to realize she meant horses. He asked if anything had happened during the night. No, it hadn't, except she'd slept poorly.

"The best thing would be for you to get out of town," said Charlie. "Go down to New York and see some plays, or whatever you do."

"I couldn't possibly, Charlie. I'm much too busy. Three of my girls are competing this weekend. Jenny's volte is lopsided and Pat's horse wobbles."

"It won't help if you're killed."

Artemis sighed. "Yes, but death would spare me the embarrassment."

The morning passed without further incident, which was either a good thing or bad. Charlie couldn't tell. It continued to snow and the wind whistled through cracks at the edges of the storm windows. That night Victor would again park his car in Artemis's driveway. He'd have a pizza and several blankets. His pistol, a black .45 semi-automatic Chief's Special, would be beside him on the seat next to his phone. Artemis had him on speed dial. If she called, the first thing Victor would do was shoot his gun into the air. "It will create a diversion," Charlie said, "and alert the deputy." The barn had an alarm system, but not the house. In any case, the police would be on their way.

Eddie Gillespie stopped by around eleven. He made no mention of the previous night's intruder. Charlie gave him a ham sandwich. Eddie sheepishly promised to be there that evening in time for dinner. What were they having? Charlie wasn't sure. Eddie promised to spend the night on the couch. Charlie was touched by his change of heart. Was it out of loyalty, friendship or a sense of duty?

But Eddie's wife was still in Florida. "I get lonely by myself and I can't cook," he said. "And like you said, I need the money. Just don't get me killed."

Charlie tried to calculate how the killer would respond to his failure of the previous night. Would he lie low or would he rush forward to finish his work as fast as possible, thinking the police wouldn't expect it? As for the killer's identity, he was sure it was Paulie Durkin, the army ranger. Was he absolutely positive? Pretty positive, at least almost.

Afer Eddie left, Charlie went to the computer to try to track down Durkin, but no way could he get a quick answer from the Veterans Service Records in the National Archives. He'd have to write a letter and wait, or e-mail a form and wait, or fax a form and wait, or contact the New York Veterans' Affairs office and wait, or hire an independent researcher and wait, or drop everything and fly to Saint Louis to visit the National Personnel Records Center and stand in line. Or, in order to look through the member directory of the Ranger Register, he'd have to contact the U.S. Army Ranger Association in Fort Benning. Or maybe he could hunt out a vet or a former ranger to help him. With Emma's help, he also visited the 75th Ranger Regiment's Facebook page, where he began to sift through names, searching for men who'd been in the rangers at the same time as Durkin. Whatever he did, it would be a long process and he needed the information about Paulie Durkin immediately. "Argle-bargle," said Charlie. "It's all argle-bargle."

Shortly after two o'clock, Charlie drove across Saratoga to Hutchins's modest Cape Cod, having called the police department and learned that today Hutchins had again called in sick. It was still snowing and trucks were either plowing or scattering salt. Charlie took pleasure in thinking he might interrupt Hutchins taking a shower or having sex with his wife. And as he leaned on Hutchins's doorbell, he arranged his face into an expression of kindly innocence.

A small dog yapped manically. This was followed by Hutchins

shouting: "You'll get no treat; you'll get no treat!" Then the door opened.

"What kind of treats d'you give your dog?" asked Charlie.

"What the hell do you want now?" Hutchins wore a white terry-cloth bathrobe. Balancing on one slippered foot, he tried to push away a small Maltese with the other. The dog hopped back and forth, evading him.

Charlie raised his voice over the dog's yapping. "Have you learned who broke into my house?"

"We're working on it." Hutchins bent down and plucked the little dog up into his arms. It began furiously licking his face.

"You personally?"

Hutchins wiped his nose on his sleeve. "I'm staying in touch by phone. I get regular calls." He kept bobbing his head to escape the dog's pink tongue.

Charlie thought he detected a touch of apology in Hutchins's voice. They were still talking through a crack in the door. "Will you let me in? It's freezing out here."

Hutchins grudgingly opened the door about two feet and Charlie slipped through. He heard the sound of a daytime game show on TV and the sound of dishes clattering from the kitchen. The little dog bounced around Charlie's feet. "What's the dog's name?"

"Ozzie. It was my grandfather's name."

Charlie nodded sagely. "Was he a cop?"

Hutchins ignored the question. "Just tell me what you want and get outta here! I want to go back to bed and take a nap. I'm sick, for chrissake!"

"I thought policemen never slept."

"That's postmen."

Charlie took off his hat and unzipped his coat. "What have you done about looking for Paulie Durkin?"

Hutchins looked vaguely embarrassed. "This Paulie has no record. I ran a check on him. I'll get a photo from the military tomorrow, or the next day. Are you trying to do my work for me? The sheriff's investigators are giving him a lot of attention. We just can't locate him. But our theory that the killings are connected to the horse-napping remains a strong possibility."

"You going to keep a closer watch on my house?"

"That's our plan." Hutchins paused to blow his nose.

"Why don't I feel relieved? This guy's an army ranger. He can probably blow through you guys like blowing a dandelion clock."

"Give me a break, Charlie, we're doing what we can."

"What about Campbell and Artemis?"

"The sheriff says one or more deputies will be at their places all day and night. And Campbell has those dogs, plus his security guy's an ex-cop. And he's got an alarm system. Artemis is more of a problem, but besides the deputies, the troopers will keep a close eye on her. She'll be okay."

Charlie still didn't feel relieved. "Victor's parked all night in her driveway so don't arrest him."

"Is he armed?"

"I believe he still has his pistol license."

Hutchins's frown was his default facial expression. He used it now. "Just what we need is to have that wild man shoot up the scene."

On Facebook with Emma's help, Charlie found the names of four men who had probably been rangers with Paulie Durkin. He was able to talk to two of them. Neither remembered Paulie, nor would they give Charlie the names of others to call. Charlie had introduced himself as a PI and they hadn't liked that. Both said he would have to go through official channels. It was like talking to the same person twice.

Around five o'clock, Charlie drove out to Rosemary's diner. The shotgun was on the seat beside him, as well as a box of shells. It was still snowing and several inches covered the pavement. Plows were out and there was little traffic. His wipers smeared the snow across his windshield. He needed new blades.

Part of Charlie wanted to return home, pick up Janey and Emma and head down to Orlando for a few days to be jollied by Walt Disney's oversized mice and ducks. This part of himself he called his bad part. His good part wanted him to hide in the snowy dark and wait for an army ranger who might kill him. What's wrong with this configuration? he asked.

Victor was asleep in the king-sized water bed he shared with the Queen of Softness. He lay on his back in his Las Vegas pajamas and snored, while the water rocked gently to his breathing. His dentures were on the bedside table, smiling affably at Charlie.

Charlie shook Victor's foot. "Hey, wake up."

It required increasingly violent shaking before Victor woke. "Cut the shit!" Then he saw Charlie. "Jesus, Charlie, I was up all night."

"You didn't sleep?"

"Just a few quick catnaps. Anyway, I was too scared to shut my eyes."

"Did anything happen?"

"Yeah, it started snowing. Some troopers stopped a couple of times. The sheriff's deputies changed shifts. And one of her stable hands was wandering around between five and six."

"Which one?"

"I couldn't tell. But I didn't see anybody else, I swear it."

"And you'll be back again tonight?"

"I promised, didn't I? I'll just take a few more blankets. Is it still snowing?"

Charlie nodded. "There'll be a lot of it."

Charlie's next stop was at Fletcher Campbell's. A sheriff's deputy was leaning against his Impala, smoking a cigar. He held up a hand for Charlie to stop.

Charlie lowered his window. "Havana?"

The deputy's eyebrows shot up. He was a thin guy with a gray, cadaverous face. "Say again?"

"The cigar."

"Nah, it's a Romeo and Juliet. You can go up."

"You seen anything?"

"Not a peep. It's a wild-dog chase, as far as I'm concerned."

Charlie parked and waded through the snow to the front door. The security guard, or retired cop, answered the bell. He was more somnolent than suspicious. He escorted Charlie to Campbell's office at the back of the house. Campbell looked up from his desk.

"You went out earlier?" asked Charlie, brushing snow from his coat.

"I'd some errands, that's all." Campbell leaned back in his swivel chair in front of the picture window. Like a bull's-eye, thought Charlie.

"Make sure you carry your cell phone next time."

"Stop mothering me, Charlie. I'm still here. Nobody got me." He gave what Charlie thought of as a forced laugh, more a pleasant cough than a laugh.

"Glad to hear it. D'you remember what I said about the break-in at my house this morning, or were you asleep when I told you? We could have been killed."

Campbell pushed a hand through his shock of white hair. Maybe his red face got a little paler. "I remember all right. Those beer cans were a good idea."

Charlie nodded. "My daughter thought of that."

"But, Charlie, machine-gunning your own coats and jackets! The cops will have a field day with that sort of foolishness!"

"It was a single shot from a shotgun. I fell." He assumed that Campbell had been talking to Lieutenant Hutchins or maybe the sheriff's men. "Is there anything else you can tell me about Matthew Durkin?"

"A wimp, like I said, unless he got angry. He got in a fight with another guy one morning, a bigger guy. I had to pull him off. I never knew what it was about. But you must have talked to him."

"I remember very little. I was only around him for a couple of days and then he was arrested. He seemed mild and soft-spoken, even shy, though it might have been the drugs."

"Maybe his son takes after him."

"I doubt it. His son's an army ranger. The best thing would be for you to go to Miami for a week or so."

Campbell returned to his boastful manner. "I'd be a coward to do it."

"Better a coward than dead. So nothing happened last night?"

"One of the dogs barked once, which put us on alert. But nothing happened."

This didn't make Charlie happy. "Can you get another security guy?"

Campbell reached back, drew his revolver and put it on the desk.

It was a shiny Colt Python with a six-inch barrel and a nickel finish. "How many do I need, Charlie? An army? Two of my stable hands are armed and I've got Leon at the front door; I've got dogs, and sheriff's deputies are parked outside. I got video cameras. I even have a safe room with a steel door. But the whole business strikes me as bullshit. Even if someone's prowling around, you're the only one who thinks it might be Durkin's kid."

Charlie began buttoning his coat. He could tell that Campbell was frightened but trying not to show it. "I'd feel better if he hadn't been a ranger."

S itting in his Golf in front of Campbell's house, Charlie considered what to do next. His socks were wet from the snow and he felt chilled. He wanted to drive over to see Artemis, but he'd talked to her earlier in the afternoon and there was nothing left to say, except to tell her again to be careful. In fact, the last time he had called, she'd said, "Charlie, this is just what you said before. You're being excessive. The sheriff's deputies are parked outside. I give them tea and cookies."

So Charlie didn't have the courage to call again, or at least for another hour or so. Instead, he called Victor.

"I got here about ten minutes ago. I'm in the driveway with my gun in my lap and there's a deputy by the barn. A trooper stopped by five minutes ago. Already I'm bored. Talk radio gets shittier and shittier."

"I hope you're keeping the radio low enough to hear anything suspicious."

"Charlie, I'm keeping it so low I could hear a crow fart."

So Charlie headed back to Saratoga. He hated these times of waiting. They made him feel lonely, stuck by himself with nothing to do. A dark hiatus, he called it. These were the times James Bond used to screw beautiful women. Then he laughed.

Janey had gone to the mall and Emma was visiting a friend. Charlie was alone in the house with Bruiser. He sat on the couch, holding the dog with one hand and the Benelli with the other. When Janey got back about seven, she began making spaghetti carbonara, adding peas, mushrooms and pecorino Romano. Eddie Gillespie showed up around eight and immediately sat down at the dinner table.

"None of the food in my house is interesting." He pushed the mushrooms to the side of his plate and passed on the green salad.

After dinner, Charlie moped around on the second floor for an hour or so, while Eddie sat downstairs watching sitcoms. He had a high, nasal snicker, and each time, the sound felt like a needle poked into Charlie's ears. Eddie had also brought a small police radio that crackled constantly.

Because he'd slept little the previous night, Charlie went to bed around ten, stuffing toilet paper in his ears and putting his head under the pillow so he wouldn't hear Eddie's noise. He dreamt he was trying to swim in an Olympic-sized pool with lane markers and LCD timers. But instead of water, the pool was full of sand.

When Eddie shook his shoulder several hours later, Charlie briefly dreamt he was falling downstairs. Then he opened his eyes. Janey flicked on the light.

Eddie stood by the bed waving his crackling radio. "There's

trouble at Fletcher Campbell's! The troopers and the Saratoga sheriff are on their way out."

Charlie jumped from bed. His eyes felt gluey. "What sort of trouble?"

"Bad trouble. Somebody's missing."

Pulling on his jeans, Charlie began looking for his boots. "What time is it?"

"Around one thirty."

"You're going out there?" asked Janey anxiously. "It's still snowing."

"I can't help it." Charlie picked up the Benelli and headed for the stairs.

"Wear a scarf!" called Janey.

Twenty

The security lights illuminating Fletcher Campbell's front yard were nearly eclipsed by the flashing red, blue and amber lights of an ambulance and a half-dozen police vehicles parked in the circular drive. The colors dyed the white front of Campbell's house and tinted the falling snow, while the house windows themselves remained dark. Police radios chattered to one another, reminding Charlie of a pond full of sex-crazed frogs in spring. Sheriff's men strung yellow tape around the house, the barn and all the space between. Forensic guys hurried back and forth. Officers with flashlights went in and out of the house, and a small crowd had gathered by the entrance of the barn. Charlie took a flashlight from his glove box, tugged his Red Sox cap firmly down onto his forehead and tied his blue scarf tightly around his neck. Best to leave the Benelli on the seat, he thought. Then he made his way toward the barn. The path was a smear of prints from the deputies' and troopers' duty boots. Falling snowflakes glistened briefly on the muddy surface and then vanished.

A New York state trooper stopped him as he approached the tape.

The trooper wore a bright yellow raincoat, and something like a hat-condom covered his Stetson.

"No press," said the trooper.

Charlie shook his head. "I'm a PI. Hutch called and told me to get down here right away."

"Hutch?"

"Lieutenant Frank Hutchins, Saratoga Department of Public Safety. He's expecting me. Come on, already." He handed the man his driver's license and tried to recall the names of any troopers he might have met if Hutchins hadn't as yet arrived, but his mind drew a blank.

"He's down at the barn." The deputy lifted the yellow tape so Charlie could get through.

He found Hutchins among a circle of men just inside the barn door. Charlie had no doubt about what was in the center of the circle. Looking between the men, he saw a lopsided pool of blood, gleaming in the glare of the lights. Horses whinnied and stamped in their stalls. Then, looking further, Charlie saw the soles of a pair of ornate Western boots. Fletcher Campbell, Charlie knew, never wore cowboy boots.

He touched Hutchins's arm. "Who is it?"

Hutchins turned, glared at Charlie in moral outrage. "What the fuck are you doing here?"

"You know perfectly well what I'm doing here." Charlie tried to sound calm and reasonable. No way was he going to let Hutchins make him leave.

"You're a civilian, for crying out loud. Go home!"

Charlie took a step forward to get a better look. "Campbell's a friend of mine and I'm working for him. Who's the victim?"

"Campbell's security guy, Leon Hufnagel. He used to be a

Saratoga cop. He didn't even have a chance to draw his weapon. Got him from behind."

Charlie didn't recognize the name. He took a step closer. Hufnagel was sprawled on his back. His throat had been cut from ear to ear. The front of his heavy, sand-colored coat was puddled with blood that oozed onto the barn floor. He seemed about fifty, and his thick, square face looked as if he were trying to lift several cinder blocks. Charlie guessed he'd been killed in the last hour. "Who found him?" he asked.

"A sheriff's deputy heard a shout and came to investigate. Hufnagel was already dead. Nobody else was around. Look, Charlie, you gotta get out of here. I don't care if you're working for Campbell. This is the sheriff's case. I'm just a guest." Hutchins sneezed and wiped his nose on a gray handkerchief. "And I should be home in bed!"

"Talk to Campbell. I'm sure he'd want me here." This was nothing Charlie really believed.

"He's not in his house. We can't find him. He and his wife have disappeared. And no cars are missing."

"Are there footprints?"

"There might have been, but the troopers and sheriff's men have tramped all over the place and made a mess of things. All I can say's there're no prints in the snow going off into the fields."

Charlie remembered the darkened house. "And the lights?"

"The wires were cut. National Grid's on its way out. The security lights have their own power source."

"What about the dogs?"

Hutchins sneezed again. "One's dead. No one's seen the other."

Several nearby deputies kept giving Charlie suspicious looks. He rose up on his toes, stiffened his back and tried to look imposing. He wasn't going to leave till he knew more about what had happened.

"And you went thoroughly through the house?"

Hutchins didn't get a chance to answer as a large red-faced man in plainclothes interrupted them. It was the undersheriff: an official being officious. Charlie remembered that his name was Maroni, but he didn't recall his first name.

"Who's this guy, Hutchins?" Maroni had a professional growl: half gravel, half distrust.

The lieutenant gave a slight, forbearing shrug. "He's from Saratoga."

"Is he a cop?"

Hutchins became less happy. What was Charlie? An interested citizen, a Nosey Parker, a gate-crasher?

Charlie spoke up: "I'm doing investigative work for Campbell. The guy who killed Hufnagel also tried to kill me. You've got to send another car . . ."

Maroni stared at Charlie from under heavy lids. "I don't 'got to' do anything. How d'you know who killed Hufnagel? You a civilian?"

Hutchins's discomfort increased. "Charlie's been nosing around from the start. I'll tell you about it . . ."

The undersheriff pointed a fat, red finger at Charlie's nose, as if this were the very purpose of fat, red fingers. "Get the fuck outta here, civilian, or you're in a mountain of shit!"

Charlie tried to think of an answer that would let him stay longer. Then he asked calmly, "Have you found Campbell's panic room?"

"His what?" Maroni looked at Lieutenant Hutchins, who shook his head.

The surprise and perplexity expressed by Hutchins and the undersheriff gave them a woodenheaded likeness, which it pleased Charlie to see. He adjusted his voice to express brusque, machinelike focus. What he thought of as a cop voice. "Campbell's got a panic room somewhere in his house. You didn't know about it? I figured he'd let you guys know. It's where he and his wife are hiding, if they're not dead." Though his exterior expressed certainty, Charlie's interior was full of doubt.

So Charlie, Lieutenant Hutchins, Undersheriff Maroni and a deputy by the name of Różycki made their way back to the house. Różycki had mentioned that his uncle Witold had built a panic room in his house in Phoenix, and Maroni had invited him along for his technical advice. Their flashlights crisscrossed the muddy path and sparkled off the falling snow. There was no more talk about Charlie getting "the fuck outta here." After all, he, too, seemed knowledgeable about panic rooms.

But once inside, Charlie was unsure what to do next. The house remained dark. They stood in the hall and flashed their lights around the living room, but nothing stood out as a suitable hiding place for a secret room: no bookcase or tall mirror, no questionable paneling or false fireplace.

"Let's start with Campbell's study," said Charlie.

"Good idea," said Różycki.

The lights suddenly came back on as they entered the hall. Charlie started, as if caught doing something illegal. Glancing back, he saw that their boots had left a muddy trail on the burgundy Persian carpet with its field of blue and beige rosettes. He seemed the only one to notice. The police officers continued down the hall, clumping their feet.

The door to the study had been broken open; yellow splinters of wood were scattered over the carpet. On the wall to the right, a picture window looked out onto the snowy dark. In front of the window stood an antique mahogany partners desk with nine drawers on either side and a green leather writing surface. The leather padding of the mahogany swivel desk chair was the same shade of green. The color, Charlie realized, of the Campbell tartan. The seven-piece desk set—letter tray, pencil cup, memo pad and suchlike—also had green leather, as did the handle of the brass letter opener. On the far side of the desk was a bronze statue of a racehorse with a bridle on a green marble base with its head turned approvingly at whoever might be sitting in the desk chair. A small plaque on the base was engraved with the name "Bengal Lancer."

The two mahogany visitor's chairs were also covered with green leather. Charlie recalled sitting in one of them the previous fall after Bengal Lancer had been stolen and it brought back disagreeable memories.

On the wall across from the door, a second window looked out toward the barn, while on either side were paintings of racehorses. The saddle pads and jockeys' silks again showed off Campbell's green-and-blue tartan. Across the room from the desk, a seven-unit mahogany bookcase rose from the floor to the ceiling. Only the center unit held books. Other units held trophies of various sorts: loving cups, plaques, medals, framed certificates and colored ribbons. Half were for horses. Other awards were for different sports—curling, golf and haggis hurling. Still more were for successes in business and civic affairs. Close to the bookcase were two leather pub chairs angled toward a flat TV on the wall near the door.

"This guy's got some kind of fixation," said Hutchins, still snuffling.

"I bet he gets most of these from lawn sales," said Różycki.

"So where's the secret room, Mr. Civilian?" asked Maroni.

"It must be behind the bookcase," said Charlie, trying to sound knowledgeable. Różycki agreed with a nod.

Charlie walked over to one of the units and tugged at it. Nothing happened. Then he reached over a shelf between two loving cups and knocked on the back panel. It sounded solid.

"Where's the keyhole, Charlie?" asked Hutchins sarcastically.

"They don't have keyholes," said Różycki. "They've electromagnetic locking systems. You got to turn something or twist something or push something. It can be as simple as a chess piece or one of these little horse statuettes. Or he might use a hidden iris scanner—that's what my uncle's got."

"What about hinges?" asked Maroni. "Does the door swing out?"

"My uncle's door rotates on car axle bearings," said Różycki, "and underneath it's got a special caster roller for extra support. And some have double doors."

So over the next five minutes they twisted, lifted and poked the loving cups, plaques, medals and the rest until Maroni said, "This is a fucking waste of time."

"Not necessarily, sir," said Różycki politely. "There's a small camera hidden at the top of that second unit on the right."

"I don't see any fuckin' camera!" said Maroni. But then they saw it: a small lens poking out from under the belly of a racehorse statuette.

"Is he watching us?" asked Hutchins.

But Różycki couldn't answer that. In any case, the presence of the camera encouraged them to keep looking.

Charlie inspected the books in the center unit. After finishing with the bottom three shelves, he began with the fourth, lifting out three thick volumes of *A History of Clan Campbell* by Alastair Campbell of Airds. Nothing happened. On the shelf above were James

Wylie's three-volume *History of the Scottish Nation or The History of the Celtic Church from Pre-historic Times to Medieval Times*, John Tweed's *The House of Argyll and the Collateral Branches of the Clan Campbell: From the Year 420 to the Present Time* and eight volumes of Scottish history by John Prebble: *Glencoe, The Highland Clearances, Culloden, The Darien Disaster* and others.

Charlie began to tilt the books backward one after another; then he paused to leaf through Prebble's history of the Battle of Culloden. Despite being in a rush, despite being eager to find Campbell, despite being desperate to get to Artemis's farm and make sure she was safe, Charlie wished he could sit down in one of Campbell's soft chairs and read about Culloden and the defeat of Bonnie Prince Charlie as the world and its many dangers faded away.

The impulse was brief. Then, a few seconds later, when he tilted back the top of *The House of Argyll and the Collateral Branches of the Clan Campbell*, there was a movement. With a whisper, the center unit of the bookcase began to slide out and pivot to the right. Charlie jumped back, got tangled up in his feet and stumbled to the rug. His fall was the only noise until the undersheriff said, "What the fuck?"

Behind the bookcase was a gray steel, vault-style door. In its center was a bolt-throwing mechanism with a five-spoked steel wheel about a foot and a half across. Above the wheel was a small screen. The wheel began to turn and in another moment Campbell stood before them, red-faced and breathing hard. In his left hand he held a shotgun, while tucked in his belt was his shiny Colt Python.

"It fucking took you long enough," said Campbell. "I was watching you."

"Then why didn't you open the goddamn door?" demanded Hutchins.

"I thought the guy was still around. The power outage shut down the ventilation. We both felt sick. We could of suffocated in there! You catch him?"

Glancing at the police officers, Charlie wondered if he was the only person who had a fleeting desire to push the door shut with Campbell on the other side. Then, over Campbell's shoulder, he saw his young wife, Ursula, her pretty face tense with fear.

"Who're you talking about?" said the undersheriff. "Your security guy's dead. He got his throat cut in your barn. What's going on here?"

"Jesus," said Campbell. "I told him to get in here to the safe room, but he said he could handle any trouble. Poor dope."

This particular expression of sympathy pleased no one.

"That still doesn't explain what's going on," said the undersheriff.

Ursula Campbell pushed past her husband. She was a tall blonde in her late thirties. Her small smile was as friendly as a cocked mousetrap. "You have to be finding out about this person," she said with her accent. "I saw him in the hall. He wanted to kill us."

She explained that she and "Fletch," as she called Campbell, had been in the study watching TV. At some point Campbell had asked her to get him a beer from the kitchen. Going into the hall, she saw a young man in a hat and raincoat on the other side of the living room. "He was a complete stranger to me," she said, "and I required to know why he was in my house."

The man had shouted, and she'd run back to the study, locking the door behind her. Then she and Campbell retreated to the safe room.

After a moment, Maroni inquired: "What'd the guy shout?"

"'Are you ready to die?'"

Charlie was silent as he considered his reaction to such a

question. Sheer terror, he expected, with the hope he wouldn't wet himself.

"You see a weapon?" asked Maroni.

Ursula nodded. "He had a knife, a large hunting knife."

"Can you say anything else about what he looked like?" asked Lieutenant Hutchins.

"He was tall and he looked strong. I was frightened."

Charlie touched Hutchins's arm. "I'm going over to Artemis's. Get Maroni to send more men over there."

Twenty-one

Although Artemis's property was close to Fletcher Campbell's, her driveway was at least two miles away and her house was several hundred yards off the road. It was still snowing and perhaps eight inches had fallen. Against the hillside and along the hedgerows, the wind had sculpted the snow into drifts. Charlie had called Artemis when he left Campbell's, but she didn't pick up. He called again when he turned into her open gate, but again there was no answer.

The driveway was deep with snow, but another car had come through fairly recently. Although Charlie didn't know the driver, he was afraid it might have been Paulie Durkin. And what might be the consequences of that? He kept the wheels of the Golf in the furrows made by the earlier car and gunned the motor, yanking the wheel as his car swerved back and forth.

The glare of the snow in his headlights made it difficult to see any distance, but soon he saw the sheriff's deputy's white-and-red Impala parked at the side of the drive, with its motor running and its windshield wipers beating back and forth. Charlie pulled up behind it and got out of his Golf. He expected the deputy to lower his window, but there was no movement. Charlie approached the car and rapped on the driver's window. There was no response. He tried the door and pulled it open, thinking he'd find the deputy asleep. The interior light came on. The car was empty.

Charlie stepped back and looked down at the snow, assuming he'd see footprints, but they weren't clear; or rather, the snow had been disturbed, but any obvious prints were being covered again. However, in his headlights, he could see a trail of indentations leading along the drive. Perhaps it was one person's prints; perhaps more.

Returning to his car, Charlie tried to reverse, but after a few feet the wheels began to spin and his car came to a stop. He tried to move forward, but again the wheels spun and whined and he stopped. He reversed again and advanced again as his wheels dug themselves more deeply into the snow. Then he gave it up. The Golf would have to stay where it was.

Charlie retied his scarf, pulled down his cap and drew the Benelli toward him across the seat. Its cold metal on his bare skin felt like a burn. He kept his gloves in his coat pockets, thinking they would only be a hindrance if he needed to reload the shotgun. As he opened the car door, the overhead light went on and there was a ding-ding noise signaling that the keys hadn't been removed. He groaned, grabbed the keys and got out, making sure not to slam the door. Then he stopped and listened. Could someone be waiting nearby? He heard only the wind.

Charlie made his way toward the house. Windblown flakes stung his cheeks and he shuffled ahead in a half crouch. Shortly he realized that no lights were on, not even the big outside light mounted over the barn doors, or where he thought the two barns must be. Everything was dark. He tried to think of a rational cause for this. Perhaps the snow had brought down a wire; while that might be likely, he didn't believe it.

Up ahead, Charlie saw Victor's snow-covered Mercedes parked to the left side of the drive. A hazy cloud of black diesel exhaust drifted back to mix with the snow caught in the beam of Charlie's flashlight. He shuffled forward. With the light in his left hand and the Benelli in his right, both his hands were numb with cold. He attempted to grip the shotgun in the crook of his arm and worried that he might drop it.

Then, looking up, he received a shock. Just beyond the Mercedes, he saw another car. It was Janey's red Mazda6. Had she driven to Artemis's house when he'd driven to Campbell's? He struggled to move faster, but the combination of wind and deepening snow was like a hand pressed against him.

Coming up behind the Mercedes, Charlie told himself that Victor was surely clutching his Chief's Special, ready to fire at the slightest provocation. He rapped several times on the trunk to alert Victor of his presence. Then he pushed forward along the right side to the door. The heater was blowing at full power and the windows were clear. He peered through the glass. Victor was not inside.

Charlie continued toward the Mazda. Maybe Janey and Victor were together. The motor was off and the windows were frost-covered. Snow had already covered the windshield. Charlie pulled open the door. The car was empty. He again flashed his light around the snow near his feet, looking for footprints, but only vague indentations led up the drive.

He turned back to the Mercedes, meaning to get inside, warm his hands and use his cell phone. Again he received a shock. Radial cracks extended from two bullet holes in the middle of the windshield. The wipers swung back and forth across them. Charlie hurried toward the door, slipped and fell against the hood. The Benelli slid away from the crook of his arm and skated across the slick surface. Lunging after it, he grabbed the pistol grip just before the shotgun slid into the snow on the far side. He lay there for a moment, catching his breath and feeling the vibration and warmth of the diesel motor beneath him. It was almost comfortable. Then he slithered back off the hood and got into the car.

There was no blood. The gun had been fired from inside the car. A few shiny specks of glass were on the dash, but his light reflected off more bits of glass on the other side of the window, glistening among the drops of melting snow. So Victor had fired at something or someone with his .45. Charlie sniffed, thinking he'd detect gunpowder, but he only smelled potato chips.

He dug out his cell phone and called Janey. Eventually voicemail picked up, so he called again. He expected that she was with Artemis, but he couldn't imagine why she'd be there.

This time a sleepy voice answered. "Yes?"

"Where are you?"

"I'm in bed, of course. What is it?"

"Why's your Mazda out at Artemis's?"

"Are you serious? Wait a moment."

Charlie heard footsteps, a door opening and more footsteps.

Janey came back on the line, breathing heavily. "Emma's not here. She wanted to drive out to Artemis's so she could ride for an hour or two before school. I told her she couldn't. I didn't think it would be safe. She must have taken the car. Where is she? Is something wrong?" Janey was almost shouting.

"No, I don't think so."

"That's not a very comforting answer, Charlie."

"I just haven't seen her yet, that's all. She's probably with Artemis and Victor. I'm out at her place now, but it's snowing hard and the power seems to be out. I'll call you later."

"Wait a minute, what happened at Campbell's?"

Charlie had hoped to avoid this part of the conversation.

"Tell me," Janey continued, "what's going on?"

"I gotta go. Campbell's okay. I'll call back when I know more."

"Wait . . . !"

But Charlie didn't wait. He didn't want to tell Janey his fears and what had happened at Campbell's farm. He didn't want to say that a man had had his throat cut. Instead he again called Artemis. The phone rang and rang and then switched to voicemail, which only told him to leave a message. Next he called Emma. The call went straight to voicemail. A mechanical voice said that it was unable to take his call right now. Then Charlie called Victor and got one of Victor's jazzy messages: "Hey, hey, hey! Maybe I'm here, maybe I'm there, maybe I'm nowhere. Catch me if you can!"

"Fuck you," muttered Charlie, ending the call.

He wanted to phone Hutchins, but he didn't have the lieutenant's private number. So he called the police station. Charlie identified himself and said he needed to talk to Hutchins, that it was very important. The officer on duty said that she couldn't accept private calls.

"It's not a private call!" shouted Charlie. "It's an emergency!"

"Shall I transfer you to 9-1-1?" Her tone was clipped; she hadn't liked being yelled at.

Charlie lowered his voice and tried to sound reasonable. "No, I'm sorry. I just saw him out at Fletcher Campbell's farm, where a man was murdered. Now I'm at the next farm down the road. It belongs to Artemis. Something's wrong. A police officer is missing and, and . . . a car's been shot up. Please call Lieutenant Hutchins and tell him we need help . . ." Charlie asked himself what else he could say without sounding like a nutcase. "Hutchins knows I'm here. He told me to call him, but I don't have his private number. Just call him, for Pete's sake!" He was shouting again.

The officer's response was chilly. "I'll see what I can do." The connection went dead.

Charlie rubbed his jaw and wondered if pounding his head on the dashboard would make him feel better, but the relief, he knew, would be brief. However, while making his separate calls, he'd kept one hand and then the other pressed against the dashboard heating vent. Now they felt almost normal. So at least I've temporarily saved myself from frostbite, he thought with some irony. Again he called Artemis, Emma and Victor; again they didn't answer. Where were they? He pulled his cap firmly down on his forehead and retied his scarf. Why was the house dark, what had happened to the lights? Climbing out of the Mercedes, he decided to find out.

Charlie flicked off his flashlight to see if he could get used to the dark so he could approach the house without being seen. But the clouds were impenetrable and there was no glow from the moon. He couldn't even see the snow, which beat against his face. Moving forward, he felt his way along the side of Janey's car and then into the further vacancy of the invisible driveway. Once more he flicked on the light. He felt a sort of caffeine rush; a prickling of the skin that he realized was adrenaline. He welcomed it. The feeling would keep him warm.

A rtemis's sprawling ranch house was built on the side of a hill and, as Charlie approached, the highest side slowly grew visible through the storm: a two-car garage and above it was Artemis's wide living room. His hands were nearly numb with cold again. He had tried to warm them by turning off the light for a minute or so and sticking one hand or the other into his coat pocket, which entailed moving the shotgun from one hand to the other and putting the flashlight in the empty pocket. It was like, he thought, some ridiculous dance. Then he'd turn the light on again to get his bearings and the process would start over.

Parked in front of the garage was an older-model Honda Civic. He guessed it belonged to Paulie Durkin. Were these the tire tracks he'd been following? But no, Charlie remembered the Honda being parked outside the dressage barn late Monday afternoon. The car belonged to Richie. He felt a sense of relief. He glanced inside; the car was empty. Shutting the door, he took a few steps toward the house and stopped. But who *was* Richie? Artemis had hired him back in September, more than a month before Charlie had run into her at Home Depot. Yes, but who *was* he? Artemis said he was a good worker and didn't talk much. She'd said she felt lucky to have him. But that meant nothing. Why was his Honda parked by the garage? Charlie's relief began to fade.

As Charlie approached the back entry next to the double doors of the garage, he kept imagining someone lurking just outside the beam of light or hurrying up behind him with a knife. Twice he spun around, swinging the light in an arc and trying not to slip. But he saw no one. The hairs on the back of his neck seemed permanently in a stand-up position. His stomach felt as it once did when he'd climbed the extension ladder onto Janey's roof to find the source of a leak. He'd been forced to sit motionless on the shingles for five minutes just to settle his nerves. His knees hadn't simply felt weak, they'd throbbed.

Reaching the house, Charlie stared up at the darkened picture window of the living room. Artemis's dinner party had been less than a week ago, but now it seemed in the far-distant past. He expected the back door to be locked, but it was open. Changing his grip on the Benelli, he pressed his flashlight along the short barrel, awkwardly holding them together while keeping a finger of his right hand near the trigger. Another silly dance, he thought. Then he stepped inside.

Water from melted snow had puddled on the cement floor of the garage and wet footprints led across to a second door and the stairway. Charlie thought they must belong to Richie, but the idea brought no comfort. The two names went back and forth in his mind: Paulie or Richie, Paulie or Richie? Next to the door was a light switch. Charlie flicked it and nothing happened. He shone his light back and forth. Artemis had two vehicles: a 1982 Porsche 928S and a gray Toyota Tundra. Both were in the garage, and the Porsche was under a red car cover for the winter.

Across the garage next to the door leading upstairs, Charlie saw the metal box with the circuit breakers. Switching off his light, he made his way toward it in the dark. Then, as he shifted the shotgun to his left hand, he bumped a snow shovel leaning against the wall. It fell to the floor with a clatter. Charlie crouched and listened. There was no noise but the wind. Then he sighed. Had he always been so clumsy?

Reaching the metal box, he flipped the toggles. Nothing happened. Whatever was wrong with the lights, the problem wasn't here. Maybe the wind had knocked down a wire after all, or maybe it had been cut.

Charlie climbed the stairs to the kitchen, trying to make no noise, though why it mattered after all the noise he'd already made, he had no idea. What he really wanted was to sit down on the stairs and rest.

He hated being terrified. His terror was like a second person, a smaller person, thrashing around inside him. But if the footprints he'd followed through the garage were Richie's, then he'd nothing to worry about. Wasn't that true? And that was when Charlie realized he was wrong. Possibility had moved to probability to certainty. Richie and Paulie were the same man. Charlie paused on the stairs. He wanted to turn around and go back outside. He wanted to take the shovel that he'd knocked to the floor and shovel his car free. He shifted his weight from one foot to the other. He could go outside and wait for the police. Then he paused again. He thought of all that had occurred since he'd found Mickey lying dead on his sidewalk. The images were like lights flashing past him. Safety couldn't be a choice. He had to move upward.

The kitchen door was open. He raised his shotgun and stood still, listening. He knew for certain no one was asleep. He wasn't sure they were in the house or even alive. He thought of those cop shows where the cops had lights attached to the barrels of their shotguns. If Charlie had to shoot quickly, he'd either have to drop the light or fire with one hand, which meant the kick of the shotgun would throw off his aim. Had things always been so complicated or was it age, as he stumbled forward from one senior moment to the next? He thought again of the term Victor had once used: "the dwindles."

Charlie moved through the kitchen and into the living room with its large picture window. At least the house was carpeted and his feet made no sound. He stood at the glass with his light off, but he could see nothing—no distant lights that might signal approaching police vehicles. Turning, he walked quickly through the dining room and den, keeping his light pointed down at the floor. Nothing was out of the ordinary. No overturned tables and chairs, no blood on the rug. Even so, he felt he was being watched from just beyond his light.

Negative thoughts, he told himself. He tried to push them away, but they only took a step back and waited.

The trouble was that if Richie or Paulie Durkin had been a ranger, he'd only have to wait. He could probably kill Charlie with just his little finger. Despite the Benelli, Charlie felt like a fly hunting a hawk.

Along one side of the house, looking out toward the two barns, Artemis had a garden room about twenty feet long and eight feet wide, with a slanted glass ceiling and glass walls. The plants were towering "jungley things," as Charlie called them, with spiky green leaves. There was also a large yellow hibiscus, which Artemis had identified for him, and an oversized, multiheaded red geranium. Along with the plants were white wicker armchairs and four wicker tables. Artemis called it her "cocktail solarium."

Shining his light around the room, Charlie thought of how obvious the light would be to anyone outside. Then, as the light traveled across the glass, he noticed something to the left of him. Again he felt a little surge of adrenaline. Moving closer, he identified two bullet holes about chest high. There was no glass on the tiles beneath the holes, and Charlie knew the shots had been fired from inside. As he touched a hole with his little finger, he guessed the bullets were .45 caliber. The holes had probably been made by Victor's Smith & Wesson Chief's Special.

Charlie pressed his light against the glass to see what might be outside. But there was nothing: no body and no blood. Just snow. So possibly the snow was covering something, like a corpse, or possibly Victor had fired at someone standing out in the yard and missed, or possibly something else. Turning out his light, Charlie decided he had too many possibilities. He saw nothing from the glass. Again he hoped to see approaching headlights, but he saw only darkness.

Hurriedly, he left the garden room and went down the hall to the bedrooms. Artemis's room was empty, but the bed was unmade. The closet door was open; some clothes had fallen from their hangers and several pairs of shoes were knocked about the floor. This didn't suggest that someone had searched the closet; rather, someone had been in a rush to get dressed, just as the unmade bed might suggest that Artemis had been sleeping, but had been woken unexpectedly. Charlie wasn't sure what to make of this.

Cold air blew from someplace, as if a door had been left open. It came from the next room down the hall. Charlie hurried toward it. The door was splintered and hung from only the top hinge; just beyond, a bed and a bureau had been knocked aside. Someone had tried to barricade the door and someone else had broken through. The bedroom had been used by Emma. Her book bag for school was on a chair. A small table by the window had been tipped over and a desk light lay beneath it. The window itself was open.

Charlie leaned through the window and pointed his flashlight down toward the snow six feet below, moving the light back and forth. After a moment he saw the indentations of someone who had jumped, maybe more than one person. The falling snow obliterated any footprints, leaving only a shapeless sprawl. The indentations led off across the yard, perhaps toward the barn.

Working to calm his fears, he tried to guess what had happened as the terror within him thrashed and thrashed. He was sure that Artemis had been woken by someone breaking through the basement door and got dressed. But after that, something must have especially scared her. What did Paulie Durkin shout at Campbell's wife? "Are you ready to die?"

Then she had run to wake Emma and together they had barricaded the door. Charlie imagined their fear as someone tried to smash through. So they'd fled through the window. Had Paulie gone through the window as well? Most likely.

Charlie threw his right leg over the sill. The window seemed too small for him. His cap and winter coat, the flashlight and the shotgun—he seemed to fill most of the opening. His muscles felt stiff and reluctant. He put the flashlight in his coat pocket, gripped the Benelli and leaned out into the dark. As he drew his left leg up to the sill, he started to fall. There was no help for it. He let himself go.

Twenty-two

Charlie lay on his back and tried to catch his breath. The ground, even covered by eight inches of snow, was rock hard. Snowflakes fell across his face. Opening his mouth, he felt them touch his tongue like a caress. He wanted to whine and complain and go home, but he could do none of those things. After another moment, he rolled over and pushed himself onto his knees. Then he stood up. His back hurt and he stretched. The flashlight was still in his pocket and he still held the Benelli. He wedged the shotgun under his arm and drew his gloves from his coat pockets. To heck with bare hands. If he couldn't do damage with six shots, then he might as well surrender; might as well tell Paulie Durkin to start slashing. His fingers would be useless unless he could warm them. His lambskin leather gloves were lined with rabbit fur. Janey had given them to him for Christmas and Charlie was glad to have them.

In the dark, he could see nothing, but he sensed the house looming up behind him and so he guessed the general direction of the two barns. He began shuffling in their direction. He recalled a line of shrubs to his left and the driveway to his right, so if he got too far off track he'd end up at one of those places. He tried to count his aches and pains, but they were too numerous to itemize. He'd banged one knee against the window frame and hit his shoulder and hip against the frozen ground. And there were also other bruises. Better to forget them, he thought, better just keep moving.

As he thought this, his foot caught on something and he tumbled forward. He landed on something large, soft, lumpy and cold. Quickly, he rolled away, guessing what it was before he could find the words to articulate it. He let go of the Benelli and scrambled to his feet, thinking he'd found Victor and that he was dead. He dug in his pockets for the flashlight, cursing the thick gloves that he had just been feeling self-satisfied about.

The first thing Charlie saw when he turned on the light was a black duty boot and he felt relief. It wasn't Victor; it was a sheriff's deputy. Right away his relief turned to self-reproach and he shook his head. He wished he knew the man's name, but he didn't. But he wished he had a name to apologize to.

The body was partly covered with snow, but the dark blue uniform was obvious. He was hatless and balding: a middle-aged man with a belly. His throat had been slashed, straight through the trachea and esophagus. In the light, the shiny, pink mass of tissue and blood had an electric brilliance. Charlie shut off the light and stepped back, appalled.

But he found no comfort in the dark and he imagined Paulie Durkin lurking nearby. He fumbled with the light and again cursed his gloves, shaking one loose so it dropped to the snow. The light flicked on and Charlie spun around, expecting to see someone. But the falling snow created a white wall and he saw no one. In any case, what could he do? He'd dropped the Benelli when he'd tripped over the dead deputy and now he had to find it. Examining the snow around him, he shuffled his feet, moving in a circle until his boot bumped against the shotgun. He snatched it up and wiped off the snow with his bare hand. Then he retrieved his discarded glove.

Finding the shotgun provided him with a brief rush of gratitude. But the good feeling wouldn't last. He dug in his coat pocket for his cell phone, meaning to again call 9-1-1. It wasn't in his right pocket where he'd thought he had put it and it wasn't in his left. Frantically, he dropped the Benelli and began to search all his pockets. After a moment, he stopped. He had to accept that the phone had fallen from his pocket, that it was gone. He swung his light across the snow but saw no sign of it. He dropped to his knees and began pawing through the snow with his bare hands. His sense of failure and mortification was like a painful swelling in his gut. At last he picked up the Benelli and got to his feet. He decided that the cell phone must have dropped from his pocket when he'd fallen from the bedroom window.

Hurrying back through the snow to the house, Charlie leaned the shotgun against the wall, took off his gloves and began to search the area beneath the window. He crawled around on all fours, holding the flashlight in his mouth. He tried to be methodical, but he was too panicky. He dug through the snow, throwing it around him. He sifted it through his fingers. He patted the ground. After several minutes he stopped. He knew that Paulie Durkin was somewhere nearby, as were Emma and Artemis, as, in fact, was Victor. Were they even alive? If so, then surely they were in great danger. He had to find them, cell phone or no cell phone. The danger, or his personal danger, couldn't matter. This was something he had to repeat to himself. Otherwise he was afraid that his fear would lead him to forget it.

Soon he was again trudging toward the two barns with his flashlight in his left hand, the shotgun tucked under his right arm and his right hand in his pocket. The snow came down as hard as ever. The murdered sheriff's deputy was gradually being covered up. Charlie looked down at the man as he passed, but there was nothing he could do about him. Moving forward in a crouch, he kept sensing someone behind him. He'd spin around, raising the shotgun, but he saw no one and such turns only got him off track. Shortly, with all his turns and adjustments, he no longer knew the direction of the barn. Shining his light and turning in a circle, he saw only the shifting wall of snow.

Then he heard a whisper. "Charlie, over here."

He jumped and nearly fired the shotgun, but it was Victor. He moved in the direction of the voice and felt hugely grateful. "Where are you?" he whispered. He still couldn't see his friend.

"Right here, in the hedge."

Charlie moved forward until he fell into it. The hedge was unpleasantly prickly. "You're under the hedge?"

"Exactly."

"How'd you crawl under it?"

"Willpower."

Charlie crouched down on his knees. His pants by this time were wet from his socks to his belt. "Why are you here?"

"Come on, Charlie, you know perfectly well why I'm here. Someone wants me dead. So I'm staying here till daylight, or till the cops come. You fucking misled me about what might happen, like I could get killed."

"Aren't you cold?"

"I got my snowmobile suit. I'm as toasty as a bedbug in a whorehouse."

Charlie began to say that he didn't know Victor had a snowmobile, but then he asked, "What happened to your car?"

"I was having a little snooze when somebody snuck up and hammered on my hood. I nearly shat my pants. It was a young guy with a big knife. My gun was in my lap and I fired, but I didn't hit him. He'd ducked down out of sight. After a minute or two, I went to look for him. Like I had my gun and my light and I felt pissed that I'd put two bullets through my own fuckin' windshield. But I didn't see him again, at least not then."

"What did he look like?" But Charlie already knew it was Paulie Durkin. Who else could it be?

"I don't know; he was agile and tall. I didn't have time to study his face. I got to the house, but couldn't find anyone. Then the lights went out. Scared the shit out of me. I had my flashlight, but it was spooky. The guy was playing a game with me, making me use up my bullets. When I was in the sunroom, he threw something at the glass. I saw him outside and shot at him and he disappeared. That gave me two more shots. So I got out of there. I'd thought my days of speed were over, but I moved pretty quick. I'd fall, get up and run some more, then fall again and run some more till I ran smack into this hedge. Then I scooted underneath."

"You call 9-1-1?"

"I had a long chat with Rosemary an hour or so ago and I'm outta battery. My charger's back home. How 'bout you?"

"Dropped my phone in the snow. Couldn't find it."

Victor laughed. "We're a pair, aren't we?"

Charlie felt comforted by his friend's laughter. "Don't tell anyone."

"Fat chance. You see Artemis or Janey? I saw the busted bedroom door and the open window."

"It was Emma. Janey's not here. Emma took her car so she could go riding in the morning."

"That doesn't sound good." Victor lowered his voice, indicating his fear. "You think they're okay?"

"Don't even ask that." Charlie paused. "I got to think they're okay." He paused again. "At least you're okay, that's something."

"Don't go all sweet on me, Charlie. I'm a happily married man."

Charlie couldn't see Victor, though he guessed his head was about ten inches away. He kept getting whiffs of garlic. Squinting, he could make out a dark blur that was maybe the tip of Victor's nose. He reached out and touched it.

"Hey, what are you doing?" Victor sounded indignant.

"I was just wondering if that was your nose."

"Who the fuck's nose did you think it was?"

"Well, I'm sorry, and I'm sorry I put you in such danger. You know the sheriff's deputy's dead? He's lying over there in the snow."

Victor jerked back enough to make the hedge rattle. "Franklin? I was just talking to him earlier. Was his throat cut?"

"I'm afraid so."

Victor was quiet and then said, "Charlie, why do you do this shit? Are you trying to be a hero? You got us into a pickle."

Charlie thought in vain for an answer, but maybe there wasn't an answer. He was cold, depressed and scared, and that seemed bad enough for the time being. Better to keep his mind blank. He leaned back against the hedge and brushed snow from his face. Right then he heard a shout, more of a yell, from the direction of the barn. The hairs on the back of his neck shot up again.

Victor grabbed Charlie's wrist. "Jesus, who is it?"

Charlie pulled back. "It's a female voice. I'm going over there. You coming?" Charlie was already moving away when he'd finished speaking.

Victor didn't move. "Can't do it, Charlie. I'm scared shitless. I'll stay here and defend the fort. I got just two bullets, 'less you want to swap and give me the Benelli."

"How in the world would you think . . . !" Crossly, Charlie had started to insult his friend. Then he stopped. It was senseless to blame Victor. "So maybe I'll see you later."

"Yeah, let's hope so." Victor made a throat-clearing noise. "Sorry, Charlie."

Charlie plodded away through the snow and kept his light off. The position of the hedge and direction of the cry had given him a better idea where the barns might be located. He tried to hurry, but he kept stumbling. He didn't want to think of the yell and who had made it and what it might signify.

He calculated that the smaller of the two barns where the horses were mostly stabled was about a hundred yards away. The larger dressage barn was on the other side of the paddock. He kept his head down, shuffled forward and at last he found the smaller barn by walking into it with a thump. He fell back into the snow, making sure not to drop the shotgun. Charlie sat a moment, rubbing his head, and then got up again. He stood listening, but heard nothing.

Making his way around to the front of the barn, he found that the wide sliding door was open, though he couldn't see anything. Charlie stepped inside onto the concrete aisle and curbed a desire to turn on his light. A horse stamped in its stall and there was the drip of water from the roof, but otherwise there was no noise. He was tempted to call out for Emma, but he knew that was the worst thing he could do. Instead, he put his back to a wall and waited. A second horse was shuffling about.

"Charlie, is that you?"

It was a man's voice. Charlie ducked down and tightened his grip on the shotgun. "Who is it?"

"Richie."

Charlie turned on his light, which reflected off Richie's face. Richie put up a hand to cover his eyes. "Hey!"

Charlie pointed the light at the floor. It was Paulie, or rather Paulie and Richie were the same man. He raised the shotgun. "What are you doing here?"

"I'm looking for Artemis. I thought I heard her yell. None of the lights work."

Charlie decided to play along for a bit. "You see anyone else?"

"Just you. The whole place is empty."

"A sheriff deputy's dead. His body's lying in the snow. His throat was cut."

"You're fucking kidding. D'you know who did it?"

"A young guy by the name of Paulie Durkin."

There was a pause. Then the man said, "Never heard of him. You think he's around here?"

"I'm pretty sure of it."

"Wow, what kind of gun is that?"

Charlie shone his light on the shotgun. "It's made by Benelli in Italy. A shotgun. The marines use them." He seemed to be bragging.

"That's incredible! Can I see it?"

Charlie raised the light to the man's face. He squinted and turned his head, but he was smiling. Light brown hair stuck out from under a Yankees cap.

"You're Paulie Durkin," said Charlie, evenly.

Right away, the man raised his arm and threw a small shovel that hit Charlie's light, sending it clattering down the barn floor until it banged against something and went out.

At the same second, Charlie jumped to one side, found the trigger and pulled. The explosion ripped through the air. There was a flare from the muzzle and then the dark grew doubly dark. Horses whinnied and stamped in their stalls. Ducking down against the wall, Charlie fired again in what he thought was Paulie's direction. He moved farther along the aisle into the barn. He stopped to listen, but the horses were making too much noise: snorting and stamping. There was a neigh like a high scream. Charlie waited.

Then came a quiet voice. "Missed me."

Charlie fired again in the direction of the voice. The blast again scared the horses. There was more neighing and snorting. Charlie scooted farther along the concrete floor, crouching and holding the Benelli in front of him but close to his body. He stopped and leaned back against the wooden wall. The shotgun held three more shells, though Charlie had others in his pocket. He made no sound, tried not to breathe. The noise of the horses made it impossible to hear what Paulie might be doing. Charlie considered saying something to the other man, something about his father and what had really happened. Then he thought how stupid that was.

The horses remained fearful: kicking out and rustling around. There were three of them. One in a stall across from Charlie gave a high whinny; another snorted and stamped. Edging several feet to his right, Charlie bumped his head against a post projecting about four inches from the wall. Exploring it with his free hand, he found it was a ladder that went up to the loft above the stalls. He grabbed a rung and began to climb. When he reached the loft, he crawled forward. Then he turned and sat with his legs crossed. He didn't think Paulie had heard him, but he couldn't be sure. He slipped three more shells into the shotgun.

Then came a voice from the floor below, almost a whisper. "You killed my old man." There was no anger in the voice; it was simply stating a fact.

Charlie began to answer, but stopped. He gripped the shotgun and tried to calculate where the voice was coming from. The horses were quieting a little, but their restless agitation, pawing the floor and snorting, still hid Paulie's movements.

When the whisper came again, it was from the second loft, directly across the aisle from Charlie. "You and that bitch and Fletcher Campbell—yeah, I know you didn't knife him, but you killed him just the same." The voice was like the quiet rasp of a file.

Again Charlie was tempted to speak, but kept silent. Absurdly, he worried that Paulie could hear the beating of his heart. It seemed deafening in Charlie's ears. Stop being foolish, he told himself. He steadied his breathing and tried to listen.

The whisper came a third time, but now it came from the loft on Charlie's side of the barn, somewhere near the big sliding door. "You don't think you need to be killed like the others? It's fast, Charlie. You'll hardly feel it."

Charlie raised the shotgun and fired twice in the direction of the voice. The row of windows above the barn door shattered. Horses whinnied. At the same time, he heard a startled cry from somewhere behind him—not loud. It was more like an abrupt intake of breath. Still, it was loud enough for him to know it was a woman's voice and that it belonged to either Artemis or Emma. He guessed it was Emma. Wouldn't Artemis have more self-control no matter how frightened she was? But maybe Emma and Artemis were together. He wanted to call to them, but the folly of the thought scared him.

Then the whisper: "Missed again, Charlie." Silence and the whisper again: "It's painless, Charlie. A quick cut, a little thrashing and that's all. Both of you, and then I'll be done."

Charlie fired, aiming lower, thinking that Paulie might be lying flat on the floor. There was more breaking glass and more upset from the horses. Then he scooted backward across the loft above the harness room. It was scattered with hay, which made a rustling noise. He slid six more shells into the Benelli. Maybe he had three more shells left. At this rate, they'd hardly be enough. "Both of you," Paulie had said. Did that mean he didn't know about Emma or didn't mean to include her? And if he didn't know about her, where was she?

A minute passed in silence. Had he hit Paulie, or was Paulie sneaking toward him? Charlie kept crawling toward the back of the barn, each movement taking several seconds as he made himself stay quiet. His hand bumped some harder object. It was a hay rake. Picking it up, he threw it down to the main floor. It banged and slid along the concrete aisle. There were more horse noises. Would Paulie think he was down there, or was he still creeping forward? Charlie reached the back wall; he could go no farther. He lay down on his stomach with the shotgun pointing in front of him. Surely the police must be coming, but he knew that what seemed an hour to him was only about fifteen minutes. Even so, they had to be close. But did he have any good reason for believing that? He fought off the temptation to shoot several rounds in Paulie's direction. Maybe he had hit Paulie with those last shots; maybe he was wounded or even dead. Maybe. But he knew that was what Paulie would want him to think—the illusion of safety.

One of the horses began to whinny and stamp the floor; then another began, then the third—stamping and kicking at their wooden walls. Charlie couldn't think what was wrong, till he smelled the smoke. Paulie had set fire to the hay. Now Charlie saw a glimmer of light. He heard a noise above him and rolled over, ready to shoot. But it wasn't Paulie. In the dim light from the fire, he saw Artemis on one of the beams above him; then he saw Emma on another, both hanging on like scared cats as they scuttled forward on their stomachs toward a support post.

Charlie looked around for Paulie, but didn't see him. The smoke was growing thicker. Artemis was about a dozen feet above him. "Hurry," he called to her.

"Get the horses out!" she cried. "Open their stalls!"

Charlie had gone to the ladder, but hesitated in the loft at the top. He kept looking for Paulie, who, he thought, might be directly beneath him in one of the empty stalls or he could be just outside the sliding door. In fact, thought Charlie, he could be anyplace. All Paulie had to do was wait until the fire forced them to run from the barn.

"Hurry!" cried Artemis, running toward him across the loft. "Make sure you cover their eyes or they'll run back."

Charlie climbed down several rungs and then jumped, aiming for the middle of the aisle so he might see Paulie. He landed and fell forward on his face, letting go of the shotgun, which slid forward a few feet. He leapt forward to grab it. His face hurt and he'd scraped his hands. Paulie was nowhere in sight.

Artemis sprang past him and ran to the double door of the first stall. Emma ran after her to another. Charlie kept turning around, trying to see the entire barn. The fire made a flickering light; through the smoke Charlie saw flames toward the front. If Paulie was going to kill them, this would be the perfect place, though maybe he'd be satisfied to burn them alive.

"Charlie!" called Artemis.

He moved along the wall to the first stall door. Artemis was holding on to a horse's halter with both hands as it tried to rear up. Emma was in the next stall.

"Give me your scarf!" cried Artemis.

Charlie was still peering down the aisle of the barn toward where he thought Paulie must be. Then he undid his scarf and tossed it to Artemis, who wrapped it around the horse's eyes. It stopped rearing up, though it kept neighing and stamping. She pulled it by its halter toward the door of the stall, whispering in its ear. The fire was now burning in the loft, with flames shooting toward the roof. "Help Emma," Artemis called as she hurried with the horse toward the barn door.

In the next stall, Emma was unable to control the horse, which kicked at her, snorting and rearing up. Charlie grabbed the halter, but then had it wrenched from his hand as the horse rose up again. Emma had taken off her jacket and was trying to put it over the horse's face, but the horse knocked her aside. Leaning the shotgun against the wall, Charlie again grabbed the halter. He and Emma were both coughing. In the dim light from the fire, he saw Emma throw her coat over the horse's forehead and he grabbed a sleeve. As he gripped the halter with one hand, he passed the coat sleeve under the horse's jaw to Emma, who tied the sleeves together. The horse kept trying to break free, but Charlie put all his weight into dragging it back down.

"Lead it out of here!" he shouted. Then he picked up the shotgun and tried to shoulder the horse out of the stall without getting kicked. Emma jumped onto the horse's back, crouched over and hanging on to the sleeves of her coat, pulling them tight under the horse's jaw and across its muzzle and forehead. She dug her heels into its ribs and it jumped forward, bolting toward the barn door.

The ceiling and opposite wall were glowing red and the fire was about to break through. Charlie ran to the last stall. The horse kept kicking the wall and snorting. It didn't seem to notice Charlie as it rose up and spun on its rear hooves. Charlie grabbed at the halter and was thrown back. He stripped off his winter coat, meaning to use it to cover the horse's eyes. Then he removed his leather belt, looping it over one shoulder and under the opposite arm, and strapped the shotgun to his chest. No way was he going to leave it behind if he could help it. He didn't think about Paulie Durkin; he only knew he was out there. The stall was hot and full of smoke. He threw his coat over the horse's forehead, grabbed a sleeve hanging down the other side and pulled it back under the horse's jaw as he had seen Emma do. Then he pushed open the door to drag the horse into the aisle. Rearing up, it broke his hold and bolted back to the stall. The heat scorched Charlie's face.

A large rubber bucket was in the corner of the stall. Charlie grabbed it, turned it over and got up on top as he hung on to the horse's halter and one sleeve of the coat. Again he threw the rest of the coat across the horse's eyes and this time he was able to catch it underneath, so he held both sleeves with the halter on the near side of the horse. But as he pulled the sleeves tight, the horse lunged forward toward the door. Charlie was half pulled and half jumped onto the horse's back and he dropped one sleeve. He fell forward with his chin pressed against the horse's mane and his heels pressed against its belly. Letting go of the halter, he reached under the horse's neck with his right hand and grabbed the coat sleeve so he gripped a sleeve in each fist. Once free of the stall, the horse kicked and reared up, but Charlie hung on. He yanked the two sleeves crisscrossed under the horse's jaw and spurred his heels into its ribs. The horse stamped and shook its head, but then bolted toward the front of the barn and the barn doors. The flames were all around them and burning bits of hay fell like candles. Something large crashed down onto the floor behind them.

In seconds, Charlie was out of the barn and into the snow, still clutching the sleeves of his coat as reins and squeezing the horse with his knees and heels. He was sure he'd be thrown off at any moment.

The pistol grip of the Benelli dug into his chest. He was hardly aware of Artemis and Emma off to his right, holding on to their horses and trying to calm them, nor did he quite see the flashing light bars on the police vehicles rushing up the drive. Maybe he heard sirens. Each time he raised his head out of the horse's mane, he slipped a little to one side. The snow blew against his face. In a blur he saw Victor laboring through the snow toward the burning barn, holding onto his hat with one hand and gripping his pistol with the other. Charlie pulled back on the coat sleeves, attempting to make the horse stop, but the horse had no wish to stop.

Then, raising his head, Charlie saw Paulie Durkin on his right, running forward in a crouch. He knew that Artemis was his destination and knew he meant to slash her throat as he had done to the others. Charlie yanked a coat sleeve and the horse swerved to the right, kicking up the snow around them. With his face buried in the horse's mane, he pulled and banged his heels against the horse's ribs. Only seconds had passed since horse and rider had rushed from the barn.

Abruptly, Charlie and Paulie were facing each other from a short distance—Charlie galloping in one direction, Paulie running in the other. Charlie had barely begun to process this image when the horse struck Paulie a glancing blow, sideswiping him and throwing him aside. The horse stumbled, nearly falling to its knees, then regained its footing. But this was too much for Charlie. His grip was broken and he was jolted loose. He slipped off the rear of the horse, hitting the ground with his feet, but then was hurled forward. He tried to turn slightly so he wouldn't hit the ground with the Benelli beneath him.

Although deep, the snow was no cushion. At most, it allowed Charlie to slide forward like a sled. He struggled to catch his breath as he dug the toes of his boots into the ground. He slid to a halt, rolling onto his back.

Paulie Durkin ran toward him with a large knife held out to one side. Charlie tried to yank the shotgun free from the belt that held it to his chest, but the front sight caught on the fabric of his pants. Clutching the pistol grip, he pulled harder and the shotgun broke free. Then, in his panic, he couldn't find the safety button on the trigger guard. Paulie was less than ten feet away.

Charlie pressed the safety button and pulled the trigger, aiming low. The discharge was muffled by the storm: a loud cough. Paulie screamed and fell, but his momentum still carried him toward Charlie. Scrambling, Charlie lurched through the heavy snow to get out of the way, but he wasn't fast enough. Paulie landed on Charlie's shoulder on top of the shotgun. He was still screaming. In his right hand, he held his hunting knife, but he no longer had any interest in Charlie. Trying to pull free his right arm, Charlie pushed Paulie away with his left. Paulie was flailing and grabbing at his leg. Charlie gave one more yank and tumbled back. He scrambled to his feet. The shot had struck Paulie's left shin and foot from a few feet away and maybe just a rag of a foot remained. Paulie flailed and bellowed, clutching at the space where his foot had been as the snow turned red around him.

Now a dozen flashlights were bobbing across the snow-covered field, and in seconds Charlie saw the eager faces of the deputies. It seemed like a horse race to see who would reach him first. He swayed painfully, impressed by the range of his discomfort from the cold and the burns, the palms of his hands and his chest from hitting the ground and sliding, and other places too numerous to count. I'm a display in the museum of serious hurt, he thought.

But now the lead sheriff's deputy began shouting: "Drop your weapon, scumbag, drop your weapon!"

Charlie looked down at the Benelli, still gripped in his hand, and released it, watched it fall into the snow and disappear. He already missed it. Looking up, he was startled to see that the lead deputy was airborne and he was the target. But he didn't have the chance to consider the strangeness of it when the deputy crashed into him and they flew backward, hit the snow and slid all in a tangle.

"I think you're making a mistake," Charlie whispered into the deputy's ear.

Epilogue

Victor stretched out a finger and thumb and delicately plucked a blueberry from the surface of a blueberry muffin and studied it thoughtfully. "I really thought I'd gone nuts, Charlie, or been flung into an alternative universe where nothing nice was ever going to happen again. There you were hollering with fire all around you, bombing outta that barn on a black horse, glued to the top like a ten-cent stamp on a ten-pound package."

Charlie nodded and glanced out the window at the small mountain of snow pushed to the edge of the parking lot. The sky was blue with fluffy clouds. It was about two p.m. three days later, and only a few other people were in the diner. "Charlie, you can barely walk," Janey had told him an hour earlier. He'd only gotten out of the hospital the previous evening. But he was tired of lying in bed.

Charlie had already heard a version of Victor's story from Artemis and Emma: how he had come galloping out of the burning barn and ridden the horse smack into Paulie Durkin, which wasn't quite true. Even Hutchins had a part of the story, and Undersheriff Maroni, and probably Paulie as well. It had come to bore him. It had been an accident; the whole thing had been an accident. He'd been lucky, that's all. And in none of these versions had anyone said how much he must hurt. Janey did, when she visited him in the hospital, but she hadn't seen him come roaring out of the barn; she'd only imagined it, though she could see the bandage on his shoulder from a burn, and the bruises, a tapestry of multicolored bruises, as well as some broken bits: collarbone, left arm and three ribs. About an hour earlier, before leaving home, Charlie had taken another Percocet, but so far it only made him feel as if he were at the bottom of a deep well.

Paulie Durkin had been in another room of the hospital, which was enough for Charlie to ask for his shotgun back. But Hutchins had assured him that Paulie was handcuffed to the bed and, in any case, his left foot was gone, and part of his ankle with it. Still, Paulie's presence had been enough for Charlie to want to escape from the hospital as soon as possible, despite the warnings of his doctors.

Victor chortled some more. "If it hadn't been for the fire, I'd of thought you were a circus act. I wish I'd had a camera."

"Maybe I could do the whole thing again so you could film it."

"Nah, the barn's burned down and we'd have to find another. Besides, Artemis wouldn't let us borrow her horses."

Charlie again stared at the mountain of snow at the edge of the parking lot. For a moment he imagined it was all the snow he'd slogged through at Artemis's come back to visit him. But maybe that was the Percocet. He shook his head, trying to clear it of disagreeable images.

"I still don't see how you knew Paulie and Richie were the same guy," said Victor, picking another blueberry out of his muffin.

"I didn't, but when I saw Richie's Honda Civic it started me thinking. I'd seen a similar car parked near the Tea Kettle. It was a lucky guess, that's all."

Victor grinned, as if he knew all about Charlie's lucky guesses. "What happened to Artemis's other stable hand? What was his name?"

"Stanley. Paulie had tied him to his bed in the dressage barn. He'd nothing against him and didn't want to hurt him."

"Nah," said Victor, "I bet he was just saving him as a snack for later."

Charlie began to say that Paulie would have saved Emma as well, but he didn't know that as a fact. "Anyway, we're lucky the sheriff's cars showed up when they did."

Victor grew indignant. "Luck had nothing to do with it. I called them."

"Give me a break. You said your phone was out of battery."

"It was, but I heard this phone buzzing. It was Franklin's radio—you know, the dead deputy. So I crawled out of the bushes and tracked it down. It was hooked to his belt and I answered it. Guy on the other end was pissed when he realized I wasn't Franklin. He figured I'd stolen the radio and said he'd slap my ass in jail."

Victor paused to sip his coffee. Then he gave a little affectionate wave to the Queen of Softness perched on her stool behind the cash register.

"And?" asked Charlie impatiently.

"Oh, yeah." Victor shook his head. "I said Franklin had been murdered, that his throat was cut. So they came barreling over to Artemis's farm. Didn't even thank me for letting them know."

Charlie wondered why he'd never thought of the radio himself. "What a shame," he said. He poured a little more sugar in his coffee and stirred it with his finger. The coffee was tepid, but he didn't care.

"What *I* call a shame is how you were hardly mentioned by the newspaper. All it says is you were one of the guys that Paulie meant to kill. That's pretty hard considering what you did. They should've given you a medal."

Chief Novak had convinced Charlie that he had to stay out of the "limelight," as Novak called it. If he did, he'd get his pistol license back. If he didn't, he could be charged with interfering with a police investigation, disobeying police orders, firing a questionable shotgun (short barrel, collapsible stock) and assaulting a sheriff's deputy: the man who had jumped on Charlie at the end had twisted his ankle. Novak also suggested that Charlie could get an accessory charge for not warning the police about the involvement of Milo Rutkowski, while Milo was alive.

"Even if you beat these charges, Charlie, you'd be paying a fortune in lawyer's fees," Novak had told him. "It'd put a dent in your pocketbook."

Charlie had been sitting on the far side of Novak's desk silently hating him. On the other hand, he'd no interest in seeing his name in lights. It would require too much handshaking and fake smiling, too much phony gratitude.

No, if there was a star, it was Hutchins. *The Saratogian* had described how he'd been first on the scene when Mickey was murdered, that he'd doggedly continued the investigation when others had given up, that he'd discovered the link between Mickey and Paulie's father, and then had helped the sheriff's department and the state police in tracking Paulie down, even though Paulie was a ranger and knew a hundred ways how to kill a person.

"It makes me want to vomit," said Victor. He put two fingers into his mouth to show how it might be done.

"The people I care about know. Others, too. It's not as if it never happened."

Victor leaned forward and lowered his voice. "I probably shouldn't tell you this, but Emma and I worked up a great story for the high school paper coming out tomorrow. Pictures and the whole nine yards. The cops won't just have egg on their face, they'll have the whole fucking chicken. No-Neck Novak'll bust a gut."

There goes my pistol license, thought Charlie.

"And *The Saratogian* will be all over this. I bet they give you a ticker-tape parade."

But Charlie and Janey had other plans. While in the hospital, he'd told her about Gene and Mary Lou McCarthy's second motel, the Tea Kettle, Too, down in Saint Petersburg. It sounded worth a visit. They could rent a car, and after coming back from the beach, they could go for a splash in the motel pool before cocktail hour. Then they might toss a couple of T-bones on the charcoal grill. Emma could come down for a long weekend and even bring Bruiser.

So Janey had gotten busy buying tickets. They'd leave in a week and Emma could stay with Artemis. To heck with Victor's ticker-tape parade. Charlie could lie on a warm chaise longue under a beach umbrella, listen to the breaking waves and rest his bones.

About the Author

STEPHEN DOBYNS has published twenty-three novels, a book of short stories, fourteen books of poems and two books of essays on poetry. *Saratoga Payback* is the eleventh mystery featuring Charlie Bradshaw, a sometime private investigator in Saratoga Springs, New York. Dobyns's previous novel, *Is Fat Bob Dead Yet?*, was published in 2015 by Blue Rider Press. His most recent book of poetry is *The Day's Last Light Reddens the Leaves of the Copper Beech* (BOA Editions Ltd, 2016). Palgrave Macmillan released his second book of essays on poetry, *Next Word, Better Word*, in 2011. Two of his novels and two of his short stories were made into films. He has received a Guggenheim fellowship, three fellowships from the National Endowment of the Arts and numerous prizes for his poetry and fiction. He spent two years as a reporter for the *Detroit News*, from 1969 to 1971. Between 1995 and 2008, he published about thirty feature stories in the *San Diego Reader*. Dobyns has taught for many years in the MFA Program in Creative Writing at Warren Wilson College. He has also taught at Sarah Lawrence College, Emerson College, Syracuse University, Boston University, the University of Iowa and half a dozen other colleges and universities. He was born in New Jersey in 1941. He has three children and lives in Westerly, Rhode Island.